Polite Sex

Polite Sex

JAMES WILCOX

HarperCollins*Publishers*

Although this novel is set in New York, with references to Louisiana, none of its characters represents or is based on persons living in either of these states, or indeed anywhere. All events and personalities are imaginary.

FIRST EDITION

Designed by Cassandra J. Pappas

Library of Congress Cataloging-in-Publication Data

Wilcox, James.
  Polite sex / by James Wilcox. —1st ed.
    p.   cm.
  ISBN 0-06-016356-9
  I. Title.
PS3573.I396P6   1991
813'.54—dc20   90-5597

94 95 NK/HC 10 9 8 7 6 5 4 3

" 'All recollected times undergo . . . foreshortening, and this foreshortening is due to the omission of an enormous number of facts which filled them. "We thus reach the paradoxical result," says M. Ribot, "that one condition of remembering is that we should forget. Without totally forgetting a prodigious number of states of consciousness, and momentarily forgetting a large number, we could not remember at all. . . ." ' "

—William James quoted in
Daniel J. Boorstin's *The Discoverers*

To Steve Beauchamp
and to Elizabeth Zintl

part one

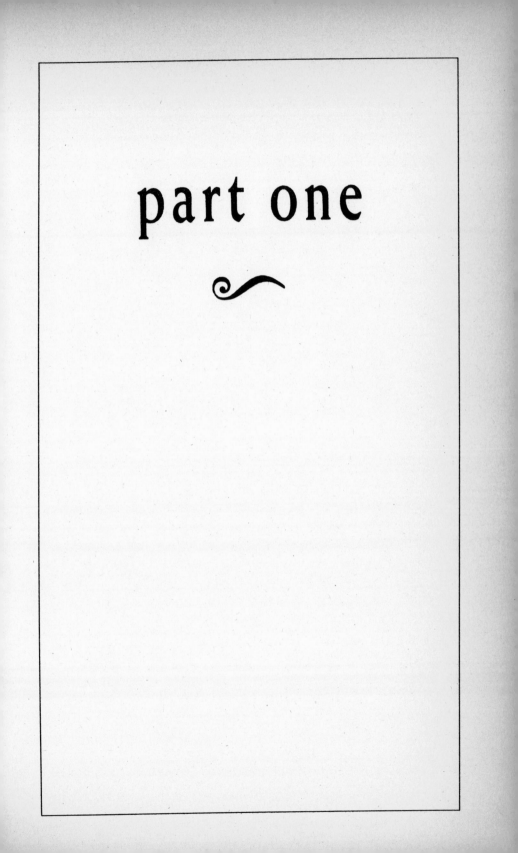

one

After graduating from Smith in 1971, magna cum laude, Emily found herself a studio on East 92nd Street, just off Park, for $180 a month. Everyone told her that she had made a big mistake, that she could have gotten something much larger on the West Side. But Emily had no patience for apartment hunting. She had taken the first that didn't have a bathtub in the kitchen. That was where she drew the line. Yes, the apartment was narrow, and you might have to walk sideways around the sofabed when it was unfolded. But the slick wood floor looked fine without a rug—she couldn't afford a decent one yet—and the previous tenant had left behind a bookshelf, a little wobbly, but respectable.

Emily was making ends meet as a glorified receptionist at Mark Four, an independent production company near Times Square. She could have taken a job with more prestige, if not more money, as an editorial trainee at *Seventeen*. But she had a chance of becoming story editor at Mark Four in six months or so, which was when the present story editor was planning to leave. In the meantime, when she wasn't answering phones or typing labels, she was reading scripts and galleys for a dyslexic boss, who seemed to prefer oral reports on them.

"Does he ever yell at you?" Clara asked about this boss late one afternoon in the lobby of the Algonquin. Emily had suggested they meet there for drinks rather than the cocktail lounge of the Travel Inn on 42nd Street and Tenth Avenue, Clara's idea. Clara was accompanying her mother on a tour of Historic New England, sponsored by the Colonial Dames of Tula Springs, Louisiana. It would have been easier for Clara if they had met at the motel, since she didn't have much time to change before the bus left for Mystic, Connecticut. But Emily had been firm.

"Yell at me? Of course not."

"No one has the right to yell at anyone."

Emily shrugged. Sometimes Clara could sound both obscure and obvious, all at the same time. But she was sweet, without a mean bone in her lovely body. Her senior year at Tula Springs High, Clara had been third runner-up in the Miss Louisiana pageant. Emily, her classmate then, could not fathom why she hadn't won, unless it was because she had dropped her baton in the twirling routine. But now, with more seasoned eyes, Emily could see that Clara's beauty was already dated, too plastic for the seventies. Indeed, there was something touching about the girl's lacquered hair and crimson lips, a naiveté that made Emily feel protective—and faintly homesick.

"Do you think anyone has the right to yell at anyone?"

"Hm?" Emily tapped the silver bell on the end table beside the faded plush armchair she was perched upon. Her martini was almost on empty. She would need a refill soon. "Yell? No."

Clara was thinking of her fiancé, who had yelled at her for going on the Dames tour with her mother. In fact, he had punched her on the arm, giving her an ugly bruise, which was why she had to wear puff sleeves. But she was determined to forget about her own problems for the time being, and focus on Emily. Emily Brix was the sister of one of Clara's all-time best friends, Martha Brix. Clara and Martha had worried about Emily all through high school, because she hardly ever went on dates and spent all her time reading and studying. Her sophomore year, Emily became famous and unpopular for writing twenty-five pages on *Silas Marner* when all Miss Jesse required were three. She was always ruining the curves in whatever class she was in. Then, when Emily took it in her head to apply to an all-girl school up North, Clara and

4

Martha just about gave up on her. How did the girl expect to meet anyone decent and eligible at a place called Smith? It conjured up in Clara's mind a drab group of class brains, all destined to become old maids, babysitters. And from the looks of Emily now, it seemed to Clara that all their worrying had not been in vain. Emily's skirt hung wrong on her, and like some sort of librarian, she hadn't an ounce of makeup on. As for her hair, that fine whitish blonde, yes, it had always been difficult to style except for that brief period when ironing was in. But did she have to wear it in a braided bun now, just like old Miss Barlow, their first-grade teacher? Tears had welled up in Clara's eyes when she had greeted Emily in the lobby. The poor dear looked so forlorn, so out of place.

"Oh, Em, you little skunk," Clara said gently, with a squeeze to her hand. "I don't know how you survive up here. It's so dirty and loud. Everyone is always yelling at you." In a neighboring chair a frail old man, sallow and rumpled, received a pitying gaze from Clara's sparkling blue eyes, her best feature, according to the licensed deportment instructor who had given a talk one day in home ec, Clara's minor in college. Never would Clara have walked into such an iffy establishment as this hotel on her own. There was something shady about it, run-down, that made Clara question her friend's judgment.

"Now, Em, you must let me pay for these," Clara said when the portly waiter loomed upon them. "Another brandy alexandra, please, and she'll have another martini, but this time straight up like she said, remember? Thank you so much." She gave Emily's hand, and then her own raven hair, a reassuring pat.

Being rather small, Emily was used to being petted and treated as a child. With Clara, for some reason, it did not bother her. It was only with certain men that she resented this patronizing familiarity. Her boss, for instance, had an unfortunate habit of giggling whenever she presented an oral report. Last week, rather sternly, she had asked him to restrain himself, if possible. So far, with only one or two lapses, he had succeeded in doing so.

"Did it upset you when we came in, Em, and the waiter made you show an I.D.?" Clara inquired after Emily had finished telling her about a play she had just seen, something about marigolds from outer space. Clara had tried hard to follow, but her mind kept straying to the bruise on her arm, and a red-faced man to her left kept looking at her, and the waiter had just put down the bill, which was simply a sin, charging so much in a place like this. But she was determined not to let all this spoil a good time.

"I don't know. It happens every now and then."

"Well, all I know, Em, I would have been tickled pink if he had carded me. Enjoy it while you can, girl."

"Yes, it's new. I got it at Saks." Emily frowned at the skirt that had cost an arm and a leg. She had bought it specially for the meeting with Clara, but now she was afraid that the length was not right for a petite woman like herself. With a sigh she went and hung it in the closet.

"Nice," Lucas commented as he pulled out the sofabed.

After Clara had rejoined her Dames, Emily had suffered an attack of loneliness. Lucas was the third person she had called, the only one free for dinner on such short notice. She didn't know much about him. He was old, forty or so, and did some sort of graphic design for medical texts. When she had tried to explain how sad Clara had made her feel, he had listened patiently, barely touching his shepherd's pie. "I never realized how much I've changed. Clara used to be such a big cheese, so popular and all. I was so excited about seeing her. And I wanted so much for her to be proud of me. I even dropped a couple of names. I told her about sitting next to Jon Voight at a screening, and she just looked at me. Never heard of him before."

After washing up in the bathroom Emily took the yellow air mattress she would sleep on that night and began to fill it, mouth to tube. She was not sure it had been a good idea to let Lucas sleep over at her place. He lived in Madison, New Jersey, though, and would have had to take the PATH to Hoboken, and then the Erie Lackawanna from there at midnight. In the muddle of one too many Irish coffees at Clancy's, a midtown bar with a cheap buffet, she had made the offer, half hoping he would turn it down. But surely he must understand that she had no romantic interest in him. She just felt sorry for his having to get home so late on a week night. He looked pretty worn out, as it was.

"Let me do that."

"It's all right, Lu, dear. Stay put."

"You sure you don't want to use the bed? I can sleep down there."

"Hush."

Swinging his long legs back onto the spartan mattress—he could feel the springs beneath—he decided it would have been much better if he had taken the PATH back home. Undoubtedly, once they had settled down, she would start up again about how lonely she was. The next thing he knew, she would be there in bed, wanting to be cuddled. Girls nowadays, especially Emily's generation, were so free and easy with their bodies. It was a real trial for someone like him, who wanted to remain faithful. Judy, his wife, was on the road so much, keeping up with her accounts. He couldn't wait till she was promoted to a desk job in the city. They would be able to commute together every day then, and he wouldn't find himself on strange, procrustean beds, his feet sticking out.

"Lucas," Emily called out softly after she had finished huffing and puffing and had turned out the lights, "you want to know something? Ever since Nixon bombed Cambodia I haven't had a decent night's sleep. I have a feeling he's insane, that he's going to blow up the world. Clara, when I told her this, you know what she said? She said she thought I was being disrespectful."

"Well, what did you expect?"

"I guess you're right. But still, how can any thinking, feeling human being not know that we're right on the edge—that there's a good chance there'll be no tomorrow? It hits me mostly at night, this sense of a huge void. I'm scared of the future. I'm scared there isn't any such thing as a future. It makes me feel so old."

He took a deep breath. Here it comes, he thought. She's going to pull the helpless little kid routine: Do you mind if I crawl into bed with you, Lucas? I'm scared of sleeping alone. And from where, half drunk, was he supposed to summon the willpower to say no? It wasn't fair. He wanted to be good—deep down, he did. Could he help it if some women found him so attractive?

Unable to see her from the sofabed, he lay perfectly still, his ears pricked for the sound of rustling sheets. A dull glow from the street slatted his bare chest, and once or twice he tensed as the building's vestibule door—only inches from Emily's own—slammed shut.

"Lucas?"

"Yes?"

"Remember what I was asking you about at dinner? That part?"

"Bobby-Boy?"

"What should I do? I can't make up my mind."

Emily had enjoyed some success at Smith with her acting, putting on a one-woman show composed of monologues from Seneca's *Medea* and *Hercules Furens*, Corneille's *La Mort de Pompée*, and Racine's *Phèdre*, all translated by herself. Encouraged by her classics professor to continue her acting after college, Emily had worked up the courage to go to a few auditions during her lunch hour at Mark Four. But the only part she had been offered, after a whole summer of trying out, was in a play that would open in October in a Chelsea garage. She was supposed to be a twelve-year-old Appalachian boy who seduces his father. Even before discussing this with Lucas, she had been quite sure that she was going to say no. Aside from the role being morally repugnant, she would have to get her hair cropped. Lucas had told her both of these excuses were lame. She would probably look good with cropped hair, like Jean Seberg in *Breathless*. And as for morality, wasn't the play fervently anti-war? Wasn't that the whole point of the production—to help stop the war?

The bedsprings creaked as Lucas shifted on the thin mattress. "Is it the nude scenes? Is that what bothers you?"

"No," she lied, anxious that he might think her unsophisticated. But the idea of being sodomized in public—simulated though this might be behind a pastel scrim—did disturb her, especially since she was a virgin. More than one potential boyfriend from Amherst, Harvard, or Williams had given up on her when they discovered she would have none of the sexual revolution. No matter how many arguments she heard—and some of them were quite persuasive, intellectually as well as emotionally—she could not relinquish her long-held belief that sex was supposed to occur between man and wife, period.

"I mean," she added after a few moments' silence, "if I didn't have to be a boy, if it were just man-woman, you know . . ."

"Good old father-daughter sex."

"Well, yes, that's bad enough. But like you said at dinner, it's all for a cause. Half the box office is going to Vietnam Vets

Against the War. And I've been thinking about it. I've never really done anything positive to help. I always hung back at school. I wouldn't even sign a Kent State petition, not because I didn't believe it was wrong. I was neurotic about my grades back then, scared that somehow if the dean saw my name, or if I went to Washington and marched, if the administration found out, the school administration . . . I was so easily cowed by authority back then, it's unreal. I used to be such a wimp. So, Lucas, maybe it's time I put my body on the line."

Lucas's heart was thumping violently. Any moment this sweet little honey would be snuggled up beside him. But she was due for a surprise. He was going to be strong. He was going to tell her that he would not have sex with her. Waking up with a hangover was going to be bad enough. He was not going to add to it the miseries of guilt, especially since Judy would be getting home tomorrow evening. How would he ever be able to face her?

"Emily, there's something I've got to say. Promise me you won't get mad. I don't want a big scene."

"What?" She knew what was coming, what she had been dreading all night. Why couldn't a man be a friend? Why did they all have to prove how goddam virile they were? "What is it?" she added impatiently when he didn't respond right away. Her hand was at the collar of her threadbare flannel nightgown.

"If you get in bed with me, that's all it's going to be. There won't be any sex."

"Shut up and go to sleep, Lucas."

"You're mad."

"Not mad. Just disappointed."

Good heavens, he wondered, turning over on his side. Was he *that* irresistible?

Huddled together on 42nd Street, the Colonial Dames peered anxiously into the gloom for some sign of the bus. Against the advice of Mrs. Tilman, two of the Dames had ventured a few blocks east on their own to have a look at Times Square. When they returned, Mrs. Lloyd Simms, who had a reputation for being a cut-up, and Miss Charlotte Rae Jones, her fifty-nine-year-old sister, were the center of attention. They both claimed to have gone inside a girlie bar, but Mrs. Tilman knew better. The pair had most likely just walked a block or two into that dreadful neighborhood, gawked at a few neon lights, and turned right around. In the meantime, the bus might have arrived, and they could have kept the whole group waiting. As if they hadn't waited long enough as it was. The bus was supposed to have left the Travel Inn at seven on the dot, but then the driver found he couldn't open the door. Something was wrong with the compressor. At eight Mr. Stan Wyszynski, the Blue Bird tour guide, had herded them back onto the sidewalk for the new bus's imminent arrival. After a half hour he had allowed them to return to the cocktail lounge until further notification, which came at nine. Now here it was 11:06 P.M., and the new bus still hadn't shown up. Mrs. Tilman wondered if they ever would see New England.

"I'm worried about Emily," Clara said to her mother, who had separated herself from the cluster of women surrounding Mrs. Simms and Miss Jones. Some of the women were tipsy from the long wait. Their laughter grated on Mrs. Tilman's taut nerves. She couldn't help wondering what sort of example they were setting the younger generation, which, on this trip at least, consisted of a single representative, her daughter.

"I think I'll go call her."

"Oh, Clara, must you? You might miss the bus." Glancing over at Mr. Stan, who was counting the suitcases lined up at the curb, Mrs. Tilman added, "And I don't want you sitting next to that man on the bus."

"What man? Him? Why would I—"

"Because you've been too nice to him. You can't be so nice to people up North, Clara Edward. They might get the wrong idea."

"No one has a right not to be nice," Clara stated defiantly. During this trip she had discovered that she didn't like her mother as much as she thought she had. Back in Tula Springs Mrs. Tilman had seemed so much easier to get along with. But the minute she had stepped onto the plane in New Orleans, her mother had become almost like another woman. To begin with, Mrs. Tilman had insisted upon bringing along three pairs of glasses, one for reading, one for distance, and a pair of bifocals. Over Atlanta she had misplaced the bifocals, and had turned around to ask the man behind her if he would search under her seat for them. "When I finish my dinner, Ma'am," he had said. "Enjoy your dinner," Mrs. Tilman shot back, to Clara's complete and utter mortification. She had never known her mother to be so rude.

"Everything all right, ladies?" Mr. Stan asked with a wink as he strolled over to them.

"Oh, fine. Forty-second Street is charming this time of night."

Mrs. Tilman was the wife of a prominent physician in Tula Springs, where she never had to insist on the respect due her. Up here, though, was another story. There was something about this Mr. Stan—as he would have them call him—that made her feel common. And who was he to tack on the "Mr." as if he were in charge of a bunch of Campfire girls?

Clara was beaming warmly at the tour guide to make up for her mother's sarcasm. She was not quite brave enough, though, to say anything to him. The poor man must have a desperately hard life, she imagined. He had a beautiful voice, just like someone on an FM station, but his polyester blazer was too large for his skinny frame, and his gray bellbottom slacks had a few pale stains—spot remover, no doubt, that had not worked. She wondered how he managed to be cheerful and witty to one busload of old ladies after another. There was no ring on his finger, so he must go home to an empty apartment, cook his own dinner over a two-ring burner, and then spend the evening in front of the TV set, wishing he had a girlfriend to hug, someone to make his life less bleak . . .

"Clara Edward," Mrs. Tilman said urgently under her breath, startling her daughter out of her reverie.

"What?"

"Stop staring. The very idea."

Mr. Stan had been summoned by Mrs. Jenks, the oldest member on the tour, and Clara's eyes had apparently followed him.

"I wasn't staring."

"Come," Mrs. Tilman said, taking her arm, as a worried-looking couple, not in their group, ventured out from the motel lobby. Mrs. Tilman was simply trying to get her daughter out of their path, but Clara yanked her arm free.

"Ow! That hurt." Mrs. Tilman had grabbed her right on the

bruise, the one her fiancé had given her. Tears welled up in Clara's eyes. She had not told her mother about the bruise, mainly because the invitations had already been sent out, and the bridesmaids' gowns had been ordered. Clara did not want to upset her mother at this late date. And besides, F.X. had apologized for hitting her. He said it would never happen again. He even put his hand on the Bible and swore it wouldn't. He just loved her so much, that was the trouble. He couldn't stand having her away from him.

"What are you doing? Let these good people pass."

"I'm going to call Emily."

"Wonderful. Miss the bus."

"Mother, please. I'll be right there in the office. Just run over and knock on the door. I can't go anywhere without knowing she's O.K." Clara had been calling the apartment all evening, hoping to entice Emily over to the motel for a cup of coffee. But there had been no answer, and Emily had said nothing about going out.

Inside the office Clara was referred to a pay phone in the adjoining coffee shop. Realizing that she had relinquished her purse to her mother, who, in the interest of safety, was carrying it inside her tote bag, Clara approached a stout middle-aged woman eating pea soup at the counter, and asked in a soft, polite voice if she might borrow a dime.

"I know he loves me, except that the way he looked at me when he hit me, the rage in his face, I just can't get it off my mind, Minna," she was saying a few minutes later after she and the lady had gotten acquainted. Minna Burns, who had not only given Clara two nickels but had offered to buy her a cup of soup, a hamburger, anything she might like, turned out to be one of the nicest people Clara had ever met. And she had led such an interesting life, too. Minna had been a John Robert Powers model, had worked as a coat check girl at the Copacabana, and danced with Ann Corio, someone who used to be famous back then.

"Not at first," Clara was saying as she sampled a spoonful of Minna's soup. "At first I thought New York was so loud and dirty. And everyone seemed so rude."

"That's a myth. You'll find some of the warmest, friendliest people in the world here, darling. They'd give you the shirt off their back."

"Well, if they're anything like you . . ." Clara smiled sweetly at the face that, yes, could have been beautiful once. The woman wore so much makeup, though, that it was hard to tell. And she had on sunglasses and a scarf over her head.

Clara was explaining more about her feelings for F.X. when she felt a twitch on the back of her cashmere sweater.

"Give her back those nickels," Mrs. Tilman whispered after Clara had introduced her to her new friend.

"But mother—"

"I've got a dime. Here, give me the girl's number. I'll phone her myself. And you, Clara Edward, you better get back outside. Mr. Stan said any minute. You'll pardon us, Miss Burns."

As she dialed, Mrs. Tilman held the phone a half inch from her ear. Actual contact with a public phone, especially in a big city, was ill-advised, she felt.

"Hello, Emily, is that you?"

Another grunt, this time distinctly masculine.

"Kindly put Miss Brix on the phone."

"Uh, she's indisposed."

Mrs. Tilman looked hard at the receiver. On the other end of the line Lucas was regaining his shaken confidence. He had feared the worst, that somehow Judy had gotten this number. But more fully awake now, he realized this was impossible. Judy did not even know Emily existed, had never heard her name. In fact, even he hadn't been sure what the last name was.

"Who is it?" Emily asked timidly from the air mattress.

"Huh?"

Emily had also dozed off. Awakened by the ringing, she had lain there on the floor in an agony of doubt. She was sure it was Leif, the director, demanding an answer then and there. And she still couldn't make up her mind if it was morally right or not to be Bobby-Boy.

"Here," Lucas said, stretching toward her with the phone. But the cord wouldn't reach.

"Yes, hello?" Emily said doubtfully after hopping onto the bed.

"Emily? This is Mrs. Tilman. Clara's concerned about you. She's been trying to reach you all evening."

"Oh, hi, Mrs. Tilman. How are you? I went out to dinner.

13

And then I . . . I invited a few people back for coffee, to the apartment."

"I see."

There was an awkward pause, during which Emily realized she was leaning against a beefy leg, and enjoying it. Starting, she sat up and removed herself from the bed. But to continue the conversation she was forced to lean over the bed, over his body, in a position that made her feel quite foolish.

"I'm sorry I didn't get to see you, Mrs. Tilman. It's been a long time."

"Yes, dear. I'm sorry, too. Very sorry."

Emily shifted uneasily. "It was so good seeing Clara."

"She was happy to— What is it, Mr. Stan? The bus? It's here? Is Clara— What? Everyone's waiting for *me*? Fine, I like that. Emily dear, I must run. You be careful, hear?"

"Yes, Ma'am. I will."

two

Mark Four's suite of offices was next door to a large and garish topless bar whose doors never seemed to close. The hawker who stood outside handing out free drink coupons had made the mistake of whistling once too often at Emily on her way to work. Though filled with trepidation, she decided on a certain crisp September morning—the morning after Mrs. Tilman's call—that she had reached her limit. With an abrupt about-face she informed him, as calmly and politely as possible, that if he dared to whistle at her one more time she would spray him with enough Mace to kill a cow.

As she strode away, instead of feeling triumph, she was stricken with guilt. His brown face, pleasant in its way, had taken on such a look of shock and pain. He was an Indian, probably a Hindu, and she might have insulted his religious beliefs, she feared, by referring to a cow. Yet she hadn't meant to say that. It had just slipped out. Oh, she hoped he didn't think she was being racist. She really and truly hadn't noticed his color until it was all over.

Somewhat muddled and upset, Emily composed herself in the ladies' room before going into Mr. Cooper's office to report on a script she had read the day before. Jean-Luc Godard being

15

her favorite director—she had written a thirty-page paper on *Vivre sa Vie* at Smith—the screenwriter did not fare well. Her denunciation of his ineptitude was crisp and to the point. "All in all, a clumsy attempt to cash in on the success of *Butch Cassidy* with a patently obvious feminist tract. This distaff buddy picture is neither good box office nor good art, though it has pretensions to both." So ended her oral report.

Mr. Cooper tapped his aristocratic nose for a moment before commenting, "Of course, you realize that it's under option."

"This? Who would be dumb enough to buy . . . ?" Even as she was saying it, an inkling of the correct answer made her feel lightheaded. Mr. Cooper's pursed lips confirmed her distress.

"You should have told me," she said bravely. "You know I've only been reading first submissions."

Though he was neither lean nor tall, Mr. Cooper's bearing, along with his clipped Oxbridge accent, gave him an upper-class aura. Yet at the same time he was an unusually emotional man, at least when it came to tears. More than once he had closed his door to weep in solitude, while Emily, out at her desk, would be fending off calls in a state of pity, dismay, and irritation.

"I wanted an opinion from an expert," he managed to say finally.

"Expert?"

"A women's libber."

A somewhat grim smile clouded Emily's cherubic face. She could not stand that term. It sounded so smug and condescending, especially when a man used it. "Mr. Cooper, if you wanted an expert to read it, you could have gotten Gloria Steinem. But if you wanted a human being, then . . . And besides, I didn't go into any details. There were some scenes that I found very engaging, such as the one in the dry goods store. Now if the author were able to get that kind of pacing into the rest of the script, where there's a nice give-and-take, not so many long speeches— well, then, I think you might just have something."

"What dry goods store?"

"You know, where the murder takes place."

"What murder?"

"The midwife, she's shot in the dry goods store by the blacksmith. It's the climax, what everything has been building toward."

"Oh, right. Yes."

Emily remained standing before the blond, kidney-shaped desk while he jotted something down. Then he swiveled his leather chair to face the windows, which afforded a glimpse, if one's head was craned, of Central Park. Not knowing whether she had been dismissed or not, she took a step or two over the Axminster carpet toward the door.

"Miss Brix," he said, his back still toward her.

She waited for him to go on. When he didn't, she said, "Yes?"

"Miss Brix?"

"Yes, Mr. Cooper."

"What's the name of that script again?"

"The one I just reported on? 'Ma Henry and Mrs. McByrd.' "

"Ah, yes, just as I thought. You've reported on the wrong script. That isn't the one we have under option. Why waste my time with such trash? A simple rejection would have sufficed."

"But this is what you told me—"

"Tell Heather to give you the proper script. I can't stand it when she bungles things like that."

Back at her desk Emily realized that she could not go on working for this man at the expense of her sanity. Perhaps the time had come to throw in the towel. Acting, after all, was her real ambition. She had always dreamed of making it big someday, reinterpreting Webster, Ibsen, and Strindberg for the contemporary stage. The trouble was, she also had to pay the rent. Even if she accepted the part of Bobby-Boy, she would not see a cent, since the producer was donating all acting fees to a peace fund. Yet hadn't Leif, the director, told her that the man playing Bobby-Boy's father was in a lot of commercials? Maybe if she got to know him, he would help her break into that field. Of course, the whole idea of TV commercials was a little nauseating to her. But if it gave her the chance to do serious theater, perhaps she could swallow her pride.

As she dialed Leif, she instructed herself to be firm. She knew Leif was dying for her to play the part. What she would say first to him was no. This would put her in a position of power. Then when he begged her to come aboard, she would give in by degrees. First she would tell him her idea about making Bobby-Boy into Bobbie-Girl. After all, she really didn't look like a boy. O.K., so she might not have the world's most astounding measurements, but she still had all the right curves. (In fact, the more she thought about it, the more insulting it seemed. It was a good thing Leif had explained that the boy was supposed to be very effeminate.) Next, she would make him promise to do away with the nude scenes, at least hers. It would be much more effective to suggest an incestuous relationship with a few offhand remarks, and leave the rest to the audience's imagination.

"I've made up my mind, Leif," she said after they had discussed the *Pentagon Papers* awhile. "I can't take the part. I'm sorry, but if you really want—"

"Oh, Emmy, that's super. See, we've already decided to use a real boy, this absolutely marvelous lad from the Living Theater. You wouldn't believe he's sixteen. I mean he really does look twelve. With you—well, you know you did look sort of old, you have to admit. But you're a sport, and we're so glad you called. Ciao, bella."

Emily did not see Lucas for another three weeks, and then it was by chance at a screening of *Klute*. In that time she had felt herself mature so rapidly that it was almost as if a different person were nodding pleasantly to him, a few rows ahead. There had been another spate of lunch-hour auditions, and she had even seen five agents who specialized in commercial bookings. A friend from Smith had suggested she enroll at Juilliard or the Yale Drama School, but Emily's parents didn't have the resources to support her any longer. It was all they could do to scrape up enough to repay the loan from Smith, which, along with a partial scholarship, had made it possible for her to afford the rather steep tuition.

But aside from nothing materializing, not a single offer in two weeks, what bothered her the most was the feeling that maybe, if she kept at it, she just might succeed—not in serious theater, but with a series of Bobby-Boy compromises. In a way, she was relieved that things hadn't worked out with Leif. What would have become of her integrity, her self-esteem, if she had been able to fool herself into thinking that an almost pornographic role was morally acceptable? One Bobby-Boy would have followed another, with a series of hairspray and deodorant commercials paying the rent, questionable means justifying a noble end, Shaw or Brecht, or perhaps a role in a serious art film. Yet who was ever going to let her play Saint Joan or the Good Woman? And when in God's name would she ever pick up the phone and hear Ingmar Bergman asking her to join Ingrid Thulin and Bibi Andersson on the set?

"In other words, what it all adds up to is a case of sour grapes," Lucas commented, after she had explained herself at some length. It was Emily who had suggested they walk over to Clancy's after the screening. She had come by herself, using Mr. Cooper's invitation. Lucas was with a friend, a gray-haired subsidiary rights director, who had to go fix supper for her children—or so she claimed. Emily detected a bit of disappointment in her voice when Lucas had made no effort to include her in Emily's invitation.

The first drink dulled the stale odor from the buffet, where cabbage, pork, hashbrowns, brussels sprouts, and shepherd's pie surreptitiously overcooked and disintegrated in the steam-table trays. Clancy's was something of an anomaly amid the skyscrapers of Rockefeller Center. Before the sixty-story monoliths had gone up, Clancy's had been a neighborhood hangout, its shamrock-green tin siding as unpretentious as its handpainted sign. Emily imagined the land on which it sat was worth a fortune. Yet it was still possible to eat a hefty dinner for three dollars and buy yourself a martini for a buck. Lucas was the one who had introduced her to the place. She would never have ventured in on her own.

"What?" Emily asked, leaning over the Formica table. The din from the bar, where a group of night watchmen downed their breakfast beers, made it necessary to listen hard.

Lucas was about to repeat "sour grapes," but with a shrug thought better of it. He had decided that he was never going to see Emily again after that night he had spent at her apartment. What with the hall door opening and closing at all hours, he had barely gotten a wink of sleep. As if that wasn't bad enough, he had been tensely waiting for her to join him in bed, especially after that phone call when she had leaned against his bare leg. There was nothing worse than a tease. And yet what puzzled him was that, for the most part, she seemed quite the opposite of a tease. In retrospect he had downplayed this quality to himself, her earnestness, until he was reminded of its appeal at the screening. When she had asked him in such a straightforward manner, without the least bit of feminine guile, to grab a bite with her, he could not resist.

"You said sour grapes, didn't you?" Emily prompted. "I suppose that's what it must sound like to you. But that isn't it at all. I'm determined to do something with my life. I haven't given up at all. There's so much inside me that I want to express, so much beauty and pain—but at the same time, I've got to be realistic. I'm not going to lay these things out for other people to walk all over. To begin with, let's be honest. I'm no knockout. When I go for an audition, there aren't any tongues hanging out. I'm short, not terribly well-built."

"You're really quite a dish, my dear."

"Stop it."

"No, I mean it. Your skin, and the way your eyes, they're so dark for a blonde, almost black, aren't they? Believe me, men notice you."

Emily suppressed a wave of pleasure. Gnawing on a strand of hair, she regarded him a moment as he signaled for another round. Had he been totally serious about her looks—or was there a note of irony in his voice? As a girl Emily had always suffered from being so slight. She feared all through high school that she was not the least bit attractive—and this had kept her from the stage. Even though she had had a passionate desire to act, it had been a guilty secret back then, something she dared not reveal to her classmates by trying out for the senior play. But at Smith, gaining more confidence as she endured the horror of mixers, and found herself being asked to dance, to go out on dates, she had worked up the courage to try out for smaller parts. And eventually, her senior year, she had presented her one-woman show, which had made her something of a celebrity at her house. Except for a few radical druggies, all her classmates had been deeply impressed by her work.

"Look," she resumed when the drinks were set down, "if there were someone able to make something of my particular appeal— I suppose I must be the type that grows on you, sneaks up on you—if there were an American Godard, I'd have it made. But just look at who's making movies nowadays. It's all hopelessly commercial. I've told you about Mr. Cooper. What more can I say?"

With a shrug Lucas bit into a brussels sprout, washing it down with Cutty Sark. It was sad to see someone so young— twenty-one, twenty-two?—give up so soon. Usually these young hopefuls lasted until they were thirty, sometimes even forty, before they cried uncle. He had known plenty of them in Paris ten years ago, girls from Ohio, Indiana, stunning creatures who infiltrated all the right parties, desperately smart, starving for the tiniest morsel of legitimate work. Giving up on Paris, they would migrate to Rome, where they might be extras in a sword-and-sandal flick. Then back to Paris again for another crack at landing a role in something that mattered, a real art film. After all, if Jean Seberg could do it, with her atrocious French . . .

Lucas had had money back then, half a million inherited from his father with no strings attached. In Paris this was enough to make him a bigshot, a producer with options on half a dozen avant garde scripts, none of which was ever made. But that didn't seem to bother anyone. He was courted by a horde of would-be Godards, Bressons, who graciously allowed him to pick up their tabs and the tabs of friends and friends of friends. It was a glorious time, of grand talk and grander plans for conquering the artistic world, everyone sharing a profound contempt for anything smacking of Hollywood. And, at the conclusion of a five- or six-hour dinner, after six or seven bottles of Pommard, there were the hugs, the kisses, the indiscriminate love and fellowship that boundless hope encourages.

Sometimes with Emily he would try to revive these times, feeding her hopes and dreams with an enthusiasm largely simulated. Deep down, he did not really believe she could ever make it as an actress. Yes, he had tried to goad her with "sour grapes." But there was something dishonest about carrying this taunt too far. Perhaps it was better that she face up to reality sooner rather than later. Maybe she would somehow manage to make more out of her life than a house in Jersey and a daily commute to the city. How horrified he would have been if anyone in Paris had told him this was to be his future. And yet here he was, not horrified at all. It was indeed possible, this sort of life—wasn't it?

21

For a few minutes they said nothing, devoting themselves to satisfying their hunger. Though he was on the verge of becoming downright fat, Lucas had a large enough frame to support a great deal of weight and still look rugged as an ex-ballplayer. He marveled at what Emily, just a wisp of a girl, could put away, her face frowning with concentration.

"You play billiards?" he asked over coffee.

She shook her head.

"Come on, then. I'll learn you how, girl."

She should have known that he was not going to take her to the Union League or some such club. Lucas was always coming up with surprises, such as when she had found out he worked for a textbook publisher. After all he had told her about his days in Paris—this had been during a wedding reception at Goethe House, she a friend of the Smith bride, he a distant relative of the much older groom—it came as such a shock to find out he was now just a production assistant for medical texts. And he didn't appear at all dismayed by this change of fortune. In fact, he even seemed to enjoy the effect the ending, as he called it, had on his listener. As he was talking about his past, having actually eaten artichokes with Jean-Paul Belmondo and driven Anouk Aimée home from a party, Emily's hopes had soared. She thought she had finally met someone who might be able to help her out, besides being a possible friend. The "ending," though, calmed her down again. After all, it should have been obvious that he was too kind, too decent, to wield any power in that world.

"Is it safe to go here?" she couldn't help asking, as they emerged from the taxi on 14th Street just off First. The billiard parlor on the second floor, El Cuate, did not look inviting through its grimy plate glass windows. Emily took hold of his arm as they walked past a gated-up karate supplies shop to the stairs.

"Don't be chicken. Come on."

As she had feared, she turned out to be the only blonde in the smoke-hazed room. Almost every table was in use, the sallow light making the Hispanic faces hunched over the worn baize look pale and drained. Every fiber of her being was on guard. She nudged him away from a table that was too close to a pair of six-foot women in elaborate wigs with tattoos on their cheeks. After a short wait, during which Emily dared not look at Lucas for fear of showing her resentment, a bleary-eyed older man, who had been playing alone, signaled that his corner table was free. In a low voice Lucas told her as he chalked up his cue that the man was probably Cuban. He could tell by his accent.

"Now, what you want to do first . . ." He racked up the balls. Despite his Paul Stuart blazer and Choate tie—a boy's tie really, from his prep school days—Lucas did not look out of place. He had a rumpled, defeated look and, what she noticed for the first time, a glint of malice in his eyes.

"Here?" she asked after he had muttered some vague instructions about holding the cue. "It feels so funny. All right, give me room." She stiffened, took aim. The cue ball exploded, ricocheting with ineffective force all over the table.

"Stroke it, don't murder it."

"I am."

Emily could not get over the feeling that she was being stared at, yet when she glanced up, no one seemed to be paying them the least attention. Nevertheless, she was still not happy with him for bringing her here. Probably he wanted to show her that he wasn't bourgeois, even if he did have a home in Jersey. It really wasn't necessary, though, as far as she was concerned. She was getting a little weary of friends proving they weren't middle-class.

After she had sunk the cue ball for the second time, Lucas commented, "Think, you're not thinking." There was an edge to his voice, he knew, but the more he tried to disguise it, the sharper it became. He was beginning to worry that maybe this joint wasn't such a hot idea, after all. What if someone made trouble—and she looked under so much strain. He had wanted to show her what the real world was like, though, and had thought it worth the risk. Of course, she had never made a racist comment around him, but she still couldn't hide the fact that she had grown up in a white-bread world. She had admitted at the Goethe Club—where he had picked her out as the most enticing girl in the room—that she did not have a single black friend in Louisiana. And that she had never participated in a civil rights march down

23

there—though, to be fair, her father had made the family go without supper when they learned of the murder of the three civil rights workers in Mississippi.

Perspiration beaded her nose. He had to hand it to her; she was trying. And her aim was improving. "Take it easy, Miss Emily. Don't jerk. That a girl." He glanced over and saw the Cuban by the door. The man did not look dangerous, but he did have an eye on Emily. Lucas scowled, and the Cuban looked away.

"I used Mr. Cooper's invitation," Emily was saying while Lucas lined up a shot. "He can't stand Jane Fonda. Did I tell you—he's got me making suggestions on a script he's bought? Tightening scenes, things like that. It's kind of exciting, thinking my ideas could actually be used."

The Cuban finally left. Lucas felt less on edge now, though he was far from being relaxed. It was getting late, and he wondered when she was going to suggest staying over at her place. Judy was in Rochester and wasn't due back for another two days. But why should he put himself in another awkward position? Perhaps this time he should say no and take the PATH on 14th. If he wrapped things up now, there was still time to catch a train from Hoboken.

"I thought you didn't like him," Lucas said, adjusting the cue for her. Leaning close, he felt a distinct chill of pleasure. "That Cooper fellow, didn't you say he was nuts or something?"

"Oh, he is. He drives everyone around the bend. Heather, the story editor, she can't take it any longer. She and her boyfriend are planning to buy a cabin in the Adirondacks and live off the earth, soon as they save up enough. She's going to weave her own bedspreads and make her own dishes, grow their food. See, she grew up in Queens and she's, you know . . . Starved for space. She wants to look out her window and see mountains, stuff like that."

Only half listening, he glanced at his Rolex.

Emily, who herself had not really been attending to what she was saying, worried about what was going to happen next. She hated to go home alone. He was such an interesting man. But if she asked him this second time, it would mean something different. It wouldn't have the spontaneity of the previous time. "Getting late."

He grunted. "Want to pack it in?"

With a shrug she stashed her cue stick on the rack.

Downstairs, after he had paid, he pointed out two whorehouses, dismal-looking buildings that made her wonder about men. They strolled farther west, past darkened shops selling vinyl motorcycle jackets and tube socks, until they got to Luchow's, where he asked if she would like to stop in for a nightcap. "It's one of those grand old places, when Union Square used to be the center of New York. They even had a film studio on this street. Lillian Gish made some movies here."

"Does your wife know about me?"

It was the first time either of them had ever mentioned Judy to the other. Lucas had not even been sure Emily knew he was married. But apparently she had found out from a friend.

"What's there to know?"

Emily's heart seemed to swell painfully. She could not believe she was talking like this to a married man twice her age. It didn't make the least bit of sense. What could have gotten into her this evening?

His gaze, hard, almost cruel, remained fixed on her. "What's there to know?" he repeated.

For a brief moment or two Emily could almost feel Jean-Luc Godard's presence. The setting was perfect, so were the actors. If only this tender, dangerous moment could be transfigured into black and white—then she could go through with it.

Yet again, "What's there to know?"

"Nothing, I guess. Better hurry, Lucas. You'll miss your train."

three

When she got home from the billiard parlor, she immediately dialed Hugh. Somehow an experience never seemed quite real or fully formed until it was discussed with Hugh. He understood so much about life. It seemed he had read everything and could quote from Greek plays, Chaucer, almost anything, at will. Around him Emily felt her horizons expand, and she would delight in the way he helped her discover the archetypical beneath the often confusing flow of sensation and emotion. That evening, for instance, he would be able to help her find a pattern in the muddle of her relationship with Lucas. Hugh would explain the tug the older man was exerting, her flirtation with an underworld, a Hades, that everyone, according to Hugh, must explore at one time or another.

Though she wasn't able to reach him that night, she did get through the next morning. To her relief—there was so much she wanted to talk about—Hugh said he would have time between classes to drop by her office for lunch. In his second year at Union Theological Seminary, Hugh had no intention of becoming a minister. Most ministers, he felt, were hopelessly compromised by their parishioners. A tendency to want to please one's congregation invariably led to a subversion of the Word. Any authentic witnessing could only be accomplished, he had told Emily more than once, in the secular world.

"So I told him no, absolutely not. I said, 'Leif, I don't care how big a role it is, I'm not going to do it.' "

"He wanted you to play a boy?"

She nodded. "A twelve-year-old boy who seduces his father."

Hugh was hunched over on Mr. Cooper's leather couch, a roast beef hero on his knees. While her boss was in Los Angeles, Emily felt free to use his office, though he had never given her explicit permission to do so. Anxious for some sign of approval, she regarded her friend intently as she devoured her roast pork hero smothered in mayonnaise and coleslaw. With his soft frizzy hair, blonder than Art Garfunkel's, and pink boyish skin, he had an amazingly innocent look that was belied only in profile, when his strong, aquiline nose brought out a more manly aura. When Emily had first met him at a Smith mixer, she had not thought he was particularly attractive until a friend or two had commented on her catch, as they put it. Hugh had been drunk when he asked her to dance. Later he had thrown up in the bushes outside the Dean's office. Yet despite all this he somehow managed to come across as being quite refined, almost English.

"Anyway," she prompted, "I think I'm beginning to see your point."

He looked up, his mouth stuffed and slightly agape. This refinement of his stopped short of table manners. When Emily had once questioned the way he ate, Hugh had given her a disquisition on the evolution of table manners, the gist being that they were decidedly a bourgeois invention. Though historically he was perhaps in the right—look at the horrors the cleanliness and propriety of the German middle-class pointed toward, he had observed, citing *Steppenwolf*—she still couldn't get over the feeling that one could chew with one's mouth closed and yet refrain from sending people to the gas chamber.

"What point?" A few crumbs exploded onto Mr. Cooper's treasured Axminster.

"About acting. It is a pretty strange career."

"Profession," he corrected, reminding her of his belief that acting was essentially a sublimated form of a slightly older profession. He had argued this without guile or rancor, marshaling facts and quotations from Boethius to Artaud. Her protests had been emotional, even somewhat hysterical, based on a gut feeling that in its purest form there was true glory in such a career. But she could not prove her point intellectually with him.

Returning to the question of Lucas, she hoped to prod Hugh into making a few comments on the situation. She had sketched in her evening at the billiard parlor for him, while they were waiting for the deli to send up their sandwiches. But he had seemed preoccupied then, and had little to say.

"Every time I see him it's almost like he's a different person. When I met him at Susan's wedding reception, I thought at first he was just another stockbroker or something. Then he tells me about having lunch with Delphine Seyrig in Paris. Then the next thing I know he's picking out a typeface or something for textbooks." She dabbed at a shred of coleslaw on her cheek. "Last night, though, there was this mean look to him. It was the first time I was scared of him—and sorry, too. Like he's been hurt real bad. All these feelings were churning around inside me."

"Does he want to have an affair with you?"

"I suppose. He's middle-aged, married, you know the type. I have to discourage him a lot. But I'm afraid of discouraging him too much."

"Why?"

"Because he might run off. He's too old-fashioned to know how to relate to a woman without sex. He can't understand just being friends. It's a shame, too. I think I like him a lot."

"What about his wife?"

"He never talks about her. And he doesn't wear a ring. If it weren't for Lucy—"

"Feldman?"

"No, Lucy Barnstone. She works for *Glamour*. We have lunch every now and then. Anyway, she told me Lucas's wife is very prim and proper. She was the one who reined him in after he spent all his money in Paris. He would have gone to pot without someone like her, setting limits, managing the money for him. And Lucy told me that Judy—that's his wife—she'd probably kill anyone who got too close to him."

"You like to live dangerously."

"No, I just don't like bossy women. I think Lucas deserves a bit of fresh air every now and then. Sometimes it seems to me like he's being smothered. He's trying to be Mr. Suburbia and he's not. This wild streak in him, it seems like a very precious thing to me, something that needs to be embraced, accepted. Judy is trying to pretend it doesn't exist—that's what's killing him. I think it could be a source of great creative energy. He's got a lot to give. And by the way, I have nothing to be ashamed of. I could look his wife right in the eye, you know. We haven't done a thing—not even shaken hands."

"Oh, listen," he said after the story editor had poked her head in the doorway, made a wry face, and gone away. Emily was a little disappointed in Hugh. He wasn't up to par this afternoon, conversation-wise. She wished he would make more of an effort to be fascinating. But something was obviously on his mind. He could only feign interest in Lucas.

"What is it?"

He looked glumly at his hero before taking a bite. His mouth full, he could proceed: "De Morgan is coming back in a few days."

"Oh. Well. What are you going to do?"

"I don't know."

Hugh had been subletting an apartment in what was really Spanish Harlem, though there were a number of Columbia students scattered throughout the neighborhood. Emily was too scared to visit him there unless a male friend went with her. It was frustrating not being able to see Hugh as often as she wanted, especially since he seemed to have so little free time. She was almost glad now that Bill De Morgan was coming back from the Peace Corps in Libya. It would force Hugh to find a more reasonable location to live in, or so she hoped.

"Well, if you need a place to crash for a while," she ventured.

"Your place is so small."

She shrugged. "It might do till you find another. You shouldn't be forced to rent something just because you don't have time to look around."

"You're on the East Side. It could be a hassle, you know. But I guess . . . You really don't mind?"

"No, it'll be fun. And I promise I won't bother you. I'll let you study as much as you want."

"Well, you're sure it's O.K.?"

"Oh, yes, sure. Listen, I get pretty lonely sometimes. It'll be nice to have someone to talk to."

As he bit into his hero a gob of mayonnaise squirted onto his sneakers.

"Hugh?"

"Yes?"

"Do you realize you have on two different pairs of shoes?"

He glanced down at the grimy sneakers, one of which had a hole in the toe. "Huh?"

"That one has green stripes, the other blue."

"Oh, well, anyway," he said, wiping off the gob.

Returning home from the office one evening Emily found a pair of jeans on the kitchen counter, two opened and one unopened suitcase on the living room floor, shirts draped over the shower curtain rod, and books piled everywhere, including on the sofa and the canvas director's chair. Feeling prey to a vague sense of panic, she poured herself a glass of wine and cleared a space on the window ledge, where she was small enough to perch, hugging her knees. Yes, it would be wonderful having her best friend live with her, she assured herself. Hugh was the only man she had dated who hadn't made sex an issue. When she had told him no, the night of the mixer, he accepted it with drunken equanimity. The truth was, she was not really physically attracted to him. He was too much like a brother to her, and she feared that sleeping together would ruin their unusual, intense rapport.

Hugh had spent two years at Oxford before transferring to Williams, where Emily used to visit him on those weekends he didn't have a real date. Up until meeting him, Emily had been dreadfully homesick in Northampton, calling Tula Springs at least once a week, often in tears. She was having a difficult time making friends with other girls. Some of them tried to be nice to her, but in a patronizing way that made it hard for her to open up. It was almost as if, being from Louisiana, she was considered backward, a little slow. And in a way, she was. She found it hard to keep up with their conversations, all the allusions to people and places she had never heard of (Bendel's, Hobe Sound, Miss Porter's, Sneden's Landing) or if she had, not quite grasping their significance. Like knowing schoolbook French and then trying to join in a rap session with hip Parisians, Emily realized how stilted, tentative, even amusingly quaint she could sound. Then there were those who assumed she was racist, giving her a gentle dig whenever the subject came up—or not so gentle. One budding friendship with a lovely senior from Maine seemed to hold out some hope her sophomore year. She was so flattered by the older girl's attention and thrilled to the marrow that there was someone else who confessed to being as lonely as she was. But when Emily heard rumors that the senior was a lesbian, she backed off from her and spent more time studying and writing papers.

Then came Hugh, who made most of the girls she used to hold in such awe seem silly and shallow. Hugh made fun of their pretensions to culture and society. He himself considered Harvard and Yale gauche, Williams being the only school he had applied to in the States. Even Oxford didn't escape his scrutiny. He found it entirely overrated, and pointed out to Emily a number of grammatical errors and misquotations in a don's highly lauded book. Half the English undergraduates seemed queer and weren't; the other half didn't and were. Hugh was glad to have gotten England out of his system. He had fallen in love with all things English at St. Paul's, his prep school in New Hampshire, but had come to realize what an ass he had been. Emily hung on Hugh's every word, secretly thrilled when he described having tea with a duke's son. "You have no idea what foul breath is . . . And his teeth, I can't begin to describe them. Green, literally green."

While sipping her wine, Emily tried to silence further misgivings about Hugh's move. The most time they had spent together at a stretch was a Williamstown weekend. And there they had been able to take the loveliest drives in Hugh's Audi to Bennington or Mt. Greylock. How would they get along here, day after day, in such a drab apartment? She hadn't bothered to make the place nice, not just because she hadn't the money, but also because she only considered it a way station. With a raise, she would move on. Here, with no fireplace (Hugh's off-campus apartment had had one), no view, would she begin to seem ordinary to him? Would he begin to wonder why he put up with this girl who wouldn't even sleep with him? This anxiety made her realize just how much she valued his friendship. She made up her mind to do everything she could to make his stay as pleasant as humanly possible.

It was a nuisance to blow up the air mattress every night, so after a while Hugh was sleeping on the floor with only a cushion or two and a blanket. Emily arranged herself guiltily on the sofa without pulling out the bed. She would have been happy to sleep on the floor so he could have the bed, but he got testy when she tried to insist on this. Her concern about being too much in the way gradually diminished, mainly because Hugh spent so much time at Union's Burke Library. There were days on end when she barely had a chance to say good night to him. His mother, though, was a different story. She not only phoned the apartment on a regular basis, but also called Emily at Mark Four. Mrs. Squires had a way of speaking of Hugh as if he were a good friend, not a son. Assuming that he and Emily were sleeping together, she managed to put Emily in an awkward position. Whenever Emily tried to make it clear that she and Hugh were just friends, Mrs. Squires—or Lettice, as she preferred to be known—would seem affronted. Lettice was somewhat proud of being with it, and didn't appreciate Emily's attempts to sugarcoat reality. The more Emily protested, the more insincere she sounded, even to herself.

"You gave her my work number?" Emily asked one evening as she was washing her one good sweater in Woolite in the salmon bathroom sink. Hugh was a few feet away, drying the supper dishes. Emily had been pleasantly surprised to find him home when she had unlocked the door. He had even cooked dinner, lamb chops smothered in pinto beans.

"No," he said after careful consideration. He wanted his reply to be completely honest.

"Then how—"

"She must have called information. Mark Four's listed, isn't it?"

"Lettice is wonderful and all, but sometimes she does go on."

"I'll speak to her about that."

"Oh, no—don't do that. I can handle it." Emily mused a moment as she ran more water into the basin. Had she offended him by criticizing his mother? "It's no big deal, you know. I really do like her a lot."

"Who?"

"What?" Emily turned off the tap in order to hear better.

"Never mind," he said from the other room, where he realized he had been drying the same glass for an inordinate amount of time. He was trying hard not to be nervous, but the time had come to lay his cards on the table. Being with Emily these past ten days had convinced him that his hunch about her was right: She was absolutely reliable, trustworthy, someone he could stake his life on. There was no one else he felt this way about, aside from Lettice. Here was a woman who did not exhaust him with her wiles, her need for attention. Neither was he distracted by passion or lust, which could so easily cloud one's reason, making one accommodate one's entire life to a totally unsuitable female. He knew, after all, that it was better to marry than to burn. And Emily would let him be himself. He could get on with his work without having to endure any more blind dates, expensive restaurants, long sexy legs attached to empty heads. Of course, he would be totally honest with Emily when he declared his love for her. He was not infatuated; he did not have an adolescent crush. This was instead a calm, abiding love, one that would grow over the years, the love that was meant to exist between a Christian husband and his helpmeet. Emily was not to mistake this love for that medieval invention, romance, and all that entailed. He wanted to be absolutely clear about this so that they would both know what they were getting into.

Setting aside the glass, he asked if she would mind stepping into the living room.

Emily, who was draping her sweater over the side of the tub to dry, smiled to herself. There was something so quaint and formal about Hugh, almost Victorian. Combined with his dirty jeans and his appalling way of eating, it made for a disconcerting charm.

"Yes, my dear, what is it?" she inquired in a stagy voice as she made her entrance from the bathroom.

With a sheepish smile he motioned her to the sofa. He was in the canvas director's chair, looking unnaturally at ease with his legs sprawled out before him. Usually, he crossed his legs when he sat, and rarely slouched.

"I thought it was time we had a talk."

"Of course, sir."

"Emily, please."

"I'm sorry." His solemnity seemed to bring out the imp in her. She composed her face and hid her bare toes in her hands as she sat Indian-style on the cushions.

Adjusting the lampshade beside him, he cleared his throat. "I'd like to read something to you."

"Will it take long?"

"No—why?"

"I wanted to file my calluses." Emily's new half-heels had given her calluses near the big toes.

"Don't file, please," he requested, opening a book, "not now." His voice sounded husky. He needed a glass of water, but decided to forge ahead regardless. "What I'm going to read is about the Troubadour poetry that appeared at the end of the—" He cleared his throat again, more violently this time.

"Are you all right?"

"Fine. In Languedoc at the end of the eleventh century."

"Oh, Hugh, I've always had trouble with the eleventh century. Couldn't you read something a little earlier, like the ninth?"

"Please, Emily. Bear with me. 'The sentiment'—of this poetry—'the sentiment is love, but love of a highly specialized sort, whose characteristics may be enumerated as Humility, Courtesy, Adultery, and the Religion of Love.' "

Emily experienced a tingle of pleasure, sharpened by the least bit of shame. So Hugh was coming through, after all. He was finally going to give her relationship with Lucas its due.

" 'The lover is always abject,' " he went on, his legs now crossed in a gentlemanly manner. " 'Obedience to his lady's lightest wish, however whimsical, and silent acquiescence in her rebukes, however unjust, are the only virtues he dares to claim. There is a service of love closely modelled on the service which a feudal vassal owes to his lord. The lover is the lady's "man." He addresses her as *midons*, which etymologically represents not "my lady" but "my lord." The whole attitude has been rightly described as "a feudalisation of love." It is possible only to those who are, in the old sense of the word, polite.' "

"Hold on a minute," Emily said, trying to digest this in terms of Lucas. He really wasn't very polite, but then again, she hadn't been very whimsical with him either.

"May I?"

"Go on, yes."

" 'Only the courteous can love, but it is love that makes them courteous. Yet this love, though neither playful nor licentious in its expression, is always what the nineteenth century called "dishonourable" love. The poet normally addresses another man's wife, and the situation is so carelessly accepted that he seldom concerns himself much with her husband: his real enemy is the rival.' " Hugh set the book aside while Emily pondered the "dishonoura-ble," a term she thought unfair, at least in her case.

"You know who this is, of course," he said after an awkward silence.

Emily thought hard, but before she could come up with a wrong answer, he generously supplied, "Lewis. *The Allegory of Love.*"

"C. S. Lewis, right. Well, really, Hugh, I don't see what it has to do with my case. It really doesn't describe the situation very precisely, does it?"

"No, not at all. In fact, it's just the opposite of the way things are. I mean, this is the root of all the nonsense that's thrown our way in movies and novels and on TV. All this romance, it's all—when you get right down to it—dishonorable. It's not the way things were meant to be between a man and a woman. Is it any wonder, Emily, why the divorce rate is skyrocketing? All these notions we have in our heads, they're all about adultery, the religion of love. That's what happens when you idolize something that's basically comical. You have an impossible ideal to live up to. And so everyone feels like a failure. Love is not meant to be a religion. Do you agree?"

His intensity threw her off balance. "Yes, I suppose so. But actually, it was never that way, I mean, you don't seem to un-derstand about us . . ." She and Lucas had only just flirted with love. Now here he was blowing it all out of proportion, making her seem so unethical.

"Emily, I do understand." His heart was thumping wildly. It wasn't going to be as difficult as he had imagined. Yet still, a man only proposed to a woman once in his lifetime; it was an appallingly significant event. "Listen, I think, in these circumstances"— he gestured vaguely toward the army blanket on the floor—"it would make sense if we tried to define how we really feel about each other."

"Oh, you mean you and me?"

A frown creased his forehead. "Emily, I think it's time we admitted how much we mean to each other. I think I want to— to be with you."

Hearing these unexpected words, so unsettling, Emily experienced a curious mixture of disappointment and joy—joy that he really cared for her so much after ten days of such close quarters; disappointment that he, like every other man on earth, it seemed, could not be satisfied with a platonic friendship with a woman. So now he wanted to sleep with her. And yet he knew what her feelings were on the subject. She had been so clear from the very beginning.

"Hugh, do you really think it's such a good idea?"

"Look, all I know is that I've never met anyone like you. You're really a good woman, Emily. I don't mean that in any trite sense of the word. Only in its deepest sense. I don't think you'd ever disappoint anyone. You're engaged in life in a way that's so earnest and valiant. I admire you so much, I did from the minute I met you."

Her heart filled with pride, which she tried to disguise. "Oh, you were drunk when you met me."

"In vino . . ." Saying these things aloud had made him like her even more than he had imagined. "Besides, I'm not drunk now."

"I don't know. You're making it so hard."

"Please, Em. I think I love you."

She hated to sound like such a prude. Here was a man who really cared for her, probably the best friend she would ever have in life. If she said no, if she didn't sleep with him—well, it would never be the same. He would leave. He would find another woman.

"I guess, I mean, if you really must . . ."

"Oh, Em, we'll be so happy. I promise."

She thought sadly of her dream, of being a virgin on her wedding night. Perhaps that was what it meant to grow old, to relinquish one dream after another. Glancing shyly up at him, she tried to imagine what it would feel like to be in his arms. After all, she hadn't been physically attracted to Lucas until she had actually touched him that night, leaning almost unknowingly against his bare leg. Maybe it would be the same with Hugh. Maybe, even though she thought she was drawn to darker men, tougher, more rugged, maybe she would discover that Hugh was just as wonderful and exciting. How could she know unless she gave him a chance? Was she always going to live in a fantasy world, a tease to married men? Wasn't there something a little hypocritical about such technical purity?

"All right, Hugh," she said finally, looking him right in the eye, "I'm game."

It was not the most flattering consent he could have imagined issuing from a bride-to-be's mouth. Nevertheless, he determined to remain cheerful and optimistic. "Well," he said, getting out of the chair, "I guess I should call Lettice."

"What?"

"I want to tell her."

"Oh, Hugh, is it really necessary?"

They exchanged a similar look of distress mingled with puzzlement.

"Emily, it's not something we want to keep secret, is it?"

"Why not? I don't see why you must tell her everything. There's something unnatural about being so open with your mother."

"You mean you don't want her to be there?"

"Be there?"

"At the wedding. Honestly, Em, what's gotten into you?"

A slight croak was the only reply she could manage for the moment. Hugh regarded her with curiosity. "You O.K.?"

"Uh," she replied with an attempt at a smile. "Uh . . ." again, as she hurried to the bathroom for her file. All she could deal with now, she knew, were her calluses.

four

Clara was disappointed. It was evident in her voice when she heard that she wouldn't be able to stay with Emily while she looked for an apartment of her own. "I've got a roommate now to help out with the rent," Emily said flatly, refusing to go into any details for the moment. Emily herself was bewildered about the precise status of her living arrangement and had no stomach for long-distance explanations, especially since Clara had called her at Mark Four.

"You really mean to move to New York?" Emily went on, turning the conversation away from herself as quickly as possible.

"I've decided I want to be a model."

"But Clara, it's such a rough business. There's all sorts of seventeen- and eighteen-year-olds, you know. People usually don't start out at your age."

"I know. But I have contacts. There's this friend of mine who said she'd get me in. She used to be a John Robert Powers model."

"What's that? Listen, aren't you supposed to be getting married? You told me— Excuse me. (I gave it to Mr. Cooper the day before yesterday. He can't say he doesn't have it.) Clara? What about your fiancé?"

"I'd rather not talk about him now. Anyway, I've already got my ticket and—"

"Please deposit eighty-five cents for the next three minutes, or your call will be disconnected. Thank you."

"Oh, Em, I don't have any more change. I'm at the Shell station, my batteries. I'll call you later."

That evening at the apartment Emily complained at length to Hugh about Clara's impending move. He was not as sympathetic as she thought he should be. So don't see her if you don't want to, he said. Emily tried to explain that this was not possible. Clara was one of her sister's dearest friends. And besides, you can't ignore someone from your own hometown.

"Why are you in a tizzy, then?"

"I'm not in a tizzy. It's just that it's hard for me to think straight when she's around. I only saw her for a few minutes when she was here with her mother, but anyway, it was very confusing. She reminds me so much of my past, and she doesn't understand a thing about all the changes I've been through since then. So it's like I'm two people at once. See, I used to be this little mouse. I was always so polite and deferential, and I used to think she was just everything, she and her friends. And, like when she comes, she's going to want to talk about hairstyles and makeup and clothes, and she'll just drag me down, know what I mean?"

"Yeah, I mean like sort of," Hugh mocked.

Emily realized that she had already started to revert, drawing out her vowels, gabbing far too much. She was not pleased with herself at all.

"You know what I think, why you're in such a swivet?"

"No, Hugh."

"It's me. You don't know what to say about me."

"Why should I worry what Clara thinks?"

"Well, she'll tell your family, won't she?"

"Tell them what?"

"Exactly. That's the point."

Ever since the proposal Emily and Hugh had been living in limbo. Her initial reaction, after the shock had worn off, had been something like anger, though she was unsure why she should have felt this. Trying her best to keep the tremor under control—her hands had actually been shaking—she had emerged from the bathroom and calmly, rationally, asked him not to call Lettice. The whole idea of marriage, she explained, was absurd. She was not planning to get married until she was around thirty, with her career established. And she wanted a long courtship, giving her plenty of time to make up her mind. How could he just drop this on her out of the blue, without even once taking her out on a proper date?

Hugh had remained unperturbed. Simply by hearing her out, he made her realize how quaint her objections sounded, like something a spoiled Southern belle might say. And when he had told her, fine, he would move out that very evening, she had begun to doubt her anger even more. After all, she was no longer a girl. She was a grown woman. Maybe this was the way things really happened in this day and age. A man takes you to dinner, and if you don't put out afterward—how she hated that phrase, put out— he thinks something is wrong with you. Was it any wonder that she had been reluctant to have any real dates since moving to New York? And the competition. For every decent guy there seemed to be twelve anxious women. The reality of big-city life was so much grimmer than she had pictured it to be at Smith. What could she mean by alienating this perfectly wonderful man?

"I haven't told you this, but you know, I really didn't have to move in with you. Fay has an extra bedroom in her apartment."

"Good for Fay," she had replied. Though she had never met the woman, she knew that Fay had been after Hugh for years. Their families had neighboring summer homes in Bar Harbor, and Hugh had joined her one summer for a barge cruise down the Loire. "Fay is a little heavy, I heard."

"Who told you that?"

"Lucy."

"Well, she just lost fifteen pounds."

"Oh, Hugh, let's not be childish. Of course you don't have to leave tonight. I just need time to think, O.K.?"

And the more she thought about it, the less impossible the idea came to seem. Perhaps she did worry that Hugh came from a broken home, Lettice having divorced his father and remarried. But when she brought this up, he said he thought his parents' bad example gave him an advantage. He knew just what not to do—

and he planned on not doing it. For he, like Emily, did not believe in divorce. Marriage was forever. Another thing that gave her pause was children. She simply could not imagine having children for another ten years, at least. Again, Hugh was right with her. He thought it would be tremendously irresponsible to even think of bringing children into a world that was on the verge of total destruction.

"I guess I am silly to let Clara upset me like this," Emily said after some time, during which his breathing had become regular, as if he might have dozed off. They were lying side by side on the sofabed, an arrangement he had suggested shortly after the proposal. Still beset by doubts, Emily had hoped that physical contact might settle the question once and for all. But Hugh had surprised her. He told her he had no intention of making love until she agreed to marry him. It was what she had always wanted, wasn't it? Not quite sure what to make of this, Emily acquiesced, though reluctantly. Soon she became used to his warmth, the sweet smell of his very white skin. It was she who first initiated cuddling. Light massage was also her idea. She was amazed at the muscles in his arms and chest, the shoulders. Never before had she imagined him as being strong, and yet he was, naturally so, without having to use weights or other such nonsense. If at first she was troubled by a vague feeling that all this might somehow be wrong, almost incestuous, the taboo gradually began to lend a certain spice to the cuddling. Desire, she was learning, was by definition perverse. It yearned for what could not be, for the "dishonourable." Was it any wonder, then, that she had never desired this man before, the very epitome of honor and goodness?

"Hugh, are you asleep?" she whispered in his ear.

When he turned over, away from her, she was almost angry. Why wouldn't he put those silly scruples aside and take her? Now. Against her will. She wanted to know what it would be like. She wanted to know.

"When you think about it, there's something weird about paying people to be who they aren't. That's essentially what acting boils down to, right? We all have this great urge, almost an erotic urge, to escape the limitations of the self, to run away from who we really are. For me, Genet provides the link between eros and acting. Have you ever seen *The Balcony*? Well, anyway, in that the prostitutes carry out elaborate roles for their clients, who also play complementary roles themselves. And the undertow throughout is that climax cannot be achieved unless the script is followed exactly, precisely, to the letter. The more elaborate the fetish, the further removed from anything connected with sex. In fact, it's possible to take this to its logical conclusion, an entirely sexless fetish, the climax postponed indefinitely. Say a man visits a whorehouse, but he wants the woman to remain fully dressed and to act the part of a clerk in a dime store. He instructs her what to say beforehand. No four-letter words, nothing but the most innocuous conversation, maybe about makeup, the merits of various brands."

"I've always liked Revlon myself," Clara put in, the glazed expression in her eyes being replaced with a spark of interest. "I try to avoid oil-based now, you know."

Bundled up against the damp chill, Clara and Emily were resting on a bench in Central Park. At this hour, just before dusk, two, maybe three separate games of touch football were winding to a close, the one at the far end including a couple of women in sweatpants and rugby shirts. Clara and Emily watched one of the women squeal as she was hauled into the air by the center and subjected to an airplane spin.

"Anyway, let's not talk about makeup," Clara urged. "I get tired of girl talk."

Determined not to be dragged down into banality, Emily had tried her best all day to elevate the tone of the conversation. This latest attempt was a rehash of something she and Hugh had discussed one night before falling asleep.

"Does someone live there?" Clara asked brightly, gazing up at the stone castle on the rocky outcroppings above the pond. Seeing her friend's expression, she hastily added, "That was dumb, wasn't it? I know no one lives there. I don't know why I say things that are dumber than I think."

It had been a discouraging afternoon. *Times* Classifieds in hand, the two had wandered from Yorkville down to Kips Bay and Gramercy Park, back up to Gracie Square, down again to Murray Hill and up finally to Lexington and 89th, where Emily had chided Clara for not taking a charming one-bedroom over a Merit Farms deli. But Clara, prepared to go as high as $375 a month, had objections that could not be overcome. She required an exposed brick wall, plenty of light and counter space, two full-sized closets, and a deep tub. To make matters worse, Clara was wearing alligator heels and complained incessantly about how hard the sidewalks were. It was she who had begged Emily for a rest as they trudged through the Park to look on the West Side.

"The West Side is not as nice," Emily had warned before they set off. "It's not as safe for a woman, you know."

"I don't care. I want to see it anyway."

"Let's get a cab."

"No, we got to walk."

"I thought your feet . . ."

"I'm not a baby."

While they were sitting on the bench Emily mentioned that perhaps it was not a good idea for Clara to smile and say hello to strangers they passed on the street. "You sound just like my mother," Clara chided, rubbing her feet. Only Clara would have thought of wearing stockings and heels to go apartment hunting. Casting a furtive glance at Clara's hair, stiff as a Queens matron's, the blush, green eyeshadow, coral lip gloss, the plucked eyebrows, unnaturally arched, Emily thought sadly how impossible it was going to be for Clara to break into modeling. Before long she would probably be heading back to Louisiana.

"Now I can say I walked through Central Park," Clara said as they resumed their trek. "It's what the real New Yorkers do, isn't it?"

Emily nodded absently. She was scanning the clouds above the bare and brown-leaved limbs, wondering if there was a chance it might snow. The still dark moments before the first few flakes always cast a spell, reminding her of the magical day it had snowed for a few minutes in Tula Springs. She had been nine then, beside herself with joy. Every winter after that she used to pray for snow, but God never answered until she packed herself off to Smith, by which time she no longer believed in him anyway.

"Oh, look," Clara said, giving Emily a nudge. They had emerged from the Park and were heading south when a black man, tall and elegant, leaned over to kiss a white woman he was putting into a cab. Both of them had on matching zebra boots.

Emily stiffened. "What?"

"Didn't you see?"

"The boots? Nice."

The black man was walking toward them now, alone. Emily decided that if Clara made a racist remark after he passed by, she would let her go on looking for an apartment by herself. There was a limit, after all, to how accommodating she could be.

"Hi, how are you?" Clara called out as he strolled past.

"Evening, ladies."

When he was out of hearing distance, Emily said through clenched teeth, "Clara!"

"What? I was just being friendly."

The street lamps were on by the time Clara had rejected a large studio on Riverside and wanted to go back to her hotel, the Barbizon on East 63rd, for a good long soak. But Emily insisted they take a look at the one bedroom in the Seventies, off Central Park West. She had determined sight unseen that Clara was going to like this one because she, Emily, could not endure another day of apartment hunting. She had so little time as it was, and she'd be darned if she was going to let her entire weekend be eaten up.

The address turned out to be a white brownstone with lovely bow windows that Emily exclaimed over even before they were out of the cab. When the super let them into the fourth floor rear apartment, Emily remarked how lucky Clara was to have southern exposure. And she pointed out how nice the terraces of the opposite brownstones would look in the spring when the plants would be in bloom. Clara did admit that the closet space was acceptable, and there was even an exposed brick wall. But the kitchen was cramped and the tub didn't seem deep enough.

"Well, I'll tell you this, you'll never find a place this good for three-fifty, not anywhere on this island."

"I thought you said the West Side was unsafe?"

"Not this part. This is one of the nicest blocks in town. A lot of models live around here. You'd be crazy not to take this. It's going to be snapped up the minute we leave."

"But the kitchen . . ."

"Look, who has time to cook? This is New York. You're going to be run ragged. All you'll want is a pizza or Chinese to go."

"Models live here?"

Emily glanced at the super, hoping his English was rudimentary. He was not just thin, but emaciated, with an Eastern European face, it seemed. Perhaps Croatian.

"This area is full of show-biz types, I read somewhere. I tell you, Clara, you're making a huge mistake. I've seen a lot, you know, and I'll tell you right now that you can spend the next five years comparison shopping but you'll never find anything this good."

"But I'd rather live closer to you on the East Side."

"You've already looked at everything there."

"Not everything." She wrinkled her nose, sniffed, as if she detected an unpleasant odor. "And besides, when am I going to meet your roommate? I think it's sort of mean you didn't ask her to have dinner with us tonight."

"He's busy," Emily said, after some hesitation. "He's got a paper to write."

Clara's blue eyes grew dark with interest. "Oh, Em, you little skunk. I just knew it had to be a he." She gave her a conspiratorial smile that did not sit well with Emily. "Don't worry, girl. I'm not going to say anything. Except Martha, you've got to let me tell Martha. I'll just die if I don't."

"It's not what you think, Clara. See, we're getting married. He's my fiancé."

"Oh, Em!" Clara squealed as she rushed over with outstretched arms. "I just knew you could do it. I knew it!"

Puzzled by the meaning of this, Emily let herself be hugged and kissed by her teary-eyed friend. She was also confused why she had chosen this particular moment to make up her mind about Hugh. But she supposed she must know what she was doing—on some level. Otherwise she wouldn't have said it, would she?

The super looked on from the radiator, where he was perched, one skinny leg folded over the other. Somewhat self-conscious, Emily glanced over and saw he had lit up a joint.

"What's that funny smell?" Clara asked, once she and Emily had disentangled. Turning to the super, a young man, she added, "It's your cigarette. Oh, it's making me sick."

"Hey, like it's cool," he muttered, snuffing it out on the radiator.

Primly, Clara said, "Thank you," then tacked on a very unnecessary smile, which made the super run his dirty fingers through his lank unwashed hair.

"Come look at the bathroom again," Emily urged, wondering if this apartment was such a good idea after all.

five

Lucas had no windows in his cubicle on the thirty-second floor, but he could have looked across the hall and seen through the smoked glass of a more prestigious office a brief, ecstatic whirl of ascending snowflakes. His eyes, though, were focused on the line art clipped to his light table. Shifting on his stool, he guided his X-acto knife across the pica ruler, deleting an inch of boils. The assigned text, sexually transmitted diseases, was due back to the compositor the next day. One block west and six blocks north Emily was telling Mr. Cooper that it would be highly unlikely for a grown woman to go roller-skating just after hearing that her husband, whom she loved, had choked to death at the Four Seasons. Mr. Cooper defended this scene by bringing up Ryan O'Neal, who went ice-skating when Ali MacGraw died. Turning to the window, but not noticing the snow, Emily said she didn't think he actually skated, and besides, why would Glenda Jackson suddenly take up roller-skating? Mr. Cooper was getting ready to pitch the revised script to Jackson's agent and thought this would be a poignant touch, roller-skating. As for Hugh, he was taking notes on Bonhoeffer in the Union library and for some reason was under the impression it was June— at least for a moment or two as he was dating his 5×8 card. Only

Clara saw the brief flurry as she was lugging groceries home from the Pioneer supermarket on Columbus Avenue. Pausing a moment to rest her arms, she stuck out her tongue for a taste of snow.

Clara had not moved into the apartment Emily had urged upon her, but into a brownstone two doors down, where Anton, the super with the joint, was also the super. The tub here was deeper and the closets slightly larger. Clara, though, was still dismayed by what people had to settle for in New York. A surgeon who had been in the Navy with her father had asked her to dinner with his wife at their Park Avenue apartment. What with the reputation Park Avenue had, you would expect at least one sweeping staircase, a ballroom or something. Instead she had been shown into an apartment as ordinary as they come, with only two bedrooms and no separate dining room! Poor people in Tula Springs had bigger homes, including Emily's parents. Well, the Brixes weren't exactly poor. But Mrs. Brix had made most of Martha's and Emily's clothes from Butterick patterns she had bought from J. C. Penney's—and then, when it came time for Emily to get married, they hadn't even given her a church wedding, much less a proper reception. Of course, Emily took all the blame herself. She told Clara that she and Hugh didn't believe in all that nonsense. Which was why they had gotten married by a judge, a friend of Hugh's mother. Clara had cried at the civil ceremony in the judge's chambers, where there wasn't even a single bouquet. She was so happy for Emily—Hugh looked like such a sweetie, a perfect angel—but at the same time she felt funny about how fast everything was happening. One day Emily lets on she has a roommate, the next it's a fiancé, and then a week or so later she's married. And Clara couldn't help feeling sad for Mr. and Mrs. Brix, neither of whom had been able to make it up North for the ceremony. Mrs. Brix had been with her mother, who had taken a turn for the worse in her nursing home in Monroe, Louisiana. Mr. Brix had purchased a bus ticket for himself, but at the last minute had come down with the Hong Kong flu. Now if Emily had only taken her time, if she hadn't insisted on rushing into things, then maybe her parents could have done something for her. Clara would have been glad to lend them her mother's punch bowl and silver service and advise them on inexpensive, but very lovely, floral arrangements.

The more Clara thought about it, though, the less convinced she was that money had anything to do with Emily's fifty-yard-dash to the altar. As a matter of fact, Emily didn't seem at all happy like a bride should be. Wasn't this the high point of a woman's life? And yet when Emily had told her she was getting married, there was some hesitation in her voice, a certain look in her eyes. It reminded Clara of the time they were seniors at Tula Springs High and Dotty Hemmy had come to gym class and told everyone she was going to get married that weekend. They all acted like it was so wonderful even though Dotty, who was a medium, had to wear an extra large tunic.

Clara, of course, would never dare ask Emily anything outright about her condition. Emily could be prickly, especially when it came to morals. (Some girls in high school, the faster set, had even called Emily a prude.) Clara would have liked to reassure Emily, tell her that she didn't think any less of her for being human. Times had changed, after all. But she knew that Emily would have taken offense at this kind of talk. She was such a private person and didn't let people get close. That was the way it had always been, even with her own sister Martha. Martha had told Clara several times that she felt Clara was more of a sister than Emily had ever been. This made Clara feel sort of sorry for Emily. From then on she determined to do everything she could to bring the girl out of her shell.

So when Emily had told her that she and Hugh were going to spend a quiet Thanksgiving alone, Clara had gotten an idea. She would invite Hugh and Emily to her apartment, as well as that friend of Emily's, Lucas Carlesi, who sounded so interesting, even though he was married. Truth be told, Clara herself was feeling lonely. It would do her good to have some smiling faces around on this first Thanksgiving she had ever been away from home. If her career had been working out better, she might not have spent so much time brooding about Tula Springs and F.X., her ex-fiancé. But she had only gotten two jobs so far, one demonstrating a cordless hair dryer at an appliance show in the Coliseum, and the other modeling thermal underwear for a trailer park magazine. F.X., in the meantime, had been calling, trying to make her believe that he would never hurt her again. But after that last date in Tula Springs, when he had twisted her arm so hard in the car, she knew she had reached her limit. No man was ever going to make her go down on him—she didn't care how dreamy he looked. That was for whores and floozies. If F.X. couldn't be satisfied with normal sex like God intended, then he would have to go bark up another tree. Fortunately, her mother had agreed—once Clara had confessed all the details—that such a marriage would be inconceivable. Mrs. Tilman was only upset that she hadn't been given more of a warning. Mortified because the invitations had been sent out and announcements had appeared in all the papers, Mrs. Tilman had been easy prey for Clara's suggestion that she move away. Filled with qualms about her daughter living alone in such a city, Mrs. Tilman nevertheless could see the advantages of her being as far away from F.X. as possible—and the town's wagging tongues.

Emily arrived an hour early on Thanksgiving with one mincemeat and two pumpkin pies from a German bakery in Yorkville. She felt a little guilty about not contributing more for the dinner, but after all, this whole thing was Clara's idea. She herself was dubious about mixing such a disparate group. Lucas she hadn't seen for weeks, but she was curious to meet his wife. They had talked a few times on the phone, Lucas and she, mainly because she stubbornly refused to give up on the idea that a woman could, in all good conscience, enrich her life with male friendships. Nevertheless, she was anxious about how Hugh and Lucas would react to each other, and probably wouldn't have agreed to come to Clara's at all if, at the last minute, Hugh's mother hadn't called to ask about Emily's plans for Thanksgiving. Mr. Squires, Hugh's stepfather, was having his daughter and son-in-law to dinner in Litchfield. Rodney, the son-in-law, was in the CIA which, according to Lettice, was enough to make anyone lose his appetite. Trying to get out of having dinner with Lettice, Emily had told her that she and Hugh were going to a friend's—at which point Lettice had invited herself along. Emily put up a mild protest, but when it began to seem that Lettice was getting miffed, Emily backed down, agreeing that Clara probably wouldn't mind at all.

"You look delicious," Clara commented, as she basted the turkey.

"Oh, Clara," Emily murmured with becoming modesty. But,

indeed, she did feel that perhaps marriage was agreeing with her. It hadn't turned out to be such a shocking change, after all. People made far too much of the married state, as if one were suddenly transformed into a different creature altogether, from caterpillar to butterfly—or rather, in most cases, from gay, flitting butterfly to humdrum, sluggish housewife.

"Well, it does," Clara said a little peevishly. She knew it was not polite to brag about one's own cooking, but she had been up at five to put the turkey in the oven and thought she deserved some credit.

"No, Em, what are you doing?" Clara called out a few minutes later as her friend removed a plate from the table by the potted palm.

Emily explained what she had explained once before over the phone: It was only Lettice coming, without Hugh's stepfather.

"I know. That plate's Anton's."

"Anton?"

"You know, the super. He had nowhere to go today."

"Oh, Clara, how could you?"

It was bad enough with Lettice inviting herself over, but to throw in that Croatian on top of it all. Emily decided the line had to be drawn somewhere. "I think you should call this Anton and tell him it won't be possible. Tell him Hugh's mother, at the last minute . . ."

"Well, Mrs. Vanderbilt, if you're too good for him, you call and explain. I happen to think he's nice."

Emily was still self-conscious about her new surname. It looked so grand, especially on the Tiffany stationery that Hugh's Bar Harbor friend, Fay, had given them as a wedding present. In the office Emily still went by Brix, worried that if Mr. Cooper heard she was a Vanderbilt, she would never see another raise. Of course, Hugh was not destitute. He had enough money of his own to go to Union for the rest of his life. But the Vanderbilt name itself meant almost nothing, financially speaking. His father was from a relatively impoverished, though genteel, branch that looked with horror upon the marketing of the name, first by Amy, then Gloria. It was Hugh's maternal grandmother, who, when she died, would leave him rather well off, as he put it. In the meantime, he and Emily were still living in the 92nd Street apartment, an exacting space for two. Yet Hugh discouraged Emily's attempts to find more room for them, claiming that most of the world's population lived six or seven to such a room. And besides, Hugh would remind her, they would have to throw out all of Fay's expensive stationery if they changed their address so soon. The least they could do was wait a decent interval.

"All right, Clara," Emily said, competing with a bad rendition of a phrase or two from a Grateful Dead song, a neighbor, no doubt. The walls, she thought, must not be as substantial as they appeared. "It's your dinner. I was just making a suggestion."

Lettice was the first to arrive. Her dull copper hair drawn back smartly into a French bun, she pressed Emily to her coarse tweed jacket, which left an imprint on Emily's cheek. Clara, who had met Hugh's mother in the judge's chambers, received a firm handshake and a comment about the apartment's stale air. In a moment the windows overlooking a twiggy garden four floors below were wide open.

"So, Clara Tilman, what have you got to say about East Pakistan?" Lettice demanded as she adjusted a sash.

Clara cast a worried glance at her potted palm. The somewhat brittle fronds stirred as the room was briskly ventilated. "East?"

"Yes, my dear, East. India just invaded it the other day. I'm quite put out. I phoned my friend Mr. Sanjiva to find out just what is going on, but I could hardly understand a word he said. He's in Calcutta, you know, and his office is practically in the street. It's no wonder he never accomplishes a thing. I knew him during the war quite well. You know, of course, that I was posted to Calcutta, and I don't mind telling you I nearly had a scandalous affair with him. He was dreadfully good-looking back then, but his English was miserable. It was a real turn-off."

Smiling demurely in the general direction of the older woman, Clara murmured something unintelligible.

"What's that?" Lettice's smile was somewhat more aggressive.

"I said I don't think I've ever been to Calcutta."

"You don't *think* you've been?" Lettice gave Emily a conspiratorial wink.

"Where's Hugh?" Emily asked. It was an idle question, for she knew he was uptown studying until the last minute. But she hoped to steer Lettice away from the subject of India, which always made her sound somewhat imperialistic.

"Hugo? Isn't he here? I thought he was here." Lettice looked about her, disgruntled. She had used his actual given name, which her son loathed. "Well, whatever, I need to take a pee."

While Lettice absented herself, Emily lowered the sashes on all the windows, promising Clara that yes, she would take the blame if Lettice objected. "I don't think she likes me," Clara would interject from time to time as she and Emily got on with the preparations. Emily tried to reassure her, but could only do so half-heartedly. For she knew that Lettice admired only practical, down-to-earth women like Emily herself. It had been such a relief to find herself not just accepted, but instantly loved by her mother-in-law. Lettice took her side if she and Hugh happened to disagree, and admonished him when he seemed to take Emily for granted. All this was gratifying to Emily. Yet she couldn't help feeling that the love and admiration she professed in return were somewhat forced from her, like tribute from a subject people.

"What's going on in there?" Emily asked in a low voice as she and Clara worked side by side in the kitchen, not far from the bathroom door. Lettice's mirthful bark could be heard even with the blender going full blast.

"Oh, I forgot." Clara's doughy hand went to her mouth as her blue eyes widened. "Anton's taking a bath."

"What?"

"The boiler is being cleaned in his building, so I told him he could use my tub."

"Clara, him? You let that . . . Why didn't you say something to Lettice?"

"I can't remember everything." She gestured helplessly at the oyster stuffing, candied yams, salad, spinach soufflé, cornbread, flowered radishes, cauliflower, scalloped potatoes, baby peas. Clara had not stinted. There seemed enough for twenty. Rapaciously hungry, Emily had to restrain herself from plucking more than three or four shrimp from the salad when Clara turned to check the turkey's thermometer.

Emerging from the bathroom Lettice announced to the girls, "What a charming young man. Do you realize, Emily dear, he and I were in the same dorm at Vassar?"

Emily didn't know quite what to make of this, but before she could inquire, Clara was answering the buzz on the intercom. Through a haze of static Emily recognized Lucas's voice. She decided it might be well to review who he was for Lettice's sake. "These are the people from Madison, New Jersey, Lucas and Judy Carlesi. He's a draftsman for medical books, and I think Judy might have voted for Nixon—I'm not sure—so maybe we shouldn't talk politics."

"Don't fret, dear," Lettice said, giving her daughter-in-law's head a pat. "Your friends are all delightful, I'm sure."

"Well, they're not really friends per se. I don't know them that well at all. In fact, I'm not really sure why they're invited."

Clara gave her friend a look, which made Emily somewhat defensive. The slight chill in the air was dissipated, though, the moment the door was answered. Both women seemed to vye with each other in being warm and hospitable as the guests were introduced. But Clara gained a slight edge when Hugh turned up, just a minute or two later, with a last-minute guest.

Hugh's companion was his friend Fay Terrace, and Emily thought it was terrible of her husband to do this to Clara. They barely had enough room at the table as it was. Nevertheless, Emily decided not to make an issue of it, and greeted Fay with a brisk, Lettice-like handshake. The girl was indeed as heavy as she had heard, not at all a threat, Emily decided. Hugh explained that he had stopped by Fay's on the way home from the library and found her stretched out on her sofa with a cold. He didn't think it was right that she should spend Thanksgiving that way, and practically forced her to come. Fay did look miserable, her nose red, a drab shawl over her ankle-length granny dress. Soon she was inundated with a flood of advice from Lettice, who steered her toward a window for a breath of fresh air.

After an initial word or two about the weather, Hugh wandered away from Lucas and his wife to join Clara and the freshly bathed Anton in the kitchen. "We brought you this," Judy said as she presented Emily with a bottle of Dom Perignon and a jar of Iranian caviar.

"You mean for Clara. I'm not really the hostess, you know."

"Lucas has wine for Clara. This is a little wedding present."

"Oh, I couldn't."

Lucas looked annoyed, but Judy was gracious. "It's nothing, really. Go ahead. There. We're very happy for you."

"Well, thanks so much. Why don't we all share this now?"

Judy's frank, unaffected good humor soon put Emily at ease as they sipped the champagne beneath Clara's expensive palm. Unusually plump and almost as short as Emily herself, Judy nonetheless managed to look stylish, her pretty features set off to good effect by the expert, natural-looking cut of her strawberry blonde hair. Emily nodded agreeably as Judy went on about the leisure-wear company she worked for. Much of her time was spent representing the firm at trade fairs or wining and dining the account executives of specialty stores for the larger-sized woman. She confessed to Emily that it was only within the last five years that she had come to terms with her hips. She had tried every diet under the sun, but nothing took. Now, with the help of Silva Mind Control, she had learned to accept herself as she was.

"Did you meet Lucas in Paris?" Emily asked, hoping to include him in the conversation. He was perched on the arm of the sofa, looking uncomfortable.

"That's right." Lucas nodded agreeably.

"Honey, what do you mean?" Judy took his hand and squeezed it. "You know we didn't meet in Paris. We met in that fish and chips shop in Earls Court."

"Earls Court?"

Turning to Emily, she said, "Isn't he romantic? Lu"—she released his hand—"London." Back to Emily: "I was doing odd jobs back then, typing, filing, trying to forget how miserable I was. My mother had just died, and I couldn't finish college. The strange thing was, Lucas always assumed I was so competent, even from the very beginning. It was so weird, meeting someone who thought of me that way. After a while, I started to believe it myself. His finances were a mess, you know, so I took a course in accounting. The next thing I knew, I was handling all his business affairs, doing his taxes, writing checks. Then after about two years of this, I realized I was in love. He was living with a bombshell then, an aspiring actress, sultry, whiny—"

"Caviar?" Clara interrupted, coming over with a plate. Emily, Judy, and Lucas took healthy portions, and Clara moved on.

"The actress?" Emily prompted.

Judy swallowed. "Her English was terrible, and Lucas never did learn how to say anything but 'check, please' in French."

"That's not true," he put in, though without much conviction.

"Well, all I know was that I had to have this man. He was like a god to me. I worshipped him, literally worshipped him. It was either trap him or die." She drained her glass before going on. Emily was fascinated, but also a little embarrassed for Lucas. His wife's candor no longer had a lighthearted ring to it. She was speaking from the heart. "So when the bombshell started leaving notes for him or babbled too fast for him, I would do a bit of subtle mistranslating. And vice versa, when Lucas wanted to say something to her. Before long there was a riproaring explosion and goodbye, bombshell—hello, Miss Judy."

Emily was so disconcerted by this revelation, her face stricken though she tried to smile, that Judy hastened to reassure her. "Oh, don't worry. I confessed to Lucas a month after he fell in love with me. It's an old story. Right, honey?"

"Hm? Yeah. More champagne, Emily?"

But it wasn't just the insensitivity of telling such a story in front of her husband that bothered Emily. And to someone who was a virtual stranger. It was also the fact that Judy could almost boast of her deception. The woman didn't even possess a rudimentary sense of right and wrong. She sounded totally amoral.

"No thanks, Lu—Lucas. You finish it up."

"Lu tells me you're an actress," Judy was saying to Emily while Lettice carved the eighteen-pound turkey.

"Who's an actress?" Lettice demanded from the head of the table.

"No, not really," Emily said hurriedly, in a low voice. She and Hugh had neglected to mention to Lettice that Emily had once had certain aspirations. What was the point? Emily's increasing workload at the office made it impossible for her to go to any more auditions, especially with a husband to look after. And besides, as far as Lettice was concerned, acting was beneath contempt. As for working for a production company, this Lettice could condone. A woman needed a career, after all—though, of course, it would have been much better if Emily were involved in a slightly less egregious trade.

"She's like a model, not an actress," Anton said, pointing a loaded fork at Clara. During cocktails Emily had learned that Anton had indeed gone to Vassar the first year they had admitted men, but dropped out to get in touch with reality.

"Clara's going to be famous someday, I'm sure," Emily said, trying to divert the spotlight from herself.

"Oh, I'm not either."

"Sure you are."

"Come on, I'm not." Clara looked expectantly at Emily, who for some reason decided not to lob the ball back. In any case, Lettice was busy with Fay again, chatting in confidential tones that excluded everyone else at the table. Emily supposed they were deploring the tourists in Maine or some such nonsense. She really couldn't understand what Hugh could mean by bringing Fay along. Unless it was some childish way of getting even. *You want to have dinner with Lucas? All right, fine, Em. I'll have dinner with Fay.*

Sitting on Emily's left, their legs accidentally brushing against each other from time to time, Lucas was feeling a little foolish and old in the double-breasted suit Judy had made him wear. He knew no one would be dressed up, and he was right. Hugh was in jeans and a khaki workshirt, Anton with a Countess Mara tie over his teeshirt. And there Lucas sat with the very latest European tailoring, lapels out to his shoulders, a wide, muted psychedelic tie, all of which Judy had picked out for him at Bloomingdale's. Of course, Clara was all duded up, but from what Emily had told him about her, that was to be expected. She was, though, quite a stunning woman. From Emily's description, he had had no idea how gorgeous she would turn out to be. The turquoise eyes and jet-black hair were quite a combination. Of course, he had to be careful not to look in her direction too often. He could feel Judy's eyes upon him almost every moment, though she was adept at pretending to be interested in whomever she was talking to.

"Well, I had a degree in graphic design before I went to Paris," Lucas said to Hugh after he had asked how he came to be working at LT & M, the textbook publisher. "I was doing freelance work for them before my father kicked off and left me a wad of dough. So when my movie career fizzled out, I had some contacts there, and they took me back. Now I've got my own office."

"Did it seem humiliating, going back?"

Lucas studied him a moment before answering. The boy was being straightforward, he concluded, with no intention of sounding snide or malicious. "No, not really. There were a lot of new folks who didn't know me. I enjoyed being anonymous again. And there's something nice about a simple life, everything regulated. Don't get me wrong, Paris was a blast, a real head trip. But a party that lasts almost seven years, well, there's a lot of wear and tear on the old bod. You appreciate going back to school again, vacation's over."

"I was in Europe, too, for a while. Burgos, that was great."

While Hugh went on to describe some of his experiences there, Lucas decided that the boy was not so bad after all. In his mind, whenever Emily had talked about her husband, Lucas had pictured a wispy snob very aware that he was a Vanderbilt. But Hugh, once you discounted his boyish looks, had a nice masculine aura about him; though he wasn't self-effacing, he did seem to be interested in what you had to say. Emily, as a result, went up a few notches in his estimation. Of course, you still couldn't escape the fact that she had married for money. He had to hand it to the little devil—she had certainly pulled the wool over his eyes. All that talk about career and morality, and all the while she was playing the oldest of female games: how to marry a millionaire.

Going into the kitchen for more cornbread, Clara tried to make up her mind if her party was a success or not. On the plus side, everyone was talking, Lettice with Fay, Hugh and Lucas, Lucas's wife Julie or Mary or something and Emily, and herself and Anton. On the minus side no one was eating the cauliflower or the candied yams, and Lucas seemed dull and old, not at all like Emily had described him. Though she thought Anton was nice, she still felt left out, on the fringe of her own party. Worse yet, the dull ache of homesickness had not abated, and she was afraid that after everyone had left, she might call up F.X. and let him sweet-talk her into changing her mind.

"Here you go," Clara said as she put another square of cornbread on Emily's plate.

Emily grunted, her mouth full of dark meat.

Poor girl, Clara thought sadly. She seemed to be eating for two.

six

❧

It was Emily's promotion that made it impossible for her and Hugh to fly down to Louisiana for Christmas. Mr. Cooper hadn't even waited for Heather to save up enough for a move to the Adirondacks before he announced in an interoffice memo that Emily Vanderbilt (yes, she had finally told him she was married) as of December 20, 1971, would be replacing Heather Bernstein as East Coast Story Editor. Emily had her own office now (though without a window) and letterhead stationery. Mr. Cooper even presented her with an American Express card for the lunches he expected her to have with agents and editors. Because Mark Four could never come up with the option money to compete with a major studio, they had to rely on smarts and personal appeal, both of which Mr. Cooper assured Emily she had.

Although Emily had some qualms about it, she let Lucas persuade her that Judy would be delighted to help her buy a few outfits. Ever since college Emily had lost all confidence in picking out a suitable wardrobe for herself. At Smith she realized that the skirts and blouses her sister had thought so darling were indeed just that. Compared to the simple yet elegant basics from Lord & Taylor, Bonwit Teller, or Bergdorf Goodman that many of her classmates sported, she looked hopelessly cute. On the other hand, the radical chic of jeans and peasant blouses never did look right on her either. Heather had adopted this look for the office, but her legs were long, the jeans skintight, and she accessorized so well with bracelets and necklaces that she managed to look dressed up.

"I need a few things for business lunches," Emily explained to Judy on the steps of St. Patrick's, where they had agreed to meet one day at noon. "If you could give me a few ideas. I was thinking we might go next door to Saks."

Judy shook her head. A Gucci scarf, giraffes, protected her lovely strawberry blonde hair from a gritty wind that gusted to forty miles an hour in the canyon of skyscrapers a block or two west. "That place isn't you at all. Come."

Emily was carted off to a drab-looking second-story shop on Madison Avenue, where they were buzzed in by a faded English-woman with a runny nose. Judy had explained to Emily on the way over that she could not wear anything in the least bit mod or fashionable. She was too cherubic for that. What she needed were clothes that anchored her, made her look like a real con-tender. After savagely blowing her nose, Miss Purvis, the shop owner, selected two mannish tweed suits for her and four high-collared blouses as well as a black string tie and a slim bowtie. Not daring to protest under the baleful headmistresslike glare while she was being fitted, Emily did manage a sotto voce protest to Judy over the severity of both the look and the prices. Putting an arm around Emily's shoulder, Judy told her to consider this pur-chase as an investment for the future. Material like this would last forever. And because the cut was classic, they would never go out of style. Still not entirely convinced she was doing the right thing, Emily went ahead and paid—or tried to. Miss Purvis would not accept a personal check. Then, rather than let Judy put it on her Visa ("No problem, honey. Just pay me back when you can.") Emily produced the American Express card Mr. Cooper had given her.

To thank Judy for her help Emily had planned to take her out for an early supper that evening. But Judy said she had to get home to cook dinner for Lucas's mother, who was driving out

60

from Forest Hills to New Jersey. They made plans to get together soon, but Emily knew this was an idle promise on her own part. She was loaded down with work, all the projects Heather had been in the middle of—and wouldn't you know it, but her mother was insisting on coming up to New York for Christmas.

"She could sleep on the air mattress," Hugh suggested when Emily brought up the subject again that evening. She had been worrying the impending visit, like a dog with an old sock. His remark now could not be dignified with any sort of comment. The idea of her mother sprawled on the floor only a few feet from them—what could he mean by this?

"How about a hotel?" Hugh said finally, after reading his wife's mind.

"If you want to pay for one, fine."

"You know I can't."

"Well, mother won't be able to afford one either."

"You just got a raise, didn't you?"

"Right, I'm rolling in money. Seventy-five hundred a year."

He paused as he unbuttoned his khaki trousers. "Good gravy, is that all you make?"

"Hugh, you never listen. I must have told you that three or four times."

"Oh."

"Anyway, I think I decided. Maybe you should crash with Fay for a few days while mother is here. O.K.?"

Emily wanted to show Hugh how much she trusted him. At the same time, this might somehow make up for the lunches she had had with Lucas after she had gotten married. And the phone calls. Not that Hugh had ever complained. She had hoped that the three of them might spend time together, but Hugh always came up with some excuse if she suggested having Lucas over. In any case, she wanted to demonstrate that she approved of his friendship with Fay. "I'm sure Fay can share things with you I wouldn't be able to," she had bravely volunteered one morning before going to work. "Your childhood memories, those are very precious. I think it's one reason why most marriages fall apart. You put far too much pressure on one person to be friend, lover, companion, mother, father. It's actually pretty neurotic, this

61

American fear of friendship. Men, too. My father's never had a real friend, male or female. Men should learn to open up to each other."

"Well?" she said now, waiting for Hugh's response.

"Fay? Why not? I don't think she'll mind." She couldn't see his face, but he didn't sound too happy. That was good.

As they lay in bed Emily stopped worrying about her mother's visit (What would Hugh think of her? How would she find time to show her some sights?), and started worrying about her lunch date for the next day. Mr. Cooper had told her to go through Heather's calendar and keep any appointments she might have. It made Emily uneasy to call someone who was expecting Heather and substitute herself. In fact, the subsidiary rights woman she was meeting sounded downright cold on the phone. She had a feeling that this woman might be a good friend of Heather's, and was taking a dim view of her, Emily's, promotion.

"Mr. V?"

"Huh?"

"You're not mad, are you?"

Hugh usually swung a leg over her as soon as they were in bed. They would cuddle for a while as a preliminary. On their wedding night she had been so tense and anxious that he had suggested they take it easy and progress step by step to actual intercourse. He wanted her to get used to him so that when she was ready to have him inside her, she would be entirely at ease. With a steady commentary from him ("Not so hard, gentle, it's very sensitive there.") she learned how to give him pleasure with her hand. A couple of weeks later he deemed her ready for oral instruction. Here he met some resistance. Emily felt there was something immoral and perverse about doing this. Unperturbed, Hugh read aloud several passages from Norman O. Brown. They sank in, and Emily was soon quite an adept, though with lingering doubts about its propriety.

"Why mad?"

"You don't have to go to Fay's. It was just an idea."

"No, it's O.K."

"You are sweet, Mr. V. You know that?"

She stroked his fine blond hair, bleached almost white in the pale wash of streetlight that seeped through the blinds. As he nuzzled her breasts, she wondered again, happily, at how much they had seemed to grow in the past year. She had been so flat-chested at Smith, and now she was more than respectable. Why had her body taken so long to mature?

When he was on top of her, she thought she could feel him against her thigh. Hoping that she didn't seem tense, she braced herself for the first sharp thrust. She was determined not to cry out, not to discourage him in the least. She wanted this to be the night she finally graduated. Since he didn't like condoms, she had taken the pill for the first time in her life. Now she was fully prepared. Let him make her a proper wife.

"Yes, Hugh, good, good."

Opening her eyes she was disconcerted by the look of agony on his face, as if it were taking all his concentration to answer some immense question, one that decided the fate of the world. And it wasn't just his face. Every fiber of his strong, lithe body seemed tortured by this question, an either/or that admitted of only one solution. She was about to tell him to stop, take it easy, relax, when she felt the damp patch blossom on her belly.

They lay silently, side by side, as his breathing returned to normal. Then she reached for the ScotTissues they had learned to keep handy by the bed.

Mrs. Dolly Brix was a hefty, vigorous woman who was secretly afraid of her oldest child. To begin with, she could never under-stand how Emily could be so petite when she herself had been forced to fight the battle of the bulge all her life. Granted, Emily's father was not so tall, but he was far from being trim. As a child Emily had had a malnourished look, which was the bane of Dolly's existence. The cupboards were always stockpiled with Little Deb-bie cakes and Jane Parker cookies, and at mealtimes Dolly would cater to the girl's every whim. Mr. Brix loved beets, but since Emily could not stand the sight of them, they were banned from the table. (Mr. Brix sometimes ate beets by himself in the bed-room.) If one food category touched another on the plate—say peas (vegetable) against the ham (meat)—Emily claimed her throat would close up. To make things easier on herself, Dolly purchased a set of flamingo dishes with built-in compartments. Mr. Brix hated the flamingos, which he considered low class, but that was the only style they had at the five-and-dime.

Dolly had known Emily was a genius almost from the moment she was born. What agony such a tiny thing had caused Dolly, who was in labor thirty-nine hours. But once she held her in her arms, she could see in the stern, wizened face a fierce intelligence that must have come from Dolly's side of the family—more specifically, Dolly's Uncle Joe T, who wrote poetry in French and never got married, poor man. By two Emily was talking in complete sentences, subject, verb, and predicate. Dolly would never forget the day Mrs. Ratcliff, whose father had been decorated in the War Between the States, had dropped by with some hand-me-downs her great-grandchild had grown out of. "Tell Mrs. Ratcliff thank you," Dolly had urged Emily to say to their eighty-year-old neighbor. Emily, who must have been only three then, had the strangest look on her face. "What's wrong, sweetcakes?" Mrs. Ratcliff asked. She had on one of those hats with grapes and cherries and Emily, of course, did not approve of fruit of any kind, wax or real. "My uterus hurts," the child finally blurted out.

Well, Dolly had nearly died. She had no idea where Emily could have learned such a word. After a conference with Mr. Brix, Dolly concluded that Emily must have taught herself to read. This meant that when Emily was ready for school, her mother was required to make frequent visits to ensure that the teachers were not holding her back. The most difficult year was fifth grade. Miss Melvin had taken an instant dislike to Emily, probably because Emily was always asking questions that the woman wasn't able to answer. Emily would come home in tears, worried to death about her grades, and spend hours and hours outlining geography lessons. Better believe, Dolly was going to get to the bottom of this. She marched herself over to the principal, and demanded that Miss Melvin either straighten up her act or resign. Dr. Leves, the principal, confirmed that Emily was a precocious child and promised to have a talk with Miss Melvin. When Miss Melvin died of cancer a year or so later, Dolly had to admit that she felt a little guilty. But what can you do?

Oh yes, Dolly could go on forever with all the worry this

child had caused. But the main thing was, they had both survived her upbringing, she and Emily.

"Now, when I heard my Em was going to marry a Vanderbilt, let me tell you, I just sat down and had myself a good cry. I knew everything would turn out all right in the end. You got to have faith, that's what it all boils down to." Mrs. Brix patted her son-in-law's hand, while Emily looked on helplessly. The recital of childhood foibles had been bad enough, but to cap it with a line like that was really a bit much.

"Mother, I've already told you, Hugh is from a branch that really isn't very . . ." Her voice trailed off. It seemed so impossibly vulgar to explain like this.

"All I can say, Em, is that when I told the taxicab driver to take me to Vanderbilt Avenue, well, I nearly popped my buttons."

Emily had decided that she and Hugh would meet her mother for drinks at the Yale Club, which was only a couple of blocks from her afternoon appointment. Mr. Cooper had told Emily that she should feel free to sign his name and account number anytime she wished to use the place. Hugh had objected at first because he would have to wear a coat and tie, but Emily finally managed to talk him into donning his one and only suit, a gray J. Press that was a little tight on him. Mrs. Brix arrived almost an hour late, because the Carey bus from JFK had to make a detour in Queens, and then it took her so long to get a cab. Hugh greeted her with a big hug and kiss that surprised Emily. He was usually not so demonstrative, not even with her. And when Mrs. Brix started up about his surname, he was good-natured enough to smile and make a few deprecatory remarks that only endeared him more to his mother-in-law.

With this initial embarrassment out of the way, the old affection crept back into Emily's heart. At times her mother held such an attraction for her that Emily had to be careful. If the full force of her need were ever admitted, she suspected that her mother would back off, frightened. Normal, everyday love Mrs. Brix was expert at giving and receiving. Emily could subsist on this, and did. But at Smith a deeper ache was revived, a child's yearning for the sound of her voice, the sight of the ivy print of one of Dolly's old dresses, smudged with flour from her plump hands. In the wonder of a New England fall, when colors were etched against a sky as harsh and gorgeous as a scholastic ether, Emily would wander about the campus stricken with remorse. She would remember the times she had made her mother feel small, correcting her pronunciation, acting horrified when Dolly didn't know who Camus was, or Giraudoux. It would seem impossible then, as a freshman with no friends, that she would ever be irritated by her mother again.

For a moment or two Mrs. Brix gazed about at the Yale Club's grand floor-to-ceiling windows, the ornate molding, leather sofas, and solid brass lamps, before exclaiming softly to herself, "That's two beards I saw since we came in—no, three. And look, a plastic ashtray." A little louder, in Hugh's direction: "Now if I were in charge here . . ."

"Pardon?"

"Oh, nothing." Mrs. Brix adjusted herself in the green leather armchair, her finger tracing a rip where a small wad of padding blossomed like a cotton ball. "It's so sweet of Yale to let travelers just walk in like this. I've always thought New Orleans should have some sort of rest station. Like when you're through shopping and you got to wait for the bus. Well, you know, Hugh, you just can't sit by yourself in the Greyhound station. There's a certain element that—"

"Mother," Emily interrupted, "you have to belong here. You can't just walk in."

"Silly me. I forgot Hugh went to Yale."

"Actually, I didn't."

"But you did go someplace fancy now, didn't you?"

Hugh shrugged.

"Oh, he's so modest." Mrs. Brix sighed, her eyes blurring with emotion.

"Are you all right?" Hugh asked as his mother-in-law drew a petite embroidered handkerchief from her vinyl purse and dabbed at her eyes.

Mrs. Brix nodded, then blew her nose. "It's just such a relief to see what a fine young man you are. I'm so happy."

Leaning forward, Hugh took her hand and held it awhile. Emily couldn't help noting that he had never done that with her.

But she was pleased nonetheless that he was being so kind to her mother. He was truly a good man.

"Tell me, Hugh," Mrs. Brix said, once the wave of emotion had subsided, "what is Emily like?"

Both Emily and he looked puzzled.

"I mean, it's so hard for me to think of her as an executive. And by the way, Em dear, you must promise to take me with you to the studio tomorrow. Mrs. Hawkins told me don't bother coming home unless I get her some autographs."

"Mom, it's just an office building. There aren't any stars or anything."

"Imagine that. Just an office building." Mrs. Brix fingered a necklace that Emily, with a curious pang of shame and pleasure, recognized. The fake rubies she had picked out herself when she was eleven, paying for the Christmas gift by not going to the movies for two months.

A while later, interrupting herself in the midst of talking to Hugh, Mrs. Brix turned to her daughter and said, "Are you sure?"

"Sure?"

"That it's just an office building. Maybe there's some parts you haven't seen."

Emily ignored this, allowing her mother to resume her conversation with Hugh. For some time now she had needed to go to the ladies' room, but she was uneasy about leaving the two of them alone. There was no telling what sort of strange ideas her mother might put into Hugh's head regarding her. Being physically present, Emily believed, did put some sort of brake on her mother's imagination. But once out of the room . . .

"Em dear." Her mother craned her head to look at her. "Where ever did you get such an outfit?"

Emily was wearing her new tweed suit for the first time. Feeling self-conscious and defensive about it—oh, it did make her look like a very repressed and embittered spinster, and she never should have let Judy talk her into it, but it was too late now and far too expensive not to wear—she calmly replied, "We better get going, don't you think?"

"Mother hasn't finished her margarita," Hugh observed.

Mother? Emily thought, giving him a look.

"Where's the fire, Em dear?" Mrs. Brix gazed solemnly at her swollen ankles. "Let your mother catch her breath."

"But Clara will be waiting for us at the restaurant."

"It's not even seven-thirty," Hugh pointed out.

Mrs. Brix consulted her Lady Timex. "For me it's only six twenty-two, no three. I'm an hour younger than both of you. Now where was I reading that if you keep on going east real fast, near the speed of light, you'd end up expanding or something. I think it was the Delta magazine, but don't hold me to it. Which reminds me, Em, thank you so much for the Christmas present. She got me *Middlemarch* in hardcover, Hugh. I'm really liking it, though the woman is certainly long-winded. There's parts I would cut. Last year she gave me *To the Lighthouse*. I didn't like it as much as *The Voyage Out*, though. *Family Circle*, that's what it was."

"Pardon?"

"*Family Circle*, that's where I read about flying east real fast."

Clara was waiting for them at Le Cheval Blanc, a five-minute walk from the Yale Club. She and Mrs. Brix fell into each other's arms like refugees in a World War II documentary. "I thought I'd give you some time to be alone with Emily and Hugh," Clara said when Mrs. Brix asked why she hadn't met them earlier for a drink.

It was a little disconcerting to see how much her mother seemed to unwind around Clara. Bringing her up-to-date about Martha, Mrs. Brix seemed so much more natural, her old self. At the Yale Club Emily had been fooled into thinking her mother was having a marvelous time. But Mrs. Brix had been constrained, uncomfortable, it was evident now. Emily was somewhat saddened by this, though she was also glad to see Dolly enjoying herself.

As a rule Emily didn't drink in the presence of her parents. At the Yale Club she had nursed a ginger ale, which helped mitigate the effect of a hangover. (She and Lucas had had dinner the night before at Clancy's, with one too many Irish coffees to top it off.) So she could not be expected to be overly pleased when her mother ordered a bottle of Cabernet Sauvignon that cost eleven dollars. Her protest, though, was met with a hand in the air. Dolly explained that as she was taking everyone to dinner, she had a right to choose the wine.

"But, Mother, you can't pay for us," Emily said, genuinely concerned about her parents' finances.

"Em, let Mother alone," Hugh said.

"We can't let her pay."

"Why not?"

Emily thought of her father clipping coupons for macaroni and cheese dinners—and Hugh asked why not. He simply had no conception of the way most people had to live.

When the check arrived Mrs. Brix spent a good deal of time auditing it. "What's this BA stand for?" "Did someone have clams? I don't remember clams." "Five bucks for a piece of fish? Why at home I could fix you the same thing for a quarter, I kid you not." Emily endured this stoically, while Clara made repeated attempts to slip Dolly a twenty. The waiter hovered, a chilling presence to Emily, who was trying hard not to imagine what he must think of them. She had spoken a bit of French with him just before dessert, and had been gently but firmly corrected when she used the wrong gender for window. Of course, she knew all along it was feminine—any child would. But how could she explain to him it was just a slip of the tongue?

After everyone had retrieved their coats, scarves, caps, and gloves, and Mrs. Brix had wondered aloud how much to tip the lady—"Do you think ten cents per coat is fair? I mean, after all, it's not a very hard job, is it?"—there was something of a muddle before they exited. Dolly had not realized she would be evicting Hugh from his own home, so she insisted on getting herself a room at the Commodore, right next door to Grand Central. Emily explained that it would be no trouble at all, that Hugh had already dropped his suitcase off at a friend's earlier that day. But Mrs. Brix would not hear of it.

"You can stay with me," Clara offered.

"Oh, I wouldn't think of it."

"Miz Brix, I insist. I would have asked earlier, but I just assumed you had a place."

"No, Clara Edward, I couldn't."

"Now Miz Brix, you're not staying in some old hotel while I'm around."

Several more rounds of protest and invitation were necessary before Mrs. Brix felt right about accepting. In a bitter wind they returned en masse to the Yale Club, where Mrs. Brix retrieved her luggage from behind the front desk. Leaden with fatigue and anxious about work the next day, Emily gave her mother a hug and kiss, as did Hugh. Then because of the cold—it was nineteen degrees, someone in the lobby had said—she and Hugh splurged on a cab back to the apartment.

"Do you think I'd look good in an Afro?" Hugh commented as they raced up Park Avenue.

"Oh, Hugh, really." Emily's mother had made that suggestion during dinner. It had come from out of the blue, the suggestion, while Emily was trying to steer the conversation away from her childhood. But no matter how hard she tried, her mother, egged on by Hugh, would always swerve back with a trivial anecdote.

"You better call Fay," Emily said.

"Huh?"

"You'll want to tell her you won't be coming over."

"Oh. Right."

"And remind me to reimburse Cooper for the drinks."

"Huh? Oh, the Yale Club. You know, your mother is great. I really like her." He sat there musing a moment, unperturbed by the jolt of potholes. "She's not like you at all."

Emily wasn't sure how to take that. Glancing at the meter, she began to calculate how much the fare would be by the time they got to 92nd Street.

"You're much more like Lettice."

"What?"

"In a way you are, Em. You're both sort of tweedy."

"Oh, Hugh, I think you've hurt my feelings."

"No, no, I didn't mean anything negative. I was just thinking about genes, how sometimes they don't seem to have any bearing."

"Driver, right side, near corner, please."

Mrs. Brix had to take a breather on the way up to the fourth floor. Clara was carrying her guest's vanity case, the heavy fiberglass suitcase with wheels being left downstairs for Anton to bring up in the morning. "Here, let me take that," Mrs. Brix said as she puffed on a landing. Clara, of course, did not relinquish the vanity case. "How nice," Mrs. Brix added with a nod toward a print Clara had never noticed before, an ochre cat.

Once they were inside the apartment and Mrs. Brix had exclaimed over the potted palm, Clara made some instant hot chocolate while Mrs. Brix freshened up. Coming out of the bathroom, Mrs. Brix was presented with a steaming mug with a treble clef on it. Clara told her she would sleep in the bedroom, but Mrs. Brix insisted that the couch would be fine. "Now Miz Brix," Clara admonished and soon they were locked in another round of politeness, which was only broken when, saying something about not wanting to be a burden, Mrs. Brix sank down onto the couch, her eyes welling up with tears.

"Oh, Miz Brix, you sleep anywhere you like, hear?" Clara said, worried that she might have been rude.

"It's all right, dear. It's not you. I've been holding it in all evening." She dabbed at her eyes with her embroidered handkerchief. "If Emily only knew how much she's hurt her father and I. To run off like this and get married, no church, no relatives. We could have given her such a wedding, too, my little baby. Oh, Clara Edward, I don't know what's got into you young folks these days. Look at you, causing your poor mother all that heartache."

Clara remained silent. Even though the accusation stung, it didn't seem the time or place to talk about her own problems.

"Why, Clara, why would she do this to us? She's the light of our life. We've gone into debt to send her to school, and this is the thanks we get."

Clara sat down beside her and took her hand. "That's just it. Emily didn't want y'all to have to spend a lot of money on a wedding. That's what she told me."

"You believe that? I credited you with more sense than that. By the way, I better call Mr. Brix. He'll be worried about me. You know him, worries about everything. That's why he can't travel. He's always afraid something terrible's going to happen to the house if we leave it behind. Can't miss a day of work, either. The whole insurance business is going to collapse if he's not there holding the fort. I say it's a fine thing he can't even take the time to meet his own son-in-law, but he blames it all on Emily. He's a proud man, Mr. Brix. Won't budge an inch. He says she could have come home with Mr. Vanderbilt if she wanted. Anyway, here I am left in the middle."

After a brief collect call, during which Mr. Brix expressed concern about the bill, Mrs. Brix resumed her talk with Clara.

"Oh, poor Em," Mrs. Brix said after they had both danced around a certain issue for a while. "I have to admit, it was one of the first things that occurred to me. But then I thought how strict Emmie could be on that subject. Dear, she wouldn't even allow me to discuss the facts of life with her."

"Well, that's just the type that ends up that way." Clara didn't mean to sound vindictive, but she was still smarting from the heartache comment.

Sipping their hot chocolate side by side, both women had a faraway look in their eyes. "I'm beginning to see it all now," Mrs. Brix said finally. "Emily was punishing herself. She made a mistake, so she blames herself, doesn't allow herself a proper wedding. If only she had talked to me first."

"It's not going to be easy, raising a child in New York."

"No. I imagine she'll want to move back to Louisiana. Hugh could find himself a church, I'm sure. He's going to make a fine preacher someday. Such a bright young man."

"Are preachers supposed to be rich?"

"Oh, that won't make a difference. Besides, Emily says he isn't really rich."

Clara pried her heels off. "Is that true?"

"Baby, I don't know what's true anymore. All I know is I got to watch my P's and Q's around that girl. She's very high society now, I reckon."

Together they pulled out the convertible sofa and made the bed with baby's breath sheets that Clara had picked up at a white sale at Macy's. Clara then washed out the mugs and wiped the kitchen counters while Mrs. Brix changed into a one-size-fits-all kimono from her vanity case. Using the mirror on the inside of the case, she ran a comb through her cropped brindled hair, which was ideal for travel. No fussing with hairdryers, curlers. Just wash and towel dry.

As she stretched out on the sweet-smelling linen, Mrs. Brix discovered that, tired as she was, she was too wound up to fall asleep. With a sigh she heaved up onto an elbow, switched on a lamp, then swung a leg marbled with varicose veins over the edge of the mattress. The vanity case was next to the palm. As she padded across the room, it suddenly hit her: Why, Emily was ashamed of them. That was the reason there had been no wedding. She was afraid that Hugh might change his mind if he saw what her parents were like.

But no, Mrs. Brix argued as she reached inside the case for the book. Emily was too well brought up to think something like that. And besides, what was there to be ashamed of? They might not be rich, but they were well-mannered, cultured, intelligent. Didn't Mr. Brix read Latin and forbid TV?

Yes, he did. But you, Dolly. What about you? You talk too much, don't you? You never know when to stop. And how many words did you mispronounce tonight at dinner? You saw Emily wince, didn't you? Don't deny it.

Mrs. Brix stood there a moment, frozen in doubt.

No, she finally decided. It was the other thing, Emily's getting herself pregnant like that. She must have known it would be like a knife to her father's heart. He had raised her to respect all the old-fashioned virtues, and then for her to rush off to the altar . . . Mrs. Brix had spent hours trying to reason with her husband. Emily had, after all, done the right thing, hadn't she? She wasn't living in sin or giving a child up for adoption. But still Mr. Brix had refused to join her on the trip to New York. He had a grudge against Hugh, refused to deal with someone who would take advantage of his daughter like that. Which was why Mrs. Brix had had to invent the story of the Hong Kong flu. She couldn't tell Emily or Clara the truth about why Mr. Brix didn't go to the wedding. And why she had to explain again tonight to Clara about Mr. Brix. Of course, it wasn't all a lie. He didn't enjoy traveling at all. But if he had respected Hugh, he would have come with her this Christmas. That much she knew.

With a sigh Mrs. Brix returned to bed, where she adjusted the light so that it would fall squarely on the page. She had assigned herself a chapter a day of *Middlemarch*. With all the waiting at Moisant Airport—Mr. Brix had dropped her off almost two hours early to allow for possible engine trouble on the way to New Orleans—she had nevertheless only made it through six pages. Her conscience wouldn't let her rest until she had fulfilled her quota. And of course, she had to read every word. Skipping felt like cheating to her.

Around two A.M. Clara went into the bathroom for a glass of water and Sominex. She found it hard to sleep in the city. The floor creaked, pigeons sometimes fluttered against the window, and the bedroom radiator clanked. Once she thought she heard someone at the door, F.X. maybe, come to take her home.

On the way back to the bedroom Clara detoured to the living room, where she switched off the lamp beside the sofabed. Then as gently as possible, she lifted the hardcover from Mrs. Brix's ample, heaving bosom.

seven

In order to spend time with her mother Emily had to reschedule lunch with a William Morris agent. She hoped Mr. Cooper would not find out about this. He was worried about the big agencies, thinking they unloaded their B projects on Mark Four, and he wanted her to see about changing this state of affairs. Be that as it may, Emily was more concerned at the moment with his giggling, which had blossomed forth again after having lain dormant for several weeks. Rumors had started to circulate that the reason Emily had been promoted so quickly was because she was having an affair with her boss. Consequently, it was more important than ever that Mr. Cooper, a married man, treat her in a businesslike manner. And she told him so, point-blank.

"Oh, dear," he said with mock distress, "and I heard that you got the promotion by stabbing Heather in the back."

"What?"

"It seems, Mrs. Vanderbilt, that you have the reputation of being a cutthroat. You'll stop at nothing to claw your way to the top."

Emily was so nonplussed that for a moment or two she couldn't speak. Then as tears pooled in her eyes, she said quietly, "But that's not true. I never—"

"Of course you never. You know that and I know that. But it's a handy reputation for a sweet young lady like you to have. The sharks might treat you with a little more respect."

Emily had had this talk just before meeting her mother and Clara at La Fondue, a nearby restaurant with fast service and bargain prices. She kept playing it over in her mind, each time coloring it with a different shade of emotion, now outrage, later bewilderment, then even a furtive amusement. At the same time she was trying to keep up her end of the conversation with her mother and Clara.

"Are you still going out to auditions?" Mrs. Brix asked as she dipped a chunk of beef into the fondue pot she was sharing with her daughter.

Emily replied in a more subdued tone of voice. Two strangers, both eating alone, were sharing their table. It was one of the drawbacks of the restaurant, which was always packed for lunch.

"No."

"What? I don't understand. Are you giving up on acting?"

"Mom, I barely have time to get my office work done. I have to bring manuscripts home every night."

Clara swallowed a forkful of her Swissburger before observing, "Emily, you're so smart, you could do anything you wanted."

"Indeed she could. But you know, Clara, Mr. Brix was always against the idea. He told Emily that the theater was no place for a lady."

"Oh, Mother, that has nothing to do with it."

"Now me," Mrs. Brix went on, "I always told Em, you've got to follow your heart. Me and Mr. Brix had more than one set-to about this acting business. I told him if that's what Emmie truly wanted to do, then he had no business making her feel bad about it. Same thing with Smith. Mr. Brix was scared to death letting Em go off all by herself. He wanted her to go to Sophie Newcomb. But I put my foot down there. I said Em needs to broaden her horizons. And as far as the money goes—well, God's planned it so that we'll always worry about money, no matter how much you have. I told Mr. Brix we'd manage somehow. Oh, dear," she added to the young woman sitting at the end of their table, "would you mind passing the salt? Thank you ever so much."

The woman did not look up from her magazine as her arm,

sprinkled with moles, delivered the salt with a mechanical jerk. In a more subdued tone of voice Emily asked whether her mother had seen any sights this morning.

"No, but the police were very kind."

"The police?"

Jointly, Mrs. Brix and Clara filled Emily in on all the details, often talking at the same time. On their way to the Empire State Building Mrs. Brix had remembered her suitcase, so they had asked the cabdriver, who was Russian, to take them back to the apartment. When they couldn't find the suitcase, they had taken another cab to the precinct station and filed a report of stolen property. Back at the apartment they had run into Anton, who was mopping the halls. Yes, he had seen a suitcase that morning and had stored it in the basement. Back to the police they had gone to make sure no one was falsely arrested.

Emily knew that the other woman at their table, the one not reading a magazine, was listening to every word even though she appeared to be absorbed by her chocolate cheesecake. Feeling protective of her mother—the woman was trying to hide a smile as she dabbed at some chocolate on her hollow, rouged cheek—Emily leaned closer, hoping she would lower her voice. But Mrs. Brix seemed to want to include everyone when she talked, and even nodded encouragingly at the two strangers from time to time. It was a blessing when first one, then the other, asked for her check and left.

"Do you think we could go to the Pan Am Building after lunch?" Mrs. Brix asked.

"I've got to get back to work, Mom."

"Maybe you should meet us there for drinks. There's a heliport on the roof. I was hoping Clara and I might be able to talk one of the pilots into giving us a little spin over the city. Imagine how exciting that would be."

"I don't think they'd do that."

Mrs. Brix winked. "I bet if I slipped one of them a fiver."

"Excuse me, please." Clara stood up. "I'm off to the ladies'. My contacts are itching."

"Such a lovely young woman," Mrs. Brix said as they watched Clara ask a harassed-looking waitress for directions. "I'm planning to leave her a traveler's check under my pillow. Twenty dollars."

"Oh, Mom, please don't do that."

"Why not?"

"It's insulting. And besides, you don't have that kind of money to throw around."

Her mother started to protest, but then seemed to visibly slump with a little sigh. "Clara tells me that's the problem, money."

"What?"

"Why you wouldn't let your father and I give you a proper wedding."

Without Hugh or Clara to act as a buffer, Emily felt strangely vulnerable. "Mom, don't you understand? You and Dad have done so much for me already. You're in debt because of my college— and Sandy told me Dad's having a hard time making ends meet."

Sandy was Emily's thirteen-year-old brother, who sometimes called her on the sly from Tula Springs when he was depressed.

"Your father is having a struggle, Em. Business is not so good, I admit. But a wedding is a once-in-a-lifetime event. We could have managed."

"But Mom, it's not fair to Sandy. He's worried about college himself. And Martha says she doesn't have any clothes to wear. How could I possibly expect you to put on some huge extravaganza for me?"

"It wouldn't have had to be huge. It could have been a nice quiet family wedding, something that would have made your aunts and uncles very happy and proud. But I suppose that Aunt Jenna might not quite be up to snuff when it comes to the Vanderbilts. Her grammar always did embarrass you."

"Mother, that's not fair. Especially when I asked you and Dad to come up. But neither one of you did."

Mrs. Brix fingered the false ruby necklace, which seemed a little tight. "Dear, as you know, my mother, I thought she was dying. And your father got that flu."

"Please, Mother, don't. Sandy's told me."

"Excuse me?"

"I know Dad wasn't really that sick. And I know he told you not to come, too. You would have flown up, right? But he's mad at me, isn't he?"

"Em," Mrs. Brix said gently, wringing her hands, "please try to see things from his point of view. He loves you so much. You're

78

the world to him. And he's really such an old-fashioned man. He doesn't understand a thing about the sexual revolution."

"Mom, he—"

"Well, he doesn't. I tried to show him an article in *Life*, and he flung it across the room. But Em, I don't want you to worry about your father. He'll come around, I guarantee. When he sees what a fine young man Hugh is, he'll forgive him quick enough."

"Forgive him?"

"Well, you know," Mrs. Brix said, blushing violently, her eyes averted. "These things do happen. It's much more common than you think. Why, Em, if you'd only talk to me, I could tell you about people my age. It's not just your generation, you know."

"Mother, what in the hell . . ."

"Oh, please, Emily." Mrs. Brix's plump hand went to her heart. "Don't be mean to me, not here."

Somewhat abashed, even though she wasn't being mean at all, Emily said less sharply, "Are you saying, you think I got married because I had to?"

"Well, honey, sweetie, what other possible explanation can there be for the way you've behaved?"

It was Emily's turn to slump, deflated, as the realization sank in.

"Em, are you all right? Would you like a drink?"

She shook her head slowly. "It's just . . . Oh, Mom, here I think I'm making things so nice for you and Dad. You don't have to worry about money or anything. I'm not out dating all sorts of creeps or living with someone. I'm doing exactly what Dad would have wanted me to do, getting married right after college, and to a man in a goddam seminary. Here I'm trying to be so good and normal and considerate—"

"Oh, you are good and normal, dear," Mrs. Brix said, reaching across the table with her napkin to dab at her daughter's eyes.

"It hurts me so much that Dad would think that about me." Emily's lower jaw trembled as she grabbed her mother's hand and clung tight to it. "He knows how much I . . ."

"Em, Em, please, it's all right." Mrs. Brix was a bit flummoxed. How could she ever have doubted her daughter's integrity? "I told your father he shouldn't jump to any conclusions. But you know how stubborn he can be. Well, you just better believe he's going to get a piece of my mind when I get back. I told him he should come with me, you know. I said, 'Mr. Brix, stop your worrying about the money.' "

Seeing Clara approach, Emily released her mother's hand and straightened herself in the unpadded wooden chair.

"I had to take them out," Clara said, sitting down. "Now I can't see a thing."

While they waited for the check to arrive, Clara asked Mrs. Brix if she would mind going back to her apartment for her glasses before they went up the Empire State Building. Mrs. Brix agreed, but deep down, she feared she never would see the promised view of three states. Imagine coming all this way and not seeing a single sight . . .

"Can we count this as a business lunch, Em?" Mrs. Brix asked as she took the check from the waitress. "Shall we put this on that card of yours? We did talk about movies, didn't we?"

"Mom, you know better. We'll just divide it up."

"In that case, I'm taking Clara out. And you too, dear."

"Mother, please. Let's just divide it in two. I'll pay for Clara."

"Oh, no, Em," Clara protested. "Let me take y'all out. I'd really like to."

"No, Clara. You've been so nice to have mother."

"Hold on, girls." Mrs. Brix flapped a hand at the waitress. "I want to ask what this thirty-five cents is. Did anyone have something for thirty-five cents?"

eight

For most of her life Emily had suffered from a peculiar form of self-consciousness that had little to do with shyness or deference, but rather with place. One afternoon in Algebra II she had found herself mesmerized by the sight of Missy Simms, a C student, at the blackboard. "I'm actually here, now," she was thinking with nightmarish intensity, "in this same room with Missy, who is actually here, now, finishing that equation. But it doesn't seem real. I can't really be *here*."

This sensation was a paler version of a feverish trance she had endured in second grade. Waking before dawn on a springlike Monday, she had run drenched in sweat into the bathroom, where she started screaming. Dolly and Mr. Brix had appeared almost immediately. "It's just a bad dream," her father kept reassuring her as she wept, aware of their presence, yet somehow not awake. The clammy tiles, the toilet bowl, the claw-footed tub, her parents themselves—all this was monstrous to her seven-year-old mind, an abomination. Yet at the same time nothing could be more ordinary, more familiar. She was there, yes, and yet she couldn't really be there. Bile left its trace in her mouth, a memory rather than an actual taste. She wanted to die, and yet she knew that she was condemned to live forever, herself always. The spell had lasted only a few minutes—she had gone back to bed in her father's arms and awakened in the morning, bright and refreshed—but the fear that it could occur again lingered.

No episode had ever been as crippling as that night's. When the feeling would creep up on her later, in adolescence, she had learned to let it run its course, knowing it wouldn't last forever. Home from Smith on holiday, especially soon after the flight, she might suffer a bout of Algebra II at the dinner table. Martha, Sandy, her father, mother would seem for a few awful moments like dream figures, figments of her imagination. If she tried hard enough it seemed she would wake up to another reality, one that was easier to believe in, more fully rounded. Of course, she dared not try. Rather, she would play the part of dutiful, loving daughter, hiding her distress.

It was at Smith that Emily found some relief from these spells. Oddly enough, the cure was found onstage, when she could immerse herself in a role so totally that she had no room left over for herself. Yet there was always the danger that something might go wrong, a delayed lighting cue, a memory slip. Then the self-consciousness would return with a vengeance. She would see herself trying to be someone else and feel at two removes from reality.

Once or twice she tried to discuss this aspect of acting with Hugh, to help him see how the stage might have a therapeutic effect for her. But somehow the conversation would veer, and he would end up explaining how men were more naturally alienated from their bodies. Women, according to Hugh, were centered by the womb. They had the ability to feel at home with themselves. Which explained why they could read an endless variety of magazines—*Ladies' Home Journal, McCall's, Glamour*—that would drive a man up a wall. Actually, Emily herself had little patience with magazines that gave tips on how to brighten up a room. She was afraid to admit this to Hugh, though. He might begin to question her femininity, something she was still sensitive about. Growing up, she had never shared Martha's innate interest in makeup and grooming. Her sister could spend hours tending to her body, the dresser top loaded with jars, tubes, and bottles that made Emily feel so inadequate.

Nevertheless, perhaps as a result of being married, Emily was noticing some improvement, a less frequent occurrence of Algebra

II. The most recent had been with her mother and Clara during the lunch in December at La Fondue. Emily had not been fully aware of it at the time, but when she got back to the office a sense of normalcy returned, making the lunch seem a little unreal by contrast. Perhaps it had been the result of seeing her mother out of context, in New York. In any case, it certainly wasn't as strong a sense of dislocation as she had felt before.

Not long after her mother's visit Emily found herself staring in the mirror one chill January morning at a pimple that had blossomed overnight beneath her right cheekbone. That evening at supper she noticed Hugh's eyes straying to it from time to time, though he did not make any remark. Emily had always enjoyed a clear complexion, even as a teenager, and thought it rather odd that at her advanced age, she should have to contend with such nonsense. Admittedly, after ten days it did clear up of its own accord. But then a week later another emerged, this time closer to her nose. Now it wasn't just Hugh's eyes, but also Mr. Cooper's that would drift toward the blemish during a conversation. She tried a variety of teenage ointments—to no avail. Although she realized it was ridiculous to devote any thought at all to such a minor problem, she did. During a lunch with an editorial assistant from Pocket Books, she felt as if the pimple were half the size of her cheek, and scarlet. It wasn't her imagination, though, that the young man, who was actually sort of cute but could only talk about the Knicks and Jimi Hendrix, had glanced at the spot several times. Emily realized then and there something had to be done about it.

"I'm not sure it's fair to call Bonhoeffer irrelevant," she was saying late one evening on the southbound 104 bus. Beside her Fay Terrace, in her knit cap, khaki pants, and black basketball sneakers, could have been mistaken for a man. She had just had dinner with Emily and Hugh at the Front Porch on upper Broadway and was now on her way to spend the night with a new boyfriend in Stuyvesant Town. In order to give himself more time to study, Hugh was staying over at Fay's, which was much closer to the Union library. Emily herself was going to transfer in a few blocks to a crosstown bus, but in the meantime was glad to have a minute or two alone with Fay. The woman was interesting, totally without nonsense. She could see why Hugh felt so comfortable with her.

"After all," Emily resumed, avoiding the gaze of a bearded older man seated across the aisle. It was freezing out, yet all he wore were jeans, sandals, and a flimsy blouse with a mandala embroidered over the chest. "After all, where do you think *The Secular City* came from?"

Hugging herself, Fay said, "You don't mean to tell me you take Harvey Cox seriously?"

"So I'm an ape. But he's right, you know."

"I thought you didn't believe in God, Em."

"I don't, not the Lutheran God I had shoved down my throat. My father's Danish, or at least his parents were. Anyway they imported the gloomiest, most vindictive God imaginable. But like Cox says, an atheist is closer to the real God than any of the suburban idols we might set up. In any case, there shouldn't be a split between the religious life and the secular—don't you think? We've got to make every moment religious. Here, right here, this is just as significant as some trumped-up Baroque altar." She patted the vacant blue molded seat next to her, keeping her face slightly averted. Although Fay had reassured her at dinner, Emily was still uneasy about the way she looked.

Before meeting Hugh and Fay for dinner, Emily had gone to Bloomingdale's in search of a medicated foundation—if there was such a thing—that would camouflage her pimple. Before she knew it, she found herself in the hands of an analyst who had taken a fancy to her. Rickie, a severe-looking young grandmother with a shag cut, declared she would break house rules by giving her a free makeover. Emily explained that all she wanted was an unnoticeable base—and Rickie agreed. No makeover. Just a base. But after Rickie had found a suitable base, she pointed out that Emily had large pores. That was why she was getting pimples in the polluted city air. What she needed first, before applying the base, was a cleanser. Then it seemed that Emily's dark brown eyes were unbalanced by her very fair skin. She needed some sort of framing device to give a more measured transition. "Otherwise, love, you're going to look startled all the time, like Bambi." And by the way, her very very blonde hair, taken together with her very very pale skin tone, it really did make Emily look—if one could be totally one hundred percent frank and honest—well, just a tee-tiny anemic.

An hour and a half later Emily was escorted to the fifth floor, where Rickie helped her apply for instant credit. The total might have seemed indecent to Emily—$139.64—but, after all, this was an investment. She would never have to buy so much again, at least not in one blow. All this sounded reasonable to Emily until she saw the look on Hugh's face. Even without knowing how much it had cost, he seemed to be in shock.

"What's that brown on your cheeks?" Hugh had asked while Fay munched on a stick of fried zucchini. Emily was a little late for dinner, and they had already ordered an appetizer.

"Blush. Cinnamon blush."

"You can't be serious, Em."

"But, Hugh, I have very anemic-looking skin. I need something for my eyes."

"Honey, I don't know but, well, you look like a manicurist or something."

Fortunately, Rickie had supplied her with waterproof mascara, which came in handy when Hugh made a second reference to manicurists. As Emily dabbed at her tears, Fay chided him for being so insensitive. What was wrong with being a manicurist anyway? Fay wanted to know. Then she went on about how hopelessly class-conscious he was. "Of course, you'll be one of the first to be shot when the revolution comes."

"I'm a C.O.," he protested. "They can't shoot a C.O."

"Hugh, you're such a liar. You know you just had a low draft number."

"Well, if I didn't, I was going to be a C.O. That's true."

Fay sighed. "C.O. or not, you're doomed. No one can look like you and not be shot. No way."

As soon as she got back to the apartment, Emily went straight to the bathroom, and with her linguini-stained ski parka still on, scrubbed all the makeup off her face. Later, wrapped in a boy's flannel robe, she settled down with a script from the office while trying hard not to feel foolish and miserable about what she had just spent on herself. If Hugh were coming back to the apartment that night, she would have confessed the full amount and promised not to wear the cinnamon blush again.

"I was just thinking about you," she said, pleased and amazed that he would phone at that very moment. She had picked up immediately, knowing by a womanly sixth sense that it had to be Hugh.

"Does that mean he's there?" a woman's voice came over the line.

"Uh, Hugh?"

"Lucas, I would like to speak to Lucas."

Having recovered, Emily placed the voice now. "Oh, hi, Judy. No, he's not here."

"You're sure?"

"What? Why would he be here? It's almost midnight. Is something the matter?"

"He probably just missed his train. I'm sorry, Emily. I hope I didn't disturb you."

"It's all right," Emily said, a little sullenly, and then went on in a vaguely conciliatory way for a moment or two, as if to appease Judy for something she, Emily, had done. Brightly, stiffly, Judy informed her that everything was fine. She just happened to get home a day early from a trip to Dallas and was a little concerned where he might be.

After hanging up Emily brooded a while, feeling ill-used. Judy had not spoken to her as one married woman to another. Indeed, she had made Emily feel like a regular at Maxwell's Plum. The very idea that she would think Lucas might be at the apartment at this hour—it was insulting. Emily considered phoning Judy back, but weariness overcame her. Without bothering to pull out the bed, she curled up on the sofa, an afghan over her, and was about to drift off when the buzzer gave her a nasty start.

"Yes?"

"It's me."

"Who?"

"Me, come on."

"Lucas?"

She hesitated. She did not want to let him in, but she was worried about her neighbor across the hall, Mr. Pears, a middle-aged bachelor, who left notes under their door from time to time. Apparently he was able to overhear everything said on their intercom, which several times had awakened him from, as he put it, "a sound and necessary repose."

When da-deedee-da-da *da da* blared out childishly several times, Emily, huddled in the afghan like a peasant woman, pressed the button marked "Door."

"Hi," Lucas said, breezing in. "Just thought I'd drop by, say hello."

Twenty minutes later he still had on his mink-lined cashmere overcoat, the fur balding in spots if one looked closely. Emily had vented her annoyance at such an intrusion. ("It's not just me I'm thinking about, Lucas. What about Hugh? What if he were trying to get some sleep and you came barging in?") And she had told him about Judy's call. ("You're kidding. She's back? Well, it's cool. I told her I sometimes hang out at your place, if I'm late or something." "But that's not true, Lucas. You haven't been here since I've been married." "Yeah, right. But I thought if I missed a train some night, you wouldn't mind. And she wouldn't worry.")

Getting her second wind, Emily went to the stove to boil water for instant coffee. Lucas's eyes were glazed, and he was slurring some words. She was concerned about sending him off to a PATH station in such condition. He would be easy prey for a mugger.

Sprawled on the sofa Lucas contemplated his Churchill loafers, wondering why he hadn't noticed before how beautiful they were. Such lines, what craftsmanship. Glancing up at Emily, her back to him as she opened a cupboard, he thought she had wonderful lines, too. And wasn't it wonderful, as well, that her husband wasn't around. Life was truly wonderful. Now he could talk to her freely, even though he didn't mean to disparage Hugh in any way. Hugh was a fine boy. A perfect husband for Emily. Wasn't it glorious how everything always seemed to work out in the end? Yes, life was grand if you gave it half a chance. He mustn't let himself be dragged down by negative thoughts. After all, here he was with her best friend. Emily would know how to advise him about her. What to do . . .

Lucas, of course, was thinking of Clara Edward Tilman. After the Thanksgiving dinner, Lucas had taken her out to lunch once or twice to counsel her on the pitfalls of the modeling racket. Then there was the late supper at La Goulue and the problem of making it in time for the last train from Hoboken. So he had to spend the night at her place—all perfectly innocent. But a week later he had missed another train. That evening during dinner in Clara's apartment, he realized something was happening to him. He wanted her, but not just in a crude sexual way. The sex they had that night was almost incidental, somehow not enough.

It was this Lucas wanted to talk about with Emily. He needed to know what it might mean, where it was leading. Since he had been married to Judy, he had never slept with another woman. Every Sunday he had been able to go to communion with his mother at St. Aloysius in Forest Hills. He loved Judy. He cared for her deeply. She had saved him from certain ruin and put his life back together for him. Yet all this seemed strangely unreal, like the love he was supposed to feel for Mary or Jesus, folks that you are so indebted to that you can only feel guilty when thinking of them. With Clara there was an urgency he hadn't felt before, a spontaneity. Now a day hardly went by without his experiencing new heights—and depths—of emotion. Death suddenly became a reality rather than an abstract concept. Every moment with her, without her, seemed so precious. Even the production supervisor at work, a real prick, was looking different to him. There was something poignant and sad about Sal's competitiveness, his desperate striving for power.

"Have you heard from Clara recently?" he began, somewhat lamely, when Emily handed him a mug of coffee. His heart was so full, yet something about Emily, the look in her eye, made him back off a little.

"No. Why?" she said flatly.

"I don't know. I happened to run into her tonight, and we—"

"What? Where?"

"After work, I bumped into her on the street and so I—we had a drink or something."

"So?"

"Well, you know, she's really a stunning girl. I mean, if a

88

guy weren't married, I could see how he might fall for someone like her."

In a voice that would have been much louder, were it not for Mr. Pears, Emily said, "I really can't believe what I'm hearing. You mean to tell me, you have one drink and you're ready to—"

"Hey, take it easy. I'm not saying me. I meant a guy who, you know . . ."

"Don't bullshit me, Lucas. You have your eye on her, right? Well, let me tell you something. If I hear you've started pestering that girl, Judy's going to get an earful—understand?"

Earful was something Emily's father would say, a word she heartily disliked. But it was too late to amend it.

"Hey, babe, you don't have to fly off the handle."

"Don't call me babe."

"All right, calm down." He fumbled with the mug, spilling some coffee onto the arm of the sofa. She had managed to get him a little steamed. After all, he had come to her as a friend, willing to trust her with a secret that could ruin him. And this was the sort of reception she gave him, Miss Holier Than Thou. "I'll pay for this."

"What?"

"The sofa. If it's stained, I'll . . ."

"Look, Lu, I'm sorry. I didn't mean to come on like gang-busters." Another word her father would use. "But for Christ's sake, be real. You're married, almost half a century old."

"I'm forty-three."

"Whatever, it's a dead end. So all right, I can see how you might be attracted to her physically. But sex is such a small part of any real relationship. You know that, don't you?"

Like a kid he sat there pouting. Emily had to resist the urge to muss his hair. There was something so endearing about that look on him.

"Lu, dear, if you only knew. You're a victim of advertising, of all the trash spewing out of Madison Avenue. They make every man feel as if he isn't getting enough. There's this impossible, unreal idea of sex. And it's warping everyone's brain. It's madness, true madness." She felt frustrated, knowing how trite and preachy she must sound. If only she could be more specific, tell him about the quiet love she shared with Hugh. The real turning point in her feelings had come right after Hugh and she had finally succeeded in having good old-fashioned missionary position intercourse. From that day on she had felt small chunks of suppressed anxiety and reserve melt away. With sex no longer an issue, she and Hugh learned to feel comfortable with each other. Friday was the night, usually, for their lovemaking especially after a Liebfraumilch dinner in Yorktown. The rest of the time they were satisfied with cuddling or massage. In a way, she was still resentful that sex had been made to seem as spectacular and forbidding as Mount Everest, when in actuality it was more like the sandbox in your own backyard.

"I wasn't talking about sex," Lucas said after sipping thoughtfully from the mug.

"Come on."

"The reason we had a drink," he said, hoping to cover his tracks, "we were celebrating. Clara got a TV thing."

"A set?"

"A part on TV."

"Oh, you mean a commercial. How nice."

"No, no." He heaved himself up off the sofa. Digging into his pocket for his gloves, he said, "A show. A real show."

"You don't mean she's going to act? Lu, are you sure you're all right?" she added with an anxious look toward the door. "Maybe you should have another cup of coffee."

"No, Judy's—I got to get home."

Casually, trying not to seem too curious, Emily said at the door, "She's not acting, is she? Some sort of game show, maybe?"

"No, it's like this. She was in a grocery store the other day and she started talking to this dame in the checkout line, and the lady turns out to be a casting director for one of those soaps. So Clara went to see her the next day and—Anyway, I wasn't supposed to tell you all this."

"Why not?"

Lucas shrugged. "Clara's very sweet. I think she didn't want to make you feel bad."

"Feel bad?" Emily gave a very good imitation of a laugh. "I think it's wonderful."

"Good, so do I," he said going out the door. "By the way, would you mind ringing Judy now and telling her I'm on my way?"

"Sure," Emily said distractedly. But after she had bolted and chained the door, she felt a sudden surge of anger. Why should she have to play the beard for him? Let him do his own explaining.

nine

❧

Sometimes it seemed to Clara that she might as well be living in Moscow, what with all the lines she was forced to stand in. That's what communism amounted to, Clara remembered from a sociology class in college—waiting. If it wasn't a line at the post office, the Chase Manhattan, or a box office, then it was sitting for hours on end in the Tenth Avenue studio where they taped "My Life to Live." With a call time of 7:30 A.M. there would be only a half hour of actual rehearsal before lunch, the rest of the morning spent thumbing through magazines or gazing anxiously at the monitor, wondering if she was where she was supposed to be. In the afternoon she would change into wardrobe, wait an hour or two, sometimes three, before going through blocking on the sound stage. Then, after yet another wait, her scene would be shot, usually in ten minutes or so.

Though she was an Under Five, Clara did worry about her lines, which never exceeded four. The problem was with the kind and doddering actor who played Dr. Kensington, an obstetrician who had murdered two of his patients. As his receptionist Clara would often be fed lines from a previous scene and suffer a false sense of déjà vu. On the days she was not on call, Clara would check with her modeling agency to find out if the go-sees left with her answering service were legitimate. She had to be careful with Chanell Guys & Gals, since they tended to book soft-core shoots for their clients, something Clara wouldn't even consider. Of course, this did not make her *très* popular at the agency, and they would often keep her on hold for five, ten minutes, when she phoned.

Although she had only lived in New York a few months, Clara thought of herself as an entirely different person from the naive smalltown girl who had said hello to strangers on the street. She had matured incredibly fast, and no longer saw life in her mother's narrow-minded way. This was what she tried to get across to her ex-fiancé, F.X. Pickens, who had shown up not long after she had landed her role in the soap opera. Of course, his presence in the city was upsetting, and Clara felt the need of advice from friends about how to deal with him. Iris, the nice makeup artist on the set—the mean one told Clara that she was getting crow lines from smiling so much—Iris said it was simple. All Clara had to do was tell him to get lost. And if he didn't stop calling her and following her, she should go to the police. Rebecca, the neighbor who had seen F.X. once on the stairs, had told Clara she would be glad to take him off her hands. Like most women, Rebecca had been bowled over by his looks, which was how F.X. had managed to make so much progress with Clara herself, before she realized what a creep he was. As for Emily, she predicted he would fade away of his own accord. Pretty girls were a dime a dozen in New York, she let Clara know. He would be distracted by one or another soon enough. It was only Lucas, though, Emily's friend, who really seemed to understand. He didn't ever cut her short when she went into detail about her feelings, the tenderness and pity that got mixed up with the fear and anger.

"Like if I stop and think how old he is, it makes me feel sorry for him," she explained one afternoon when Lucas, who had left work a little early, dropped by the studio for a chat. They were in a cramped cinder-block dressing room, the makeup lights glaring even though Clara, except for an occasional minor adjustment, was finished with them.

"How old is he?"

"It's not that I don't feel ancient myself. I mean there were two sixteen-year-olds trying out for this print ad yesterday with me. But let's face it, he's twenty-eight. And on top of that he's gray but won't admit it. I found some Grecian Formula in his cabinet back home one day, in Louisiana."

Lucas managed a dim smile. It was an unthinking comment, he reasoned, one not aimed at his own gray locks. Yet if she cared for him even half as much as he cared for her, could she have said such a thing in front of him?

"And all he's ever done," she went on from the cot, where she was perched with a *Cosmopolitan* on her lap, "he worked for a Ford-Lincoln-Mercury dealer, his father-in-law's. He was married once right out of high school, but it was dissolved. He's Catholic, see." She glanced up at the monitor. "Oh, and plus he used to sell insurance. It's really sad, a man that age, hasn't found himself."

Leaning toward the mirror to check her lips, she caught a glimpse of Lucas's weary face. F.X. had never held her afterward. But Lucas, when it was all over, had taken her in his arms, cradling her, making her feel so safe and secure. And his tenderness, his regard for her before the lovemaking, and during, it was such a revelation. F.X., the only other man she had ever slept with, had handled her so roughly and used four-letter words. Yes, she had slept with Lucas out of pity that time. Her defenses were down from too much wine at dinner, and he seemed so sad, so needy. And old, looking almost as old as her father. But it hadn't turned out like she had expected. She found herself responding in a way she thought only happened in the movies. And this was deeply disturbing, because she knew it wouldn't be right to go to bed with him again. He was not only married, but happily married.

"Now, you know what he wants to do? Last night F.X. says to me—"

"Last night?" Lucas moved a little to his right to avoid his own reflection in the mirror. "I thought you decided not to see him again?"

"He was waiting on the stoop for me when I got home. I had to talk to him. Anyway, he wants to try acting now. He said if I could get a job on TV, anyone could. So he made me promise to set up an interview with Grace. She's the casting director I met at the Pioneer."

"Not a good idea, Clara. It's not very professional."

"I know. But I thought it'd make it easier to never see him

again. I did hurt him a lot. He really wanted to marry me, you know."

"Hey, the jerk used to beat you up. Remember?"

"Not beat me up, just get a little rough sometimes."

"I tell you, I ever see him lay a hand on you . . ."

The door banged against the wall as Iris strode in, muttering, "The way he orders me around . . ." Flipping off the lights on the mirror, she squatted in front of Clara and peered at her face. Lucas had been introduced to the makeup artist once before. He found her abrasive. And she was far too old—in her early forties, he guessed—to be wearing a mini skirt and spike-heeled boots.

"You know, I'm going to sic the union on him if he doesn't watch his step," Iris went on. "He thinks just because—"

"You going?" Clara mouthed to Lucas, who had retreated to the door. He gave a little wave and left.

Clara watched as Iris tidied up the counter in front of the mirror. She had a way of making everything she did, even if it was only tweezing a brow, seem important. And everything Iris said sounded urgent.

"For you." Iris slipped Clara an envelope as she got up off the cot.

"Me?" The handwriting was unfamiliar, and it wasn't her name. It was addressed to the character she played.

"Dear Kimberly," Clara read, Iris looking on over her shoulder, "I like the way you do your hair, but I wish you'd stop wearing that bow. May God bless you and praise you forever. Sincerely, Mrs. R. J. Fenolk, Sioux City, Iowa."

Looking up from the flower-bordered stationery, Clara asked, "What's this supposed to mean?"

"Well, kid, you just got your first fan letter."

"Really?" Clara stared at it again. Then she began to worry about the large white bow the stylist taped to her hair every day. It was supposed to be something of a trademark for Kimberly.

"Then show it to Don," Iris advised when Clara expressed her concern. Don was the stylist and was fairly touchy about his work.

"The letter?"

"Right. Let him know that other folks besides me find it ridiculous."

"I didn't know you didn't like the bow, too. Why didn't you tell me? Do I really look stupid? Oh, Iris, you've got to help me. You know how Don is. He'll just yell at me. Please, you know him, talk to him."

"I don't have time."

"Iris, sweetie, friend." Clara put her arms around Iris, who with a sigh and a face pink with pleasure, gave in.

"Oh, all right," she huffed as she broke away. "Now let me out of here. I got work to do."

Emily was a little annoyed when Clara made the request over the phone. It made no sense that she should have to introduce Clara's ex-fiancé to her boss. Mr. Cooper wasn't interested in anyone who wasn't a star, especially a male anyone. Furthermore, Emily wasn't getting along so well with him, not recently. He had not bought a single book or script recommended by her. And he complained to his secretary, who wasted no time in passing it along to Emily, that she wasn't aggressive enough in scouting out new properties. With all this going on, the last thing Emily needed to do was drag a friend of a friend into his office.

"Clara," Emily said, mustering all her patience, "F.X. should be seeing agents. Cooper's not going to do him any good. And besides, why are you helping him out like this?"

"Well, I tried to get him in to see this casting director, but she's in L.A. now, and I thought if I could do one nice thing for him I wouldn't have him on my conscience anymore. See, I talked to Minna about him, and she said I should try you out next."

"Minna? Who's Minna?"

"Minna Burns, the friend who got me into Chanell, my agency. I told you about her. She's the lady I met at the motel when Mama and I were on that sightseeing tour. Minna came over for dinner last night, and we started talking about things I could do for F.X., and—"

"Listen, Clara"—Mr. Cooper had just walked into her office—"I'll call you later, O.K.? Bye now."

Fingering the sandy handlebar mustache he had recently sprouted, Emily's boss handed her a letter she had written for him. It was meant to raise the spirits of an Iranian banker, who was getting cold feet on a project already in production, a remake of

Sayonara set in Reconstruction Georgia. "Still not there," he said.

Emily's face was impassive. At first she had thought it was an honor to compose the letter for him. It seemed he might be grooming her for a more responsible position, letting her know the ins and outs of the business. But then it occurred to her that this was taking time away from her real duties of acquiring properties. How could he expect her to do this when he pestered her with his secretarial work?

"I put in everything you said, Ronald."

Gazing out her door, he seemed about to leave. "What? Yes, like I said. Needs more zest, more punch." With a Mont Blanc pen, he wrote in a childish hand above one of her lines, "The Chicargo Tirbune called HEAVEN SCENT a 'mindblowing adult thriller.' "

"Come on, Ronald. You can't say that."

"Indeed?"

Riffling through a stack of folders, she came up with a photostat of a review of Mark Four's most recent film. "It says," and she read aloud, " 'The flick may be mindblowing for a third-grade audience, but as an adult thriller it is a predictable rehash of a Sixties mindset, passé now and . . .' "

"All right then." He leaned over the letter and made a few marks with his pen. "There."

She regarded the change a moment. ". . . called HEAVEN SCENT a 'mindblowing . . . adult thriller.' "

"Now it's an exact quote. Retype this, will you, so I can send it out this afternoon."

After he left, Emily sat in grim silence ignoring the next two calls on her line. She had no intention of being a party to such stupid tampering with the truth. Everyone knew *Heaven Scent* was a bomb. Why couldn't he forget about it? Yes, she would go into his office and explain that it was better left unmentioned. But what if he still insisted on the misquote? Was it really that important? After all, this wasn't an ad. It was just a private letter. But, at the same time, something inside her was deeply offended.

"Hugh, I've been thinking. Maybe we should stay put."

They were eating on the couch, their plates balanced as usual on their knees. They had never gotten around to buying a table, but even if they had, it would have made the apartment intolerably cramped. As it was, there never was a time when Emily felt the apartment looked neat, not since Hugh had moved in. Two of his suitcases were stuffed behind the director's chair and four boxes of books had yet to be unpacked. Where would they go? Even the bathroom had books stacked on the sink counter next to the mouthwash.

"Hugh?"

He finished chewing before saying anything. It was one concession he had made for her recently, not to talk with his mouth full. "This is great. You were the one who talked me into taking that place. Now you're backing out?"

Only a touch of annoyance was noticeable in his voice. He was in far too good a mood that evening to let her vagaries upset him. When she had come home from work the first thing he had done was to thrust his paper on the philosophical hermeneutics of Schleiermacher into her screenplay-laden arms. Dr. Kluth had given him a glowing report, declaring in a bold, legible hand that he had "an astonishing critical facility whose iconoclasm was balanced by a judicious use of primary source material."

"It's not backing out. I still love that apartment more than anything I've ever seen. And I think we could be so happy there with all that space."

Clara had been the one who had found the apartment for them, a one-bedroom on East 64th Street, with a garden in back, all for only $355 a month. It belonged to Anton's mother, who rarely, if ever, used it. Clara's super had gone to work on his mother after Clara made a big fuss about what good tenants Emily and Hugh would be. For tax reasons Anton's mother had bought a condominium in Dobbs Ferry, where she now lived, but she was reluctant to give up the rent-controlled apartment in the city. She was afraid she might find Dobbs Ferry too boring and want to move back. Furthermore, she could not sublet her apartment— legally, that is.

Anton managed to convince his mother that it would be safer to have people living on 64th Street, especially since she had left behind furniture and carpets that would be well worth stealing. When Mrs. Peterson learned that Hugh was St. Paul's, that was enough for her. Her late husband was St. Paul's and had left the school a generous bequest in his will. But even with this go-ahead, Emily and Hugh remained doubtful. Emily did not like the idea of an illegal sublet, and Hugh was uncomfortable about paying so much rent. Clara's enthusiasm, though, was unrelenting. She could not believe that they wouldn't jump at the chance for high ceilings, a full-sized kitchen. How could they stand living another minute on 92nd Street, with a fully furnished garden apartment waiting for them?

After seeing the garden with her own eyes, Emily began to listen to Clara. Was it really illegal, since there would be no written contract between them and Anton's mother? Indeed, it remained Mrs. Peterson's apartment. She could move back in anytime she wished. Why should Emily worry about a greedy landlord who was out to gouge every cent he could from helpless tenants. As for Hugh, he, too, was impressed with what they would be getting for the money. And when Emily explained how much they would save by eating in, he began to relent. It was indeed true that Emily and Hugh spent far too much eating out in restaurants, simply because it was such a trial to cook in the studio. But what finally did the trick for Hugh was the sight of a real bed. He was so damned tired of pulling out the sofa at home, and in the morning trying to cram it back together again with its faulty joints.

"What is it, then? Are you having scruples about being illegal again?"

She set aside her plate of lamb chops smothered in pinto beans. Since he was the chef that evening, she would have liked to have eaten everything on her plate. But her stomach was in knots. "Please don't use that word. You know it's not illegal."

"Well?"

"Remember yesterday I told you about that quote Cooper wanted doctored?"

"You get so wrapped up in these little things. It's not that big a deal. And look"—he playfully slapped her hand—"you hardly ate a thing. Here I slave over a hot stove for you and . . . "

"All right, stop. I'm sorry." Emily herself was puzzled at the depth of her depression. It was amazing how awful Cooper had made her feel, like some common criminal. And Hugh, who was so good, what would he think of her? Why did she feel so totally unworthy of him?

"Em?" Setting aside his own plate, he reached over and smoothed away a tear. "Come on, take it easy, honey. It's all right."

"Sometimes I just wish it were all over. I don't want to go on."

Putting an arm around her, he pulled her close. But even though she nestled against his chest, she did not feel safe, secure.

"Today, this morning, I decided I couldn't do it. I just couldn't live with myself if I lied about *Heaven Scent*."

"But I told you, that was his lie, not yours. You can't be responsible for everything."

"I know. But I can be responsible for what I do. And look, I thought a lot about how to do it. I didn't want to make Cooper feel bad about it. I'd be offhand, humorous. And I was. I mean when I went into his office this afternoon, I wasn't at all self-righteous or priggish. I brought it up only after discussing other business. And then—you won't believe. When I told him, he, he . . ."

She felt his bicep flex as he gave her a reassuring hug. "Take it easy, Em."

Though she knew it was ridiculous to let that little man affect her so, she couldn't help herself. The pain was real.

After a moment she was able to continue. "He reached in his drawer and took out an American Express bill—mine. A statement from January."

"Yours?"

"The bills go right to him. I didn't know that at first, though. When he gave me the card, I thought I'd be billed and then . . . See, I went shopping with Judy once—"

"Lucas's . . .?"

She nodded. "My tweed suits, I didn't have enough cash so I put them on my card. I was planning to pay back Mark Four, of course. When I got the bill, I was going to write a check. Then when the statement never came, I guess it slipped my mind. But Cooper's been thinking about it all this time. Instead of coming and asking me about it, he's held on to it. And he practically accused me of being a thief. It was awful, Hugh. I wanted to die. He just wouldn't believe that it was an oversight."

"The son of a bitch. I ought to go have a talk with him."

"No, let me handle it."

"Who does he think he is? The nerve of that guy."

While Hugh brooded, she took the dishes to the sink and began to wash up. It was comforting to see how upset he was— at least, at first. But when he decided to pass up dessert, she became uneasy.

"You know it was a mistake."

He glanced at her as he stuffed a book into his overloaded knapsack. "Mistake? How can you—"

"Me, I mean. What I did."

"Forget about that. It's him I'd like to . . ."

"But you do understand. I had so much on my mind and I just assumed the bill would be coming."

"Em . . ."

"I would never do anything to embarrass you like that."

"Hey, calm down."

"You look so mad, Hugh. Where are you going?"

"To the library."

"Can't you study here tonight? I don't want to be alone."

"I told you I had to go out."

"Oh, yes. You're right." Somewhat timidly she helped him shoulder the pack and then stood within hugging distance at the door. Looking expectantly into his eyes as he backed out of the apartment, clumsily, because she was in the way, she heard him say, "Of course, you have no choice now. You'll have to quit."

"What?"

"You can't go on working for someone who accuses you of being a common thief."

Hearing those words coming from him—common thief— stirred up a vague panic, which she immediately tried to disguise. "Oh, come on," she said cheerfully. "He didn't call me that, really. I was exaggerating, you know me. And anyway, we can't afford to have me quit."

"Sure, I see. That's why you don't want to move now."

"Well, I was a little worried what might happen if he fired me. But he probably won't. These things happen all the time."

She had followed him out into the hall, where she still hoped for a kiss, a squeeze. "We're moving, Em," he said to the glass door of the vestibule. "I don't care if we have to borrow from

Lettice, but we're going to have that apartment. No cheap two-bit producer is going to keep you out of there, I guarantee."

She stood there a moment after he walked out. She wished she had asked him what time he would be home.

Emily and Hugh were advised to move in discreetly, a box or two at a time. And if a neighbor should happen to see them, they were to say that Hugh was Mrs. Peterson's nephew, just visiting. The top drawer of the dresser should be left alone, with Mrs. Peterson's things intact, just in case the landlord should make a surprise visit. And, of course, Emily should make sure that a few of Mrs. Peterson's dresses were hanging in the closet.

None of this made Emily very happy. She asked Hugh if they were really going to enjoy feeling like intruders in their own home. But it was a useless question. They had already broken the lease on the 92nd Street apartment and lost their security. And furthermore, Hugh was not pleased that she had still not worked up the gumption to quit her job. He did not seem to understand that she needed more time to consider. In any case, how was she supposed to make a rational decision in the midst of moving? Wasn't it enough that she had agreed to the move?

Having a slow week, with no call time on the set and only one audition, Clara volunteered to give Emily a hand with a few boxes. To save money Emily suggested they use the subway rather than a cab, and she bought Clara a token. Perhaps they were too ambitious with their first load, a box of paperbacks that they were unable to shove under the turnstile. It being rush hour, the clerk in the booth scolded them over her loudspeaker about blocking the flow. Clara was ready to give up, but Emily, with a mighty heave, managed to squeeze the box through the narrow passage.

"I can't believe no one stopped to help us," Clara was saying some minutes later when they had deposited the box in the foyer of the 64th Street apartment. "Not a single man."

"We'll take clothes next trip. Hugh can get the rest of the books tomorrow. He's got a friend from Union who's going to help out."

The next load they took by cab, and then walked back uptown for one more, Hugh's underwear, shirts, and socks. Emily was relieved that they didn't run into any neighbors, though she was not sure if some curtains on the third floor didn't part as they were getting out of the cab. Safe inside she chained the door and hurried to the kitchen sink to wash the grime from her hands and face while Clara used the bathroom.

Though it was almost seven, it was still light; she decided it might be nice if they ate in the garden. The locusts had not put out any leaves yet, and the stone jardinières held only a few sprouting weeds, but to Emily, who had plans for growing herbs, flowering shrubs, tomatoes, green peppers, it was as luxuriant as a rain forest. Scrubbing the glass-topped garden table with ammonia and water, she soon forgot about the parted curtains and had to agree with Clara, who carried out two cushions for the wrought-iron chairs, that she would have been crazy to give all this up.

"I feel like a grown-up here, a real adult," Emily was saying a little later after she had brought out the Porterhouse steaks and fried potatoes.

Clara poured wine from Mrs. Peterson's decanter into two stem glasses. "I just know you and Hugh are going to love it here. Tell you the truth, I was worried about that other place. It was so tiny. Two people couldn't live there for long without being at each other's throats."

"Hugh and I thought of it as temporary, like camping out for a while. I guess that's how we survived."

"Now you can start to live."

"Right."

In jeans and a workshirt, without any makeup on, her hair hidden beneath a red kerchief, Clara was somehow easier to talk to, or so Emily imagined. Emily herself hadn't bothered to change out of her office clothes, a silk blouse and beige pleated skirt that had gotten a spot on it from one of the boxes. Emily was worried that it might not come out, even though Clara had reassured her several times that it would.

A breeze stirred the ivy on a neighboring terrace and made the down on Emily's arm rise. Relishing the chill, she poured herself another glass of Gallo Hearty Burgundy. "Are you going to finish that?" she asked, eyeing Clara's half-eaten steak.

Clara was full, so Emily decided not to let it go to waste. She was still hungry, with only bones and gristle on her plate.

"I don't see how you can eat so much and stay so tiny."

"It's my metabolism. Every day I use up thousands of calories by worrying."

"Worrying? What have you got to worry about?"

"You're kidding."

"No, I'm serious. You've got it made as far as I'm concerned. A wonderful husband, a job, now this place."

"Clara, I'd give it all up just like that for—I mean the job. I'd quit in a second if I could, well, do something like you're doing."

"What? Be in a silly soap?"

Emily felt something inside her yield, surrender, the same something, perhaps, that had fought so hard against Cooper. "Silly? Clara, you waltz into town not even wanting to be an actress, and the next thing I know you're on national television. Sure, it's probably a dumb show. But I'd give my right arm to be on it."

Smiling sadly, Clara said, "I knew it. I was afraid all along you'd hate me for this. I'm still not sure what I'm doing there. Any day I expect to be fired. One of the guys in wardrobe told me—no, it was Iris, she said she thinks Dr. Kensington might strangle me next week. She heard one of the writers talking about it."

"Well, at least you'll have a credit."

Whether it was a sudden surge, or simply that she had just become aware of it, the chirping from a neighboring garden seemed unusually loud. Querulous calls, proud, hesitant, joyful, mechanical, they were hard to define. Distracted by this wholly other, unseen in tree limbs beyond the wall, Emily did not attend to the more familiar voice until the tone became more urgent.

"What's stopping you?"

"Huh?"

"Come on, Em. If what you really want to do is act, then what's the matter? Do it."

"I can't." She reached for the wine. "Not now. Hugh's still in school. It would be unfair—I mean it will seem like I'm using him. I'd have to quit my job. There's no way with all the work I've got that I could find time for auditions." She had not told Clara about the contretemps with Mr. Cooper over the American

Express bill. But this, too, made her feel it would be hard to quit. The more she thought about it, the more it seemed it would be an admission of guilt if she resigned. And she would give up any right to unemployment benefits, money which could come in handy now.

"So what's to stop you from getting a part-time job?"

"Hugh won't want me going to auditions. And his mother, she'll have a fit."

"Hugh will understand. He's not a dope. Just make it clear what you want, what you have to do." Twilight began to induce a mild myopia, blurring Clara's features so that she seemed a bit more remote. "As for his mother, what's it to you, girl?"

"Well, she does control his money. Hugh has to wait until he's thirty before he's in charge."

"Great, so you're going to wait until you're thirty before you start living. I like that." Iron legs scraped over the bricks as Clara pulled closer. "Listen to me, Em. Ever since we were girls, I knew there was something different about you. You're not like most girls—"

"Thanks a lot."

"Hush, let me finish. I just didn't understand back then. I was too naive. But I've been thinking about you a lot lately. It's like being here, away from home, it's opened my eyes. You're really something special, girl. I have a feeling you're going to be someone someday. I'm going to say I knew her when."

"Clara . . ." Emily protested, softly.

"Back home I never knew you wanted to be an actress. So it seemed weird when your mama told me that was your dream. But one thing I know: if that's what you got your heart set on, then that's it. You're going to do it, and do it big. For heaven's sake, if someone like me can land a part, just think what you could do if you put your mind to it."

Emily discovered that they were holding hands. She hadn't realized this at first, and now felt a little self-conscious about it. "But your looks . . ."

"That's just an excuse, and you know it. I'm not tall enough. I'm not pretty enough. Well, as Daddy would say, hogwash. How on earth do you think you landed Mr. Vanderbilt, huh? Explain that one to me, Miss Ugly. I know about a dozen models who would give up everything for a man like that—including me. You think I enjoy being an old maid? I've got half a mind to pack it in and go back to darling, insane F.X. One more night of eating alone, sleeping alone—oh, it's a blast, honey."

That morning Emily had awakened with the thought that she might be struck by a bus on her way to work. It had seemed a comforting thought at the time, the only solution to her misery. Now it seemed perfectly natural, the boundless hope that filled her heart. On impulse, before she had time to think about it, she leaned over and gave the hand that held hers a kiss.

"I won't hear that sort of talk," Emily was saying a few moments later as they cleared the table. "You're not serious about going back to that moron?"

"No, course not, but . . ." Clara seemed to have faded. Talking about herself had drained her voice of the energy and conviction she had lavished upon Emily.

"Clara Edward," Emily said in a perfect imitation of Mrs. Tilman's throaty voice, "we'll have none of that, young lady. Enunciate. Stand up straight."

With a wistful smile Clara held open the French doors. Loaded down with dishes Emily stepped imperiously into the bedroom. "Come, child."

They were at the sink, Clara washing, Emily drying, when it happened. Emily set down a stem glass, still wet. It suddenly occurred to her that she was cured, that she needn't ever worry again about Algebra II. Someone might be watching her, but that someone would no longer be herself. No, that god was dead, that severe, judgmental, Cartesian idol was gone for good. And of all people, it was Clara who had brought her this good news.

"Em?"

"Mmm?"

"You O.K.?"

"I'm quitting."

"Huh? Pass me that plate, will you?"

"Tomorrow, first thing, I'm going to tell Cooper off. That's it, I'm through."

With the back of a sudsy hand Clara wiped a strand of hair from her eyes.

"Well, aren't you glad?" Emily said, taking up the glass again. "Say something, girl."

"I'm glad, sweetie, yes. Only does it have to be tomorrow? Can't you wait until you introduce F.X. to him?"

"You're hopeless, a real basket case. Oh, all right. I'll introduce the creep to the bum first. Then I'll quit. Now are you happy?"

Clara shrugged. "I just want to get him off my conscience. Then I'll be able to go on."

"What do you mean, go on? You got someone on the back burner already?"

"No, no, nothing like that."

"You know, it's funny. Not long ago Lucas stopped by our apartment and—"

"Lucas? Let's see, is he the one from Thanksgiving? That old guy, sort of fat?" It was Dr. Kensington's receptionist talking, a fey voice that Emily had heard a week ago when she had stayed home with the flu. Clara probably didn't even realize what she sounded like in her attempt to cover up. But she managed to confirm the nagging doubts Emily had had about the two of them ever since Lucas's visit. It saddened her, but she was far from being disheartened. With so much hope inside her she could almost smile. Clara, too, would be cured. She would get over the man, with Emily's help, and see what he really was all about. Then Emily would be on the lookout for someone more suitable. Hugh had some nice-looking friends at Union. She would give a dinner party soon—next week.

On the way out of the building the two of them did encounter a neighbor in the vestibule, an older woman in a smock and pearl choker. She was having difficulty getting her mailbox opened and cursed drunkenly, unconcerned that she was observed.

"Doll, give me a hand, will ya?" she demanded in an almost masculine voice, as if there were only one of them trying to get by.

Feeling somewhat illegal again, Emily tried to hurry Clara along. But Clara fiddled with the box until it opened, and only then emerged onto the sidewalk, where Emily was waiting to give her a good scolding.

part two

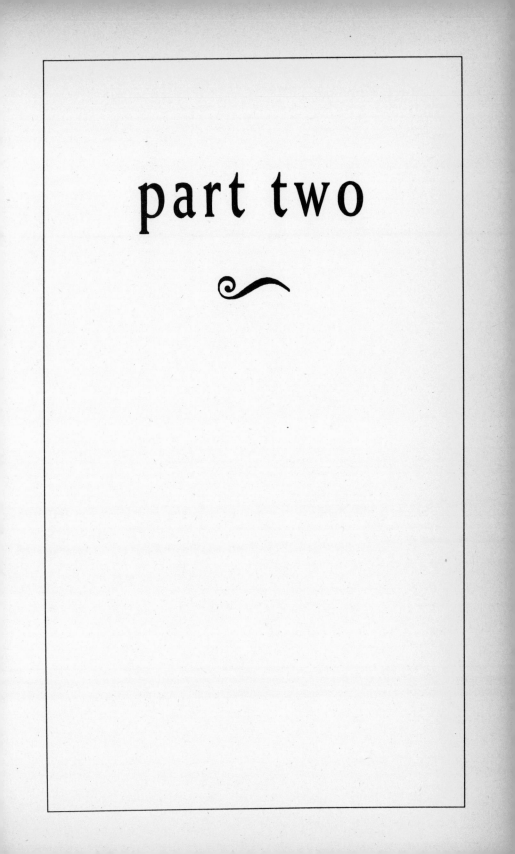

ten

When Emily got home from work, she was tempted to cancel her dinner plans. How nice it would be to soak the ache from her bones in a hot bath, then spend the evening in bed, reading and dozing. The only trouble was, she couldn't remember the name of his hotel. It sounded Japanese when he had said it over the phone, but she hadn't bothered to take down the number. That meant that she might as well get dinner started.

By chance it turned out that she had all the ingredients for her specialty, the chicken dish she could put together almost automatically, without having to think. It was a relief, for she had been afraid that she might have to trudge down five flights for a jar of cream mustard. The recipe was a modification of one that had appeared in the *Post*, a paper that she wouldn't have been caught dead with. The super had left it behind one day when he had come to replace a washer in the clawfooted tub that took up so much space in the kitchen. Out of curiosity she had glanced through the tabloid, savoring a few moments of outrage when she came to the editorial page, then finding herself intrigued by a recipe for veal. Having no veal on hand, she had substituted chicken, and thyme for dill. The result was a hit with every man she served it to. Women, though, tended to be more cautious in their praise. Granted, it was a little on the rich side, with its cup of heavy cream, stick of butter, wine, and sharp cheddar cheese. Though she never divulged the ingredients, her female guests always complained of guilty consciences afterward.

Despite the tub, over which a plywood board was placed for extra counter space, the kitchen was good-sized by New York standards. It separated the modest living room from the even more modest bedroom. The floor plan, actually, was similar to that of the shotgun shacks in the poorer black neighborhoods of Tula Springs. Emily's shack just happened to be located six stories high in one of Kips Bay's few remaining tenements. Emily had taken over the lease from Lucas, who had used it as a bachelor pad when he left Judy. After he remarried and moved to the West Side, Emily found herself surrounded by Slavs and Poles, some of whom didn't even seem to understand English. It was only later that the landlord began renovating the apartments, young stockbrokers and aspiring advertising executives gradually replacing her more ethnic neighbors. Although the landlord offered to give her $3,000 in cash if she moved out, Emily held on. At $215 a month the apartment was a bargain, even if it was a pain in the neck to remove the plywood (and the pots and pans stacked on it) every time she wanted to bathe. And it was rent-stabilized.

Aside from the rent, the best thing about the apartment was the light. Being higher than the brownstone across the street, her apartment with its southern exposure could actually grow far too warm on a clear winter day—the living room, that is. The kitchen and bedroom, with single windows that looked out upon a grimy brick wall, an arm's length away, were appropriately dank and chill. She spent most of her time in the living room, often falling asleep on the loveseat beneath her herb garden. Once she had even managed to grow tomatoes on the windowsills; but later, when she tried again, she could not succeed. She would often wonder how she had done it, and some friends who had not seen the tomatoes with their own eyes did not quite believe her.

Though it was a treat to spend an evening alone, Emily was a loyal friend and would troop out to Queens, if necessary, for a christening or surprise anniversary party. Most of her friends were also colleagues at work, a test preparation center that helped people achieve higher scores on the SAT, PSAT, LSAT, GMAT, GRE, NCLEX, CPA, and BAR. It was surprising how many people who worked there lived in Queens, but she supposed that their salaries made Manhattan impossible. Most of her friends took the "E" train or the Flushing line. She was lucky enough to be able to walk home in fifteen minutes.

"You do this . . ." Breathing hard, he motioned down the hall. "Every day?"

"Come on in, you ninety-eight-pound weakling." Standing up on tiptoes she gave him a peck on the cheek.

"A few little stairs," she said after closing the door behind him.

F. X. collapsed onto the loveseat. "Must be . . . seven flights."

"Five, my dear."

They were taking up right where they had left off, Emily somewhat wry and self-assured to counter his enormous ego. With large doses of irony, most of which had eluded him, Emily had been able to maintain, if not a real friendship, then a comradeship of sorts with F. X. She had not seen him in almost ten years, ever since he had given up on New York and moved back to Louisiana. A couple of times, when she was visiting her parents during the Christmas holidays, she had tried getting in touch with him. But he had been out of town when she phoned his brother's house. And she hadn't left a number where she could be reached.

"So this is it." He nodded at the room, where the evening light cast a dull luster on the few good pieces she had salvaged from her marriage, the teak coffee table, the cherry sideboard, a Charles X chair.

"That's right, you've never been here, have you?"

"Last time I saw you you were on Sixty-something."

"Fourth."

"The place with a garden, chandelier in the dining room. That was quite a pad."

"It wasn't ours, the furniture and stuff. We were just squatters. But it was nice. I did fall in love with it."

"You know it's cold out there," he broke in, before she had finished her sentence. "And I was sweating like a goddam pig when I left New Orleans. Thought I was going to miss the plane, too. No one told me about Daylight Savings until the last minute. I was goofing around and the next thing I know it's an hour later than I thought. Didn't even have time for a shower before I left. Then it doesn't matter anyway. The fucking plane's an hour and a half late."

This was more like the F.X. she had known, the gentleman who had shown up at her office in lizardskin boots and the tightest jeans she had ever seen on male or female. She had been so embarrassed by him that she had sneaked him out to lunch before Mr. Cooper could see him. The whole point, of course, was for him to meet her boss—at least, that was what she had promised Clara. But the girl had not prepared her, aside from saying how good-looking he was. Yes, he was that, though in so obvious and brazen a way that Emily found it unseemly, even faintly repulsive. She certainly did not want Mr. Cooper associating her with F.X. before she handed in her resignation. It must be done properly, with dignity, so that Mr. Cooper would realize just what a horrible creep he was.

Perhaps this was why she now felt slightly off-balance, less certain if their old routine of trading good-natured insults would sustain them through an entire evening. The truth was, F.X. did seem changed, and not just outwardly, though this too was evident. After all, he was at least forty-five. In place of the muscles he had been so proud of—and which she had always found ludicrous—there was a lean look, and his face did not seem as pretty-boy perfect as she remembered. Hard to believe, but this, combined with his graying hair and unremarkable coat and tie, made him appear almost distinguished. Exchanging small talk with him over a glass of wine, she had to remind herself that this was the same man who had treated Clara so badly, the only man she, Emily, had ever called a pig—and to his face.

It was probably because Emily had let him know, at that fugitive lunch so many years ago, what a miserable excuse for a man he was, that F.X. called her up again. Of course, she would have continued to fend off his invitations for lunch or a walk in the park if she hadn't found herself in the same production with him at the Hoof and Mouth Rep on West 13th Street. This was a year or so after she had been fired from Mark Four, a humiliation that she thought she would never recover from, especially since it could have been avoided. All she had to have done was to quit as she had planned. But unfortunately, Mr. Cooper had run into her and F.X. in the lobby as they were headed out to lunch. F.X. had had the gall to introduce himself as a good friend of hers and had gone on to ask if Ronnie (yes, he had called him Ronnie!) wanted to join them for a bite to eat. Later that afternoon when Emily had gone to Mr. Cooper's office to explain who F.X. really was, Mr. Cooper had asked her, almost before she had gotten a word out of her mouth, if she had been looking around for another job: It would be most advisable if she did.

Lettice had come to the rescue with a part-time position for her at the Renseleer Foundation, which doled out grants for the upkeep of worthy historic preservation sites. Seated at a boulle desk in a brownstone off Madison, Emily tried to keep from dying of boredom by learning Juliet and Portia by heart. In her spare time she would rush to auditions, turning down nothing, no matter how inane it seemed. That was how she ended up as a Rhinestone Maiden at the Hoof and Mouth's production of a campy version of the *Ring*. She had two lines, which gave her some dignity at least. F.X. had none. He stood around in a leopardskin bikini, flexing his muscles on cue. The rehearsals were long and arduous. Two directors quit in a fury over last-minute rewrites. Emily usually took the subway home with F.X. late at night, happy for his protection. They had so much to complain about—sets that would fall apart, an insulting stage manager, freezing dressing rooms—and often the talk would continue long into the night. She was usually too keyed up to go to sleep right after rehearsal; and Hugh had said he didn't mind their talking in the living room while he slept. As long as they kept their voices down.

"Lucas blasted through here," Emily explained as she pulled back the curtain. F.X. squeezed through the hole in the bedroom wall which led to a room—a closet, really—with a toilet, no sink.

"See that door there?" she went on. "It leads to the hall. That used to be the only entrance."

"You mean this wasn't private? Anyone could walk in?"

She nodded. "He couldn't take it, though—having one of the old ladies tying up the place in the morning. So he pounded out the bedroom wall and padlocked the door."

"Must've freaked the landlord out."

"Better believe. There was supposed to be a big court case, and Lucas was going to be evicted. Then he got married, and I settled with the landlord, paid him a few bucks. It was worth it to me, having my own bathroom. Then he went ahead and gave everyone bathrooms anyway, the landlord. Except me. I ended up saving him money."

"So what are you going to do, kid? Stand there and watch me whip out my dick?"

Emily stuck out her tongue and let the curtain fall.

Though he was a notorious womanizer, F.X. had never made a pass at Emily. This was fine with her, because if he had, that would have been the end. The only thing that had bothered her was that Hugh had not, at the time, seemed the least bit jealous of their friendship. She and F.X. could talk till two or three in the morning, and Hugh would never betray even a hint of suspicion, as if F.X. were the perfect gentleman. Or rather, as if she were so sexless that even someone as promiscuous as F.X. would not be attracted. Thinking about it now while F.X. relieved himself of some of the wine he had drunk, she wondered if perhaps she could have been using him back then to taunt Hugh. For it was around that time that Hugh had seemed to be drifting away from her, losing interest.

Partly, of course, it was her fault. She knew what he thought of acting, yet she continued to go to auditions. They never argued about it. Hugh refused to discuss the issue. Indeed, he even told her more than once: If that's what you really want, Em, then go ahead. I'm all for you. But there was no conviction in his voice. Quite possibly, she would have preferred a screaming match to this tepid endorsement.

At that time Hugh was working harder than ever at Union. The more praise he got from his professors, the earlier he would rise to begin studying. Emily would never forget the day she had gone uptown to bring him a notebook he had to have. Just outside the library she found him surrounded by a coterie of admirers, all seeming to vie for his attention. For a moment or two she stood apart, unobserved. Two women were plain, another lovely, middle-aged, and there was a gray-haired man in jeans. Were they flirting, she might have understood. But the respect they treated him with, the deference, made her uneasy.

Later that day she asked him if he might like to have a friend or two from Union over for dinner. But he refused again, even when she assured him that it would be just them, not Clara. She had given up trying to matchmake with any of Hugh's friends, mainly because Hugh seemed so proprietary about anyone from Union. Emily wished he would give her a chance to get to know them. But the only person he would invite to the apartment was Fay Terrace, who did not treat him with reverence. In fact, quite the opposite. She was harshly critical of any of his virtues, which she called into question time and time again. Emily happened to think that they were real virtues, his patience and tolerance. It was almost as if Fay, who had found a job in advertising, a highly paid job, was his hairshirt.

"So I guess you heard."

"Heard what?"

"Come off it, Emily. You know."

The chicken had been a success. F.X. had practically licked the serving plate. Now he was halfway through a second bottle of wine, an expensive Pinot Noir that she had been saving as a gift for the LSAT instructor's fifth wedding anniversary.

"You want dessert now?" she said, instead of lying—or telling the truth. She had heard. Clara had phoned her from Los Angeles years ago—was it 1979? 1980?—to tell her she had landed a part in a pilot about a boxer who had twin chauffeurs, both female. Almost as an aside, she asked if Emily had heard that F.X. had been arrested for selling coke at a dinner theater in Louisiana.

"Yeah, I'm a jailbird. You're sitting here with an ex-con."

"Oh, F.X., why make such a big deal about it?"

"You're right," he mocked, imitating the way her hand had flitted into the air. "What's so bad about being in the pen for two years? My dear, it was simply divine."

"I'm sorry. I didn't mean to make light of it." She fingered the grainy edge of the herb box. "I know it must have been a nightmare."

He sat there for some time, staring down at a cushion, his Adam's apple rising and falling in gulps.

"F.X.?"

"So thanks for writing. Thanks for coming to see me."

Emily had no answer at first. What could she say? Well, F.X., we were never really friends. I just saw you off and on, hardly at all after the *Ring*. Or: I didn't know where you were or what really happened. Clara only mentioned something about a trial. She was on the West Coast then, and we hardly ever talked.

"I'm sorry," she said, after a moment or two.

"Sure." His black deep-set eyes fixed her with a look that was almost menacing. "I just thought you might be a little different from those good buddies of mine, the ones who dropped me like some fucking hot potato."

Gently, she offered, "You didn't even tell me when you left New York. No goodbye, nothing. And then when I heard, well, I was going through my own sort of hell. I guess it was selfish of me, but I couldn't think of anything but Hugh and me. We were separating then. I was a wreck."

She waited for him to ask what had happened—why hadn't it worked, the marriage? But he just sat there, which in a way was a relief. Something so painful and complicated, how could a man like him ever understand? "By the way, you never told me: What are you doing here in town?"

His strong cleft chin resting on a fist, he didn't reply until she repeated the question. "*Phantom of the Opera.* This girl I used to know, she's in the show. Got us some tickets."

"You're with someone?"

His broad shoulders gave a shrug.

"Don't you think she's going to wonder what you're up to tonight?"

"You're just like her, you know." He raked his fingers through the thinning waves of salt and pepper hair that had once seemed— to Emily—as dark and luxuriant as Clara's. "Every time I try to say something important to Francine, she's got to start nitpicking. So what do you say, Emily? Want to let me talk? O.K., then. It's like this. I've been doing a lot of thinking lately, trying to figure out what's happened to me, why my life, you know, it hasn't been anything like I thought it would be. I keep on thinking there's this good part that's coming, that all this shit I've been through, it's leading up to something real good. The real thing. Then I remember I'm forty-five and I sort of freak. I mean I can't really believe I'm this old. It's—What the fuck?"

The phone had rung. Reaching behind his back for the receiver, Emily caught a whiff of cologne, a pungent scent that oddly enough did more to remind her of the old F.X. than he did himself. "Yes, hi, I'm here, but I can't . . . No, Allen, listen. I've got a friend over. Let me call you back. I'm sorry, I know. Bye, dear." Stretching again to place the receiver back in the cradle, she brushed closer for a better sniff. The old F.X. and she, the Rhinestone Maiden—how precious it all seemed to her now, though still embarrassing. "I'm sorry. Go on."

"Know what my career is now? Seating people in a goddam restaurant. That's what I've been aiming for all these years. Far Oaks."

"My mother always drags my dad there for her birthday. It's a plantation, right? I hear it's real nice."

"Real nice, yeah. There's this real nice guy who greets you and asks real nice if you have a reservation and—Let it ring!"

With a muted groan she reached behind him again while he glared sullenly at the handwoven Kurdish rug. "Yes, just a minute," she said before holding out the receiver. "For you."

With a scowl on his face he listened a moment, then grunted. "Wait a minute," he said, after another pause, "I never said it was a man I was having dinner with. You just assumed it when I said friend. And by the way, how the hell did you get this number? Oh, that's real nice. My pants. Listen, who cares, Fran? I told you before we left I was going to have one free evening. Emily. Emily Vanderbilt. No, I'm not kidding. I've known her for ages. Blonde—that's right, blonde. See what I care!" He slammed the phone down.

"Give me the number," she said, reverting to the severity she used to practice upon him. "I will not have you treating another woman this way. Come on."

"Hey, give me a break."

"I'm going to call and explain who I am. The number, please."

"Relax. I'll take care of it myself. Later."

"The number, please."

"Number, please, number, please. What are you, some sort of fucking operator? Ease up. Let me finish what I was saying. You know, I got some rights myself. You women, you act like you're the only ones entitled to fair play. Well, it works both ways, understand? Look at Clara, I got more talent in my little finger than that woman has in her entire brain. And who ends up on 'Circus of the Stars'? Me and Fran were sitting at home the other night and who comes prancing around the ring with a bunch of shit-eating Pekingese? I mean the tricks were awful. She didn't know what the hell she was doing."

Not owning a television, Emily had been spared. "I'm sure Clara was forced to do that. Her ratings are sagging."

"My God, a woman her age in tights. It was obscene. Her butt was so big they nearly split when she leaned over. And she had a neck brace on, too."

"What?"

"She couldn't hold up her head otherwise, she had so much makeup on."

"Men are so bitchy."

"What? Listen, I worked hard, much harder than she ever did. Tell me where the justice is? Huh? I'd like to know. 'Cause it ain't here on earth, baby. That's for sure."

"I can't believe how childish you sound. All right, so Clara's gotten a few breaks. But she's worked hard herself. And besides, her success—or whatever you want to call it—what does that have to do with you? There's no connection at all. I mean you're acting as if her success *caused* your failure."

He shot her a look. "So you admit, I am a failure."

"No, no, I didn't mean that. I just— Hey, you want dessert or not?"

"I guess so."

"All right. I'm going into the kitchen to heat up some sauce. When I come back, I want you to have phoned Francine, understand? Apologize for being so rude. Don't you look at me like that. You do it or you're not getting any dessert at all."

Pouring himself more wine he said, "Yes, Ma'am, I promise."

"You got your fingers crossed. Uncross them, you silly boy."

"Fuck you."

Emily stormed out of the room in mock fury. In the kitchen

she couldn't help smiling to herself and humming. It was just like the old days.

She thought about leaving the dishes until morning, but since this was something she always thought about and never did, she dutifully reached for the detergent and ran the water. F.X. had devoured the entire pan of apple cobbler with brandy sauce, and despite her urging, refused to call Francine. In fact, he had left in a bad mood, without even bothering to say thanks for dinner. Yet as she scrubbed the crust from the aluminum pan, she felt herself missing F.X. in a way she never missed Allen—Allen, who was so charming, considerate, and intelligent, the best of friends.

She awoke in darkness, pigeons rattling the sash of her bedroom window. They usually stirred at dawn, though not infrequently she had been awakened at two or three in the morning. She felt as if she had just lain down, the dishes put away only minutes ago. Yet the luminous dial read six.

Before going to bed she had cleared the plywood board of dishes. In her nightshirt she now slid the board from the tub and ran the hot faucet. When the water finally warmed, she inserted a rubber drain stop and let the tub fill to its usual six inches, which was when the water turned cold again.

Sometimes as she walked to work, or back, she would notice a particularly plain or heavy woman and wonder, Do I look like that? Though she did not look anywhere near forty, her face remaining fresh, unlined, Emily had put on weight, especially in the haunches. Soaping her ample breasts, she was careful not to squeeze for fear of encountering a lump. Martha had had a scare only a week ago, a shadow on her mammogram. But it had turned out to be a cyst, benign. Everyone had been so grateful. Her mother had cried on the phone. Emily, too, had shed a tear, though her feelings were more complex. On the same day as her sister's good news she had overheard a young male temp at work refer to her as "the dumpy one." It had come as such a shock, for up until that moment she had considered herself still attractive, if a bit overweight.

By seven-thirty she was ready to leave. She was always the first to arrive at the institute, savoring a quiet half hour or so when she could work up a lesson plan without interruptions.

"How much you rake in?" F. X. had asked when he had finished the cobbler the night before.

Around twenty-two a year, she had admitted.

"You got to be kidding? Hell, even I do better than that."

"But I like my work," she had told him. Locking the door behind her now, she gave this reply some thought. Yes, in general, this was true. Of course, there were days when she did get fed up—when the director audited her SAT classes to make sure she was being "lively and engaging," or when he added more to her administrative burdens than she cared for. But from a bird's-eye view, she was content, she supposed.

eleven

❧

As he waited for Emily to get her change from the Korean clerk at the dry cleaner's, he glanced over his shoulder once, twice, causing the middle-aged West Indian behind him a moment's unease. Emily noticed all this in a fitting mirror and had to squelch an urge to comment once they were outside together. It was Mr. Brix's first visit to the city, and perhaps he wasn't even aware that he was staring at people. Emily trusted this would stop once he got more used to his surroundings.

"I don't know how Mom got you to come," she said after he refused to let her carry any of the skirts or blouses, the plastic crackling in a steady breeze.

"It was my idea. Of course, your mother would have liked to come. But her back is acting up again."

Genuinely touched that he had traveled such a distance for her, Emily was nonetheless disturbed by the suddenness of the visit. It was not like her father to do anything without weeks, months, of planning, re-planning, and usually in the end shelving the idea altogether. She could only hope that nothing was wrong at home, that he wasn't going to drop some bombshell about Martha or Sandy. Or her mother.

"She is all right, isn't she?"

"Oh, fine. It's just that the operation hasn't helped any. She feels just as much pain as before. The doctors just can't figure out what to do. I tell her she should be proud. She's got John F. Kennedy's back. But you know your mother. She never did like the man. It says don't walk," he added as they crossed Third Avenue.

"You got time if it blinks."

It was cool for April. She was afraid the raincoat he wore— far too short for him—was not enough. And it had such an odd plaid pattern. How in heaven's name had he ever picked out such a thing for himself? His brand-new white patent leather shoes were another matter. A lot of businessmen in Tula Springs wore them, so she supposed her father was making a stab at being fashionable. But a green plaid raincoat that barely reached his knees—with epaulets yet?

All five flights he took at a steady clip, the dry cleaning draped over his slightly hunched back. She knew it was sheer willpower that propelled him, and urged him from time to time to take it easy, rest. Almost seventy, he was never one for exercise, though he did on occasion rake the pine needles in his front yard. That, too, he would do at a pace that worried Emily and her mother. They were sure that in his haste to get the chore over with, he would keel over dead.

Once inside the apartment she put on a kettle of water for tea and then made the proposal she had been mulling over that morning. Mr. Brix had traveled coach on the Crescent from Louisiana, which meant sitting up for nearly thirty hours. He had looked so dazed and exhausted when she had met him at Penn Station that she could not bear the thought of his going through such an ordeal again. "Now listen, Father, I don't want an argument. I've made up my mind that you're going to have a room on the train back. And I'm paying."

"Don't be silly. You hold on to your money."

"Please let me do this."

"I wouldn't hear of it. Such nonsense."

"At least let me call and see if there's a space."

He had not taken off the raincoat, which was bunched about his waist as he sat. "Call? Oh, that reminds me. When you went out this morning a young lady phoned. I've got it somewhere."

Reaching inside the pockets of the raincoat he produced a pen holster, a flyer for a Chinese restaurant, a small bottle of glue, and a wad of coupons, one of which was examined more closely. "Yes, here it is. I wrote it here on the back of this, which I was planning to give you. Seventeen cents off a four-ounce jar of Sanka. Do you drink Sanka? Anyway, she's at the Kitano Hotel, Room seven seventeen. Francine Joiner, I believe. Who is Francine Joiner?"

Emily had drifted into the kitchen. "I don't know." She reached for a tin of Fortnum & Mason Prince of Wales.

"Why the big sigh?"

"She's some friend of a friend I've never met."

"F. X.?"

"How did you know?"

"He called right after and told you to ignore the young lady's call. So I asked him what he meant by that. I didn't like his tone of voice. Sounded like a smart alec. Emily Sue, I hope you're prudent when it comes to friends. In this day and age you can never be too careful."

She set the Limoges cups on a tray from Tiffany's, her best, before saying, "My machine was on. You really didn't have to answer."

"But I was here."

"Yes, I know. But those were personal calls." She paused a moment, trying hard not to feel like a teenager. "F.X. is just a . . . He's someone from back home who was in town and decided to drop by."

"I thought the name sounded familiar. He's the fellow who was supposed to marry Clara Tilman, right?"

"Yes, Father, about three centuries ago. Let's sit in the other room," she added, motioning him away from the tub he had perched on.

"I hope you and Clara still keep in touch," Mr. Brix said as he adjusted a curtain to block out the glare.

"She's got her own circle of friends. By the way, are you ever going to take that raincoat off? It's buckled. Unbuckle it first. Yes, that's it. You know, a sweater might keep you warmer. It's a bit cold out. Let's look for one this afternoon—"

"This is lined, Emily. The finest quality. I looked all over Baton Rouge, New Orleans." He held the raincoat up for her to admire. "You wouldn't believe where I ended up finding this, something just right for a Northern spring. Give up? A block from my office, that little place next to the hardware store."

"But, Father, isn't that a dress shop?"

"Unisex. Outerwear is unisex these days. Besides, everything in there was sixty percent off. They have to make way for the fall line. And I'll let you in on another secret. Miss Cleo, the lady who owns the place, she said she's always been partial to State Farm. She's sending her brother over to see me when I get back. I've got just the policy for him."

The tea having steeped, Emily poured as Mr. Brix held out his gilt-rimmed cup. His hands, gnarled by chronic arthritis, did look like those of a seventy-year-old. But aside from them he seemed remarkably unchanged from her childhood days. Though somewhat overweight, pear-shaped, he had a will of iron, a boot-camp self-discipline that canceled out any first impression of softness. How often when she was growing up did he remind her of his clichéd, but factual, boyhood on an Iowa dairy farm. Every morning he was up at, yes, four to help his father milk the cows. Then there was the obligatory three-mile trek to the freezing schoolhouse, with grades one to eight in the same room. Too poor to attend college, he had nonetheless taught himself to read Horace and Cicero after putting in a ten-hour day as a dry-goods clerk. Nothing mattered to him more than that his children be given what was denied him, a first-class education. Which was why Emily and Martha, and later Sandy, were roused from bed at six every morning for a Latin lesson before school. Martha would much rather have taken Spanish during school hours—the only language offered there—but Mr. Brix considered Spanish low-class and too easy. He felt the same way about prejudice, and once smacked Sandy on the ear for telling a joke with the word "nigger" in it—smacked him so hard that Mrs. Brix had burst into tears and fled the table.

"Ah me, ah me," Mr. Brix said, as was his custom after taking an initial sip of tea or coffee—or indeed any beverage. "Did I ever send you that interview, in the paper back home, the one where Clara talks about combining motherhood with a career? If not, I'll have Mother get—"

"You did."

"Maybe you and I could drop by this afternoon, pay her a visit? I'd like to tell her how much Mother and I enjoyed her on 'Circus of the Stars.' "

Emily paused in her search for the tea cosy. "You bought a television?"

"Well, you know your mother can't get around as much as she would like to—her back. So I broke down and got her one for our anniversary." He rubbed a painful-looking knuckle. Sometimes he winced, but never had he complained of this affliction. "I've spotted Clara on three commercials already. One of them came on during 'Wheel of Fortune,' so she must be doing pretty well. Just dandy, I imagine."

"Father, you don't mean to say you watch—"

"Well, your mother likes me to keep her company when I can. And you have to admit there's some pretty smart cookies on 'Jeopardy.' "

"I'm afraid I can't admit that."

"Pardon?"

"I don't own a set."

"Oh, that's right. Clara said something about that."

Emily spotted the cosy, right beside her on the loveseat all the time. "Clara what?"

"I called her this morning, you know, when you were out."

"Oh, Dad, you didn't." Emily's polite formality broke down. She couldn't believe what she had just heard. "Please tell me you didn't."

"Your mother gave me her number and told me to be sure to look her up. Clara sounded just delighted. She's expecting us at four."

Emily and Clara had not spoken in over a year, ever since that unfortunate dinner party when Clara had accused Emily of flirting with Lucas. Of course, everyone knew that Clara was insanely jealous of her husband. She never asked unattached women to dinner—Emily being the one exception. Though the accusation was ludicrous—Emily didn't have the slightest interest in him—it still hurt. And it really didn't matter that Lucas had called several times afterward to apologize. He was not the one who had insulted her.

"I'm afraid you'll have to call her back," Emily said, recovering her composure. "We're going to the Morgan Library this afternoon. The Voltaire letters you wanted to see . . ."

"There'll be time enough for that. We better check on the wallpaper first."

"What wallpaper?"

"I was thinking a little wallpaper might cheer this place up. They have so many wonderful designs these days. And I'll be here to help you put it up. As a matter of fact, Clara told me she has some samples. She's just redecorated her bedroom. Pardon? You say something?"

Emily thought she had groaned inwardly. But apparently she had made some sort of noise. "More tea?"

During a late and delicious lunch neither wallpaper nor Clara was mentioned. Emily, though, was too well acquainted with her father's ways to sink into complacency. So it was hardly a surprise when, emerging from the kitchen with their coffee, she found him leafing through the Yellow Pages. Calmly she said, "You know it's not allowed—legally."

"Nonsense."

"Shall I show you my lease? It specifically says no wallpaper can be hung."

Mr. Brix seemed to meditate upon this. "Some country," he mused aloud after closing the book. "You can buy a submachine gun to mow down schoolchildren, but wallpaper?"

Emily smiled and laid a hand gingerly upon his shoulder. Growing up she had not been encouraged to express physical affection with her father. Indeed, after her first period, when her mother had snuck a box of Tampons into her dresser drawer (without a single explanation!) there had been no more goodnight hugs from her father, much less kisses.

Despite several cups of coffee—too many, really—they found themselves in a conversational doldrum. Emily had anticipated many long talks with her father on this visit, a chance to sort things out, to be frank. She knew he felt terrible about Hugh. "It's a tragedy," he would say whenever she was home for the holidays, "a real tragedy. I don't think I'll ever really forgive myself. I should have been more supportive, talked some sense into the boy." And Emily, somewhat disingenuously, would say it had nothing to do with him, her father. Of course, in her heart of hearts, she could not help harboring some resentment. On her own turf in New York she imagined it would be so much easier to air this anger, get rid of it once and for all. But at the same time she couldn't help feeling slightly foolish. Practically forty, she should certainly have learned to take responsibility for her own emotional life. To blame her father in any way seemed so childish.

"You don't suppose Hugh might want to have dinner one night, do you?"

"Dad, I don't know how you can be so—" She stopped herself just in time. Stupid, she had almost said. It was strange how he could revive the pain as if the divorce had been just yesterday, not almost fifteen years ago. All she had gone through to attain her present state of calm acceptance—the years of therapy, self-help books by the dozen, a bout with an addiction to Valium—all this seemed like nothing. Without letting him see her face, she collected the cups and marched silently into the kitchen.

"Do me one favor," she said, just before he settled himself on her bed for a nap. "Don't ask me about him. Not now."

"I'm sorry, daughter. I didn't realize you still . . ."

One warm December evening in Tula Springs, Emily, half drunk on eggnog, had confessed to her mother that it was during the time Hugh was converting to Catholicism that she realized how much she feared she loved him. What she couldn't bear admitting to her mother, though, was that she had gone to Hugh, pleaded with him to reconsider. They could still make a go of it. Hugh was not unkind, but firm. Their marriage had been a mistake from the beginning. Neither he nor Emily had had the slightest conception, he told her, of who they were, what they wanted. The only reason he might seem attractive to her now, he explained, was because she was afraid of change. Neither of them would have a future if they stayed together, he assured her. They would be mired in the past, living out all sorts of neurotic fixations. Enough damage had already been done, terrible, irreparable harm to an innocent life. Even Emily had to admit this—and she did.

Setting an extra blanket by the bed her father was stretched out upon, she smiled briskly, almost professionally, like a stewardess. "Call me if you need anything. Now get some rest."

*   *   *

She did not know what to expect as they rose to the fifteenth floor in the art deco elevator. Her heart pounded almost as if she were meeting a blind date. If Clara turned out to be cool and condescending, well, Emily had resolved to endure it for her father's sake. He seemed to have his heart set on this visit. Nothing she said could deter him from making the trek up to Riverside and 112th.

"Father, your trousers," Emily commented, as they waited for the door to be answered.

"What? Oh." He zipped his fly, which must have been open on the 104 bus as well.

A moment later Clara was saying, "The place is a mess," so casually that it was almost as if Emily dropped by every day. With a flush of either pleasure or embarrassment Clara gave Mr. Brix a hug, then said something about how nice Emily looked.

Beaming, Mr. Brix did not bother to adjust his bifocals, which had been knocked askew by the encounter. Following Clara down a wide hall, he and his daughter emerged into a room at least twice as large as Emily's entire apartment. Specially installed windows reaching from the floor almost to the ceiling afforded a spectacular view of the Hudson. The furniture was sparse, tasteful, in unusual California pastels. Emily had no idea what Clara could have meant by mess, unless it was a pile of magazines scattered over one of the outsized couches.

In jeans and a man's wrinkled shirt, Clara made Emily feel overdressed, for she had chosen to wear her best skirt and blouse, both silk, from Bergdorf's. Her friend Allen had given them to her for her birthday last year. Not only were they exquisite, just the right colors for her complexion, but they fit well. The cost—she had wandered into the store to satisfy her curiosity—had appalled her, but she supposed it would have been rude and inconsiderate to return them.

"Now when people say come over for tea, do they really mean tea or what?" Clara was saying to Mr. Brix. "Here, let me," she added as she straightened his glasses. "What I mean is, would it be all right if I had a drink?"

"By all means," Mr. Brix said, his usually dull eyes positively aglow.

"Oh, thanks. That means you got to have one, too. I never drink alone."

"Just tea for me," Emily inserted as Clara busied herself at a lacquered table with a bottle of scotch and another of seltzer. Though her derrière was perhaps a bit prominent, Clara had a figure that a woman half her age would be proud of. Emily marveled too at her face. With little makeup Clara managed to look in her early thirties, her dyed tawny hair cut in a boyish style that Emily could never have gotten away with, fashionable though it was.

"Now I hope you don't mind this scotch," she said, handing a Waterford glass to Mr. Brix. "It's Clan MacGregor, the cheapest Lucas and I could find. We drank it for Lent and then decided to stick with it afterward, at least, I did. If we have anything good, it's so hard to stop, you know. I just blow up like a balloon."

"Say, it's not bad at all. Really good." Emily looked doubtfully at her father, who all but smacked his lips. Rye was his drink, not scotch, but Clara hadn't bothered to ask.

In a few moments Clara was back from the kitchen with a cup of tea, microwaved, no doubt. But somehow she had remembered just how much milk and sugar Emily liked.

"Mrs. Brix said I should tell you how much we enjoyed you on 'The Circus.'"

"Oh Lord, Mr. Brix. I'm so embarrassed. They made me wear a wig. And Priscilla bawled me out about the costume. It was so skimpy, but I had no choice."

"I hope I'll get a chance to see her," Mr. Brix said.

Priscilla, Clara's thirteen-year-old daughter, was never around when Emily made one of her rare visits. Emily had to admire Clara, grudgingly, for bringing her up at all, especially when it wasn't necessary. What cool. But surely it would have been more charitable to remain silent. Emily had enough to endure as it was.

"She and Lucas drove out to Montauk to check on this place we're thinking of renting for the summer. It's quiet, secluded, none of the Hamptons nonsense. I just can't stand—" A crash from somewhere down the hall made her wince. "Oh, that man, I could kill him. He's building shelves in the bedroom, making the biggest mess. And all he wants to do is talk about his psychology course.

He goes to Baruch and loves Karen Horney. By the way, Em, I've got a sample book for wallpaper. You want to take a look?"

Emily explained about her lease while her father, rather unhelpfully, encouraged her to ignore it. Really, he did not seem at all like his usual, slightly morose self.

After Clara, who had only taken a few sips herself, had refreshed Mr. Brix's drink, she said, "I wanted to have you both for dinner tonight, but I got an RCIA meeting."

"How nice!" Mr. Brix exclaimed, though Emily was sure that he, like herself, hadn't the slightest idea what this meant.

"It's classes in Church doctrine," Clara went on to explain, unbidden. "Lucas and I think it will be good for Priscilla if I make it official. I mean, I've been going to mass with them, but I really haven't taken the plunge."

Emily was thoughtful while her father, following his own brand of logic, asked Clara how deep the Hudson was at this point. She couldn't help wondering if Hugh had something to do with Clara's wish to convert. The whole thing seemed so hypocritical, in any case. Lucas, after all, was divorced and remarried. And what a dreadful divorce it had been. Distraught, thoroughly wretched, Judy had accused Emily of pandering to Lucas. This actually had come out in court, that Emily had introduced Clara and Lucas at a Thanksgiving dinner and then had gone on to cover for their clandestine affair. Emily, of course, was horrified at being cast in such an unsavory role. Her main line of defense, that she herself felt jealous and betrayed, had to remain unspoken. For how could Judy understand that Emily, though somewhat enamored of Lucas, would never have considered acting upon it. It was all in her head, a chaste romance that helped her endure the more mundane and rocky moments of her own marriage.

"Let's make a date," Mr. Brix was saying as he futilely riffled the pages of an almanac Clara had brought out for him. The Hudson's depth. "I want to take you all out to a first-class dinner, money's no object. It'll give me a chance to meet Priscilla. And your husband, he sounds like such a fine young man."

"Oh, Dad, really I don't think Clara—"

"Actually I'd love to, Mr. Brix. But I'm leaving town tomorrow. Off to Honduras."

"Oh, is that that project you and Lucas were developing?"

Emily asked. Lucas was always involved in some vague way in Clara's work, if not as an actual producer, as a script consultant or location scout. The last Emily had heard, he was trying to develop an idea for a made-for-TV movie about a nun (Clara) who was murdered by the United Fruit Company during the digging of the Panama Canal.

"No, this is just for me—very selfish." Clara stretched her legs out on the couch, a bare foot dislodging the latest issue of *Vanity Fair*, which crumpled to the floor. "I'm giving myself a week there. It's a public health project. This village has no sewer system, just a ditch. I'm going to help build them one."

Emily set down her cup, which had been empty for some time. "You mean raise funds?"

"No, Em. Dig. Pour concrete, the whole shebang. Lucas thinks I'm crazy. I tried to get him to come along, but he's a little squeamish. About all he's good for is handing out coffee at the soup kitchen. We have one at our church, after mass. Priscilla is very good with the men. I'm so proud of her." Suddenly Clara laughed. Mr. Brix, who had set the almanac aside, chimed in with a laugh of his own.

"What's so funny?" Emily asked him.

He shrugged.

"I'm sorry. I was just thinking about the mess I got into," Clara said. "One of the priests at Justin Martyr asked me if I'd do some sort of ad on TV for the homeless. I hate doing stuff like that—it seems so pious and sappy. But he begged me, so I gave in and said all right, I'll do it for nothing. The next thing I know the Coalition for the Homeless is telling me I'm not well known enough to do it. They want a name. So Father Dennis starts ranting and raving to them about all the shows I've been on, and these stupid teen movies I did way back, real trash. He reeled off all the titles, things I had forgotten myself—you know, where I played a hooker or a waitress who lures the kids. It was really too much. I said, 'Dennis, darling, please, enough.' But he wouldn't give up, like the honor of his parish was at stake. So I—Oh, Mother. You remember Emily, Martha Brix's sister? And this is Martha's father."

Mr. Brix stood up, but perhaps because she was wearing a houserobe, Mrs. Tilman did not venture into the room. For the past ten years, ever since being widowed, Mrs. Tilman had been living with her daughter. Having a built-in babysitter must have helped Clara combine marriage with a career, but Mrs. Tilman was never mentioned in any of the interviews Emily's parents clipped and mailed to Emily. Mrs. Tilman smiled wanly in their general direction. She looked a little haggard, drawn, though this could be because she had just risen from a nap.

"You know I got the RCIA tonight," Clara said, wriggling her clean toes. "Lucas and Pris should be back around eight. If they're not, I want you to call me at the Parish office. I'll be in the West Room. Make Bill come get me. Are you listening?"

"Yes, dear."

"I've got some turkey breast from Zabar's. Lucas is not to eat the cream puffs. They're for Pris only. And she is to have one, that's it. Oh well, give her two if she makes a fuss. There's one beer for Lucas. You've hidden the rest, right? Good. Now remind me to give you the shopping list I made out for when I'm away. Lucas is going to have Minna over for dinner on Thursday, you remember."

"Clara, darling, I just don't know if I'm up for Minna Burns."

"Minna has no one, Mother, nothing to look forward to. And you know how she dotes on Lucas. It would crush her if you canceled. Just remember to call the ambulette a good two hours before you want them to come. And remember to alert the doorman so he can help the driver get her wheelchair off the van. I noticed that the driver was too rough last time. He can't be trusted. Now on Wednesday Lucas is eating with Nathan and his wife at Orso's. Make the reservation in my name, O.K.?"

"Perhaps we can discuss this later, dear, after your guests have left." Mrs. Tilman and Emily exchanged a furtive look. Had Clara seen it, Emily knew she would have been cross.

"Perhaps it's time, Father," Emily said, getting up.

"For what?"

"Come. I'm sure Clara has a lot to do before her meeting."

After Mr. Brix had hugged his hostess rather warmly and after Clara and Emily had put on a good show of a friendly leavetaking, Mr. Brix seemed to wander aimlessly about, straying as far as the bedroom that was being redecorated.

"Father, what are you doing?" Emily inquired.

"My coat. I can't—"

"You didn't wear it, remember."

"Oh, but Em," Clara protested, "it's chilly out today. Let me give him something. Lucas has a sweater . . ."

"That won't be necessary," Emily said, ushering her parent to the door. "He'll be just fine."

twelve

M r. Brix left on a note of compromise. Though he refused to let his daughter book a roomette for him on the Crescent, she did discover that for only $35 extra he could be accommodated in a sleeper. This he paid for himself, after Emily reassured him that the economy room would be tiny and practical, not the least bit luxurious. On the walk over to Penn Station, a few blocks west, Emily found herself light-hearted, hopeful, and only slightly perturbed when a rack of calf-length moiré skirts almost rolled over her father's foot. "Que tu es bête!" the young Haitian black man propelling the rack commented. Emily shot him a brilliant smile, which made him sullen, uncertain.

As soon as they had walked down the steps of the out-of-order escalator, she realized that, to survive, her hope required low humidity and a gentle scudding breeze against a bluish backdrop. There in the stale passage to the waiting area, clogged by the almost palpable smells of fried food, she felt oppressed, her good humor sorely tried when her father stopped to admire a toy frog that made repeated flips in the middle of pedestrian traffic. The station itself, undergoing renovation in a haphazard way, had the feel of an endless rest room, though without the comfort of stalls or sinks. Wanting to stock up on food for the trip, Mr. Brix wandered off to a Roy Rogers.

"What happened?" Emily asked when he returned empty-handed to the seat she was holding for him.

"Not finished yet—building it."

They were far too early, with over an hour to kill. Emily knew they shouldn't have left the apartment so soon, but her father had insisted. "You never know what might happen on the way." Wedged between a pale, teenage father with three weary, unkempt sons and a pleasant, matronly, older man who seemed on the verge of saying something, the two Brixes managed only the most desultory exchange of small talk. But even without the neighboring screams and whines, the furtive looks, Emily would have been hard-pressed to come up with anything new to say to her father. She had stated her case the night before, when he had finally come out with the real purpose of his visit. He wanted to persuade her to come home, if not to Tula Springs, then to Baton Rouge. Martha had a garage apartment that would be perfect for her. She could move right in while she looked for a job.

"But Dad, I've got a job. And an apartment."

"A bathroom in the kitchen, five flights of stairs. And look what you're earning. Emily, you deserve better, much better. You don't know how much it hurts your mother and me to think of you living this way. And you don't seem to want to improve things at all—no wallpaper, nothing."

She had protested in vain, unable to convince him that she was happy, content. And inevitably, they rehashed an old sore point, her refusal to accept any financial help—in lieu of alimony—from Hugh's mother. Lettice herself had urged it upon her time and again. But Emily stood her ground. There was no price that could be put on what she and Hugh had shared. The lump sum Lettice had proposed would only cheapen the memory that sustained her when all else began to seem meaningless or trivial.

When the track was finally announced, Emily shook her father, gently. He had dozed off, his round head lolling to one side. In the long unstable line before the gate they exchanged a tentative hug, hampered by the plastic grocery bag he carried in one hand. Already the bag had a rip from the discount Strand books that he had loaded into it. Then, as the line began its descent, he turned for a last glimpse, his eyes ablaze with a fierce, angry love. "For God's sake, at least let Clara give you some samples."

"Goodbye, Father."

Once he was gone Emily experienced a blissful sense of relief. Her life was her own again. She could do what she wanted, no second-guessing, no pausing in the middle of a busy intersection while he lapsed into thought. Her mind once again clear and focused, she was able to deal with problems that had plagued her for weeks at the institute. One of the worst was a threatened sexual harassment suit. Thor, a lithe secretary, claimed he was not given a raise because he refused to sleep with the staff accountant, Rosalie DeHaven, one of Emily's good, if not close, friends. In tears Rosalie admitted to Emily she had made a pass at Thor once— but only once. The real reason he wasn't getting an increase was because he was dumb and late almost every morning. Moonlighting as a gorilla strip-o-gram, Thor was known to actually fall asleep at his desk. Waking him up one afternoon, Emily firmly, but not unkindly, suggested that he might be interested in a more exciting field of endeavor and packed him off to see Clara. Through a friend of a friend, Clara, already back from digging ditches, managed to get Thor a position at a wholesale costumer, where within days he was promoted to sequins.

"She was nice enough about it," Emily explained when she described this incident to Allen one evening. "I think Honduras did her some good, actually. She seemed a little less uptight. And besides, she owed me one—for F.X. I told her he had stopped by last week and how good I was not to give him her unlisted number. He called twice while Dad was in town, and would say at the end, 'Oh, by the way, you don't happen to have Clara's number?' It finally dawned on me that's why he had come to see me in the first place. He'd like to pester her for a job, I bet. One last stab at fame and glory."

As she rambled on happily, it seemed that Allen had always been a part of her life, that he knew Clara and F.X. as well and as long as she herself. Yet she had met Allen only a year and a half ago, when she was buying herself a glass of wine after the first act of *Billy Budd* at the Met. She had gone alone with a ticket that had been given to Thor, who couldn't use it himself because of a last-minute engagement at a reception for Wheaton alumnae. High up in the Family Circle, Emily had been miserable throughout the first act, for it was only a few days after a man had plunged to his death from the balcony below hers. When Allen offered her a seat in his Center Parterre box, her relief easily overcame any scruples she might have had about accepting an invitation from a total stranger who happened to be crushed against her at the bar. She was afraid that if she went back to the ceiling something would happen—she would trip, the fidgety child beside her might playfully shove her, or perhaps a mysterious compulsion to end the suspense might overcome her and she would cast herself overboard. In any case, Allen proved to be a perfect gentleman. And his date, an elderly widow who was once the ambassador to a tiny country that since World War II no longer existed, didn't seem to mind at all.

"It's interesting that you didn't introduce me to your Aged P," Allen observed as she fed him one of the champagne truffles he had brought her. Sometimes he would take her to Lutèce or Le Cirque, but more often she would cook him the New York *Post* chicken, which he adored. His cheeks boyishly plump and rosy, his eyes steely blue, Allen had an impish quality which peeked out furtively from beneath his old-fashioned reserve. No one dressed better, with an understated elegance that made him seem, though he was neither tall nor in any way imposing, positively eminent. Perhaps he actually was, but because he rarely talked about himself, Emily could not be certain of this. A retired investment banker, he devoted all his time to various boards and committees for the preservation of wilderness areas. Emily figured he must be around seventy-five, which was just about the age that most men finally grew up and learned how to appreciate a woman.

"My dear," she said, giving his nose a pinch, "how in the world could I explain you to Mr. Milton Brix?"

Nestled in his arms, she had angled herself in such a way that she could see a bit of the Empire State Building. The dishes were done—he had helped her wash up—and the super had promised that tomorrow she would be able to fill the tub with hot water. A new boiler had been installed in the basement. Small things, but enough to make the world seem right.

"It's funny, Allen, how angry I was for a while when Dad was here. This old resentment that I thought I had got rid of a long time ago, it crept up on me again. As if it were all Dad's fault." His hand stroked her hair, and for a moment she was lulled into silence, her eyes half closed. "I started falling into this role after a while, making him think I was still desperately in love with him."

"Him?"

"Come on—Hugh. It was almost like I wanted to punish him, Dad, by making him think I couldn't bear hearing his name. But you know how well Hugh and I get along. I care for him, I love him—yes. But I was acting almost as if I were *in* love. Spurned and rejected, poor Miss Emily, she will never give up hope. She'll win him back."

"One of your best roles, no doubt."

"I went on the road with it years ago, took it to Louisiana, played it at supper clubs all over Manhattan. It's getting a little old hat now. Time for a new production." She moved her head so that his heart thumped a bit less loudly in her ear. The rise and fall of his modest potbelly matched the rhythm of her own measured breaths. There was something mesmerizing about Allen's presence, the way he drew her out. He made her see just how much of her life involved a certain amount of posturing. At the time, when she was with her father, she hadn't felt at all insincere about her emotions. They were all perfectly real, unpremeditated. And yet later, when she talked to Allen, she would begin to doubt her feelings, which were always far more subtle, more complex, than any gesture, any line, could possibly express. How she envied Clara's ability to forge ahead, living almost entirely in the moment. When jealousy was called for, there it was, pure and innocent, untainted by any sense of the ridiculous. Forgiveness, too, was easy, unfeigned.

"I don't know, it just seems weird to me how everyone I know is turning Catholic," she was saying a few moments later, after Allen had finished using his white linen handkerchief and had zipped up his trousers. "Hugh I think I can understand. It was all part of his getting in touch with his body. He loves the sacraments, the earthy, pagan feel of the Church. And, of course, it horrified his mother—that was a big part of it, too. He had to make that break from her. They were far too close. But Clara, I'm sure she's never given any real thought to what it all means."

Allen had folded the stained handkerchief and was slipping it into his elephant-hide briefcase. "She went to Honduras, didn't she?"

"Sure, she genuinely does want to help people. But what does that have to do with the Church? Why can't she just *do* it and forget all the hocus-pocus?"

"People can't seem to live without the hocus-pocus."

"You do." Though Allen looked the ultimate Wasp, he was a German Jew. After his bar mitzvah, he said, he had rarely been inside a synagogue. "And me."

"You," he said, smiling sadly, "you could use a little hocus-pocus in your life."

"It was sweet of you, Allen. But please, no, don't ever bring it up again." Before dinner that evening he had presented her with the keys to a friend's apartment in Sutton Place. It would be hers for two years, rent free, while his friend studied trecento art in Padua. Two bedrooms, a terrace, a doorman, and she wouldn't have to give up her own apartment if she didn't want to. Allen, in any case, would only be a block away.

He would not take the keys back that evening. Next time she saw him, though, Emily planned to slip them into his briefcase.

Hugh assured her that there would be no one else tagging along; it would be just him. He had called her at work, which meant if she were to make it across town on time, she wouldn't be able to go home first to freshen up. It was always like this with him, a last-minute notice that he was available for an hour or two. Depending on her mood, she would sometimes say no, even though she wanted to see him and had no other appointments. But if her self-confidence was low, she couldn't help feeling slighted by the way he squeezed her in almost as an afterthought.

She was lucky. There was no wait for the shuttle at Grand Central, and when she got off at Times Square, the Number 1 was in the station. As soon as she stepped inside, the de-graffitied doors rumbled shut as if the train had been waiting specially for her. Since she had allowed fifteen minutes for transferring from one train to another, she arrived too early at the parish office.

"Couldn't you call him?" she asked the somewhat obtuse receptionist who had buzzed her through two sets of glass doors.

"Father Vanderbilt is occupied now."

"I know, but—"

"He's hearing confession."

Though the woman was as heavily made-up as a cocktail waitress, her dyed hair teased into a beehive, she managed to convey a nunlike severity that made Emily feel vaguely defensive. Retreating through the doors she turned her face away from the steady gaze of the video cameras that recorded all entrances and exits.

Once outside the parish office she wandered around the corner to the church's main entrance. Though the portal was almost black with grime, the spires above had a certain grandeur. Nineteenth century neo-Gothic was usually so tame, but here at St. Perpetua asymmetry reigned with one stunted spire, windows balanced neither in number nor height, giving the building a correct sense of being unfinished, incomplete. She was about to settle onto the steps when she noticed a movement in the shadows near the massive carved doors. A man approached, his belly distended like a starving African child's, his dark face flushed and full. "Drink," he muttered, holding out a green pint of wine. "Drink, gordacita."

With a polite refusal she hurried inside.

"No customers?" she said, peering into the Reconciliation Room, where he sat alone, reading. The converted confessional, ornately carved outside, was fiberboard inside, a single bulb hanging from the tile ceiling. In jeans, a workshirt, his shoes kicked aside, Hugh grunted happily as they embraced, his paperback digging into her breast.

"Keep an eye out," he said, once she had settled into the folding chair near the door. "If anyone comes . . . ."

"Sure. You look tired."

With an explanation Hugh dog-earred the fat book, Shelley Winters' memoirs—"I just found it lying around, you know"—and set it aside. Chunky in an agreeable, masculine way, his blond hair receding, he sometimes seemed to her to be the father of that boy she had loved, or rather, an uncle. For he himself could look back at his old self with a certain bemusement that suggested a more distant relation. No matter how angry the boy might have made her, it never seemed right to take it out on this man.

"It's Cy. We had another run-in at dinner last night."

Emily drew a blank until he reminded her that Cy was the new pastor.

"He gave us the tight-ship routine. No air conditioning after nine o'clock, no more real lemons, or plastic garbage bags. We should use the grocery bags as garbage bags. And then he wants us to start talking about money in our homilies. That's where I put my foot down. I'm not going to start preaching about how people can toss a dollar into the basket and feel virtuous—at a time when a movie is seven bucks blah blah blah. Then I hear Max creep in at three A.M.—he's right over me—drops one shoe, turns on his rap music. Cy's afraid to talk to him, afraid he might get sued. Max is very litigious these days, very defensive."

"Is he still going to AA?"

"He says he is. I doubt it." Fingering the fringe of the stole draped over his workshirt, Hugh started to explain why he doubted it, when he interrupted himself with, "Oh, by the way, thank your friend, will you? I mean, I plan to write anyway, but if you would say something, too."

Emily looked puzzled.

"Bechstein. Sent us a right nice donation."

"Allen?"

"Five hundred for a microwave at the rectory. Thanks for telling him we needed it."

"But I didn't— I mean, I only mentioned it in passing once. Oh, Hugh, you've got to return it, the check."

"You crazy? Cy's ecstatic. He's always wanted a microwave, says it's going to cut down on food bills. Besides, how do you suppose I can talk back to him like I do? Bechstein's my trump card now."

Reverting back to Max, Hugh talked at some length about the two 7 A.M. masses he had had to say for him, the way he refused to use the dishwasher, the flask he brought with him to Cub Scouts. Emily tried her best to look interested, but apparently it wasn't enough.

"You O.K., Em?"

"Fine."

"You're upset about that check, right? If I'd known— It's already deposited, and Cy's started comparison shopping."

"It's all right, really." She glanced over at the portable screen beside her, provided for anonymous confessions. "You know he's not my boyfriend or anything."

He shrugged. "So?"

"We're just friends."

Hugh and she were close, but not quite close enough—she realized after a moment's hesitation—for her to say anything about the handkerchief. She herself was a bit confused about the issue. Surely there was something perverse about their behavior—she, fully clothed, looking the other way while Allen, himself fully clothed, found some satisfaction. Yet for the life of her she couldn't manage to feel it was really wrong. As his friend, she felt she was doing him a favor. He was elderly, after all, and terrified of all the diseases going around. Not that he had ever asked her to sleep with him—this puzzled her. And of course they never discussed the handkerchief. It just happened one evening after they had gotten slightly looped at dinner. At first she hadn't been sure what he was doing. Then she pretended not to know. And he didn't do it every time he saw her. Just now and then.

The hour was soon up, without any penitents, and they were able to leave.

"Juanito, my man," he called out merrily to the drunk in the portico.

"Maricón," came the reply, which didn't faze Hugh at all. With his arm around Emily, they hurried down the littered steps.

"I got to be back by seven for a Third World meeting, O.K.? You're welcome to come."

"Thanks, but I've got to work out a new schedule for the GRE's. It's a pain."

Even this far north, virtually in Harlem, Hugh and Emily did not escape signs of that urban blight that so distressed them, gentrification. Indeed, right next door to a Puerto Rican social club that sold used records in bins outside, was a hi-tech restaurant with mesquite-grilled swordfish ($22) on its menu. Emily and

Hugh could not resist exchanging horror stories as they walked past. Emily: You wouldn't believe this little Yup in my building— Gucci bag, a baby ad exec who thought up a slogan for a banana liqueur. She crumples the flyers she gets in her mailbox and throws them down in the vestibule, all those Chinese menus and limo ads. Just leaves them for everyone else to pick up. Hugh: We had a couple at our last Third World meeting, both lawyers in matching yellow sweaters, cableknit. Twenty-six years old, Em, and she's got this huge rock on, he's got a wedding band. I knew we were headed for trouble the minute they walked in. God, the next thing I know they start whining about the Freedom Fighters. I'm not kidding, they were wondering what we could do for them.

On upper Broadway they found a Cuban-Chinese restaurant that wasn't too crowded. The one Hugh liked was packed, but he was willing to give this one, which wasn't quite as grimy and authentic-looking, a try. The prices, at least, weren't that much higher.

Hugh's Spanish, for some reason, did not go over well with the man behind the counter. Reverting to English, he managed to get a couple of Dos Equis from him, which he brought to their table.

Emily, in the meantime, was wondering if she should mention her recent lunch with Lettice. If he knew about it, she didn't want him to think she was trying to keep it a secret. But if Lettice hadn't told him about it—which was very likely—then it was probably best to remain silent. Emily did not want Hugh to think she was meddling in his affairs by trying to patch things up between him and his mother. Of course, this was precisely what she had in mind—not to meddle, but to effect a reconciliation on a deeper level than mere civility. Lettice had still not recovered from the shock of finding herself the mother of a Catholic priest. And Emily could sympathize with her. After all, Lettice's first love had been a member of the Abraham Lincoln Brigade in the Spanish Civil War. Though he had died while crossing the street in Newport, Rhode Island, struck by a bicycle—Hugh, not Lettice, had provided this detail—Lettice always spoke as if he had been struck down by a Fascist bullet, paid for by the Vatican.

"I think it's so dishonest," Lettice had said that Wednesday at La Grenouille, "the way those Jesuits are appropriating Marx. Liberation theology, indeed."

"Hugh doesn't go along with that himself, not entirely. Besides, he's a Capuchin." Emily had to think before saying this, since Hugh had spoken sympathetically of certain Jesuits in Central America. But it was true that he had little faith in any political salvation, as far as she could gather. "No, he's definitely not a Marxist."

"Not a Marxist—don't make me laugh, dear. Hugh is to the right of Mrs. Thatcher, I'm sure." The sarcasm, Emily could see, was masking real pain. Evidently it still wasn't easy for Lettice to dislike her son. And it was this that gave Emily hope that one day she could convince Lettice to forget about her principles, admirable though they were. Indeed, Emily, too, had many of the same objections to the Roman Catholic Church, which made it something of a chore to defend Hugh since she seemed to be defending at the same time the Inquisition, the explusion of the Jews from Spain in 1492, the genocide of the Mayans and Incas, and Pius XII.

"Emily, this Virgilio," Lettice said later over crème brûlée, "what do you make of him?"

Virgilio was a lector at St. Perpetua. Hugh mentioned him from time to time, and was apparently fond of him. "He works in a hardware store, I believe."

"Yes, of course, but . . . . Did you ever get the feeling, the way Hugh talks about him, that—"

"He's married or something," Emily put in quickly. She did not feel it was right to start in on Hugh's sexuality. Ever since he had converted, Lettice had voiced doubts about her son. And when he announced his intention of becoming a priest, these doubts gave way to conviction. She was sure he must be gay. Why else would a healthy, attractive young man take a vow of celibacy—unless he simply couldn't cope with what he was? Consulting books, psychologists, gay friends, straight friends, bi friends, Lettice put up a last-ditch effort to convince Hugh that everything would be fine—that he would one day find a man to love and that she would accept him into the family with open arms. This, more than anything else, estranged Hugh from his mother. For, as he told Emily, sex wasn't the issue. He was not repressed. He was not gay. And Emily, though she, too, had had her doubts, especially right before the divorce, believed him.

"Virgilio is married?"

Emily nodded, though she was less sure of this fact now.

"Well, what does that mean nowadays? You never can tell about anyone."

"He likes him, Lettice. Let him be."

"Why would someone like a clerk in a hardware store? My God, the man spent last Thanksgiving with us in Litchfield. I thought Mr. Squires would die. His accent—not that I object to accents. Or bad grammar. But he just seemed so plain, so uninteresting. He's not even good-looking."

"Well, then, it can't be sex, can it?"

When the black beans arrived, and the moo-shoo pork, Emily was asking about Clara.

"Yes," he admitted. "I did talk to her."

"Chalk up another convert."

Hugh shoveled some beans into his mouth before replying. "I tried to talk her out of it."

"What?"

"I think something's up. My hunch is she's not going into it for the right reasons."

Could there ever be a right reason, Emily wanted to say—but refrained, looking politely interested.

"Clara, you know, is wracked by guilt. It determines everything she does."

Emily could not help smiling. How naive could Hugh be? The girl never had a scruple in her life. When she saw something she wanted, she went ahead and grabbed it.

"Hey, I'm serious, Em. She came to see me a couple of weeks ago, and I simply couldn't believe how miserable she was. I mean she looked fine, pretty terrific actually. And she did all she could to convince me that she had never felt better. But I could tell. She's tortured."

"Please, give me a break."

"It's Judy. She can't stand the thought of what she did to her."

"She said that?"

He waved his hand impatiently. "Of course not. She just told me how happy Judy is now."

"There's a bean on your cheek."

He wiped it off. "Judy has this great boyfriend. Judy has this great job—her name kept coming up. You know what she's aiming at—Clara? Two to one she's after an annulment."

"What? Lucas and she?"

"Lucas and Judy. First Clara converts. Then she begins the big campaign to ease her conscience once and for all. She'll simply have the Church say the first marriage was invalid."

"You're kidding? She didn't say that?"

"No, she didn't. But the way she was fishing around—and something Lucas had said to me last year at that dinner party. You were there, too. Anyway, I think that's their plan."

"Judy would never go along with that."

He shrugged. "One thing is true—Judy never did intend to have children. That's Clara's strong suit. A little sickening, I think, to use that against Judy. I'll be damned if I'm going to encourage Clara to convert. As a matter of fact, she's a little mad at me now."

"Well, she doesn't need you to go through with it."

"No, but I'm sure I'd be useful if Lucas tries to get an annulment. I think she was paving the way."

"You're giving her too much credit," Emily said after finishing her second beer. "Clara doesn't plan like that. She's much too . . . I don't know."

"Boy, you really get me. You think someone who rakes in what she does is Miss Innocent? Believe me, that woman knows exactly what she's doing. Always has. The other stuff, the klutzy Southern belle, it's an act."

Walking him back to St. Perpetua, Emily was thoughtful. From Clara they had drifted into a discussion of F.X. and his visit. Hugh had laughed at her description of the dinner, which for some reason she felt called upon to turn into a farce, Francine phoning every three minutes instead of just once. Why, she wondered as they ventured down an ill-lit street, why did she have to

turn F.X. into a clown? For whose benefit? Simply to be enter-
taining, to amuse Hugh?

"Sure you don't want to join us?" he asked when they got to
the door of the parish office.

"I've got to get home." She kissed him on the cheek. He gave
her a hug. It was some consolation, his arms. For a moment she
felt almost as if their lives made sense, their loneliness. Then she
was off to the subway, walking briskly, her purse firmly clamped
beneath her arm.

part three

thirteen

C lara, how could you?"
"How could I what?"
"That woman."
"She couldn't get her mailbox open. I just wanted
to help."

"You know I can't get involved with the neighbors. They
might say something to the landlord. Hugh and I are illegal,
remember? We're not really supposed to be moving in here."

With an exaggerated sigh Clara stepped up the pace.

"I'm sorry," Emily said when they got to the corner of Third
and 64th. "I didn't mean to bitch. You've been a real help tonight.
Here, take this."

As she continued to flap her hand at the traffic, Clara made
a face at the money her friend was trying to give her.

"At least let me pay for the cab," Emily said as a Checker
pulled over behind a double-parked stretch limousine, a tacky
blue.

"Don't be silly."

"Clara, take it."

"Bye, Em. I had fun." Just as the cab began to move Emily
stuffed the bills through the half-open window. "Oh, you creep,"

Clara squealed, grabbing as many as she could and throwing them back out. Twisting in her seat she got a glimpse of Emily stooping in the gutter, shaking a fist at the by-now speeding cab. Her laugh was cut short by the driver, who, with his eyes upon her in the rear-view mirror, let her know that he didn't want any funny business in his vehicle.

Clara thought this was rude of him, but held her tongue.

"I've had lots of trouble with Negroes," he was saying as they went through an underpass in the park. "Got to watch there's no funny business with Negroes, you know."

Clara wondered if he had mistook her for a black or if he was just plain crazy. What made it hard to decide was that he was black himself, unmistakably so. Perhaps he was just trying to get a rise out of her. Whatever the case might be, she was relieved when he pulled up in front of her apartment.

Alternately humming and talking to herself as she climbed the stairs ("Is everyone nuts in this town—I'd like to know."), she was looking forward to crawling in bed and making short work of the Godiva chocolates stashed away in her night table. It was a reward for not having eaten any chocolate for an entire week.

"Oh, goody!" she exclaimed when the complicated locks to her door—two Medecos, one police—worked on the first try. Sometimes it took her several attempts before she got it right, usually as a result of having failed to lock one of them on the way out.

"I'm home, sweetie," she called out cheerily to the potted palm.

"About time."

It was a moment before she saw the bare foot on the arm of the couch. A few steps closer and the angle was enough for the entire body: F.X. in jeans, a gold tanktop. She wasn't sure if she was relieved or not that it hadn't turned out to be a burglar.

"Who let you in?"

"The super."

"Anton had no business doing that." She made a mental note to murder Anton the next time she saw him. "Now if you don't mind, it's time for you to go. Good night." She was playing her mother at her most imperious, not one of her favorite roles by any means. But it was the easiest way of covering her dread.

"I'm tired, F.X.," she finally said when he just lay there, propped up on one elbow, a smile on his face. His hair, so black it had an almost bluish sheen, was tousled, wet, as if he had just showered. "Let me go to bed, please."

"Who's stopping you, babe? You've been going to bed with whoever you like, huh? Who cares if they're married or not?"

"I told you a hundred times, I have not slept with him."

"Sure, you and him are just good friends."

"I don't even see him anymore."

"Don't lie to me."

"I haven't." She tried not to raise her voice even though all she wanted to do was scream.

"Iris told me he came in to see you just the other day. At the studio. So quit your lying. It won't work with me, understand?"

"I'm not lying."

"Stop it, girl."

"What right have you to say anything to me? Get out."

"Oh, getting tough, huh?"

She knew if she stayed in the same room with him, she would lose all control. "Pardon me,".she said as she shut the bedroom door behind her. Unfortunately, there was no lock.

The pink Princess phone with the illuminated dial was on the shelf of the pink laminated headboard. Sitting on the edge of the bed she dialed as fast as she could.

"Come up as fast as you can and pound on my door, hear?"

"No."

"What? Who is this?" She had dialed her downstairs neighbor, Rebecca Clausewitz. "Hello, hello?"

"I got three pieces of gum today."

"Yes, that's nice." Trying to make her voice distinct without talking loud, she said, "Now be a good girl and put Rebecca on the phone."

"Aunt Rebecca you mean?"

"Yes, yes, put Aunt Rebecca—"

"She not your aunt."

"No, dear. Now listen, just do as I say."

"I hate you." The child hung up.

She was dialing again, Anton this time, when the door flew

open. Amazed that she hadn't screamed, Clara picked up the receiver that had slipped to the pink shag throw rug.

"Who you calling?"

"No one."

"Him, I bet. Here, give me that. I'd like to talk to this lover-boy. Lucas, huh. I'd like to ask the old lard-ass how he manages to get it up."

Quivering with rage, fear, Clara said, "Did I tell you? Emily said yes, she's going to get you an appointment with her boss." The small, sweet voice, appeasing, went on as he slammed the receiver down. Anton wasn't answering. "Mark Four's pretty big these days. They're getting into action films, things you might be good at. Emily said they're doing one in Turkey now about this secret agent. I've always thought it would be fun to go to Turkey."

"God, you're so beautiful." He was on his knees before her, his eyes boring into her with what at one moment seemed love, another, rage. "Why are you so gorgeous? Come on, tell me. I can't take it, girl. It's just not humanly possible . . . " Tears filled his eyes as he laid his head in her lap.

"Don't . . . "

"Girl, you got any idea what I went through for you?" he said, as he nuzzled her jeans. "You think it was easy getting that annulment?"

"She wanted it. Not you."

"Bullshit. Who fed you that line?"

"You did. You said she wanted to get married again and—"

"Yeah, well, the only reason I went along—it was so you and me could get married right. With a priest. Oh God, I want to screw you so bad."

"F.X., I asked you not to use that language with me," she said as she struggled to keep her jeans zipper zipped.

"You got to marry me. You just got to."

"Look, why don't you go home and get some rest? We'll talk it over tomorrow, I promise." Her hands were free; she had lost the struggle.

"I love you so much. You know that, huh? You're so fucking gorgeous."

"Oh, I forgot to tell you. Guess who stayed with me not long ago? Miz Brix, Martha's mother. She's the sweetest, nicest thing. We went up top the Empire State, and she told me when we got up there that Emily wasn't pregnant at all and I felt so ashamed of myself for thinking that. I can't wait for you to meet Emily. She's so smart and she's got the nicest husband." She had untied the red cowboy kerchief covering her head and was fiddling with it nervously as he began doing something to her that she had read about once in one of her father's medical textbooks, a perversion that the book said was against the law, even if you're married. "My mama doesn't have much use for Miz Brix. It always made me sad the way Mama would criticize Miz Brix behind her back. She told me Miz Brix's mother was a blacksmith and I said, 'Lord, I'll never speak to Martha or Emily again,' and Mama told me not to get sassy with her, and I said I wasn't going to the country club anymore, I hated all her friends who think they're so high society and gossip about each other and make everyone feel so funny 'cause they're not married. That's all they can think of—why aren't you married?" The kerchief was twisted tight as a rope, but she managed to still sound polite as could be. "So anyway Mama made me go to this reception after a golf tournament at the country club and I snuck Martha in for revenge. I would have asked Miz Brix, too, but Martha said she didn't have anything to wear for it. It would only embarrass her."

The kerchief was around his neck, but he didn't seem to notice. He kept right on with his tongue, his lips, moaning.

"I can't stand most women, I decided. Older women. Except for Minna Burns and Miz Brix. They can be so mean, without any heart." As she tightened it slowly, nothing happened. He kept right on. Then, with both hands, she jerked as hard as she could and kept up the pressure.

He looked up—his neck muscles straining against the kerchief—and smiled. "Oh, that's nice, real nice." But his eyes were stricken. Seeing them, the real hurt, she could hardly believe what she had tried to do. Perhaps that was why she sank back, exhausted, and let him mount her. Three, maybe four strokes at the most, and she exploded. It was the most intense orgasm she had ever experienced. And coincidentally, it was also the first.

While he worked away for another minute or two, she consoled herself with the thought of the chocolates in the drawer.

*　　*　　*

Emily found herself reading the same line over and over. Her mind kept straying from the script to a chilling montage of her own future. She is rejected in a casting office in a brownstone in the Village, rejected on the twentieth floor of a 57th Street skyscraper, rejected on a sound stage off Third Avenue, rejected by kind faces, frowning, cute, mean, sullen . . . Yes, this was bound to happen once she quit her job. And it would be so much harder than before, because this time she would not have anything to bolster her self-esteem. She could not tell herself, well, I'm an executive at a production company. No, this time it would be without a net. And very little, if any, encouragement from the sidelines. Certainly Hugh could not be expected to cheer her on. But she was going to do it. She was not going to give up.

"Are you sure it's such a good idea?"

"Hey, you're the one that's been telling me I should. Remember all that sour grapes business? Well, it's true. I was always making up excuses, putting acting down, just because I was terrified I'd fail. But Lucas," she said into the office phone while her other line signaled, "the time has come. I realize now if I don't act, if I don't give myself a chance to express all these things inside me— well, I won't be able to live with myself."

"Couldn't you audition at lunchtime and hold onto your job?" he said after a brief interruption, when someone had apparently walked into his office to ask about repros.

"No more hedging my bets, Lucas. I've got to go all the way, give myself totally. And none of this prissy business about bad plays, whatever. I'll take whatever I can get. And you know how snobby I was about acting classes, like no one could teach me anything I didn't know? What a moron. I'm going to find out who the best teachers are and get rolling."

"Can you have dinner tonight?" she asked after they had rehashed their positions again. "I got to talk to you about all this. I mean, I can't believe you're not being more supportive."

"Judy's bought some steak."

"What about Thursday? I'll cook."

"Well . . . "

"Hugh won't be home till late. He's all wrapped up in one of his papers, and stays at the library—" She looked over, puzzled, as someone walked into her office, appropriated a chair, which he tilted back at a precarious angle, and said, "So get off the goddam phone, girl, and say hi."

"Call you back," she said, and hung up in the abrupt manner that she and Lucas were fairly used to by now.

"How long you been gabbing? I been cooling my heels out there long enough. That dame at the front desk must have a broom up her ass. Wouldn't let me in till I told her we're engaged."

Despite herself, Emily couldn't help smiling. She had seen handsome men before, but none quite like this. The blatant way he seemed to be aware of his classic jutting jaw, his broad shoulders was, strangely enough, disarming. "So," she said, finally realizing who he must be, "I meet the great actor in the flesh. Welcome to New York, F.X."

"So where's the casting couch?"

"Down the hall to your right. Mr. Cooper, though, seems to prefer women."

His blush was as violent as a schoolboy's. "I meant yours, your couch."

"Oh?"

"Clara says you're this big cheese here."

"Very big."

He adjusted his turquoise-studded silver buckle, letting his belt out a notch or two. "You really from Tula Springs?"

"No, actually I'm from Brooklyn."

"You're shitting me."

"I just say I'm from Tula Springs for the cachet."

He regarded her a moment warily, a leg draped over the arm of his chair. "Clara said you—"

"Of course, I'm from Tula Springs, you ape." Shocked at her own audacity, she giggled in a silly way, somewhat as Mr. Cooper would.

Frowning earnestly, he said, "I never seen you there."

"I never seen you neither."

After they had cast about for friends in common, besides Clara, and discussed an English teacher they had both had in high school, Emily found herself asking if he would like to grab a bite with her.

"What about your boss?"

"He's not coming in today," she lied. It was the first time she had ever lied to anyone so deliberately. What a curious effect he was having on her, she thought, as she unlocked the bottom drawer of her desk and got out her purse.

It was at lunch that Emily reminded herself, as she bit into a too-hot morsel of beef fondue, why Clara had called off the wedding. Feeling it was wrong to be having such a good time with him—there was something about him (his naiveté? his huge, unapologetic ego?) that made her laugh—she decided it was time to take him to task.

"Twisted her arm? Hey, what's going on here?" he protested.

"Why do you think she ran away to New York?" Emily blew on the next forkful. "You're a real pig, you know."

"Tell me about it. I get a pot of scalding coffee thrown at me and I'm a pig."

"What?"

"No warning. You don't believe me, man? Here, look." In a gesture that could have come right out of a Lana Turner movie, he ripped open his cowboy shirt (snap buttons, fortunately) to display a patch of mottled skin. The extras at a nearby table did not bother to look as Emily, red in the face, urged him to cover up. The muscles were truly gross, far too large.

"Well, F.X., you must have done something."

"Just awful, yeah. I took my life savings and made a down payment on a mobile home. Thought it'd be nice to own something ourselves, not have to throw money away on rent. It was my wedding present to her, and I figured we could use it for our honeymoon in the Great Smoky Mountains. Next thing I know she's tossing this coffee at me. 'You got to be nuts if you think I'm going to live in a fucking trailer park,' she screams at me. She's lost it totally, man, so I grab her hand and maybe twist it a little 'cause she's got this goddam meat cleaver on the counter."

Looking doubtfully at him, Emily said, "You punched her once."

"Huh?"

"She was coming up here with her mother, the Colonial Dames trip, and you hit her."

"Oh, that. Did she tell you about the party I had planned, her birthday? Suppose not. I had reserved the dining room at the country club, got this printer who owes me a favor to do engraved invitations, and then at the last minute she tells me she's going up North with her goddam mother."

"So you punch her?"

"My arm accidentally hit her, my elbow. I was trying to shake loose. She had her fingernails dug into me—but I suppose she left that part out, too. Shit, I'd give anything not to love her. I've tried my best."

He wore lizardskin boots, yes, and his jeans were disgracefully tight—but even so Emily could not help feeling disturbed. He couldn't be making it all up, could he?

"That was him?" F.X. was saying over dessert when Emily had let it slip that they had passed Mr. Cooper in the lobby on the way to lunch. "Why the hell didn't you introduce me?"

"Listen, you're never going to get anywhere in this town dressed like some two-bit midnight cowboy. It would only have hurt your chances."

"Hey, this is show biz. You got to get noticed. Come on, we could have asked him to eat with us."

"Ronnie," she mimicked, "like how 'bout grabbing a bite with us?"

"Well, what's wrong with that?"

"You would have asked him, wouldn't you? Listen, boy, if I were you, I'd get me some elocution lessons before I went around meeting folks."

"What?"

"You sound like a clod, the way you slur your words."

"I know, I know. I'm supposed to sound like some fucking English fairy, right?"

"You don't have to go that far. A plain American fairy would do."

"Fuck you."

"Such eloquence, my dear. Now put away that wallet. I'm paying."

"American Express. High-powered career lady, huh?"

"Up yours."

That afternoon Emily was running off copies of a memo on the Xerox machine when Mr. Cooper emerged from the men's room.

Pretending not to notice him, she went on trying to get the pages to come out darker.

"Was that your fiancé I saw you with in the lobby?"

"What? Oh, my lunch date. An agent." She could not bear the smirk in his voice. And he was standing so close. Why did he have to stand so close?

"An agent?"

If he giggled, she knew she would scream. "An independent from the Coast."

"Was it Bauer, Lenz and—"

"This machine needs servicing, Ronald. I'm tired of wasting so much time here every day."

"Speak to Babette."

"I did. She says she's not responsible for this anymore."

The smell of his cologne was making her ill. He was hemming her in, making it impossible for her to move without touching him.

"Well, who is?"

"You're the boss."

"I can't be bothered with copy machines."

Childishly, she hit the machine with her fist. "You should make someone do it."

"All right, do it. You're in charge from now on."

He walked away, but the scent lingered.

Emily described the incident in detail for Lucas later that week when he stopped by the apartment for a drink. He was still doubtful, though. Jobs like hers didn't grow on trees. A lot of folks would give their right arm for it. Emily then demanded to know what the bottom line was: Did he or did he not believe she could make it as an actress? Yes, he said, tacking on a string of equivocation about luck, chance. And being a cutthroat.

"You don't think I can be a cutthroat?"

"No, not really."

"But I think I can. I mean, in a decent way, without really hurting anyone."

She brooded all week. How awful it would be to quit and then discover she couldn't earn a cent. All of a sudden she would be transformed into a housewife, totally dependent upon Hugh. And she knew that, of all things, Hugh would detest this role the most. He had married her because she was independent, strong. If she failed totally, wouldn't he lose his respect for her? And then he might begin to wonder why she had married him, if his money, after all, did not have a lot to do with it. Hadn't he always made fun of the girls who chased him in college? Earth Shoe golddiggers, he called them.

"What is this doing here?" Emily said aloud to herself as she walked into her office after another weekend of agonizing about her position. A rubber plant, six feet high, crowded against her file cabinet. At first she was angry about this encroachment. But then it occurred to her that it might be a peace offering from Mr. Cooper. Well, it was the least he could do if she wasn't going to get an office with a window.

A few minutes later Babette stuck her head in the door. "I hope you don't mind. There's just no room at the reception desk out front."

"It's yours?"

An Australian import, Babette had been at Mark Four only three months, during which her silky blonde hair had been clipped and Afro-ed and her long nails shorn. She was the only secretary who knew word processing—and was quite efficient at it.

"You don't mind, do you, Em? Oh, and by the way, the couch should be coming on Tuesday afternoon."

"What couch?" Emily had only two chairs in her office. Was Mr. Cooper upgrading her?

"My couch, love. It's going to be a wonderful pearl gray. I can't wait."

It took Emily a good half hour to digest this information. Then she went to the ladies' room and cried for ten minutes in a stall. Afterward, feeling more composed, she walked into Mr. Cooper's office unannounced.

"Mrs. Vanderbilt?"

"Mr. Cooper." Her heart was beating violently. She had no idea what to say. "I am not a—" She stopped herself just before she almost said "a crook." "I am not a Xerox repairman," she finally managed.

"No, I didn't think so." He regarded her in a kindly, avuncular manner. For once he seemed focused, actually there. "You've been very unhappy, haven't you?"

She nodded, her throat too choked by emotion to speak.

"Perhaps, Emily, it would be a good idea for you to start looking around for something that would make you happy. Life is too short to be miserable all the time, don't you think? Now, you're a very bright young woman. You have your whole life ahead of you. I'll be glad to give you the very highest recommendation wherever you apply."

"Thank you."

"Well, it's been nice . . . "

"Uh, yes."

Back out in the hall she consoled herself with the thought that at least there hadn't been a scene. It was the one thing she couldn't have stood, a real scene. Just let her find a dark quiet place to curl up and die . . .

fourteen

_

Hugh had a key to Fay's apartment, so it didn't matter if she was home or not. Her spare bedroom was by now his study, though she would use it when he wasn't around to work on jingles for radio ads. Fay had landed a job at Young & Rubicam, which was about the last place on earth she ever expected to end up. Her dream had been to work in city planning, but no opening was available except in Omaha, which, as far as she was concerned, might as well be the moon. At Broadway and 111th Street, her apartment was close enough to Union for Hugh to check references in the library without having to trudge all the way up from 64th Street. He was writing his dissertation and needed absolute silence to concentrate. Emily, now that she had quit her job, spent more time than ever at the apartment. Though she made a point of being as quiet as possible, he found he just couldn't make any progress with her around.

If Hugh did not meet his quota of 750 words a day, he himself realized he was not fit to live with. Fay didn't seem to take this as personally as Emily. When he brooded, Fay wouldn't try to tempt him with snacks or drinks or small talk. She would leave him alone, and go off to do her laundry, or visit her current boyfriend, an assistant D.A. in the Bronx. Unlike Emily, who constantly asked questions about it, Fay hadn't the slightest interest in his dissertation. Why it annoyed him so much when Emily made a perfectly reasonable request or offered to help, remained a mystery to him.

"Like the other day," he explained to Fay one afternoon when he had written a record 1,117 words and was feeling more sociable, "she asks if I'd like her to type up my notes or proofread. And I just sat there and pretended I hadn't heard, and then she says what's wrong, and I say nothing and go off in the bedroom."

"You're a real prick."

"I know. Then at dinner she clicks her fork against her teeth, and I think to myself, if she does that one more time . . . "

"Are you mad at her because she's trying to be an actress? You used to bug her a lot about that."

"Right. I can't figure out why, either. I mean, I never had anything against acting before, until she started asking me about it. Then I got on this kick, downgrading it, making it sound immoral."

"Real passive-aggressive behavior."

"You think?" He took the joint from her hand and inhaled deeply. "Yeah, maybe I was trying to get at her in some way. But why? I mean it's so weird. The basic thing is that I love her. She could join the circus for all I care."

"Hey, hold on. Did you hear what you said?"

"What?"

"That last thing about the circus—you don't think there's like this subdued hostility?"

"I meant . . . "

"I know what you meant, but the way it came out."

"This stuff is good," he said, handing the joint back to her. "Hostile? It's this damn dissertation. Going to drive me bonkers."

Returning from Fay's apartment, Hugh couldn't help feeling relieved if Emily was not home. He would collapse in front of the TV and watch one mind-numbing show after another, sometimes eating nothing for dinner but a bag of cheese curls washed down by wine. One day, absolutely unable to crank out more than fifty-three words, he came home early, thinking he might take Emily out to a late lunch to make up for being away so often. She was not in, though. Auditioning, the note said. And no cheese curls.

She had forgotten to buy another bag. Musing on this, he answered the knock on the door.

"Do you have any vinegar?"

It was the upstairs neighbor, Mrs. Powys. From time to time she would stop by for various spices—cinnamon, cumin, sage, oregano. Normally, Hugh would have felt sorry for her. She was always drunk and obviously lonely. But she was also a friend of the landlord's, and would ask questions that made Hugh nervous. How is your aunt, she would inquire about Mrs. Peterson—and Hugh would have to come up with some sort of lame chitchat. Of course, since Hugh and Emily had been in the apartment well over a year, it was obvious something fishy was going on. But Mrs. Powys never went too far. Just as Hugh began to feel really uncomfortable, she would abruptly change the subject.

"No vinegar, Mrs. Powys. Very sorry."

"Rosemary?"

"No, none of that either, I'm pretty sure."

"I see. May I come in anyway? I just, you know, what with Dr. Kissinger . . . "

"Pardon?"

Mrs. Powys remained in the doorway. She had gone to some trouble fixing herself up, it seemed. Her hair was uniformly dyed—often there were gray streaks—and her diamond bracelet and brooch were correctly fastened and pinned. "Well, you know, of course, Mr. Peterson, we're on the verge of annihilation."

Hugh smiled.

"Red alert, my dear. Dr. Kissinger has put our nuclear forces on red alert. The Russians have invaded Israel, I believe."

After getting rid of her, as politely as he could, Hugh discovered she had been, in the main, right. He hadn't turned on the TV or radio that day. When he did, he felt the same numbness overcome him as he watched the "Special Report"—a sense of hopelessness. By the time Emily got home, the alert had been called off. She seemed in a strangely good mood, considering what had happened that day. All she could say about it was how sweet it was of Hugh to go upstairs with some vinegar. For that was what he had done after turning off the set. He had found an almost full bottle and gone up and met Mrs. Powys's three cats and let himself be bored to death for a whole hour while she described their personalities. The thought had occurred to him that, if a nuclear war started, he would confess to Mrs. Powys that his last name wasn't Peterson, that he was no relation at all. Fortunately, this hadn't proved necessary.

"Oh, God, what am I going to do?" Emily was shivering backstage, about to go on, and whom did she see in the audience? It was enough to make her want to give up entirely.

"What's with you?" F.X. asked.

"He's here. Hugh's here. I can't believe it. How can I let him see me like this!"

In the last few days Emily had been feeling curiously hopeful about this production. It was her debut on the New York stage, and for the first two weeks of rehearsal she was certain the show was going to be a major disaster. But lately the script seemed to be coming into focus, a tone was set for all the actors. And several people had complimented her on the way she said her two lines. They said she was really funny.

Seeing Hugh changed everything. Suddenly she was looking at the set, the actors, from his point of view. How shabby and makeshift Valhalla seemed now, the columns as amateurish as a high school play's. And there was F.X. in that ridiculous polyester leopardskin bikini, giving the whole production a funny feel. And herself—would Hugh remember that she had complained about what she had to wear? Her Rhinestone Maiden costume left her rear end practically bare.

In the audience Hugh smiled bravely from the third row, hoping to encourage the actors already onstage. Twelve people had shown up for the performance, mostly older men. Of course, it was raining, and the theater was so out of the way, in the midst of the meat-packing district, virtually deserted at night save for a few transvestite hookers, one of whom had accosted Hugh as he entered. Having typed 1,232 words that day, he was simmering with repressed elation. If he only managed to do 300 words a day next week, his dissertation would be finished! Of course, he would have to spend a few weeks polishing it. But the worst would be over. Fay and he had planned to celebrate that evening with a dinner at a steakhouse, but then he had told Fay that it was Emily's opening night. "You're going out with me and the girl's got her opening night? You out of your mind? Get on over there, Vanderbilt." "But Emily said she didn't want me to come. She practically begged me." "Don't you know anything? All actors say that. Then they never forgive you for not showing up." "Really?" "Listen, you got to start being more supportive. Emily's been working like a dog, getting rejected left and right. Now here's her first big break . . . " So Hugh had found himself at "Twilite of the Gods."

Concentrating hard, he slowly began to get the drift of what was going on. Siegfried was either John Dean or Bob Woodward, Brunnhilde was Martha Mitchell. He thought Wotan might be Nixon, until he said something Hugh remembered from the televised hearings, one of Sam Ervin's lines. As for the Rhinestone Maidens, Hugh became a bit flustered at their entrance. He could not believe what Emily was allowing herself to wear, some sort of sequined get-up that had no back at all. And the soles of her feet were so dirty. Nevertheless, the sound system was excellent, and when the Chicago Symphony nearly blasted Hugh out of his metal folding chair during Siegfried's Funeral Music, tears welled up in his eyes. The tableau onstage, for a few moments at least, seemed almost noble: With her arms upraised, straining against the breeze from an ill-concealed wind machine, Emily seemed a different woman altogether, her legs somehow longer, her hair lush and golden—and what a fierce, chiseled, Nordic face. On the verge of falling in love, he was distracted by a peculiar movement seen from the corner of his eye. Two seats away from him an older gentleman seemed to be having some kind of minor fit. Worried that he might be an epileptic, Hugh glanced over and saw it was just a hand moving rapidly. And though it was warm inside, the man hadn't bothered to take off his raincoat.

Not until he had congratulated Emily warmly after the show, did it dawn on him what he had just witnessed.

"What's wrong?"

"Nothing."

"You really thought I was good?"

"Yes," he said, much less enthusiastically.

They were waiting for F.X., who was backstage talking with an agent. Hugh had agreed to go get a hamburger with him and Emily, both of whom were always ravenous after a show.

"You sure you don't mind if F.X. comes?"

"No," he lied for the second time. He understood that F.X. was from her hometown, which in itself meant quite a bit to Emily. But aside from this it was hard for him to fathom why she spent any time at all with him. Of course, F.X. could protect her. That went for something in this neighborhood.

"Once we took these beer cans, tied them all together."

"Yeah?"

"Tied them to the car, his car."

"Yeah?"

"Coach Frakes comes out of the gym, starts the engine . . ."

"Yeah?"

F.X. went on like this to Hugh for some time before Emily broke in. "I want to dance. Come on, Hugo."

Annoyed by the name, he told her to dance with F.X., who nearly turned over the tiny round table as he stood up.

It had been Emily's idea to repair to the Twinklezone after they had eaten at a diner on 14th Street. She had never been to a disco before, and a friend from her acting class had said the place was a lot of fun. Fay had once informed Hugh that not everyone who dressed in designer fashions was from Queens, but still he couldn't get over the feeling that he was in a bridge and tunnel hot spot. Emily and he seemed out of place among the Gucci loafers, she in a plain cotton skirt, he in khaki trousers and muddy Adidas. F.X., though, looked like a regular, and had Emily dancing less and less stiffly as the Three Degrees asked several times, "When will I see you again?"

"No thanks," Hugh said to a woman with an alarming resemblance to Barbra Streisand, frizzed hair and all. She had walked by with a drink and asked him to dance.

In the men's room Hugh was jiggling the keys in his pocket when he felt a strange lump. After flushing he took out the lump and stared in a semi-looped daze at a piece of tinfoil. Then it came to him. Fay had some coke—from a friend at the office— and he had talked her out of using it. Grass was one thing, but coke was too Wall Street. He had brought it with him to the play to make sure she didn't use it after he left. But he had forgotten to toss it out.

"Hey, you know Clara?"

Hugh looked over and saw F.X standing at the next urinal.
"Clara Tilman? Yeah."
"I'm in love with her, you know."
"That's nice."
"What's that?"
"Coke."
"You're shitting me. Hey, man!" F.X. reached out and grabbed Hugh's wrist as he was about to dump the contents into the urinal. "You crazy? Here." He took the tinfoil from Hugh and then dragged him over to a stall.

"Take it easy, man," he said as he locked the door behind Hugh. "Don't go flashing that stuff around in public like that."
"I was going to dump it."
"What! Where'd you get this shit anyway? Hey, where you going?"

Hugh felt he was suffocating. F.X. was crowding him against the toilet-paper dispenser. He had to get out.
"Mind if I try some? I never tried it before."
"Go ahead," Hugh said, escaping.
"How do you do this?"

Another man had walked into the tiled room. Hugh coughed and said something to the man, simply to warn F.X. they weren't alone. The man, as he stared into the mirror lined with miniature blinking Christmas-tree lights, gave Hugh a funny look.
"Loud, huh?" Hugh repeated. "Well, I better be going now. I'm going out of the bathroom now."

If it were not for the coffee-maker, Emily would never have survived at the Renseleer Foundation. Sensory deprivation was doing her in. The phone almost never rang, and very few people ever came in for Emily, as receptionist, to announce. Surely the United States must be filled with decaying mansions where Washington, Lincoln, or Arthur had slept, yet only a handful of civic groups bothered to apply. Coffee kept Emily alert enough to read, study lines, and occasionally chat on the Watts line to Boston, where a friend from Smith gave glass-blowing lessons. When she didn't have a letter to type for Mrs. Lewisham, her boss and the only other person in the office, she would write cheery, respectful letters to her parents, an occasional facetious postcard to her sister, and a more serious note or two to a cousin who was troubled by the long lines at the gas stations and wondered if this could be the beginning of the end of Western civilization. The high point of the day was a lengthy discussion with Mrs. Lewisham of what Emily should purchase for their lunch. The merits of various delis and diners were compared and contrasted, as they sifted through flyers from Chinese, Greek, Japanese, Norwegian, and one Thai establishment.

Eating at her desk one day, a feta cheese salad with kippered herring on the side, she swallowed a black olive without properly chewing it in order to pick up the phone. "Renseleer Foundation."

"Renseleer Foundation," Mrs. Lewisham's voice echoed from her office. Large, sweet, and religious, Mrs. Lewisham couldn't seem to remember that it was Emily's job to answer the phone.

"Emily Vanderbilt, please."

"I'm Mrs. Lewisham, the acting director. How may I help you?"

"Mrs. Lewisham, it's for me."

"I'll be glad to take it, dear."

"It's my agent."

"Oh, I am sorry, Emily. I've been waiting for my nephew to call and I thought this might be him. He's learning Tibetan, you know, and I promised to introduce him to Mr. Woo Yuk Cheung."

"Excuse me, Ma'am, but I'm in a hurry. Got to talk to Miss V."

"Go ahead, Herb," Emily said after Mrs. Lewisham had hung up in a flurry of apologies. Herb Rice was young, a shocking twenty. Indeed, Emily had heard rumors that he was actually only eighteen, but these she refused to believe. Though his elder partners in the agency had bona fide offices, he was required to work out of an apartment that was taken over every evening at six by an assistant librarian who commuted to Weehawken.

"You sitting down, kid? Wait till you hear this."

"Oh, Herb, don't tell me—"

"Correct. You got it. You're booked on NyQuil."

Emily could not suppress a squeal of ecstasy. This was her very first commercial—and it would be on national TV.

"Fifteen hundred guarantee. If they run the four cycles, that means six grand. Shoot date is the sixteenth, Boken Studios at

Forty-eighth and Eighth. By the way, Vanderbilt's got to go. I don't want to sell you with that name."

"Brix then, Herb. That's my maiden name."

"Forget it."

"Why?"

"Too ethnic. I think we're going to register you as St. George, Emily St. George. Get some new head shots with that name."

"Oh, Herb, I don't know."

"Trust me. I've researched this, knocked it around with Phil and Harold. They say it's a winner. Come on now, let me run with it."

With some misgivings she let herself be talked into it. Herb explained that it was only temporary. If she didn't like it after a while, she could change it back. Not to her surprise, Hugh found it a terrible idea. But he did congratulate her about the NyQuil and—whether there was an actual connection or not, she was not quite sure—began to make love to her again. Of course, this could be because he had finally turned in his dissertation. While he was writing it, he hadn't seemed to take any interest in her. It made her anxious, but she was afraid to press the issue with him, knowing what a strain he was under.

As it turned out, Herb couldn't have been all wrong about the name change. Two weeks after she shot NyQuil, he booked a print ad for Chase Manhattan, a full page that ran in the *Daily News*. Emily bought twenty-five copies from five different news-stands (buying more than five from each would attract too much attention, she figured), and mailed the ad to her parents, her sister, an assortment of aunts and uncles, the glass-blower in Boston, her apocalyptic cousin, and several classmates from Smith, as well as the once-suspect lesbian senior from Maine, who was now married with three children. It was not a flattering picture, actually. The art director had made her wear tortoiseshell glasses, and her smile was disingenuous. But she was the most prominent model in the shot, the only young woman—and the *News* had a circulation of millions.

Not long after Chase, Herb came through again with a dog-food commercial. Although it only ran in the tri-state area, more people commented on it than on the NyQuil. In it she and a beagle carried on a conversation, which had taken two and a half days to shoot. The poor thing had electrodes inserted into his mouth, and got a small stimulation—not a shock, his handler had repeatedly assured her—whenever he was supposed to talk. Emily was actually recognized at the checkout counter at Gristede's by a bag boy. And Lettice herself made a passing reference to it—a not uncomplimentary one—in the midst of a tirade about the Pakistani prisoners of war that India had finally decided to release.

"Do you think you could introduce me to Herb?" Clara asked Emily one day while they were hiding under the stairwell, waiting for Mrs. Powys to pass by. Clara was disgusted with Chanell Guys & Gals, who had lied to her about a shoot for a magazine called *Nugget*. It turned out to be a nude, and she refused. On top of that, Kimberly had been poisoned by Dr. Kensington, an off-camera murder that left Clara without a steady paycheck while she auditioned for other soaps.

Emily did want to help Clara in any way she could. But Clara already had an agent, someone high-powered, who didn't seem to have much time to devote to Clara's career. Even so, it might not be a good idea to alienate him so soon in the game. And also, she warned Clara, Herb didn't seem to handle glamorous types. He liked the girl-next-door look. "I'll do it, though. I'll call him if you really want to meet him. He's just a baby, you know."

"I appreciate it, Em."

Though Emily had said glamorous, it was with some mental reservations. In the last few months Clara had not been able to wear jeans, she had put on so much weight. And her face had broken out in splotches that her dermatologist attributed to stress. Emily gathered that the real problem was F.X. He and Clara did not seem to be able to call it quits. At the same time they were making each other miserable.

"One good thing, though," Emily commented to Hugh later that afternoon, "he's keeping Lucas at bay."

"Who? F.X.?"

"He's so jealous, keeps tab on her day and night. Between F.X. and Judy, Lucas doesn't stand a chance."

"You really think there was something between them?"

"Look, I talk to Lucas all the time. He hasn't admitted anything, but still, he's not exactly the world's greatest actor. Which reminds me, what are we going to do about her apartment?"

"Hold on. What does her apartment have to do with Lucas?"

"It's just an expression."

"But you do that a lot. You jump from one thing to the next."

"Stop being so technical."

"It sounds airhead. You're not an airhead, Em."

"Thanks."

They both brooded for a while on Mrs. Peterson's faded, elegant couch before Emily resumed in a carefully controlled tone of voice: "She can't pay the rent anymore on her apartment. Her parents want her to come home, give up."

"Why can't she move in with F.X.?"

"It wouldn't be good for her. Besides, he already has a roommate. A man."

"I don't see why Clara should be our problem." After a tense moment he added, "Must you gnaw on your hair?"

"I'm sorry."

"So Clara helped us find this place. Are we supposed to be her slaves for life?"

"The way you exaggerate. I just thought if we let her stay for a week or two . . . "

"Stay? You don't mean here?"

"She said she wouldn't mind sleeping on the couch."

"Well, why ask me? You two have already decided, I can tell."

"Do you hate me?"

"What?"

"Sometimes you sound as if you really hate me."

Hugh laughed. "I think all these commercials are really going to your head."

"What do you mean?" She was not laughing.

"You're getting very dramatic these days."

"Hugh, you've been putting me down in little ways. It's very passive-aggressive."

"Have you been talking to Fay?"

"What does she have to do with it?" Emily had indeed talked to Fay the other day, and had gotten into a brief discussion about

Hugh. She had phoned Fay's to ask when Hugh would be home for supper. "Anyway—"

"Look, let her stay here. I really don't care that much."

"You do. I can tell."

"I don't."

"I'll call Clara and tell her it's not such a good idea."

"No, I really don't mind."

"Hugh, you do. Why can't you be honest about what you feel?"

"There you go. Generalizing."

"No, I'm trying to be specific."

"Then listen to me: I don't care."

"I'm going to tell her no."

"And blame it on me, right?"

"No, I'll say it's my decision."

"You'll be lying, Em. Besides, it's not just your decision. I ought to have some say. And I say— You smell something burning?"

Emily jumped up. "The beans!"

fifteen

❧

S he won't get on!"
"What?"
"She refuses to get on the horse!"
His face only inches from Emily's, Herb Rice was
making his point so forcefully that Emily was obliged to wipe the
moisture from her cheeks. Directly across from the Flatiron Building, where Broadway intersected Fifth Avenue, the narrow island
they were standing on was crammed with lights, cable boxes,
reflectors, and a sullen crew in knit caps and army fatigue jackets,
refusing to do a thing about the manure that steamed away in the
bitter cold beneath the mare. Emily had been in her jazz class
when she had gotten the summons from her agent, who without
any explanation, had told her to get downtown pronto. It was an
emergency.

Rushing out of the dance studio in her leotards, Emily had
felt a surge of excitement that made her forget what a miserable
day she had been having. To begin with, it was her birthday, and
although her mother had sent her a blouse from J.C. Penney's
(frilled collar, puffed sleeves, chartreuse with yellow zigzags,
somehow managing to suggest a unique combination of tart and
spinster) no one else had remembered. As if this wasn't bad

enough, she was worried to death about all the money she was spending, more in this one day than she made in a week at Renseleer. Cabs alone were a horrendous expense as she raced from one audition to the next, not trusting the subway to get her there in time. And the half hour with the diction coach who was helping her sound Mexican for an important audition was an outrageous $20. On top of that was the $130 for the jazz dance classes she had just signed up for. Billed as beginner, the classes already seemed too advanced for her. It was so embarrassing to be the only one who couldn't follow the steps the instructor shouted out so rapidly. Fortunately, Herb Rice's call had come through just as they were launching into a Bob Fosse routine. Though she hoped it was a job he needed her so desperately for, Emily couldn't help feeling just as excited by the prospect of a surprise birthday party. Herb, after all, could be so sweet when he wanted.

Somehow she managed to contain her disappointment when she learned what the "emergency" was all about. Clara, as Lady Godiva, was supposed to mount the white mare held by the squat, burly trainer in medieval garb, all for a print ad for some sort of power drill. What Lady Godiva had to do with power drills—and the Flatiron Building—was left to the genius of advertising. The real problem Emily faced was that Clara, in a five-foot-long wig and little else, refused to go through with the shoot. Huddled against the side of a portable generator humming out power for the lights, she would not budge.

"She said you're the only one she'd talk to," Herb went on, running a hairy meaty hand over his receding hairline. Though he was only twenty, he had aged rapidly enough to cause his colleagues no undue concern about his youth or innocence. He even had a bona fide potbelly. "I get this insane call from Sam here, the art director, threatening to sue the pants off me if I don't rush right over and get this dame in line, *your* friend, sweetie. So what's all this primer donner stuff, huh? Who's she think she is? I pick her up out of the gutter and this is the thanks I get."

"Take it easy, Herb. I'll handle it."

Though Emily's face was stern as she approached the generator, the sight of Clara up close gave her some misgivings. This was not acting. Clara truly did look frightened, lost, and almost blue with cold.

"Oh, don't," she protested as Emily tucked her parka wherever the blonde nylon hair would allow. "You'll freeze, Em."

"I'm fine. Now, girl, what's this all about? Is it the horse? Are you afraid of the horse?"

Clara gave her a reproachful look.

"Well, if it's the costume . . . " Emily began, noting that the flesh-colored pasties and panties were actually much more modest than the Rhinestone Maiden outfit she had been forced to wear.

"I'm naked, Em. Right in front of the whole world."

"Don't be silly. You got more on than a lot of folks wear to church nowadays." Emily noticed a small crowd of onlookers across the street in Madison Square Park. She moved to shield Clara from their gaze. "And besides, what did you get all dressed up for if you thought it was so bad?"

"I don't know. I was scared they would yell at me."

"You realize how much this is costing, don't you? The crew, the horse, the equipment. Herb's going to—"

"Don't, Em. Don't yell at me, too."

"I'm not. Just try to be reasonable, honey. It's going to be all right."

They both glanced anxiously over at Herb, who had his arm around the art director, trying to jolly him up apparently.

"Em, please, don't make me. I can't. I just can't. Something is scaring me so much. I can't be Lady Godiva."

The absolute conviction in Clara's voice finally swayed Emily. She knew now where her duty lay. "Don't worry, O.K.? You go get dressed. I'll talk to Herb."

"Oh, Em, I love you. Really, you're great."

Too miserable to move, Emily remained there for a few moments, faint with hunger. All she had had time for was a candy bar after her diction class, nothing else all day.

"Em, I've made up my mind," Clara said finally, moving closer for warmth. "I can't take it anymore. I'm going home, back to Louisiana."

"No, girl," Emily snapped back, surprised at her own vehemence, "you'll do no such thing. I'm not going to let you, understand?"

"But I can't afford an apartment and—"

"You're moving in with Hugh and me—and that's that. Period. I don't care what Hugh says. And as for Herb, I'm ready now. I can take care of him."

Prepared to defy her agent, no matter what the cost, Emily was taken offguard when he informed her of the compromise he had worked out with the art director. Since it was going to be a long shot, after all, and the features of the model would not be overly important, Emily was instructed to accompany Clara ("I don't want to ever set eyes on that girl again," Herb inserted.) to the studio across the street and change into her costume.

Fifteen minutes later a shivering, blushing Emily found herself mounted on the twitching white mare—and two hundred dollars richer.

Clara proved to be a good roommate. She provided the domestic touch that Emily managed only in spurts. Yes, when auditions were slow, Emily might tidy up, mop, or fix a good meal. But most of the time the apartment seemed cluttered, as if they had just moved in. With Clara around there seemed, oddly enough, to be more space. Rarely were there dirty dishes in the sink, and never on the counters. Clara organized the cookware and utensils into recognizable categories, and with Anton's help installed a spice rack and shelves and even put down new kitchen tiles. Mrs. Peterson's clothes disappeared from the closets and dresser (again, courtesy of Anton), her novels from the tulip bookcases in the living room, and an oppressive Victorian carpet of purple roses was replaced by a smaller, lighter rug of Clara's from Blooming-dale's. The windows let in so much more light that Emily felt obliged to apologize for letting them get so grimy. Of course, Clara had all the time in the world for housework since she had not yet managed to find herself a new agent. Even so, Emily couldn't help being impressed when she came home one evening and found the dining-room chandelier brilliantly lit. It must have taken an enormous amount of time to clean the crystals; and the bulbs it needed were, Emily had thought, impossible to find.

Lettice appeared to take the new roommate in stride, though her brow would furrow whenever she asked after Clara's health. Once or twice she did attempt to question the wisdom of such an arrangement, but Emily refused to take the bait. She was en-joying a neat apartment, decent meals, and the chance to help a friend in need. Hugh, as well, seemed quite content. He hadn't complained once.

"But, of course, he's not one to complain in the first place," his mother said. "You never really know what's on his mind. I'll never forget the shock he gave me when he announced his plans to go to divinity school."

"Why was it such a shock?"

"I always thought he was an atheist. But Union, I take it, can accommodate atheists. I just wasn't aware of it at the time."

Having just read Hugh's dissertation, Emily knew that her mother-in-law was exaggerating only slightly. Hugh had no tolerance for the supernatural. His faith appeared to be—if Emily was not misreading him—in the divine mystery of human relationships, which could only be rendered in myth, not history. Emily felt comfortable with this, as it was pretty much her own way of thinking. Neither she nor Hugh went to church on Sundays, though occasionally he would go to a voodoo ceremony on Fridays in Queens—strictly for some sort of research, of course.

"In any case, he seems happy."

"Happy? After what just happened?"

Emily wondered for a moment what Lettice could be referring to. Probably the assistant professorship at Yale Divinity. The field had been narrowed down to Hugh and a woman from Stanford. The woman, a published author ten years older than he, had gotten the job.

"So, one job he doesn't get. Do you realize how many jobs I'm turned down for? Practically every day there's a blow to my ego. I've told Hugh he shouldn't put so many eggs in one basket. He's got to apply to a few places besides the cream of the crop." Her father's favorite clichés were trotted out, as they often were when Lettice was around. Why this was so, Emily could not say.

"Can you honestly imagine Hugh in Lawrence, Kansas, or someplace like that?"

"Sure. Why not?" A brief image of herself in Kansas had to be firmly suppressed before she added, "You've got to start somewhere."

"Indeed."

"You know Hugh has quite a little fan club at Union. I've seen the way they treat him—and I've been wanting to tell him that maybe it isn't so great a thing. You get such a high opinion of yourself that nothing seems worthy. And, of course, this is all compounded by the fact that really, he doesn't have to work. He doesn't feel the necessity. I give my parents everything I can to make up for all the sacrifices they went through to send me to college. When I make a buck, it really means something to me. Hugh hasn't the faintest idea what money is."

"My dear, stop being such a bore."

Emily couldn't help smiling. She did sound obnoxious. But she was speaking her mind, and it was fun. Defying her mother-in-law by becoming an actress had made it so much easier to be around her. Before, Emily had always felt she had to walk on eggs, so to speak, even if Lettice did claim she adored her. Now that she was able to pay her share of the rent, and often more, she felt no need to hold back.

"Emily, I have a confession to make. I'm actually delighted Hugh didn't get that job at Yale. Teaching theology, it really is ludicrous, a waste of time. I've been hoping, you see, that Union would get all this out of his system. Young men often have strange notions about what they want. My hope is that someday he'll see the light and go to law school."

"You're joking?"

"Not at all. Of course, I couldn't suggest this to him. He never listens to me. But still, if he could get something practical like that, just think of the good he could do. I could get him a job working for public housing projects. Or he could work with inner-city children. And I have a chum from Vassar who is dying for some legal help with her Native American foundation."

Emily picked up the Limoges teapot and poured the dregs into her cup. "It's funny. I've been thinking about law school myself . . . "

"Oh, lovely." Lettice actually clapped her hands together. "I just knew this insane urge to display oneself with a can of Lysol on TV—well, you'd have to wake up one day. It's been so distressing for Hugh, I'm sure."

"Lettice," she said coldly, "I was thinking about law school for Hugh, not me. I think he's moving toward something more practical."

A moment's silence followed. Emily rallied first: "Do you notice anything peculiar about me?"

"Pardon?"

"My teeth are chattering."

Lettice had insisted on sitting out in the garden, amid week-old snow that had hardened and blackened with the soot from the furnace of the neighboring apartment complex.

"What about her?" Lettice's brow furrowed.

"Clara's out shopping. We can talk all we like inside. She's built a fire."

"In England we never had fires in March." Lettice had recently begun to harken back to the days when she was courted by a supposedly dashing RAF pilot. A sign of old age? Emily wondered, though Lettice's hair was still copper and her stride vigorous. "Cheltingham was an icebox, but no one ever complained."

"Come," Emily urged as Lettice swatted the crumbs from her tweedy lap.

"Fay? Just a friend."

Clara put down her knitting and regarded Hugh intently. "It's funny. I never knew men and women could be friends before I came up North. Down South everyone thinks friends are very suspicious. I mean, if something wasn't going on, well, they'd think something was wrong with the man."

Hugh's fair cheeks colored.

"Oh, I didn't mean you. I believe you and Fay don't do anything, honest."

"Then you must think something's wrong with me."

"No, I didn't mean that, either. I just meant to say how much I admire you and Fay, your relationship. Emily isn't jealous at all. I know. She tells me all the time. And besides, she has that friend, what's his name."

"Lucas?"

"The old fat guy, yeah. What do you make of him?"

Hugh finished the paragraph he was reading before replying. "I like him."

"But you never have him over."

"I've been real busy."

Emily was at the Renseleer Foundation that afternoon. She had left instructions with Hugh and Clara to forward any call she might get at home. Although Emily had been turned down initially for the role of the blonde Mexican in an off-Broadway production, the play had since closed down in rehearsals because of artistic differences coupled with financial problems. Now it seemed it had been resurrected, and Emily was once more being considered for the part in "The Passion of Fred." Of course, Herb had her office number, but she was afraid someone from the show itself might call and not realize that on Wednesdays she worked.

"Do you think we should ask him over one night?" Clara said as Hugh stood up and stretched. He had stayed home, rather than gone to Fay's, on the off-chance that F.X. might drop by. Clara said she thought he would. But last-minute things always came up with him.

"Lucas?"

"We could have him and Fay. I have this recipe for six I've been meaning to try out. You and Em, Lucas and Fay, me and Minna Burns."

"Oh gosh, not her. She's too much."

"What about the lady upstairs, then?"

"You nuts?"

"No one ever asks her out. I can hear her walking around all day. Besides, aren't you supposed to love your neighbor, Mr. Ph.D.?"

"In small doses only."

"Hey, you're not going to leave that glass on the floor like that, are you?" she said as he headed for the door. Emily might let him get away with such behavior, but Clara had certain standards. "Wash it with the sponge—not the cloth. The cloth is for wiping up."

"Yes, mother."

As it turned out F.X. did not stop by that day. And Emily got no calls. Later in the week, though, Hugh was awakened from a light doze by the sound of raised voices in the living room. He picked up the book on his chest, Karl Barth, and resumed reading. He would give them a chance to be alone before going in to see him.

"He is so stupid. He keeps on mispronouncing words," Clara

was saying only a few minutes later after she had burst into the room. " 'Georgine,' he says. And he won't believe me when I say it's 'Georgian.' "

Anxious to catch F.X. before he left, Hugh refrained from asking how that word of all words had landed in their conversation. Instead, as he left the bedroom, he said, "Love thy neighbor."

"He's not my neighbor. He's my boyfriend."

"Is he?"

She sighed as she plopped down onto the recently vacated bed. "I don't know. I suppose so."

F.X. was perusing the contents of the refrigerator, from which Clara had removed, only the day before, Emily's magnetic peach and banana. She said they were tacky, and the notes they held illegible. "Got any beer, son?"

"Behind the mayonnaise."

"Oh."

In the living room Hugh listened patiently for a while as F.X. explained his theory of Clara. "It struck me just yesterday—she can't help it. It's the way her mind is. Something's like chemically wrong. She can't relate to men unless there's hostility. Between you and me, son"—here F.X. leaned forward, as though he were not halfway across the room—"I think she's mentally ill. Really certifiable."

"Interesting. By the way, I meant to ask you, this stuff you're getting from Fay . . ."

F.X. scratched his crotch. "The heroin?"

"Heroin? You're kidding." Hugh was pale, ill.

"Relax!" F.X. snorted merrily, slapped his knee. "You believe anything, don't you?"

"I meant the coke," Hugh said with a flush of anger. "I'm trying to get her to stop. She can't afford to give away that stuff like that."

"What are you talking, boy? I pay good money. She's not cheap."

"You buy from her? That's awful. What the hell does she think she's doing? She never told me . . . " Hugh wondered how he could ever have given F.X. Fay's name. He had been smashed, of course, but even drunk like that he should have known better. "Do me a favor, F.X. Lay off. Fay's got to stop."

"What about you?"

"So I tried it once to see what it was like. That's it."

"Fay seems like a big girl to me. She doesn't need a mother." He had hoisted his cowboy boots onto the coffee table. "You know something, pal? It used to worry me, you living here with my girl. What's the angle, I asked Fay. She's the one told me not to worry. Never touched her, have you?"

"Who? Fay?" Hugh suffered a brief fantasy of leaping from his chair and smashing his fist into the handsome face.

"I always figured you and Fay had a thing going."

"You forget I'm married."

"Convenient, isn't it?"

Hugh could not believe that this dope, this two-bit redneck goon was able to make him feel so angry. Surely he was beneath any sort of consideration. He had humored him far too long. It was high time this ass learned whom he was dealing with.

"Like another beer?" Hugh asked, getting to his feet.

"Gotta roll."

"Roll? There's some English muffins, I think."

F.X. looked up at the ceiling. "You're too much, man. I got to go, vamoose, get it?"

"Oh."

"He went to meet who?"

"F.X."

"What's he meeting him for? Is he going to eat?"

Clara shrugged twice. Emily knew as much as she did. One minute Hugh was working on a biography for a grant, the next he was hightailing it to a bar without even having the decency to say when he would be home. It seemed F.X.'s bad manners were catching. Clara had worked hard on dinner—stuffed flounder with brown rice and broccoli. The least he could have done was say, sorry, can't make it tonight.

"How was rehearsal?"

Emily, absorbed in her food, didn't respond until Clara had asked again. "Fine."

"Are you going to dye your hair?"

"Huh?"

"Are you going to dye your hair?"

"What do you mean, am I going to dye my hair?"

"Well, you're playing a Mexican, aren't you?"

"Clara, I told you, I'm a Norwegian raised by Mexicans. Why would I dye my hair?"

"You don't have to snap."

"I've had a hard day." Emily added, a little resentfully, since in truth she did feel henpecked, "I'm sorry."

"I tried to call you at rehearsal but I couldn't get through. I wanted you to bring home some borscht. Minna likes it when she visits."

"I asked you not to call me at work. It annoys the director. You want to get me fired?"

"I wish you wouldn't snap at me."

"I'm not snapping." After a slightly longer wait, Emily added the obligatory, "I'm sorry."

"You think the rice is overcooked?" It wasn't. Clara was fishing for a sorely needed compliment. F.X. had told her that morning that he was tired of screwing her—as he so graciously put it— on Hugh and Emily's bed, always waiting for the moment when they would be out. It was time they got their own apartment together. F.X. was sick of living with a man. When Clara told him that she didn't feel ready to move in with him yet, he had gone into the familiar routine about her being mentally ill. He was saying it so much lately that she was beginning to have her own doubts. What else could explain why she would put up with such treatment?

"It seems a little overcooked to me, maybe."

"Huh? What does?"

"Emily, the rice."

"Don't worry about it. Eat."

Clara drained the wine from her glass and poured herself some more. "Why are you acting so funny?"

"Huh? No, none for me," she said as Clara brought the bottle to her glass. "What do you mean funny? I'm not acting funny."

"You are."

"Clara, I'm under a lot of pressure. This play is really taking it out of me."

"This guy I talked to, he said you weren't at rehearsal this afternoon."

187

Emily tried not to appear disconcerted. "What is this? Some idiot answers the phone, and you believe him over me? I was there." She forked in a mouthful of fish. "They just say that because we're not supposed to get calls. I told you before."

"You don't have to snap."

"Clara, really . . . " Two more mouthfuls of flounder before it finally came: "I'm sorry."

sixteen

C lara asked me to dinner."
Switching off the electric broom, Emily surveyed her handiwork. The dustballs were gone, but she would have to scrub a sticky patch of dried molasses with steel wool.

"Did you hear me?"

Without looking at Lucas, she nodded. Sooner or later Clara was bound to have discovered that he had left Judy. Emily did not feel it would have been right to tell her this herself. She had preferred to go about her business quietly, doing what she could to make his new apartment less dreary. When she wasn't needed at rehearsals, she might stop by Woolworth's for a can opener, lamp shade, cushions, or a sauce kettle, which he would accept only under protest. Apparently, he was aiming for a monastic effect. This was fine for him, but after the trek from the rehearsal studio to Kips Bay she would have liked to sit on something other than a stool.

Emily excused herself and went out into the hall to check the bathroom door again. It was still locked. Mrs. Kosik had been in there almost an hour—and Emily was dying.

"You want to use this?" he asked when she came back in. He

189

held out an aluminum mixing bowl. "I keep it for emergencies."

"Thanks. I'll wait."

Looking for steel wool she ended up in the dark, tiny bedroom with the crucifix on the wall. Lighting a candle—there were wiring problems back here—she could find nothing but a *Playboy* on the unmade pallet.

"Well?"

"No luck."

"I mean about dinner."

"Lucas, I'm not going to tell you what to do. If you want to have dinner with her, fine, go ahead." She was tired of playing superego to his id. How many times had he told her that he had not left Judy because of Clara, as if she were some sort of thought police. Perhaps she shouldn't have let him confess that he had slept with Clara once. "We haven't seen each other in almost a year, I swear," he had told her. "Neither of us felt right about Judy. It was too much." Emily had been reassuring, though probably not as congratulatory as he would have liked.

"At your apartment, you wouldn't mind?"

"What?"

"She's asking me and Fay and Minna Burns."

"Forget it. You two do what you want, but please, not under my nose."

"But it's all over. We just want to be friends, we decided."

"A convenient time for friendship, now that you've dumped Judy. She certainly found that out fast enough."

"It's been a month. Besides, I didn't tell her."

"Who did then?"

"She said Hugh did."

"I never told Hugh. He didn't know a thing."

Lucas took a large bite of the toothpicked club sandwich that had been left over from her rehearsal that afternoon.

"You told him, huh?" she ventured.

"I assumed he already knew. I mean, why should you keep it a secret from him?" This came out between several swallows. "He just called me at work one day, out of the blue. Asked how I was, real friendly and all."

Emily couldn't help being irritated with Hugh for calling behind her back. As if he suspected her of something when all she was doing was vacuuming, mopping, and scrubbing a filthy tub in the kitchen.

After Emily had made another excursion to the hall—Mrs. Kosik was through, hallelujah!—Lucas treated her to his favorite song and dance: Judy was suffocating him. If he would have stayed with her he would have died. She was a very controlling woman and—

"Hey," Emily broke in, "she was out on the road half the time. Looks to me like she gave you plenty of freedom."

"Sure, that was part of her plan. She could always throw it in my face whenever I'd hint that I needed air. But somehow she managed to be there all the time. The house, a goddam split level, it was her, not me. And Fabrice, our maid from Haiti. She and Judy used to have long talks everytime she got back from a trip—in French. They talked too fast for me to understand everything, but it was me they were discussing. Fabrice was spying, I'm sure."

"Look, you're not going to tell me that she doesn't love you. I know she does, deeply."

"Sure, so does God. He sees everything, too. And Lord help you if you don't love him back. He'll fry your little ass."

The stool sat in its corner, unused. Emily was perched on a $3.95 cushion, her back against the wall for support. Lucas was stretched out on the pine floor, shifting positions as one after another grew uncomfortable. Since the move he had let his hair grow and no longer wore a coat and tie to work. Instead he sported tight-fitting silklike shirts, with bold designs usually reserved for women's blouses. From time to time he would pinch the roll of fat around his waist and repeat how many pounds he had lost in the past week.

"Three pounds, right, wonderful, terrific. Now listen, whatever you do, don't be a humbug about it. You're putting all the blame on Judy, when you know perfectly well—"

"Judy? No, on me. It's my fault I can't accept the type of love she's offering. And it's killing me. I wish I could. I tried my goddam best. Hell, I know she's a great lady, one in a million. I don't deserve someone that good."

Emily tried her best not to roll her eyes. This was the flip side of the popular hit single.

She did not stay long that afternoon. After she had laid some roach paper in the cupboards, she gathered up her things and headed for the door.

"I already said yes," he said with a peck to her forehead. "To Clara."

"It's my apartment."

"Then you explain to her why I can't come."

"Lucas, please. Don't be difficult."

Mrs. Kosik's door opened furtively as Emily passed down the dimly lit hall to the stairs. Apparently the woman didn't know English, for when Emily called out, "Good afternoon," to the shadow behind the crack, the door slammed shut with a bang.

They had asked for 750 words. Hugh could only come up with 500, and Emily thought these were not worthy of him. He looked so vulnerable, though, sitting there waiting for her opinion. She hadn't the heart to give it to him straight.

"Not bad. But isn't it a little short?"

"I know. I just can't think of anything else to say."

Hugh had worked for three days on an autobiographical essay for a teaching post at Philander Smith College in Little Rock, Arkansas. He could not understand why it was so hard to write about himself, especially when he was trying to be sincere.

"Maybe to begin with," Emily said, lowering herself to the bed where he lay in an exaggerated pose of exhaustion, like one of Michelangelo's slaves, "this third-person business. Why not just say I?"

"It's less egotistical."

"Not really—I don't think. And maybe, I don't know, these sarcastic remarks about your family, your parents' divorce. It's sort of jarring."

Hugh laughed, unhappy. "I was just trying to lighten things up a little."

"You know when I look at this . . . " She chewed a strand of hair until Hugh asked her to stop. "Sorry. What I mean is, if I didn't know you, I'd think that you hated religion."

"I do."

"You mean all the self-righteousness, the horrible sexist bureaucracies."

"Actually, Em, the more I think about it, the more it seems

that all that *is* religion. So I do hate the very concept of religion. There's either the authentic life—or not."

"But this is Little Rock. Do you think they'll get the point?"

"If they don't, then I don't belong there."

"Well, maybe you could be a little more specific about your objections." For a moment she savored a brief pang of nobility. After all, here she was helping him to exile her to Arkansas just when her own career seemed to be taking off. If she had ever had any doubts about her love for him, this should settle the score.

"And listen," she went on patiently after Hugh had made a few defensive comments, "I'm not sure it's a good idea to mention in the end that you are 'currently a stockboy at an A&P.' "

"Well, I am."

"Yes, I know. But if you're going to say that, shouldn't you explain why? You can't just end it that way, can you?"

Hugh was tired of giving reasons for this latest move to friends, much less strangers. He had tried to explain on paper why he had taken the job, but the reasons, in black and white, sounded a bit fatuous—so he had thrown them all out. What were they? By now he was not so sure himself. He was fed up with thinking. The field exam at Union had been bad enough, linking three theologians with one theme, discussing doctrine, a contemporary issue—in his case, racism. The doctrine? The resurrection of the dead. And then his 350-page dissertation on a spatial analysis of hope—space and time being interchangeable metaphors for completion. What a relief, after all this, to finally settle down to something real. Of course, at Clara's dinner, Lucas had poked fun at him, calling him Simon Weil. Emily had defended him vigorously, saying that he would write about his experience one day. He would gain valuable insight into the way most people had to live, without much hope, with the clock dragging on slow as molasses. Minna Burns had criticized him for taking the job away from someone who might really need it. As for Clara, she simply said that she was too embarrassed to shop at the A&P now. And Gristede's was so much more expensive.

"Would you like me to rewrite it for you?" Emily offered. "I think I could make it sound less hostile."

"Do I sound hostile?"

She nodded.

"Maybe I shouldn't try to write after work. I come home so mad. You know what he did today?"

"Jorge?" Jorge was the assistant manager, the man most frequently on Hugh's mind.

"He called Kumar a stupid nigger, behind his back, of course. Kumar just happens to be a brilliant mathematician—he's from Lahore. But he got mixed up and put the wrong price on the cake mixes, the ones not on sale. What does Jorge do? He rips the gun out of Kumar's hand and throws it down the aisle. That's it for me. I lost it. Shoved the bastard hard as I could and asked him to step outside. The manager came up then and they were holding us apart. Jorge threatened me with his friends. Can you believe he's such a wimp? Friends."

Emily had begun massaging his shoulders. Something was going on. Hugh was acting so strange these days. Even the way he talked didn't seem like him. "You should be more careful."

"It's all talk. Macho crap. Saving face." He winced.

"You sore? Take your shirt off. I've got some Ben-Gay."

When she had found the ointment and begun to rub it in, she told him that Lucas was coming over again for dinner.

"So?"

"I don't think it's a good idea. What if F.X. comes by?"

"Let them settle it themselves."

"Lucas is married. It's not right."

Hugh craned his neck around so he could see her. "You got a thing for him, don't you?"

"I like him very much. I care for him as a person."

"You got a thing."

"You know, you're beginning to sound like F.X. It's really weird. Has he been telling you I got a *thing*?"

"You're at his apartment all the time."

"I trust you at Fay's."

"Fay's an ass."

"Don't say that."

"Why not?"

"She's your best friend."

"Friend, right. All this friends shit. Did you ever think, Em— it's pretty adolescent, isn't it? When are we going to grow up?"

"Hugh." It hurt to hear him denigrate her feelings for Lucas—

and his own for Fay. Somehow this had been a mainstay of their marriage, a symbol of their love and trust for each other. There was no doubt in her mind that Hugh had ever fooled around with Fay. And as for herself and Lucas—well, maybe she had fantasies at times that he was holding her in his arms. But she never imagined intercourse or anything crude. Just loving support.

"You don't really mean . . . You've known Fay all your life."

"To your left. Harder, press down."

Hugh was indeed angry at Fay. He never should have trusted her with his secret. It was that seminar on Augustine, three years ago, that had started it all. The leader, a woman from the University of Ghana, was down on Augustine, even though he was black himself. The trouble was, he was a patriarchal black. In any case, Hugh had been thoroughly smitten with Clarisse, a regal woman with an imperious charm. She talked of the necessity for the confessed life. We must confess to one another, reveal ourselves. The only sin is holding back, since what we hold back will master us in the end. Under Clarisse's spell Hugh had found himself at Fay's, sharing a joint or two, sipping Gallo. His heart was pounding violently. Not a soul knew. And yet it was such a big part of his life. Was he ever going to free himself?

"Doesn't mean you're queer, boy," F.X. had told him not long ago. Fay had blabbed to F.X. one night when they were high. She was really sorry, she had told Hugh. She didn't know what she was doing. The coke was so good, and F.X. was making her laugh. So now Hugh was forced to share his secret with F.X. He only prayed that F.X. would keep it to himself; he was sure he would die if Emily ever found out.

"Fay promised she wouldn't tell anyone."

"Look, just looking at you, boy, I knew something was screwy. You're one of the most uptight characters I've run into in a long time. So don't blame her. I would've got it out of you, anyway."

Hugh felt he should have been offended by this arrogance, but he wasn't. Dismayed, yes. The very fact that he was sitting in a singles bar on First Avenue with a pick-up artist was bad enough. But to discuss his most intimate secrets with him . . . And to listen, believe he had some answers—Hugh thought he must be losing his mind.

"I gotta give it to you straight, boy: You are dumb, really dumb. How many chicks you slept with?"

"Me? One, I guess."

F.X. hooted. "You're not shitting me, are you? God, I love it." He reached over and squeezed Hugh's neck. "You really are something else. Here, have another."

Hugh was drinking tequila, trying to keep up with F.X. "So why did Fay say she thought I might be, you know, a latent . . . "

"Fay don't know her ass from her elbow. What the fuck you doing talking to a woman about sex anyway?"

"Well, she said, like if I fantasize all the time about two women making it, it's . . . I'm projecting my own homosexual urges on the women."

"Bullshit." F.X.'s hand slapped the wooden table. "God, you people up here are so screwed up. I never seen such an uptight bunch of twits. Look, homos don't fantasize about women. All they got on their minds is men."

"You know, when Fay and Em and this guy from Union went to see *Deep Throat*, I was really turned off. It worried me. I couldn't stand all those men. It seemed mostly about men. It was so gross. I didn't say anything, though."

"So what's your problem, man?"

"The thought of a man, normal man-woman sex. It just doesn't seem like a turn-on. I got to think about two women." Hugh was about to confess something not even Fay knew. How every time Emily went to visit her parents in Louisiana he would buy a few lesbian magazines, which would be thrown out, ten blocks away, the day before she returned. "It's almost compulsive with me, this idea. I get so turned on just by the thought that I—well . . . I don't know where it came from. Even when I was six, I remember seeing a picture in a museum, two women—"

"And you were hard as a rock. Big deal. Two women, sounds good to me."

"You mean . . . ?"

"Shit, yeah. See that broad over there—in the green tights? I bet she'd do it."

"You think she's a lesbian?"

"Who cares? Lots of girls like girls. Doesn't mean they're dykes."

"What?"

"You don't know nothing, do you, boy? Just like Clara. She caught me once with my arm around this girl I'd just met. We were walking down the street, and like Clara freaks. She knows I love her, but she still freaks out. How can I explain to her about a man's chemistry. He's got to have some release, right? So how am I supposed to function when I can get to her about once a week? These girls are just release, nothing else. By the way, don't you go telling her I was here again. I'll bust you wide open."

"You know, Kant says using another person as a means, not an end in himself, that's the worst sin."

"What does this Kant know? I'm supposed to marry my dentist? Course I'm using him. We're all using each other all the time."

"I'm not using you."

"Sure you are. You're getting a big kick out of me. You want to know why?" F.X. leaned over and pulled Hugh to him by the collar. "Because, son, I'm the only person in your life now who's not full of shit. They've been shoving shit down your throat for so long, you can't even tell the difference, can you? Divinity school. Just listen to that. If that's not crapola, I don't know what is. And what have you learned, son? Go ahead, tell me. I want to hear."

Hugh couldn't answer. It was the first time Hugh felt himself being truly honest, when he couldn't answer F.X. Maybe that was why, as Emily's hands began to massage lower, the small of his back, and then reached inside his jeans, he could say, "No."

"What?"

"Don't, Em."

"What's wrong?"

"I don't want to fool around now."

"Fine. I really don't have time anyway. I should be at rehearsal."

"I'm sorry."

"It's all right. Really. I'm late."

The day before previews began for Emily's play, Clara moved out. She had found a studio for $175 a month six blocks from Lucas.

Emily dropped by occasionally on her way to the theater in the East Village. She missed Clara's cooking, her housekeeping, but she realized that it was better for Clara to be on her own. Clara told her that she had started dating some men, and that her old agent, the one before Herb Rice, had been talking her up at "My Life to Live." There was a good chance that the writers might resurrect Kimberly. They were caught in a plot hole with Dr. Kensington, the easiest solution being that Kimberly had been given an antidote to the poison. I was clinically dead, Clara told Emily, saw this light and didn't want to come back to earth again. Emily said she would keep her fingers crossed.

Although Emily's part in *The Passion of Fred* was relatively small, it was her picture, along with the male lead's, that was used in all the advertisements. A rash of posters at midtown construction sites tested her ability to appear blasé as she walked past, particularly so when she was with Lettice, who didn't seem to notice. Emily had to lean over and pretend to adjust her shoe to give time for Lettice to look around. But even then the woman couldn't seem to focus on what was being heralded two inches from her nose. Nor did Lettice, who read the *Times* religiously every day, comment on the review that singled Emily out. "A remarkably intelligent performance by the newcomer, Emily St. George, lent a touch of authenticity to the otherwise strained and rancorous proceedings," Emily quoted to her parents over the phone, by heart. Mr. Brix made a comment about the St. George, but Mrs. Brix came through with flying colors by bursting into tears.

Hugh, in the meantime, was fired from the A&P. Lettice was privately urging Emily to get him to see a therapist. He had never raised his voice to his mother before, and yet twice in a single week he had shouted and slammed down the phone. Emily agreed that Hugh did seem to be a little more hostile these days, but she was firm in saying that it was only natural. After working so hard at Union, being something of a star, he could understandably feel bitter about not having his talents recognized by the world at large. Yes, it did worry her that he had turned down a perfectly good job at a small college in Minnesota. But hadn't he done it at least partly for her sake? He didn't seem to want to ruin her career at this point—at least, that was what he had told her.

"I wish there was something I could do for him," Emily was saying to Clara shortly after the play had closed. It had lasted only a week, but Emily had enough press clippings to make it all seem worthwhile.

"You know," Clara said, "I think men are strange. You never know what they're thinking."

"That's because they're out of touch with their feelings. Men are brought up that way. My father always thinks it's a sign of weakness to say what he really feels. And I can see it happening to my little brother. I wrote him the other day. I told him he ought to have the courage to cry when he feels like it. I'm so afraid he's going to end up just like my father."

They went on happily in this vein in Clara's dank and dismal apartment. None of the many feminine touches could disguise the fact that the building was falling apart. Clara herself, though, was thriving. Her complexion had cleared, and she was steadily losing weight. Emily asked her about the men she was dating, and found out there was a new one who worked for a Catholic charity.

"There should be something we can do," Emily agreed after Clara went on at considerable length about the number of starving children in the world, a fact discussed on every date with Mr. O'Malley.

"When you're aware of this, it makes your own problems seem impossibly frivolous. That's what Mr. O'Malley calls it, impossibly frivolous."

Emily thought it a little odd that her friend referred to her date this way, but apparently he was an older man. How much older Clara wouldn't say.

"Hugh with all his money—all the good he could do if he wanted."

"Right now he doesn't have much at all," Emily reminded her.

"Well, I mean, he's not far from thirty. Isn't that when he gets everything? You know, Em, he should talk to Mr. O'Malley. I bet if he talked to him, he'd see how foolish it is to feel sorry for himself. That's one thing I'll never do again—ever. Feel sorry for myself. Mr. O'Malley made me realize that God has blessed me with everything I need. We have a duty to be thankful. To show our thanks by giving to each other."

Emily was beginning to feel uneasy about the creeping evangelism in Clara's voice, no doubt thanks to her new paramour. Trying to bring out a more personal note, Emily resorted to banality.

"What does he look like? I don't know."

"Well, is he tall, or what?"

"Just sort of average. He's not a material type of person at all. We don't bother about looks."

"How did you meet him?"

"Lucas introduced us."

It took a moment for Emily to digest this. "He did?"

"He and Lucas went to Trinity together. That's a Catholic college somewhere. He has one of his sons going there now."

"Mr. O'Malley does?"

"Yes, he has three sons, two daughters, and two adopted Korean girls, and something else, I think, from Africa. Maybe it's just an exchange student. Anyway, you can sympathize with his wife, all she has to put up with."

"He's married?"

"Of course."

"Clara, you're dating a—"

"They're sort of spiritual dates—not really dates, you see. Anyway, I've made up my mind. I'm going to give him Hugh's phone number. Is that all right?"

Emily was noncommittal. She was too busy trying to sort out what she had just heard.

"By the way," Clara said as Emily, who had just remembered a dental appointment, emerged from the bathroom with her umbrella, which had been drying in the tub. "Don't act funny when you go out."

"What?"

"You know, suspicious. Just try to be normal."

"Clara, what—"

"My apartment is being watched. Judy's hired someone. She suspects me and Lucas, so just act like nothing's wrong."

Once outside Emily could not help smiling at her own stupidity. She had believed for a while that Clara was really serious about meeting other men. As she walked toward Second Avenue, Emily felt eyes upon her, which was ridiculous since there were only a couple of schoolgirls in sight. Nevertheless, she did not like the feeling and was glad when she was finally out of the neighborhood.

seventeen

❧

Though it made no sense, Emily was happy. None of the parts she tried out for after the play had closed came through. Herb booked her a print ad for Winston cigarettes, but little else. Hugh was drinking too much, and coming in at odd hours. He refused to celebrate his twenty-ninth birthday because Rudolf Bultmann had just died. As for Lucas, he was getting more paranoid about being followed, and discouraged Emily's visits. Her father's secretary had accidentally started a small fire in his State Farm office, which, Mrs. Brix reported, made him moody and impossible to get along with. Lettice was attacked by her own corgi, who had to be put to sleep. Clara, through her former agent, landed a role in a movie with six weeks' location work in Morocco, and Mrs. Lewisham was almost run over by an M31 bus on her way to work. Yet Emily was happy.

She had discovered a park. The trees, few and fragile-looking, possibly an Oriental species, stood in redwood planters. There was no grass, and for all but a few minutes of the day, it seemed, neighboring office buildings blocked out the sun. Water poured gently down a wall of cleverly patterned brick, so that its constant flow created its own texture and, at times, if she looked steadily enough, seemed still, a crystal pulsing with the rationed light. A cart presided over by a man as short as herself offered amazingly good coffee, Twining and Fortnum & Mason teas, and irresistible cheese and almond croissants. He had Indian features, Mayan, she liked to imagine, and though she came often and sat long, there was never a smile of recognition. This she appreciated. She could sit nearby at one of the half dozen castiron tables and not fear an intrusion on her privacy.

It was here, in the moments between auditions, and some-times, most sweet of all, when she was playing hooky from a try-out for a deodorant or floor-wax commercial, that she revived. Prodded by the sight of a handful of burnished yellow leaves against a patch of sky, her memory stirred. And there she was again, in her girlish frills, intent on getting to the right building at Smith in time for her classics seminar. What anxiety, what loneliness. Why savor it now? It had been the most miserable time in her life. She had truly wished that she would be put out of her misery, die of some swift painless disease. Yet now she cherished this time, could not get enough of it. And so she would sit not far from the Mayan, lost in a new and peculiar tenderness, a compassion for the old self so wracked by doubt and fear. She was watching herself, yes. But from a distance. And for some reason, this made all the difference.

"I don't know quite how to explain it," she was saying to Hugh one evening after he had relayed a message from Herb Rice. Herb was mad as hell at her for missing an appointment he had set up with an important casting director. Hugh quoted, "I don't need any more flighty airheads on my list," or so Hugh claimed. It really didn't sound like something Herb would say. More like a way Hugh could conveniently get a dig at her. So she had felt compelled—even though some sixth sense told her no, don't— to explain herself.

"It's hard to describe what it was like before I met you, Hugh. I was so alone that I think, if it was morally right to kill oneself, I just might have."

Hugh glanced at his watch. His class in Queens began at five. He was teaching philosophy at a private college there, and comparative religion. It was a godsend that the position had opened up recently. Now they wouldn't have to move.

"Aren't you going to eat first, Hugh? No? Well, anyway, I'm

not sure why, but all of a sudden this fall, the memory has been so strong. That pain I went through, the sense of being totally alone, somehow for the first time in my life, I'm not running away from it. I think it frightened me so much for so long that I buried it. But now, I don't know why, I feel I can face it. Embrace it somehow."

"What do you mean, totally alone?"

"That's the sense I had. Maybe it was because I was so far from home, the East was so different. I don't know. Maybe there's something just basically wrong with me."

"What do you mean, basically wrong?"

She had thrown this out half jokingly, not meaning for him to pick up on it. "Anyway, now somehow I've accepted this."

"What? That you're totally alone?"

"Yes— I mean, you know, underneath it all."

"You've been married to me for what, three, four years—"

"Five."

"Whatever, and you say you're totally alone?"

"I mean in the sense that we all feel misunderstood at times, isolated."

He was speaking in a mild tone of voice. Someone who didn't understand English would think he was consoling her. She felt, though, an obstinate antagonism, almost a bullying.

"Well?"

"I'd rather not talk about it now, Hugh. You're obviously upset about something else, and you're going to be late for class."

"It's just like you, you know, to start something and then leave it hanging. Like your acting. I mean, does this mean that acting was all a whim, that you're not really serious about it? You're going to start cutting auditions like some sophomoric . . . " He smiled in a way that any woman not knowing him would find cute and sexy.

"Hugh, please, don't."

"Don't what? Here I have to take a job with students who barely know how to read, all so you can be a star. Then what? Then when you get your way, you start goofing off."

"Please don't say 'my way.' I would have gone anywhere you wanted."

"That's easy to say now. But boy, if I had taken that job in Minnesota, you better believe, that would be it. Finito."

Finito was not one of Hugh's words. Neither was the way he was sitting, this was not Hugh, with one leg draped over the arm of the sofa.

"I would have come with you. My career doesn't mean as much as this."

"This? I thought you were totally alone. What does 'this' mean? Sounds like you were trying to tell me that the reason you got married was just to cover up your loneliness, to try to run away from it."

"That's not what I said."

"If you still feel so lonely, then what's 'this' all about?"

"I was *remembering* being lonely, there's a difference."

"The good old days, huh, before you got trapped in 'this.' "

Emily grabbed the bag of cheese curls and hurled them across Mrs. Peterson's living room. "Fine! Maybe you're right. Maybe there was something decent and honest then."

She had done it again. It was amazing how he could manage to make her look like the heavy. Getting up off the couch, straightening his tie, putting on his jacket, he had the air of a patient martyr. And she had the most insane urge to apologize. But she wouldn't this time. If she had a shred of self-respect, she wouldn't.

"Hugh, I'm sorry."

"It's all right," he said stoically, as he opened the door. Not once, of course, had he raised his voice.

"What time will you be home?"

"I don't know."

"Should I heat up those leftovers?"

"I'll grab something on the way. 'Night."

While Clara was in Morocco, Emily found herself spending more time with a woman she had known since the NyQuil commercial, a struggling actress who made a good living on the side importing crocodile hides from Singapore. Emily did not exactly consider her a friend, since Sidney could only be construed in the plural. Never, it seemed, had Sidney spent a moment alone. Eating, shopping, sleeping, these were all group activities. She even had a phone in her bathroom, a special shock-proof installation. To her surprise, Emily soon discovered that many of Sidney's satellites were not only intelligent and talented, but also fun to be with. She felt slightly ashamed of herself for having passed judgment on them earlier, as being vapid and vain, before she had ever really gotten to know Sidney. It also made her wonder about all the dogged devotion she had expended on Lucas over the years. With Sidney and her friends, Emily never had to drag herself home feeling defensive, vaguely anxious. These people were straightforward, outspoken, and had no trouble laughing at their own foibles. And the fact that they didn't pair off, that they seemed to hang around in an odd, constantly changing assortment of male and female, was such a refreshing change for Emily. She felt that she had finally graduated from the strained, ludicrous conventions of a Doris Day film to a Bertolucci.

The benefits to her own marriage went without saying. It had been unfair of her to expect Hugh to accept Lucas as her primary friend all this time, particularly since he didn't seem all that enchanted with Lucas himself. Safety in numbers applied here as well. She had always rationed herself with Lucas, making sure that Hugh got the lion's share of time. But now that sub rosa jealousy was no longer a factor, she could spend more time away from Hugh with a clear conscience. She was no longer relying on him for the entertainment and amusement that only friends could supply. Perhaps it was wrong, after all, to blur the boundaries between husband and friend. There must be a reason, in the accumulated wisdom of the ages, why there were two separate and distinct words with no root in common.

Aside from being fun, Sidney's friends really knew the business inside out. Emily felt she must have been crazy to have held herself aloof for so long. Milly's father knew Dick Van Dyke, and Milly herself had been in A Chorus Line before she broke her ankle. Sam had a speaking part in Jaws, and Faye Dunaway was reading a script Lisa had just written. Lisa had even talked to Dunaway on the phone. Cheryl had been on "The Jeffersons" twice and once on "Barney Miller." There was someone who was always talking about David Niven as if he had been a good friend; and Molly's stepmother was in Suzy's column one day in a list that included Dina Merrill and Gregory Peck's son. Of course, Emily was a little concerned about how much money she was spending on drinks and dinner with this crowd. But Hugh was finally earning something now. She had been pulling the weight for so long with so little help. It was time, maybe, that she enjoyed herself a bit.

Emily was surprised at how easy it was to be accepted. She had been in only one legitimate play, and none of them had seen *The Passion of Fred*. Yet they treated her as an equal. From the very beginning she frowned on four-letter words and refused to laugh at dirty jokes. One or two took offense at this, but in the main she was liked. Sidney, it must be admitted, did become exasperated with the way she dressed and one day took her on a tour of the shops with the best designer clothes. Of course, she knew Emily couldn't come close to affording any of them, but she wanted to implant an idea into her mind of the goal one should strive for. With this accomplished, she then showed Emily how best to approximate these ideals with minor alterations on mass-market wares. Her hair came in for the same treatment, though Emily opted for the most conservative cut allowed by Lisa, the resident expert.

After four years of illegal subletting, Emily was feeling brave enough to invite more than a couple of people over to the apartment. When Hugh was at a faculty meeting or grading papers at his office in Queens, Sidney would fill the house until it overflowed into the garden. Emily felt it her duty to explain to as many people as possible that the place was far more elegant than anything she could afford, but since no one really listened to what she was saying, or wrote it off to false modesty, people just assumed she was disguising her success. More than once Mrs. Powys complained of the noise in the garden keeping her up, but considering all the times Mrs. Powys had sung drunkenly in the stairwell over the years, Emily did nothing more than caution the guests from time to time. If Hugh wandered in, he would sometimes find someone to talk to. If not, there was a bar he liked a few blocks away. Once F.X. showed up, with some business associates of Sidney's, but Emily barely had a chance to talk to him. He was zeroing in on Lisa. Lisa liked girls, of course, but for some reason she was leading him on. With a shrug Emily made her way into the bedroom.

"Someone said you're married," a stunning young woman

remarked as she repaired her face at Hugh's desk. She had sharp, hawkish features, but with her height, her dazzling outfit, her manner, she was almost beautiful.

"Yes, I am," Emily said as Sidney walked through the French doors with some caviar Molly had stolen from her stepmother. "Sid, you think you can get that woman out there to stop screaming?"

"What?" she asked as Emily trailed after her.

" . . . unpardonable," the belle laide was saying to herself when Emily returned from the garden.

"Uh, please be careful. Try not to get any powder on my husband's papers there."

"Your husband? Are you the one that's married? I was just talking to someone who said they were married."

"You mean like a minute ago? That was me, I believe."

"Oh, what a coincidence."

Only later, after going out yet again to calm the screaming guest—she was laughing, actually, not screaming—did Emily find out that the woman at Hugh's desk was the wife of Lange Chapman. Sidney herself told Emily this, though Emily found it hard to believe. How could Else Chapman have ended up in Emily's apartment?

"Who's Else Chapman?" Clara asked on her return from Morocco later that same week.

"You never heard of her? Come on. Her husband produces all those hundred-million-dollar epics. And she's in the papers all the time. The society columns. You must have heard of her."

"I'm sorry."

How Clara could be so dense worried Emily. Whatever the reason, it was certainly making it hard to tell her story. "Look, she's one of those people that hobnobs with Cary Grant and Lauren Bacall. Everyone knows her. And didn't you read how she's threatened to sue the woman who wrote, oh what's it, that novel, *Sins of Rachel and Eve?* Sidney swears that was her sitting right at Hugh's desk."

"Why didn't you ask her yourself?"

"She was only here a minute—sort of breezed in and out."

Both women glanced through the French doors at the desk. Wonder still didn't register in Clara's eyes, which seemed puffy from jet lag. She had called the minute she had gotten in from the airport and been invited over to tea.

"She was getting powder and lip gloss all over Hugh's things. I told her to please be careful, but she was so zonked she didn't know what she was doing. It's really sad when you see these people up close. I'm sure she's some sort of addict. And you can literally feel this vacuum where their mind should be. It's like a black hole that sucks you in, this horrible loneliness and insecurity. Imagine how mixed up and insecure you must be to end up at a party at my house. Sidney told me people she hasn't heard from in years are calling her now, trying to get invited over here."

"Why?"

Emily asked herself for patience. "Because *she* was here—Else."

"Why was she here?"

"That's what we're all trying to figure out. Sidney thinks it's a combination of someone hearing I wasn't really St. George, that I disguised the fact I was a Vanderbilt, and that Molly's mother was giving the party instead of Molly. See, Molly's mother—stepmother, actually—is also named Molly."

"So?"

"Molly's mother is this big society dame and . . . Oh, Clara, I don't know. You're not any fun."

"I'm sorry. I'm so tired. And Em, you have no idea what I went through there. It was a nightmare."

Emily perked up. She had been prepared for a laborious account of how wonderful Morocco was, which was why she had tried to squeeze her story in first. "Hey, here you are making a film in one of the most exotic countries in the world, and you're complaining? I would have given anything to be in your shoes. As a matter of fact, I was so depressed when I heard you were going that I nearly cut my wrists."

"Oh, stop. I don't believe a word you say anymore." Clara made a face at her, and they both giggled. "It was supposed to be a horror film, you know. So what does that stupid cretin do, Ken? He's the director. He gets these poor Berbers to put on masks that he literally bought at the five-and-dime. I'm not kidding. You could see the strings in the back of their heads. We all nearly died looking at dailies. This isn't supposed to be a comedy, you know. And the way he treated them, like dirt. He hated me, too, right from the beginning. All he did was criticize my hair and makeup—in front of the entire crew. They'd crack up laughing when he'd make a comment about my mascara, this cheap junk that kept on running." Clara's eyes filled with tears. "The worst part was this one child. We were shooting at this abandoned sugar mill just outside Marrakech, right in the middle of nowhere. People lived there, squatters. No electricity, no nothing. Ken and the crew just barged right in and roped them off the set, actually built a fence so they wouldn't get in the way."

"Careful, your saucer."

Clara moved it away from the edge of the table. "This one little boy, he was so tiny and cute. He wore the same teeshirt every day, it said Adidas, and he would follow me around and peek out from behind the walls. I fell in love with him, Em. I'm not kidding. I've never seen such a smile in all my life. His eyes, his face . . . it was just heavenly: I cried every night thinking about him. It was so cold, and Ken wouldn't let me give him any money. He was afraid the boy would crawl under the fence during my takes. But I gave the boy every cent I had anyway—and then Ken wouldn't let me have my per diem because someone told him what I'd done and we had this awful fight, Ken and me. He called me a bleeding heart and said I'd never work in pictures again— and I said that was fine with me."

"He sounds like a monster."

"He was. Just horrible. When I said I'd wire home for money, he took my passport away. I was a prisoner, really. I was watched all the time by one of Ken's cronies. It got so that I was afraid to even wave to the little boy. I was afraid Ken would somehow punish him for getting too close to me. Then I'd go back to the hotel where there were all these fancy French tourists. I got to hate them so much, the tourists. And at night I'd dream about this horrible bird. I woke up screaming once and I was so embarrassed 'cause Midge and Ellen, they're in wardrobe, they shared the room with me, and I thought they would think I was crazy. But I couldn't help it. After Ken shot him, he kept coming back in my mind."

"Shot who?"

"The bird. See, at the sugar mill, this stork had made his nest high up on this chimney thing. He made a terrible loud clacking sound that was ruining all our takes. So Ken, he gets a gun and that's it. I couldn't believe he'd done it, and right in front of Hassad."

"The little boy?"

Clara nodded, tears running down her cheeks. "Hassad wouldn't look at me after that. He must have stayed in his hut, or something. That was the last I saw of him."

Emily, feeling silly and ashamed of herself, reached out and took her friend's hand. "Listen, Clara. I've got an idea."

"What? Don't tell me—" She blew her nose. "Don't tell me to sue him and all that. I can't bear the thought of ever seeing Ken again, not even in court. I just want to forget the whole thing as quick as possible."

"No, it's not that. I mean you really should sue him. Your rights were violated. And if you want help finding a lawyer—"

"Please, stop."

"All right, but listen. Sidney's ex-husband is coming to town next week. She's having him to dinner and—"

"Oh, Em, please. No more dates. I can't deal with that now."

"This isn't dates. I'm talking professional stuff. Murray is a director. He's done a lot of sitcoms and is sort of a big deal in L.A. And now there's this pilot, and Sidney thinks I should meet him, just in case. You never know."

"Well, you should."

"You, too. I want you to come."

"Oh, Em."

"Look, Clara, you got to start mixing and mingling. You can't expect auditions alone to get you anywhere."

"But what about you?"

"Don't worry about that. If he likes you, fine. We're so different, we can't be in competition. Look, do you think I like all this social stuff? It's totally against my nature. I find it gross. But Clara, people like you and me, we could be dragging ourselves from one try-out to the next until we're eighty and never get anywhere. We both owe it to ourselves to give our very best effort. I've been so frustrated after *Fred*, you have no idea. I thought that here, finally, things were headed in the right direction. And then nothing. It's back to square one. Herb even seems annoyed when I call. And I used to be his star client." Emily was warming her hands on the teapot. It had gotten much chillier since they had gone out to the garden. "I feel I'm so close to being recognized. And I just can't bear the thought of coming so far and then, for want of that little extra shove, giving up. Hugh agrees with me. You ought to see what he puts up with, all these people floating around here. But he knows what it takes in this world. See, you and me, Clara, we don't have that killer instinct. We were raised to think that being good would be enough. Girls are polite, they stay in their places, they're neat—but that ain't the way the world works."

"Oh, Em, please. I know you're right. But I can't, I just can't."

"Now come on. You're going to that dinner, hear?"

"If I meet another Ken, I'll die."

"Sid says Murray is really nice."

"I don't care. I think I'll hate him anyway."

"Good, hate him. But if he gives you a job, take it."

"Listen, I don't even want to be an actress anymore. The whole thing is a nightmare."

"So you're going to give up after one bad experience?"

It took some doing, but Clara finally caved in. She would go to dinner with Murray. Emily packed her off home to get some rest, and then called Sidney.

"You're joking," was Sidney's reaction. She could not believe Emily had gone ahead and invited someone without telling her first. Her relationship to Murray, Sidney explained, was extremely delicate. She had to be so careful about appearing to use him. She had invited Emily only because she knew Emily was the most discreet friend she had. And Murray had once lectured at Smith, which gave them something in common. To throw in someone like Clara Tilman— Well, Clara was nice, of course, but she was a little obvious. It was out of the question.

After a moment's thought, Emily called Clara back. Not wanting to hurt her friend's feelings, she explained that after giving the matter more consideration, she had decided that maybe it was better if Clara didn't come. "You're right about socializing. It never really got anyone anywhere. You're tired and need a break from all this."

"No, Em, you don't have to baby me. I know you're right. I can't give up now. I've got to keep on fighting."

"Yes, of course, but this dinner, it's stupid. I wish I didn't have to go myself. I was just dragging you along so I'd have someone to talk to."

"What? You have Sid."

"Oh, I know. But she'll be so involved with Murray, I'll just be a third wheel."

For a second time that day Emily was able to convince Clara of the reasonableness of her own position. So when on the very day of the dinner, two hours, in fact, before she was supposed to meet Sid and Murray at Elaine's, Sid called, Emily was not overjoyed at Sid's good news.

"Listen, I've had a guilty conscience about your friend. If you really want her to come, then tell her it's O.K."

"No, it's all right, Sid. She doesn't want to come."

"Oh, so now she doesn't want to come."

"Well, you said yourself—"

"Here I've gone to all this trouble of getting her invited. I made a doormat of myself with Murray, told him that Clara was this real good friend of mine so he'd let her come, and now she's too good for us?"

"But—"

"Listen, Em, all I can say is she better be there. If you consider me a friend . . ."

Under normal circumstances Emily was not to be bullied by veiled threats. But the truth of the matter was that Sid had gone out of her way to be nice to Clara. If the timing was off, well, the world wasn't perfect. And Emily really wanted to help Clara out. It did seem as if Clara had suffered a lot in Morocco, and the first check the producers had sent, for $4,500, had bounced. So, taking a few deep breaths to ward off a mild hysteria, Emily phoned her friend.

"Oh, that's sweet. But I'm sorry, Em. I've got a date with Mr. O'Malley tonight. We're going to hear Cardinal Cooke."

"Listen, this is a chance of a lifetime. Do you realize who Murray is? You don't get a chance like this every day. Meet us at Elaine's at nine. It's on Eighty-something and Second, you know."

"I can't. I already promised Mr. O'Malley."

"Look, Clara, don't be stupid."

"Em, please."

"I'm sorry, but all this running around with married men, I don't care how spiritual it is. It's very tacky."

"Em, you don't know Mr. O'Malley. No one could be nicer. Even Hugh says so."

Emily did not like to be reminded that Hugh was doing volunteer work at a Boys Club, thanks to Mr. O'Malley. Clara had introduced them before she went away to Morocco, and Hugh, to Emily's surprise, had found him interesting and persuasive.

"I'm sure Mr. O'Malley is wonderful. But he's a beard, all the same. You ought to have more pride, Clara."

"He's not a beard."

"He is, and you know it. And don't think that Judy doesn't know it, too. She's not a dope."

"Have you been talking to her?"

"She called me the other day. I didn't tell you this because I didn't want to upset you. But she screamed at me and called me a pimp and a beard." The hysteria, which had seemed so far away at the beginning of the call, now seemed to be marching closer, the drumbeat getting louder and louder.

"Oh, Em, no."

"You don't know what I've gone through for you. Judy reduced me to tears. I was in shock for days. You have no idea what it feels like to be called those things. Especially when you're completely innocent."

"Well, then you must know how Mr. O'Malley feels."

"Listen, Clara, if you value our friendship one bit, you'll forget about Mr. O'Malley and his precious Cardinal Cooke and get yourself over to Elaine's. I'm getting tired of laying myself down on the line for you and then have you walk all over me."

"But—"

"To tell you the truth, Sid didn't want you at first, but then, well . . . Oh, I don't know, just come."

"Why should I come if she doesn't want me?"

"Because if you don't I'll never speak to you again. Goodbye."

eighteen

e⁓

Dinner at Elaine's was destined to join those few choice memories that, try as she might, Emily would never forget. Clara had indeed shown up but, without warning Emily, she had brought along her Mr. O'Malley. Being inhabitants of different universes, Mr. O'Malley and Murray had trouble communicating at first. Neither one knew where to begin. So after a few awkward moments, they gave up entirely and talked only to the women. Smiling bravely through it all, Emily concealed her anxiety that Mr. O'Malley was going to ask one of the celebrities at a nearby table for an autograph. But when Florence Henderson stopped on her way out to chat with Murray, Mr. O'Malley displayed the utmost calm. It turned out, as Clara later revealed to Emily, that Mr. O'Malley had never heard of "The Brady Bunch."

Emily was duly punished for two weeks, during which Sidney would not return her calls. Emily attempted to explain to Sidney's answering service that Mr. O'Malley was a complete surprise to her, too. But the prickly man at the service refused to repeat the message back to her; Emily was sure that by the time it got to Sidney it was completely garbled. Clara, though she was the cause of all the trouble, did not share Emily's anxiety. She simply could not grasp what was so awful about never speaking to Sidney again.

"She's just a failed actress. And the way she talks, she ought to have her mouth washed out with soap."

"It doesn't mean anything. That's the way those people talk. Sidney's really very sensitive. And nice." Seeing that Clara was still unrepentant, Emily could not help adding, "After all the trouble she went through for you, I can't believe you invited that man along. Don't you understand how carefully planned these things have to be?"

"I do now. Every time she said one of those four-letter words, I nearly died of embarrassment."

"Come off it. You're saying the crew in Morocco never sullied your ears?"

"I was embarrassed for Mr. O'Malley, not me. He told me afterward that it was a tragedy I had to associate with people like that."

"Well, you seemed to be enjoying yourself all right."

"I can't help it if Murray only talked to me."

Clara had actually turned a few heads when she had walked in, which was saying a lot in such a place. Emily had forgotten how good her friend could look when she put her mind to it. This, of course, did not help matters with Sidney. True beauty was one thing Sidney, who was very attractive, would never forgive in a woman. Nevertheless, her heart was not of stone. After two weeks she did call Emily, and at the conclusion of a marathon conversation, during which Emily had to change ears, the friendship was patched up.

"It just teaches me something I've always known," Sidney concluded. "Whenever you try to help someone, you ought to first go have your head examined."

Though Hugh made fun of Sidney, sometimes cruelly and unjustly, Sidney never spoke of him with anything but the greatest respect. She was much impressed that Emily had not only managed to land him, but to hold onto him all this time. She herself had only lasted eighteen months with Murray—and those were eighteen months of complete and total abnegation, as she put it. Emily was inclined to downplay the accomplishment, which had never seemed like much of an achievement before. Nevertheless, Sidney's praise made her begin to wonder just how she *had* managed to hold onto him. "It's a matter of just the opposite," she would say to Sidney, "of *not* holding on. The minute a man feels you're holding on, that's when he wants to run. I've told you about Lucas, haven't I? Well, there's a case in point."

With this wisdom in mind, Emily began to worry that she was becoming a little possessive of Hugh when she wondered aloud why he spent so much time at his office.

"I suppose I ought to grade papers here, with Sidney and her gang all over the place?"

"It's only been a couple of nights. Besides, Sidney likes you a lot. I wish you'd come out to dinner with us some night."

"I associate with enough lame-brains at work."

"Sidney went to Wellesley."

"Well, I guess that shuts me up."

"Look, if it wasn't for Sid, I wouldn't be auditioning for this Jack Nicholson film. Herb didn't even know about it."

"I thought it was Lisa who set it up."

"Well, Sid was the one who introduced me to Lisa. And she rode Lisa on it, made sure she didn't forget to set up an appointment with the casting director. They want an unknown, and everyone says I'm perfect for the part. Can you imagine what this could mean to me, if I got it?"

Hugh glanced over at her from the bed. It was unlike her to sound so excited, almost feverish. He knew that she had been having a rough time lately, that she was more discouraged than she let on. Nothing seemed to be working out, as far as auditions went.

"It'd be great, Em."

Working intently on cleaning out all the hair from her brush, every last strand, she said, "Not only that, Sid made her invite me to Montauk this weekend. One of the producers is going to be there, at Lisa's. Sid thinks it'll be good for me to meet her. Whatever, it can't hurt."

Hugh looked puzzled. He had just spoken to Lisa that morning, and they had made plans to have dinner on Saturday. Emily was usually out on Saturdays with Sidney, so he figured he would be free.

"What's wrong?"

"Nothing. It just seems odd to go to Montauk when it's this cold."

"Well, it might be nice without all the tourists and stuff." She peered hard at her brush. "I wonder if I'm losing all my hair. I can't believe how much . . ."

While Emily muttered to herself, Hugh pondered the situation. F.X. was the one who had told him that Lisa was—as F.X. put it—a switch-hitter. Of course, any girl who turned F.X. down was suspected of this, but Hugh had also heard Sidney say something about Lisa once having had a female lover. Normally, he wouldn't have had anything to do with Sidney and her friends, but when he found himself coming home late one evening, just as Lisa was leaving his apartment, it seemed almost natural that he should ask her to get a cup of coffee with him around the corner. Detached from the herd she seemed an altogether different person—sharp, independent, responsible. He had asked her about her screenplays and was impressed by the extent of her knowledge, not just of films, but of literature and history as well. It was Lisa herself who had brought up her friend Nicky, a Jungian analyst in the Bronx. Lisa never came right out and said they were lovers, but he gathered as much. They made plans to have lunch together, the three of them. But then at the last minute Nicky couldn't make it. Hugh didn't give up, even though Lisa was busy and hard to pin down. He began to live on fantasies of the three of them at a marvelous dinner, the wine freeing them from their inhibitions, their attraction for each other so obvious that nothing had to be said, Lisa simply assuming he was coming home with them. Whether this was actually going to happen or not, Hugh knew that someday he was going to have to make love to two women. He was obsessed by this thought, which, try as he might, would simply not go away. More and more time was taken up by these daydreams. He even had magazines locked in his desk in Queens. It was shameful, he knew. But it seemed the only solution was to find someone, some two, and do it. That was bound to get it out of his system. After all, reality was always a disappointment. He would probably discover that it wasn't all it was cracked up to be in his own mind. Perhaps it would become as humdrum as normal intercourse. Then he could leave off with this fantasy and be a better husband to Emily.

"Is it really nice out there?"

"Montauk? That's what Sid says." Emily glanced over at him.

"Maybe I'll come with you."

"What?"

"I'm in a rut, grading papers all day, trying to write. Might do me good to get away for the weekend."

Emily crawled into bed beside him. "Now listen, honey. I've just recovered from one horrible mess, where I tried to invite someone along. I'd love for you to come myself, but Lisa, I don't know her that well. Sidney's sort of twisting her arm as it is, with me. If I suddenly spring another guest on her . . ."

"She knows me. I'm sure she won't mind."

"Some other time, huh? Not this weekend, please. Lisa scares me, I have to admit. She's so—"

"Direct?"

"That's one way of putting it."

Emily could not fall asleep right away. Maybe she should see if Hugh could come with her. After all, it was nice that he was finally expressing an interest in seeing Sidney and her friends. How many times had Sidney actually come right out and warned her about letting him spend so much time on his own? Of course, Emily had no doubts at all about his being unfaithful. Maybe, though, it wasn't such a good idea for them to go such separate ways. She should try to involve him in her work. And she should make more of an effort to sound interested in his classes and the articles he was writing.

Turning over quietly, so as not to disturb him, she resolved to ask Sidney if he could come along with her.

Emily had misunderstood. Lisa herself wasn't going to be in Montauk that weekend. She was just letting the producer use the house as a retreat for a couple of weeks. But Sidney promised that she herself would be there for dinner. She would be visiting friends in Sag Harbor and would drive over in plenty of time. Yes, she would be there before Emily arrived. But no, under these circumstances, it probably wouldn't be a good idea for Hugh to come out, too. Emily pleaded, though, until Sidney caved in. "I know I shouldn't say yes. It's not my house, after all. But O.K., Em. I'll tell them Hugh's coming."

Hugh did not seem happy with the good news. "I really can't go, Em. I already promised Lisa I'd have dinner with her here. She's catching the red-eye, so I thought I'd have her over before she goes. I'm going to try making garlic chicken for her and Nicky."

"Who's Nicky?"

"A friend of hers."

"Well, this is just great. Here I've gotten myself into trouble again with Sidney. She's going to give me another blasting when I tell her you're not coming." Emily did not press the matter, though. It was probably better that Hugh didn't tag along. Nevertheless, she was annoyed that he had made such a big deal of wanting to get away for the weekend.

"I didn't make a big deal about it. I just said, hypothetically, it might be nice."

"You're getting as bad as the others, Hugh. I'm tired of being the only reliable person I know."

A little befuddled, Emily set out on her journey. Sidney had advised her to take the Jitney, but she had heard from someone—maybe it was the thin guy who sat behind her in the soap-opera class—that the Jitney only went as far as East Hampton. Knowing a cab from there to Montauk would be exorbitant, Emily arrived at Penn Station in plenty of time for the train. In fact, in far too much time. Anxious that she might miss it, she ended up wandering for what seemed hours in the dismal lower level for the Long Island trains. There didn't seem to be anywhere to sit, and she felt funny perusing magazines since a large section of all the newsstands was given over to pornography and comic books. And the Indian vendors would eye her, making her feel that she was loitering with intent.

It was a relief to finally be off. She attempted to while the time away with a *New York Review of Books*, but the vibrating coach made the fine print a chore. In Jamaica, after a twenty-minute wait on the platform, she changed to a much older train with quaint brown cars and worn plush seats. Instead of commuting businessmen, she was now treated to an almost empty coach with a Native American family as the only other passengers. Emily wondered if they belonged to the Long Island tribe that sold souvenirs by the roadside. Sidney often brought back artifacts on her excursions to Sag Harbor, and had pressed upon Emily and

Hugh some sort of carved, feathered god that now adorned their mantle.

Amazingly slow, the train would sometimes stop for no reason at all between stations. Babylon seemed hours from Jamaica, both towns equally unremarkable, save for their names. Objective correlatives, she supposed, were fast becoming extinct. At least Clara, despite Morocco turning out to be so horrible, had the satisfaction of knowing Marrakech was actually Marrakech.

It was dark, had turned dark without her realizing it. The dim yellow lights of the car were cozy, comforting as she caught glimpses through the begrimed narrow windows of a lone house or shed amid a field or scant woods. Her companions were speaking an unfamiliar language—or perhaps a mangled English. She caught a word every now and then, as one can in a Swedish film, and wondered if the portly woman was the mother or wife of the tender-looking man squeezed against the child. It surprised her that Long Island, even at this speed, was this long. She had always thought of it as barely visible on the map, something a classroom globe might leave out entirely. Suburbia was left behind now, and the puzzling halts gained a tinge of adventure.

The Indians got off in East Hampton, leaving Emily the sole occupant of the car. Then, almost four hours after a late departure from Penn Station, she found herself standing outside a deserted terminal as a few other passengers were driven off in waiting cars. Not surprisingly, Sidney was not there. She had probably got tired of waiting, the train was so late. A little annoyed that she had no dimes or nickels, just quarters, she called Lisa's from a pay phone at the station.

After fifteen rings a man finally picked up. He said she would probably be better off taking a cab rather than waiting for someone to come get her. Emily took the address and directions down on the back of a Con Ed bill she had fished from her purse, then with another quarter (that made thirty cents in charitable contributions to the phone company) she summoned a cab.

Huddled against a wall of the station, she realized she had not dressed warmly enough. Not only did it seem a good ten or fifteen degrees colder than in the city, but a wind blew strongly enough to set a scarecrow in motion across the highway. At least she assumed the spastic dance was a scarecrow's. As she waited, her eyes would stray to the distant, just barely visible, flapping arms that a bluish light atop a telephone pole almost illuminated. If it was actually a person, she hoped he was having fun. Allowing herself a frisson or two, she then clamped down on her imagination. But she was relieved when headlights appeared.

"I'd like to go to Barton Lane, please. If you take a left here and then go about a mile to—"

"Pardon me, lady, but you can sign off. I lived here all my life."

"Oh," Emily said, disconcerted by his rudeness. But as he pulled out onto the highway, she looked on the bright side. Better a rude, taciturn driver who knew the way than an inept, friendly one who would extract small talk. Leaning back against the ill-padded seat, she soon became lost in a minute examination of all the signs and portents concerning her recent audition for the Nicholson film. Now, had Ms. Somera indeed said "very good" or "very nice" when she had finished reading? "Very good" was much better than "very nice," but the important thing was the tone. She did seem to mean it, and she had looked straight into her eyes. Not only that, Ms. Somera herself had held open the door for her on her way out. Emily worried that she should have said something more personal about herself—maybe that she knew Latin—something that would make an impression. Yet deep down inside she could not worry too much about this. Because she had been too good for Ms. Somera to ignore. She just knew the woman would be calling Herb soon, any day.

With only ten minutes' preparation—the script was a closely guarded secret—she had given the reading of her life. When tears were called for, they came right on cue—not a hysterical flood but a carefully controlled up-welling. Something wonderful had happened to her at that moment: She had finally stopped acting; she simply was. The feeling was so intense that, by contrast, her normal, everyday life seemed as meretricious as a Vegas act. Never had she experienced such an ecstatic purity of intention. And with this simply being, not acting, she had discovered a sense of un-bounded love, almost as if the audience were already there, before her, in the dark.

Emily had often wondered why salmon made things so difficult for themselves, swimming upstream in an entirely unnatural

...nce of hers had taught her that such was life. ...ng required sacrifice, often the supreme sac-...in now of her gift; there was no longer any ...nd Clara had been right about her all along. ...t, to make it more than a possibility, she was ...im upstream against her very nature. Yes, it ...e was cultivating friends with a goal in mind. How much nicer it would be to be instantly recognized for what one really was. But the world was not made that way. One had to struggle against all odds to create that audience, to spawn that vast, dark love.

"Fifteen dollars!" Emily cried, rudely awakened from her reverie. "That's more than the train from New York cost."

"Listen, lady, I don't make the rates. This here's outside my zone. You way the hell out, you know. I don't normally come this far out."

Emily had only been dimly aware of the roads as she brooded in the back. They had come a good way, through piney attempts at woods, rough fields and bogs, and finally along a dirt lane. She looked with some misgivings at a small, plain cottage. Though Lisa was not rich, she had expected something a little more substantial.

"Can you wait for me till I make sure this is it?"

"This is it, sweetheart. I ain't got all night, you know. Some of us got a living to make."

Knowing it was highway robbery, Emily handed over the $15. There was probably a good lesson in this somewhere—but how nice it would be if life, just for once, stopped playing schoolmarm.

Waves crashed unseen as she knocked on the door of the cottage, which up close was weathered and pocked.

"Hi, I'm Emily St. George," she declared bravely to a man in a filthy undershirt, his belly showing. "Lisa's friend, reporting for duty."

With a pleasant smile he indicated with a beer can, "Over there," and gently shut the door on her.

The caretaker, Emily reasoned, as she followed a clay path through stunted, twisted pines, uphill. Emerging onto a bluff, she exclaimed as the wind whipped her skirt about her waist. The stars here seemed swollen, throbbing, ready to be plucked. Freezing, she nevertheless lingered, savoring the glorious sky. Never had she experienced such wilderness, the waves sending up a drenching spray from the boulders twenty, thirty feet below. With arms outstretched, her head upturned, forgetting herself entirely, the dreary task before her, she exulted like a child, until it suddenly occurred to her that someone in the cottage not far off might see her and think her mad, dancing around like that.

It was hardly bigger than the caretaker's, but better preserved. Emily touched her hair before knocking and was dismayed at how wet it had gotten. Fifty dollars she had spent at the salon that afternoon, a fortune!

"Hi, I'm Emily St. George."

"Can I help you?"

"I'm Lisa's friend. She—"

"Lisa's on her way to the Coast, I'm sorry. I'll tell her you came by, if you want."

"No, you see, I'm supposed to— Is Sidney here?"

"Please, don't mention *her* to me on an empty stomach."

Emily managed a wry smile. "Can you tell her I'm here?"

"She hasn't shown up yet," the woman said, walking off into the kitchen in bare feet.

Emily stood uncertainly at the door until a man sitting at a dinette table called out, "Hey, will someone shut the goddam door?"

This was her invitation. She walked in, trying to make her overnight bag as inconspicuous as possible. Five or six people sat around the dinette with drinks, both men and women in jeans and flannel or denim shirts. Emily had been led to believe it was going to be something much more formal. After all, Sidney had told her she was wearing her Halston. So here she was duded up with long earrings, a cream silk blouse, and a Chanel skirt in mint condition she had bought secondhand at a Lenox Hill Settlement House auction. Death would have been a blessing at that moment. No one bothered to even look her way as she stood poised against the sink, a few feet from the dinette. No one noticed that she laughed at the appropriate moments in the conversation. No one responded to a question or two she inserted in the blank spots. She tried to look interested in what they were saying, then she tried to look, like them, bored. Surreptitiously she removed one earring, then the other. There was a lemon on the counter. She began peeling it.

In desperation she wandered into the next room, where she found a phone. She would have to call a cab—Lord, please not the same man—and ask to be taken to a motel. It was impossible to remain here another moment. If only she had Sidney's number in Sag Harbor, what a blasting she would give her. Of course, Sidney had probably done this to punish her for not bringing Hugh. When Emily had told Sidney that Hugh couldn't make it after all, Sidney had gone into a swivet, though it had seemed at the time a very tame swivet for Sidney. So Emily had not really worried that much.

"Calling Sid?" a man asked, emerging from the kitchen. Emily was trying to get information, but hung up. "She'll be here any minute."

"You sure?"

"Just talked to her a few minutes ago. She called to say she ran out of gas and she was so worried about Emmie. She wanted to make sure Emmie was picked up at the station. You Emmie?"

"Emily." She had not noticed him at the table, although he could have had his back to her. In any case, she was grateful for his kindness. And she felt a little ashamed for judging Sidney so harshly.

"Can I get you a drink?"

"Yes, I'd love one. Any vodka?"

When he came back with the drink, and one for himself, she had had a chance to look around. Aside from the kitchen, this seemed to be the only other room, a nice-sized sitting room with knotty pine walls and an open-beam ceiling. "Where does Lisa sleep?"

"The bedrooms are in the other cottage."

"You mean where that awful man is?"

"Lisa lets a lot of people hang out. He's a producer, and actually, he's not so awful."

Emily went a little red. Hadn't Sidney told her the producer was a woman? But maybe Sidney had gotten her mixed up with the casting director.

"I didn't mean 'awful' awful. He seems sort of interesting."

"He is. He doesn't like to change clothes much. Not on vacation. And he doesn't use deodorant."

"Ever?"

"Just on vacation."

As he went on about him, volunteering snippets of information, some of it pretty intimate, it occurred to Emily that this man she was talking to could be more than a friend of his. There was something very gentle about the way he talked and moved his hands. This could indeed be his lover.

"Oh, he and Lange Chapman have known each other for ages," the man was saying as Emily took a second drink from him. They had moved closer to the fire, on a comfortable, worn leather couch.

"He does? By the way, did you tell me your name?"

"Gerard."

"Lange Chapman, huh. They seem to have such different tastes. I mean Chapman produces these blockbusters and—"

"Oh, Barney can't stand Chapman's work. And Chapman hasn't a clue about Barney. See, Barney's a real artist. He immerses himself totally in his work, oversees everything. And, of course, everyone quits on him, the writer, director, set designer, because he wants to do it all himself. You either love the guy or hate him. There's no in-between."

Emily gazed contentedly at the stonework of the fireplace. The pieces fit together with no visible mortar, and yet not one looked artificially shaped. It was amazing how one edge yielded naturally to the other.

"Of course, Chapman's wife is something else," she commented.

Gerard looked at her so that she got a new appreciation of his lovely green eyes. "You know her?"

"Please, she was getting lipstick and powder all over my roommate's books. I asked her if she wouldn't mind being a little more careful, but she was zonked, thought I was two different people."

"I can't understand why she's such a big deal these days. I've never heard her say one intelligent word. And she's not pretty."

"Well, she knows how to make the best of what she's been dealt."

"I suppose."

Emily was feeling so comfortable and warm that she made up her mind not to go out to dinner with the others. A man, lean, and tanned as a hide, had come into the room to inform them that they were all headed for the Yacht Club to chow down.

"I'll wait here for Sidney," she told Gerard.

"We've left her a note," the other man said. "Get your ass in gear, boy."

Though Gerard smiled, Emily could tell he didn't appreciate being spoken to in that way. "I'll wait here with her, Henry."

"Suit yourself."

Once they were alone Emily found her heart fluttering in a silly, adolescent way. Gerard was growing on her. The more he talked, the more attractive he seemed. Not that he said anything that wise or amusing, but his blithe, easy manner was such a relief after all the undercurrents she had endured with Hugh over the years. Apparently, men did not have to be maelstroms of discontent, brooding, like Hugh and Lucas, over their fate. Gerard seemed so perfectly at ease with himself. And he had such wonderful black hair and olive skin. It was a shame he was probably gay. He would make someone such a good husband.

"Another drink?"

"I better not."

"Come on."

"Oh, all right. Say, Gerard, why don't you ask Barney to join us? He's not going to eat with them, is he?"

"I'll see."

Emily slipped off her shoes, which were damp. She wished there was a bedroom so she could change into something more suitable—and dry. She had brought along some slacks in her overnight. In any case, damp or not, she congratulated herself for sticking it out. How nice it would be, just the three of them, alone. She almost wished Sidney wouldn't show up at all.

nineteen

❧

The sledgehammer crashed into the wall with a satisfying thud.

"Is this legal? Are you allowed to do this?"

Lucas took a moment to catch his breath. "Who cares? I'm doing it."

Sweat streaked the plaster dust coating his face and bare arms. Emily realized this was not the most opportune moment for a visit, but she had little choice. She must talk to someone.

"You look beat, Lucas. Come on, take a break."

"All right."

For good measure he took another swing at the wall separating his bedroom from the bathroom. The hole was large enough for Emily to squeeze through, but hardly enough for him.

After washing up at the kitchen sink, he joined her in the living room. Emily knew from Clara that Lucas was losing heart. Judy was not letting him go without a tremendous battle. Not only did he have to contend with private investigators, his friends—Emily included—being called as witnesses, but now Judy was threatening to kill herself. This, Clara believed, was what was making him waver. He had had two meetings with Judy's psychiatrist, who had not been altogether reassuring. Even though most real suicides are not so dramatic about their intentions, there was no knowing for sure. Lucas, of course, took full responsibility for this. He had finally admitted to Judy that he was deeply in love with Clara. As long as he had pretended not to be, Judy could battle with some dignity and hope. The truth, apparently, was too much for her, as he had feared all along.

"So you go back to her, Lucas. What's that going to be like now?" Emily said as gently as possible as she poured him another cup of coffee. Even she realized a reconciliation was impossible between them, much as she had once hoped for one.

"That's not the point. I know I'll never be able to live with Judy again, not after all this. It's Clara. How can I ever marry her now? I know it'll kill Judy, if I marry again."

"No one says you have to get married."

"Clara's got her heart set on it."

"But that's not for her to decide."

"I promised her. How can I go back on my promise? And besides, she told me if we don't get married, that's it. She won't ever sleep with me again. She says she's tired of feeling wrong about sex, and I can't blame her. I feel the same way myself. There's no reason in the world why Clara and I should be made to feel like criminals, two people who love each other the way we do."

Emily had an answer for every one of his statements, but kept them to herself. How easy it was to see a friend's blind spots. It made her wonder if her own were as blatant—and if friends should indulge one another so much, fearful of seeming moralistic. She, at least, had good enough reason to keep her own mouth shut. Probably never again would she ever be able to say anything to anyone.

As Lucas unburdened himself of his doubts, claiming at one point that he had made up his mind he would never have sex again, Emily found herself envying him his space. Though the apartment was narrow and mean, it was his own. Lately, she realized that she had been hoping that Mrs. Powys would turn them in to the landlord. Perhaps she had even been hoping this months before, when she had given those noisy parties. It was the only way Hugh and she were going to find a real place of their own, if they were forcibly evicted. Otherwise, 64th Street was far too good a deal, far too comfortable, to be relinquished voluntarily.

"Before it's too late," she interrupted him at one point, when he was imagining aloud how he would force himself to live without Clara, "there's something I've got to ask you—I mean, tell. Do you mind if we change channels for a minute?"

He shifted in the beanbag chair he had recently bought, and brushed some dust from his good trousers. Apparently, he had not bothered to change from his office clothes before going to work with the sledgehammer. "Shoot."

"Something's happened, Lucas. I don't know what to do."

"Do? What's there to do about it?"

"Hold on. I haven't even told you what it is."

"You don't have to."

Emily regarded him a moment. He really did seem to know.

"So congratulations, Em. This is great."

"What?"

"You're in the family way, right? Clara began to suspect about three weeks ago."

"But I never said a word."

"She ain't dumb, you know."

"My God, she hasn't said anything to Hugh, has she?"

"Come on. She wouldn't want to spoil your fun."

"Oh, it's going to be great fun, my dear. Especially since Hugh and I haven't slept together in over a year." Her flippant tone did not prevent a tear from streaking down her face.

The beanbag chair rustled loudly as she crawled into the arms that he held out for her. There, safely nestled against his great bulk, she was finally able to cry. She had held it in for so long, the pain, terrified that Hugh would get suspicious. Now it amazed her how she could have kept up such a cheerful, efficient front ever since her gynecologist had confirmed her own suspicions.

"Are you sure you and Hugh . . . ?"

"Of course. We might have fooled around, but there was no real intercourse."

He stroked her hair. "Shhh, calm down. It's going to be all right. You know, you could always sleep with him."

"With Hugh? Don't talk nonsense, please. I'm due in November."

"That far along? My God, why did you wait so long to tell anyone?"

"It was stupid, I know." She hiccuped violently. "I just didn't want to believe it was true. I was hoping something would happen, I guess." She dug a handkerchief out of his trouser pocket. After blowing her nose, she waited awhile for the hiccups to subside. "It doesn't seem possible, even now. I can't believe it's happened to me. This is not me. It's not."

He grabbed her wrist to prevent her from slapping her belly again. On the two "not's" she had come down pretty hard.

"Take it easy, kid."

"Lucas, you don't understand. It's not some big affair, nothing like that. It was one night. Not even a night—a few hours. I don't even know his name, his last name. How can I—It's impossible, a nightmare, you've got to—"

"Calm down. These things happen all the time. We'll take care of it."

"Is it too late?"

"I don't think so. If that's what you want . . . ."

"Want? Do you think I *want* an abortion? I have no choice."

"You could—"

"What? Give it up for adoption or something? Great, then Hugh would know everything. How can I tell him that he married a slut?"

"Stop it."

"What other explanation is there? Lucas, I slept with a virtual stranger. I don't even know where he is now."

"I don't believe you."

"I don't either. But it's true."

"But you must have felt something or . . . I don't know. It's just not like you."

For the last six weeks Emily had been trying to explain it to herself. But no explanation, logical as she tried to make it, could rid her of the gut feeling that it was wrong, the child in her was. Human life was sacred, this she knew full well. Yet in her particular case she could not feel it. And it wasn't just because the child was going to ruin her career, not to mention her marriage. This wasn't it at all. She would have been happy to sacrifice both for an innocent human life. But there was no innocence here. She could feel no innocence whatsoever.

"You sound like *Rosemary's Baby*," Lucas said after she tried to express some of these feelings. "Come on, you're being ridiculous. It's not the end of the world."

She had moved away from him and was sitting across the room. "I know I'm projecting—but still, it's not me. Lucas, it's as bad, I mean I feel like it's as bad as incest, like my father . . ."

"What?"

"That's what I feel like, I don't know why."

"Your father? Was he old, this guy?"

"No, don't take everything so literally. I was just trying to explain how inside me . . . He wasn't old at all. He was thirty, that's all."

"Did he force you, were you scared? Emily, maybe you should report this to—"

"I told you," she shouted, "stop it! Stop taking everything so literally!" Hugging herself, she managed to add, "I'm sorry. I'm a little strung out."

"You don't have to talk about it."

"I do. I've got to. There's no one else. I've tried to imagine saying it to Clara, but I don't know. For some reason it's you. I trust you. No, Lucas"—he had held out his arms again—"I better stay here."

"Suit yourself. But why me?"

She regarded him steadily a moment before saying, "Because you're in hell, too."

He raised one eyebrow slightly, but that was all.

"I was wet," she began. "That was the problem. This was out in Montauk and it was cold, really cold. Don't ask me what I was doing there that time of year."

"Sidney, I take it? Her gang?"

She nodded.

"I never could understand why you spent so much time with those bimbos. Clara said—"

"Oh, never mind. Clara ought to be grateful, anyway." Clara was in Providence, Rhode Island, at that moment, playing a battered wife in a made-for-TV movie directed by Sidney's Murray.

"She is. She adores you, but still she wonders—"

"Please, let's not get off the track. Listen to me, please. I was wet and probably drinking too much and I think I hated everyone there except this one guy. When they all went out to dinner I was there alone with him. I was waiting for Sidney to show up and thought I might talk to him and his friend, a producer. But Barney, the producer, had gone to bed, and it was just Gerard and me. We sat up in front of the fire and Gerard started talking about Barney, how much he loved him. He was so open, so vulnerable, Gerard was. I've never met a man like that, someone so honest—so gentle. Lucas, I'm sorry, but all my life it seems I've been battling men. This was the first man I've ever met who wasn't defensive. No pretenses, understand, no masks. None of these undercurrents. He said what he meant. He said what he felt. He was so in touch with himself. There was a wholeness, an integrity that made him so beautiful."

"Congratulations."

"Lucas."

"Sorry. But you got to admit, this doesn't sound so awful to me."

"Listen, will you? He wasn't bad-looking either. He was dark like F.X., but not those striking kind of looks. A quiet kind that grows on you. To be honest, he was the first man I've ever met who turned me on—without touching him or anything. His manners, I don't know, something, the way he talked . . ."

"Horrors."

"O.K., big deal, right? But it was so nice for me to feel safe with someone like that." This was why, after a while, she had taken her dress off to dry when he had gone into the kitchen to fix them another drink. And why, only partially clothed, she had ended up sitting on the couch with him after Sidney had called to say she had gotten motor oil on her Halston and couldn't possibly come looking that way.

"We got to talking about Barney again, and I found out that they weren't lovers. They were just friends." This was when she had put on a sweater over her bra and zipped up her slacks. "Gerard tells me he's in therapy because he can't respond physically to men. So naturally, I ask him, what about women? And he tells me he's a virgin."

"And you believed him?"

"Gerard doesn't lie."

"Sounds like a good line to me."

"It wasn't a line." She couldn't believe how petty and jealous Lucas was sounding. Why couldn't he just accept what she was saying?

"How do you know it wasn't?"

"Because it . . . Because it took so long to get him . . . ready."

"Ready?"

"You know, uh, firm." She did not add the worst part, how Gerard had looked so miserable when it was all over. And that one little comment he had made, "How much?" At first she wasn't sure what he had meant by it, but when it finally dawned on her (Oh, how could someone so gentle, so kind, be so cruel!) she had been devastated.

"Don't you see, Lucas, I was trying to help him. I wanted him to be happy, to see that sex could be enjoyable, that it wasn't such a big deal. I told him all about my own problems getting initiated. And I told him I thought he wasn't gay at all, that he was a deeply sensitive, good man who would someday make a great husband."

"Wonderful. You're a regular saint, giving up your body for the cause of womanhood and marriage."

Yes, she had tried to make herself believe that. And him. It was so necessary for Gerard to believe that, too. Otherwise, what must he think of her?

"So, Em, that's it, huh?" Lucas said finally, after Emily had tried to say something, but failed.

The look in his eyes was chilling, the skepticism. For it made her remember correctly: The comment—How much?—had not come at the end. Rather, in the beginning, just as she had begun to tug on his zipper with her teeth. And yet she had gone ahead with it anyway, knowing full well what he meant. Yes, even with that comment ringing in her ears, she was still determined to save him.

part four

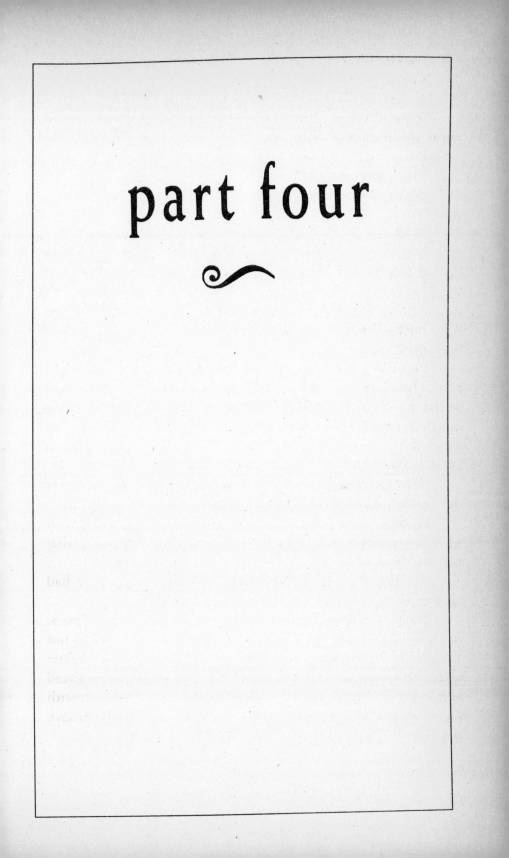

twenty

❧

Lucas blasted through here. See that door there? It leads to the hall. That used to be the only entrance."

"You mean this wasn't private? Anyone could walk in?"

F. X. really had to go, but she went right on talking, peering in. He hadn't actually planned on seeing Emily, but when neither of the old numbers he had for Clara worked—one was disconnected, the other was a former agent's—he decided he might as well look her up, for old time's sake. But he hadn't been prepared for this apartment. A bathtub in the kitchen, a bedroom two feet wide—poor thing had obviously struck out, as far as alimony went. And her career, what a shame about that. She had had so much talent, worked like a dog—and this was her reward.

"Yeah, I'm a jailbird. You're sitting here with an ex-con," he was saying after they had finished eating. Of course, this was something he would never admit to Francine. She hadn't a clue about his past. But there was no need for pretense in front of Emily. Not now, at least.

"Oh, F. X., why make such a big deal about it?"

Stunned by her callousness, he made some sort of flippant remark. Here he was opening up to her, trying to share the most painful event in his life, and she brushed it aside like that. He had forgotten what an enormous ego she had. That had always been the one thing he didn't like about her; the conversation always wound up being about her. At dinner, for instance—yes, she had gone to a lot of trouble, and the chicken was delicious. But could he get a word in edgewise? No, it was all about her hot water and this guy at work who dressed up like a gorilla or something . . .

". . . I couldn't think of anything but Hugh and me. We were separating then. I was a wreck."

F.X had tried again, and again she put him off. There was so much he wanted to tell her, too—things he had never been able to tell anyone. The afternoon he had been taking a shower, well, he probably wouldn't have been able to admit it was him. He'd say it happened to a good buddy—four guys had held him down. That tub of lard, the one whose shoes he had refused to shine, a real mental case in for armed robbery, holding up a puppy mill. They pressed a shiv to his throat while the tub of lard pumped him—and this girl here gets teary-eyed about a divorce. What did she know about real suffering? She was better off without Hugh. The things he could tell her about her precious priest. But he would keep his mouth shut about that. Let her think Hugh was a sweet little saint—that wasn't any of his business. F.X. had done a lot of things he was ashamed of, but one thing he had never done was rat on anyone, friend or not.

They reverted to small talk, interrupted by a phone call from what sounded like a boyfriend of hers. Well, he was glad she had someone. The way she had hung around the bathroom when he wanted to take a piss made him wonder if she was planning to come on to him. He had always prided himself on never making a pass at her, too. She was a nice dish, and it probably would have been fun, but he made it a policy never to mess with friends' women. And Hugh, despite all his weirdness, was a friend. Then again, he had to admit that it gave him a sense of power, back in the old days, to withhold from her something that she obviously wanted.

Pouring himself another glass of excellent wine, F.X. decided to give himself another chance. He wasn't sure why, but Emily seemed the one person he could open up to about the pen. If he could only tell her about the tub of lard, get if off his chest . . . He had been carrying it around for so long. Maybe the thing to do was to lead up gradually to it, talk about what he was doing now and then work back.

". . . this real nice guy who greets you and asks real nice if you have a reservation and— Let it ring!"

The goddam phone again.

"Yes, just a minute." She held out the receiver. "For you."

"F.X."—it was Francine—"there's this show on PBS you said you wanted to see, about the orangutans of Borneo. You can switch it on now if your friend there has a set. Is that his wife, by the way?"

"Wait a minute, I never said it was a man I was having dinner with." He tried his best to be patient with her, even when she admitted going through his pants pockets to find the number here. She was acting like she owned him, and they were just friends. They didn't even sleep together. He was getting all the hassles of a girlfriend without any of the benefits. Probably it was a mistake letting her come with him on this trip. He knew plenty of girls who were much prettier, even if they weren't as smart as Francine. How he had ever let himself get involved with a woman he wasn't physically attracted to, he would never figure out. Of course, Francine did have amazing tits, really the best he had ever seen on a woman. But she wouldn't let him touch them unless he planned on making a serious commitment.

"Give me the number," Emily said after he had hung up. "I will not have you treating another woman this way. Come on."

"Hey, give me a break." F.X. knew Emily was just trying to cover up her jealousy. Sure, it was all right for her to talk to her boyfriend. But now that the tables were turned, she suddenly wanted to get in on the act. The best thing, he figured, was to change the subject. So after a little more bantering, he did.

"I'm sure Clara was forced to do that," Emily said when he had mentioned seeing Clara on "Circus of the Stars." "Her ratings are sagging."

A bitchy comment—but who could blame Emily for being bitter? It was nothing, though, compared to his own feelings. F.X. had decided that he had never really recovered from having been dumped by Clara. It had ruined his self-confidence. No wonder why he had never been able to stay married. Three ex-wives, and each of them was nothing but a runner-up, a second-best. Probably this was the reason, too, why he had never made it as an actor. An actor needs tons of self-confidence, and Clara had smashed his to bits. Before he left town he planned to have it out with her. He was going to let her know what a wreck she had made out of his life. For months now Francine had been telling him that he had to forget Clara, and the best way to forget was to forgive. F.X. had tried his best to forgive, but discovered this wasn't possible unless the person was fully aware she was being forgiven. And the only way Clara was going to be made aware was to be confronted with her sins, in person.

F.X. thought about asking Emily now for Clara's number, but decided it would be better to wait. He didn't want to hurt her feelings by making her think the only reason he had stopped by was because of Clara.

"I'm going into the kitchen to heat up some sauce. When I come back, I want you to have phoned Francine, understand? Apologize for being so rude. Don't you look at me like that. You do it or you're not getting any dessert at all."

This blatant flirtation made him uneasy. Just what exactly did she have in mind for them that evening? "Yes, Ma'am, I promise."

"You got your fingers crossed. Uncross them, you silly boy."

"Fuck you."

If she made a pass, what was he going to do? While she heated the sauce for dessert in the kitchen, he weighed all the pros and cons. Though her figure left much to be desired, there was something about her that he found appealing—a warmth, almost maternal, that made him want to snuggle up. This was something he didn't remember about her. She had always seemed cold in the past, unapproachable. But did he really want to do more than snuggle? The answer to this would have to wait, he supposed, until they had eaten the dessert.

He ended up eating more of the apple cobbler than he wanted, probably to stall for time. Then the next thing he knew she was yawning. It was this that decided him. He refused to believe she could be tired or bored with him around.

"F.X.?"

"Huh?"

He gave her another kiss full on the mouth.

"Dear, do you really want to do this?"

"What?"

"Is this what you really want?" She did not pull away or resist. Instead she looked him straight in the eye. "I don't think you really want me."

"I do."

"You do? O.K., fine."

He kissed her again, but it wasn't working. She was right.

"Great, now you've ruined everything."

"Pardon?"

He stood up. "You've made me self-conscious. I can't function when I'm self-conscious. No man can. It's something you ought to learn."

"Don't be mad. I'm sorry."

"Sorry," he muttered, going to the door.

"I was self-conscious myself, F.X. When I get that way, I just can't . . . It was like I was watching us, this scene."

"Thanks for dinner."

"Don't be mad. I love you."

"Yeah, right."

"I do—except I don't know why. You're vain, you're a tease, you never write."

"ExCUSE me," he said, with the childish sarcasm of a standup comic.

"Someday, my dear, you're going to stop blaming everyone for your failure. And then you know what's going to happen? Right then and there, you're going to stop being a failure."

"You're one to talk about failure."

"F.X., if there's one thing I've learned tonight, it's that I'm not a failure."

"Yeah?"

"Yeah," she imitated. "See, I used to always be bothered that you never made a pass at me. Now you finally have. My life is complete."

He smirked in a sour way. "Go ahead, make fun."

"Sorry, that's all the fun for one evening." She had gone over to the door. Raising herself on tiptoes, she tried to give him a peck on the chin, but only made it to his neck.

"Good night," he heard her call after him as he hurried down the stairs.

"Listen, there's this girl who just called," the voice said over the wire with no introduction at all. "Ignore what she said, O.K. Don't say anything to Emily about it."

"Who is this?"

"Friend of hers. F.X. Pickens. You're Emily's pop, right?"

"Her father."

"Yeah, hi. So like I was saying, don't say anything about Francine calling."

"Young man, I'll have you know that I'm not in the habit of ignoring—"

"That's great, Pop. Gotta run."

Mr. Brix glared at the receiver before hanging up. Then for a good while he stood by the teak table, where the phone was. At home in Tula Springs, Dolly had always chided him for taking so long to get from one piece of furniture to the next. If he went to pick up a magazine, he would linger so long over the coffee table that she wanted to scream. And when she announced that dinner was ready, the time elapsed between his "I'm coming" and his actual removal from his armchair was so great that she always made the announcement a good fifteen minutes before it was actually ready. This he knew, of course, which was why he never came right when she called.

Before journeying to New York Mr. Brix had been warned by his wife not to drift. "Now you know, Milt, she says she doesn't have a lot of space, so when you're there, set yourself down somewhere definite. Don't go drifting around and getting in her way. If you're going to sit, then sit. Don't just say you're going to sit, understand? Emily won't be able to stand it." As Mr. Brix wandered to his daughter's window, he prided himself on having not drifted once, at least when she was around. "Then you over-exert yourself, Milt, to make up for drifting. That's what you do when you go out in the yard. Why can't you keep a nice steady pace, like Mr. Lamar next door? He doesn't run to work, and when he's called to dinner, I bet he comes." Craning his neck for a glimpse of the Empire State Building, Mr. Brix wondered why he was always being compared to Mr. Lamar. He and Dolly had never socialized with the Lamars. Mr. Lamar sold Studebakers, then Chevys. He played bridge. That was the sum total of their knowledge of him, yet Dolly was always holding him up as a paragon of husbandly virtue.

Having got some drifting out of his system, Mr. Brix settled down in one of Emily's nice chairs to await her return. She had gone out a few minutes before to use the cash machine and shop for groceries. He would have gone with her, but the dull throb in his groin discouraged him. The doctor had given it to him straight—nine months, a year at most. Dolly had wanted all the children to know right away about the cancer, but he had forbidden her to say a thing. The kids would only suffer needlessly. They had to get on with their own lives. Toward the end, maybe when he checked into a hospital, there would be plenty of time for them to get adjusted to the fact. In the meantime, while he still had his strength, he wanted to scope out Emily's situation. He had never liked the idea of her living alone in the city. He worried constantly about her safety. But of course, he knew enough by now to keep most of this to himself. If he asked Emily to please keep out of Central Park, for instance, she would probably go out of her way to stroll through it.

As for her living quarters, well, they were neat and clean. But surely she could do better than this, a woman of her abilities. It was almost as if she were purposely holding herself back. Life was so terribly short. Surely it was time she started learning how to enjoy herself. She had suffered enough from that confounded divorce. If only he could help her forget and move on.

"You know, Clara, I would never dare mention this to Emily herself," he was saying into the phone after remembering his promise to Dolly. She had insisted that he call Clara while he was there.

"Oh, it's O.K. I understand."

"Perhaps you know some nice men. From what I can gather Emily doesn't seem to have any prospects."

"Gosh, Mr. Brix, I'd be afraid to meddle. Emily's pretty much her own person."

"You've been a good friend to her, I know. And Mrs. Brix and I are so proud of your accomplishments."

"I don't think she's interested, though. She doesn't want to meet men."

"But that's not right. She's still so young and attractive. She'd make someone a wonderful wife. And I know she's lonely. I can see it in her face. She's terribly lonely."

Clara said nothing in turn.

After clearing his throat, he said, "Maybe we could all get together—"

"Oh, no, that wouldn't be possible at all. I'm sorry."

"My treat, dear. We could go to one of those nice French restaurants."

"Well, Lucas and Priscilla aren't going to be around, and I've got so much to do today. Maybe some other time."

"I know it would mean so much to Emily. You know, every time Mrs. Brix and I see you on TV, well, we get such a lift. You seem to enjoy yourself so much. Emily needs friends like you. I'm afraid her job sounds kind of gloomy. I met one of her friends from work yesterday, and to tell you the truth, Clara, she just wasn't your caliber. She was sweet, but sort of timid. She didn't have any of your spunk."

"Oh, Mr. Brix, Emily's friends are all so smart, I bet. I'd feel like a dope."

"Now, now, dear."

"Well, look, maybe . . . I mean, tea, do you like tea? Maybe you could drop by this afternoon for a few minutes."

After talking a while longer, Mr. Brix hung up, not fully satisfied with the outcome. But tea was better than nothing. Maybe it could be stretched into dinner. He knew Emily found it a strain to be alone with him, but despite his encouragement, she was not inviting any friends over to dine. The looks she sometimes gave him, as if she were ashamed of him, or worse, angry—what a stern child she was. From the very beginning she had been strict with him. No beets allowed at the dinner table—his favorite vegetable, too. And when she was a teenager, how worried he used to be when he bought a new tie for himself. He was sure she would make him take it back. Lord forbid if he should ever want to hug her. Even as a child she would always grow rigid in his arms, if not actively push him away. Well, they had gotten around it by saying Martha was his girl, Emily Dolly's. Of course, it had nearly killed him when he heard she was getting married. She had been so cavalier about it, mentioning it in an almost offhand way, during a phone conversation. Was it any wonder that he thought she had gotten herself in trouble? And then, when he learned from Dolly that Emily didn't have to get married, why, it was almost a worse blow. Because if Emily hadn't been ashamed of him, she would have let him and Dolly give her a proper wedding instead of inviting them up at the last minute. She should have gotten married at home, in Tula Springs.

Mr. Brix had to admit that maybe, because of this, he had been hard on Hugh, not very friendly when, on those few occasions, Hugh did come down with Emily for a visit. Hugh, of course, was everything he was not. Mr. Brix had always felt he didn't measure up in his daughter's eyes because he had never gone to college. And there was Hugh with Oxford, Williams. Not only that, Hugh was loaded, a Vanderbilt. Did Emily think he, her father, enjoyed scrimping and saving year after year? Didn't she think that he might like giving her fancy clothes if he could? She had always been ashamed of the family car, too, the Studebaker they had bought from Mr. Lamar. Indeed, she used to make him ride around with the windows up so her friends would think they had air conditioning. How status-conscious the girl had always been. Mr. Brix had never cared for white shoes, but when Emily was in eighth grade, he simply had to wear them. All the other fathers wore them. Clara's father wore them, Dr. Tilman. And why couldn't they go to Dr. Tilman, Emily would complain, when they got the flu? Why did they always have to go to old Dr. McFlug's crummy office? Dr. McFlug didn't have air conditioning and he was right over the Feed and Seed that sent up all those horrible smells.

"Switchboard."

"I'd like to speak with Hugh Vanderbilt, please."

"Is this a parishioner?"

"I'm his . . . A friend from out of town."

"Just a moment. I'll connect you."

Mr. Brix had hesitated before making this call. He was afraid Emily might return and catch him. But perhaps it was best to take the opportunity when it arose. Mr. Brix hadn't spoken to Hugh in years, not since the divorce. The last communication between them had been a bitter letter in which Mr. Brix had vented his unbounded disappointment in Hugh as a man. No real man would ever leave his wife, Mr. Brix had declared. Hugh must be totally without honor, without feeling, to have so casually ruined a young woman's life. "In my day a man would be horsewhipped for such behavior," Mr. Brix had said in conclusion. "My only satisfaction is that my daughter has enough dignity and honor intact not to accept one red cent from you. It would be tainted." Dolly had burst into tears when she read this over and begged him not to send it. But Mr. Brix was not to be deterred.

"Hello, Hugh."

"Yes, what can I do for you?"

"It's Mr. Brix."

Much less cheerily: "Oh."

"Hugh, you know this isn't easy for me." As if Hugh hadn't done enough by divorcing his daughter, he had compounded the insult by becoming a darn priest. Now, if that didn't take the cake . . . The gall of the boy.

"I'm in town for a few days and . . ."

Hugh was not helping him out.

". . . and I thought, I just wanted to make sure Emily was doing all right, her situation." Another pause, but Hugh remained silent. "I don't know if you're aware of her living conditions, but I have to say I'm not happy with what I've seen. Emily has worked hard all her life. She has a first-class education, and to end up like this, well . . . What I mean is, I hope you're not holding against her anything I might have said in the past."

It took a moment for Hugh to say, "If you're talking about money, it's out of my hands. You know mother disinherited me when I was ordained."

"I realize that, but a word from you might . . ."

"My mother has tried her best to make Emily comfortable. But she's been very obstinate, Emily has."

"Yes, I understand. But if she thought it meant something to you, you could sway her, I believe."

"We've talked about it many times."

"Of course, but maybe now would be a good time to try again. You can't just take a simple no on such a vital issue."

"Mr. Brix, I'm hardly the one to argue her into something I don't believe in myself."

Here Mr. Brix decided to be unhelpful. He did not fill up the pause.

"Money never made anyone happy," Hugh went on. "In fact, I believe it's a sure way to make yourself miserable."

"Well, good for you, sir. But there happen to be people struggling to make ends meet who don't have a billionaire Pope to foot their bills."

"The Pope has done a lot of terrible things, Mr. Brix, but one thing you can't accuse him of is paying my bills."

"No, I guess not. You're letting your parishioners take care of that, poor working stiffs who sully themselves selling cars and insurance, things like that. Seems to me you'd be helping everyone out a whole lot more if you didn't play at being poor, if you accepted your responsibilities like a man."

"I'm sorry, but I don't have time for a sermon now."

Mr. Brix tried to rein himself in. It was amazing how provoking the boy could be, even after all this time. "Listen, get this straight, I have nothing to say myself. I'm only calling for my daughter's sake." He winced as a painful twinge shot through his groin. "There's nothing I wouldn't do for that girl."

"I don't believe you, sorry. I think you're calling to get in another whack at me. You're still not satisfied, are you? You're afraid I might have forgotten how to feel guilty about her? Well, I have forgotten. I don't feel guilty anymore. We've made our mistakes, she and I. But we're not clinging to them anymore, hugging them for reassurance. We've learned to let go and get on with what we've got to do."

"Fine, let go, that's the answer to everything these days, isn't it? Well, sir, let me tell you something. I could have easily let go myself. You think I wanted to . . ."

"To what?"

"Never mind."

"No, go on. I'd like to hear this."

"Forget it, Hugh. You haven't changed at all, have you? You're still the same arrogant bastard. I'm sorry I called."

Somewhat shaken, he hung up. Why did the boy have such

an effect on him, almost making him say something that he knew full well was not true? How close he had come to saying, *You think I wanted to have Emily?* What nonsense. As if there had ever been such a question. Of course, Dolly had promised him when they were first married that she would be careful. But the doctors always fitted her awkwardly, with devices that hurt. And it was such a chore to get her down to New Orleans for a refitting. She was so ashamed and even feared arrest. That was what her sister had told her, that she could be arrested. Mr. Brix hated seeing her in tears, but it simply had to be done. How else was he going to get on with his project? For years he had dreamed of making a spoken language recording of his favorite passages in Latin. The idea was that the listener could follow with an English translation. An outfit in Jackson, Mississippi, had agreed to produce a first edition of two hundred 78s. In fact, he had already signed the contract and was ready to pay out his life savings of $350 for production and distribution costs when Dolly gave him the news. With a baby on the way it was out of the question that he could afford the record. No one, of course, would give him a loan. Living in a rented apartment, they had no collateral, and he was working on commission then, selling tires. Of course, he might have been a little disappointed in Dolly at first. He was only human, after all. But no father could have been happier when Emily finally arrived, right? And Dolly and he, they had made their peace long ago.

"I'm home, father."

"Oh, hello, Emily. Here, let me help you with those groceries. I shouldn't have let you go out alone. How did you ever get them up all those stairs?"

twenty-one

W ell, look, maybe . . . I mean, tea, do you like tea?
Maybe you could drop by this afternoon for a few
minutes."

"Oh, that would be wonderful."

"Come around four, O.K.?"

"Before I forget, I was thinking of getting her some wallpaper
and—"

"As a matter of fact, I've got some samples. We're redecorating
the master bedroom and, well, anyway, she's free to take a look.
I better get going now, Mr. Brix. I've got so much to do."

"Thank you so much."

"Bye bye."

When Clara hung up, she could have kicked herself for being
so soft-hearted. This was what had always gotten her in trouble
in the past, feeling sorry for someone. For a moment she seriously
considered calling him back, making up some excuse to keep them
away. But what if Emily answered? She might resent being dis-
invited. The last thing Clara wanted to do was stir up any ill
feelings. Yet how nice it had been to have Emily out of the way
for almost an entire year.

"Mommie, can I bake some cookies?"

Clara flashed a look at her daughter, who had slouched into the sun-drenched great room. She had told Priscilla that it was inappropriate for a thirteen-year-old to call her mother that. Apparently, Priscilla was going through a phase, or so Sister Joseph had assured Clara when she had visited the counselor at Sacred Heart. Girls sometimes played at being younger than their calendar years. It was nothing to worry about, usually short-lived. Clara had been advised not to come down too hard on her, to let the girl act it out with only a few gentle reminders.

"Pris—stand up straight, please—listen, sweetie, how would you and your father like to go out to Montauk this afternoon? Wouldn't that be fun?"

"No."

"You're getting in the way of the carpenter."

"Daddy said I could bake Toll House."

"Please don't pull on your chain, dear." Clara had recently presented her daughter with a small diamond attached to a gold chain, which she hoped would replace the popbead necklace Priscilla had been wearing to school. "You can bake when you get back."

Entering the soundproof study without knocking, Clara startled her husband, who had been absorbed in correcting an error.

"I can't retrieve two pages of the revised shooting budget," he said. "They just disappeared. I must have filed them wrong. The memory . . ."

Over his muttering Clara asked for attention.

"What? Anything wrong?"

"Dear, how would you like to take Priscilla out to the Island this afternoon? It seems like a good time to check on that house."

"Can't now. Sorry."

Crumbs on his desk gave her pause. Fourteen more pounds had been shed by him during Lent. Never had he looked better, and yet here he was sneaking cookies that had been expressly forbidden.

"Why are you encouraging Pris to bake?"

"Bake what?"

"You're sixty, you know, prime time for a heart attack."

"Wishful thinking."

"Lucas!"

"Joke, my dear."

"It's not funny."

"Well, you're always bringing it up."

"That's because you're always cheating." She squeezed into his lap, blocking his view of the computer screen. "Now, bad boy, let this stuff go for now and spend a nice afternoon with your daughter."

"But I've got—Ouch!"

She had been nipping at his neck. "What a baby."

"Take it easy, not so hard."

"The agent called, honey. We've got to make up our mind by tomorrow," she lied with the clearest of consciences. She would, after all, do anything for her daughter's sake.

"Tomorrow? I thought we had another month."

"Some other people are interested in renting it for the summer. We've got to move fast if we want it."

Clara was able to deliver these lines with perfect ease while worrying about the call. Had Emily put her father up to it? Was it possible at this late date that she was beginning to have second thoughts? Yes, she had been good up until now, holding up her end of the bargain. Of course, there had been that little episode a year or so ago, when Emily had gone off into the bedroom to talk to Lucas. Clara had used this as an excuse to keep Emily out of the picture. She had provoked the argument with Emily, feigning more jealousy than she actually felt—all because of Priscilla. It was around this time that Clara had been alarmed by certain mannerisms, the way her daughter gnawed the tips of her hair, for instance. Or the way she would tilt her head before giving a saucy reply. She had the same inflection, too, with certain phrases. Some resemblance, of course, had to be expected. But Clara had not counted on such uncanny mimicking when she had talked Emily out of an abortion almost fourteen years ago.

She supposed it was Mr. O'Malley's influence that made the whole idea of abortion seem so repugnant. Lucas was not supposed to have told her about it, but it wasn't hard for her to figure that something was up. When Lucas finally broke down and admitted he had made an appointment for Emily, Clara was beside herself. Lying awake night after night, she felt the unborn child's eyes upon her, his last hope—for these eyes were the piercing Berber eyes of the child in the abandoned sugar mill. Clara had failed that desert boy. Would she be able to live with herself if she failed again? Soon it became apparent that she had to take a drastic step. Emily was planning to keep the whole thing a secret from Hugh. She had no faith in Hugh's kind and good heart, his forgiveness. Clara did. She knew Hugh could not possibly let Emily go through with the abortion. There was plenty of room in his heart for another man's child.

What a shock it was, then, to witness Hugh's reaction to her news. She had always thought it an exaggeration, someone going white as a sheet. But right in front of her eyes, he did just that. No words needed to be exchanged for Clara to realize she had made the mistake of her life. It nearly killed her when, not long after, Hugh and Emily separated. She would have done anything to make it up to Emily; Clara was convinced she had ruined her friend's life. Then it had occurred to her that there was something she could do. She would accept the full weight of the responsibility, as would Lucas, who never should have spilled the beans to her, Clara, in the first place. Lucas balked at first, as did Emily. But Clara was relentless. Emily was suffering such confusion, such genuine anguish about betraying Hugh, that she soon caved in. And when she did, Lucas realized that now he had a reason to marry Clara, a good Catholic reason to do what he had always wanted to do in the first place.

So everyone ended up happy, after all. Clara, from the very first, positively adored the child, who really did not resemble her mother very much, with her mop of black hair and scrumptious olive skin. And when it turned out that Lucas wasn't able to have children himself, well, then she became convinced that God was behind the whole thing in the first place. You just had to trust in Him, that was all. Though he tended to spoil Priscilla, Lucas was nonetheless a wonderful father, and Mrs. Tilman was provided with a blessed distraction from a dull, lonely widowhood. As for Emily, Clara did give her position a lot of thought. Emily had once told Lucas that she was terrified that if she raised the child herself she would communicate to it, unconsciously, such a sense of shame that the child could never really be happy. Rationally, yes, Emily felt she could be a good mother and not let the memory of the conception prejudice her against the child. But Emily knew that feelings were rarely rational. And, besides, the fact that she had toyed so long with the idea of abortion, this in itself was enough to make any subsequent thought of motherhood problematical. In any case, Emily could rest secure that her daughter had a loving two-parent home with plenty of financial security. When Lucas's mother had died, he became well off again and this time, under Clara's orders, managed to invest the capital well instead of frittering it away. Even if Clara's career went belly up, as several times it threatened to, they would never have to worry, but simply live a little less grandly.

Both Emily and Clara had agreed that it would be best for there to be some distance between them. Emily, despite all her reasoning, was bound to feel an urge to reclaim her own flesh and blood. And, indeed, this proved to be the case. She had admitted to Lucas years later, in the bedroom during that dinner party, how dreadful her suffering had been. So Clara was proved, in retrospect, wise to have packed up Lucas and the child and moved to Los Angeles, where God seemed to smile upon her, giving her one role after another. It was only recently that the pickings had got lean on the Coast, and she was tempted by an offer from New York to play a contract role in the soap she had once appeared in. By this time Priscilla's formative years were over, and Clara could rest assured that the girl was properly imprinted on her. Only mildly apprehensive, trusting Emily to keep her distance, Clara had returned. Before they were even halfway settled, Clara found a counselor, who, in a family-style setting, broke the news to Priscilla, as gently and professionally as possible, that she was adopted. Priscilla, who had been prepared by hints and children's stories early on, took it well. As for who her natural mother was, Lucas thought that one day, when Priscilla was mature, she could be told. Clara was more doubtful about this. She was not sure that there could ever be a time when a person was ready to hear the whole story. This was why she always made certain that the girl was out of the house when Emily made one of her rare social calls. Emily's history, after all, was not one to fill a young mind with much confidence in the future. Weighing the poor child down with such a burden would be a crime. And, besides, the past, this past, had nothing to do with Priscilla. She was entitled to her ignorance. As far as Clara was concerned, it was the child's God-given right.

"So, Lucas?"

"All right, dear, I'll go. A drive might do me good. Where's Pumpkin?"

"Remember what Sister Joseph said about that?"

"Sorry."

"You're infantilizing her."

"I know, I know."

Somehow Clara survived the visit with Emily and her father. The whole time, though, she was on tenterhooks, waiting for the bombshell: "Emily told me her secret, Clara. I knew something has been wrong with her for years. Now she and I have come to take Priscilla home, where she belongs." To cover her anxiety she employed all her acting ability to appear carefree, delighted to see them both. She even forced herself to mention Priscilla whenever it seemed appropriate. If she didn't, she was afraid that she might be signaling her fear to them. It was so important that she appear confident, strong, absolutely at ease, someone not to be trifled with. Perhaps that was the reason she kept on bringing up the Church. She was telling them—quite consciously, she realized—that if they tried anything, she would bring the full moral authority of the Pope himself, if necessary, to defend herself and her child. She hadn't planned on going to the RCIA meeting that night, but to prevent herself from lying, she did go. As for Honduras, well, she did tell a partial lie. She was not going there the next day. Rather, she had to shoot in Colorado for Listermint. But she made a promise to God that if He kept Emily away from Priscilla, she would go to Honduras. Clara's general anxiety level had been raised recently by a couple of TV miniseries she had noticed in the *Times* listing, dealing with natural mothers making all sorts of fuss over earlier, hasty decisions. She worried that Emily might watch and be influenced by all the blather over a natural mother's rights. Her only hope was that Emily still didn't have a television. And that she still had a sense of honor. Life was simply unworkable if people went back on their word. Some limits had to be set.

God kept His end of the bargain, Clara was trapped. She would be going to Honduras with a group from Justin Martyr, most of whom she didn't know at all. But she consoled herself with the thought that this would look good at the annulment hearings coming up. Clara was hoping, for Priscilla's sake, that she could persuade Judy to cooperate and have her marriage to Lucas annulled. It was possible, since neither of them had entered into the union with the intention of procreating. Ironically enough, Judy had used every birth control device under the sun, unaware that her husband was sterile. In any case, with an annulment, Lucas could finally go to communion. So far Priscilla, who was well versed in Church law, had forbidden either parent to receive the bread and wine. On this subject Priscilla was much stricter than Sister Joseph.

"You only stayed three days," the child complained when her mother returned. Clara had signed up for seven.

"Mommie was sick. You know that."

"But it was only a stomachache."

Only—Clara liked that. She was so dehydrated that they had tried to rush her to a clinic on the back of a three-wheel motorcycle. It had been so humiliating, being tended by a manicurist from Justin Martyr, a real saint who never complained about the soiled bedclothes. Clara had made a valiant effort to rise and dig one day in the tiny village outside Olanchito. She was determined to help lay the new sewer pipes. But after fifteen minutes she lost control again, too ill to even be properly embarrassed. The doctor said it was the lettuce she had eaten.

"Pris, your mother nearly died."

"You always exaggerate."

Tears welled up in Clara's eyes as she checked herself out in the three-way mirror. Clara was trying to upgrade her daughter's wardrobe, but Priscilla had seen nothing she liked in Bonwits, Saks, or Bergdorf. They had drifted from store to store until they found themselves in a discount house on Sixth Avenue, Chuckles, a place Clara herself would never have set foot in. But Priscilla had expressed interest, and Clara, by accident, had come across a capelike coat that would be perfect for the somewhat tacky restaurant hostess she played in "My Life to Live."

"Mom."

"What?"

"People will see."

Clara dabbed at the tears that were embarrassing her daughter. Since returning from Honduras she found herself much more susceptible to slights and everyday thoughtlessness. Perhaps it had something to do with the despair she had felt in Olanchito. Clara had never known the meaning of the word before, the bottomless depths it floated so innocuously upon. Of course, she had seen poverty before. Her location work in Morocco, Tunisia, Java, and Colombia had given her conscience an excellent workout. But this was the first time she had felt utterly helpless herself. As she lay in her stench, too ashamed to inform Rita, the manicurist, that she needed changing yet again, she experienced a profound revulsion, not just regarding herself, but for the entire world. Stories that she had heard from villagers about illness, rape, and starvation took on an entirely different cast. In this feverish state she felt for the first time that her own suffering was nothing compared to what she had heard. And with this realization came a loathing for a world that could permit such pain. It dawned on her then that the god she had been propitiating all her life was quite literally Satan himself. There was no justice here. No peace. The only reality— something she had denied with every fiber of her being all her life—was suffering. Satan was Lucifer, was light. The only hope lay in darkness, oblivion, forgetting everything in blessed death.

"Is there a ladies' here?"

"No. You can't go here, Mom."

"I have to."

"Can't you wait?"

Horribly offended, Priscilla trudged, slouching, as her mother hurried from the store. How could she be so selfish, the child said, as she dogged her mother's steps. She hadn't even given her a chance to try anything on. "Rest Room for Customers Only," Priscilla pointed out when Clara hesitated outside a Chinese fast-food shop. Desperate, Clara turned down a side street, where she knew there were some hotels.

"Mom, not here. You can't."

"Why not?"

"You don't have a room. This is for—"

"Hush."

With a stiff smile Clara breezed past the doorman just inside the revolving brass door. Priscilla was instructed to wait for her beside the checkout desk.

It was a good half hour before she emerged. Priscilla greeted her with a stern look. At this moment Clara would have welcomed some playful infantilism. But, unfortunately, those regressions were usually triggered by her father's presence.

"Hold on," Clara said as Priscilla started for the door.

"Come on."

"I can't just now."

"What? You've been in there an hour. I nearly died. Everyone was looking at me, Mom. This is terrible what you do to me, you know."

"Dear, Mommie is still sick, my stomach—"

"Shhh!" In a fierce whisper: "Do you have to let everyone know!"

"I'm sorry," Clara whispered back. "I'm just not certain now I can make it back to the apartment. We'll have to wait."

"This is great. I'm not even going to see that blouse in Chuckles."

"Maybe. Just give me time to settle down. Some tea would help, I think. You can get a napoleon."

"I hate napoleons."

"You ate three the other night," Clara said as she sank down carefully into a faded plush armchair.

Priscilla looked disdainfully about her at the sparsely populated lobby before picking a chair at one remove from her mother. Clara had to make a little fuss before the girl changed to an adjacent wing chair.

"Algonquins were Indians," Priscilla informed her mother when Clara asked, rather distractedly, what the hotel's name could mean. Her mind was monitoring a slight twinge in her stomach. "I mean what did you think they were, Chinese?"

"I'm sorry. I didn't know."

"But how could you not know? You went to school, didn't you?"

"I went to school in Louisiana. We didn't have Algonquins there."

"You didn't know what quarks were either. The other night at dinner . . ."

"Hm?"

The waiter had arrived. Clara gave the order, tea for herself, and a mocha napoleon, counting on Priscilla to relent and admit her liking.

"What was that?" she said when they were alone again. "Quarks?"

"I really worry about your education. You seem sometimes just totally out of it."

Clara realized her daughter was simply venting a little teenage frustration. She did her best to remain patient, though the barb stung. "Honey, Sacred Heart is much more advanced than the school I went to."

"Mom, your makeup."

"What? I don't have anything on today."

"It's an inch thick. Don't you realize people don't do that these days? It's not cool. When you came to school the other day, I nearly died. Mrs. Grant never puts on anything, not even lipstick."

"Mrs. Grant doesn't work for a living, honey."

"She does so. She's a landscape architect."

"Please take your hair out of your mouth."

Priscilla was gnawing on a black curl. Soon, however, it was replaced by a napoleon, which made the girl much less crabby. How easy it was for Priscilla to switch from one mood to the next. It was a blessing. No matter how mad she might get at her mother, she was always quick to forgive. As Clara sipped her tea and listened to Priscilla chatter happily about quarks, her eyes strayed to the faint bruises on her daughter's arm. Clara had grabbed her to give her a good shaking the day before, and her daughter's skin being so sensitive, she had left some marks. Priscilla had lied to her. She had told her that she was at a poetry reading at the YWCA, when actually she had gone over to Halsey Jones's apartment with a girlfriend. Halsey was a junior at Horace Mann, far too grown-up for Priscilla. He had his own Porsche, his own separate entrance to his bedroom in his mother's apartment. Clara had to get it through her daughter's head that she was playing with fire. Did Priscilla actually think she enjoyed shaking her up like that? It was her duty, no matter what Lucas might say. Of course, Priscilla had burst into tears, screamed, threatened never to speak to her again. Yet here she was, only a day later, acting as if nothing had happened.

And yet, Clara thought bitterly, this was not the end. Priscilla was probably going to try to sneak out again. She had heard her on the phone just this morning whispering to that spoiled friend of hers, probably plotting another meeting at Halsey's. Clara was a little afraid what she might be forced to do if she caught Priscilla lying to her again.

"Let's go, Mom."

Clara's stomach felt all right now.

"Mom?"

"Just a minute."

No, it wasn't her stomach holding her back. It was that despair, as if she were flat on her back, unable to move, to help herself in the least. Nothing she did was ever going to be right. Priscilla was going to drift farther and farther away from her, never learning the truth about the world, how cruel and dangerous it was, until it was too late. And Clara would always feel the pain for this child. No matter how much she shook her, Priscilla would never wake up to reality. She would always think her mother was something of a joke, as if she really were the fatuous restaurant hostess she played in "My Life to Live." More than once Clara had caught Priscilla and her girlfriend Jessica hooting at the TV set when she was on. Of course, daytime TV was forbidden, but Priscilla never obeyed. And then, when Clara would fly into a rage, Priscilla would act as if she were some horrible, unjust tyrant. It was always Clara who would have to apologize. And apologize for what—for trying to save her daughter's life? No, it was all too impossible. Clara felt defeated. She was simply not enough. And she had no support at all from Lucas. He would always take Priscilla's side.

"Come on, let's go to Chuckles, Mom."

Clara's eyes filled with tears. "You little skunk."

"What? Oh, great, here come the waterworks."

"No, I'm all right." Coming to the decision gave her a sense of peace. She would call Emily, soon. After all, Emily did have a brilliant mind. Surely she would have some advice about how to raise a child in this day and age.

"Ready, Mom?"

"O.K., I think I can make it now."

twenty-two

Clara doesn't plan like that. She's much too . . . I don't know."

"Boy, you really get me," Hugh said. "You think someone who rakes in what she does is Miss Innocent? Believe me, that woman knows exactly what she's doing. Always has. The other stuff, the klutzy Southern belle, it's an act."

Even as he spoke Hugh realized he was exaggerating. But he had a hard time, even at this late date, keeping a clear head when it came to Clara. In a way, he had never really been able to forgive her for adopting Emily's child. It was a grand gesture that made him and Emily seem mean, unworthy. He liked to tell himself that if he had known Clara was going to do it, he might have had second thoughts about divorcing Emily. Maybe he would have stuck it out with her and raised the kid. But Emily had led him to believe she was going to get an abortion. She had said nothing about Clara until after the divorce, when all the damage had been done.

"Sure you don't want to join us?" he asked when they arrived at the door to the parish office at St. Perpetua. It was after seven. He was a little late for the Third World meeting, which he hoped Virgilio would start without him. Hugh did everything he could to discourage lay dependence on the clergy, including sometimes not showing up at all for Finance Committee meetings.

"I've got to get home."

He leaned over for a kiss, putting his arms around Emily. When they had been married, how stiff, infrequent, their hugs had been. But now that they had freed themselves from the law that required them to love, honor, and cherish each other, how natural it seemed to do just that. Emily's warmth renewed him; his blood sang merrily.

Only three people had bothered to show up. Mrs. Montague, who ran bingo in the parish hall with an iron fist, not bothering with the velvet glove, was letting Virgilio know the facts of the matter. She said it was nonsense, the idea of adopting a sister parish in Nigeria. "We've got enough problems right here without trying to clean house over there."

"We're not cleaning house. We're trying to show some solidarity." Orma Link said this, a comely middle-aged woman who had been arrested three years ago for giving sanctuary in Texas to a Guatemalan refugee.

Mrs. Montague patted the bow atop her dyed, beehived hair. Though she was the same age as Orma, she insisted on the full title, Mrs., when being addressed. By volunteering in a cancerous way for almost every committee and job in the parish, from reception desk to washing out the chalices, Mrs. Montague had garnered a wide variety of detractors. Hugh himself viewed her as an exercise in patience, as indeed a veritable Nautilus gym calling into play every conceivable sort of spiritual restraint.

"There you go again, Orma," Mrs. Montague said, "getting political. This is a church, may I remind you. We're not supposed to stick our noses in other people's business. How would you like it if a bunch of Africans paddled over here and started griping about the rats in Finnegan Hall? I'm not talking about mice. Rats, three of them sashayed right by me when me and Miss Shereeshu were setting up for bingo last night."

"We set out glue traps," Virgilio said.

Folding her arms, Mrs. Montague looked at him as if he were one of those traps. "Don't make me laugh. What we need are professionals, a top-notch exterminator. Money should be no object."

"Unfortunately, that's just what it is," Hugh put in. "We really can't afford one now."

"No, but we seem to be able to afford a microwave."

"That didn't come out of the parish funds," Orma said. "Besides, it's none of our business, the rectory kitchen."

"I have nothing against the clergy living in luxury, Orma. But I'm sure the Pope doesn't have rats running around the Vatican."

"I wouldn't be too sure of that, Mrs. Montague," Hugh said. "In any case, we're straying from the point, don't you think?"

Orma began to make a case for a village on the Niger River as the sister parish, but she was disheartened by another objection somehow linked to rats. More than once Orma had spoken to Hugh about expelling Mrs. Montague from Third World, so Hugh avoided the looks Orma was giving him while Virgilio and Mrs. Montague discussed D-Con. Perhaps the best way of handling it, he mused, was to reschedule Third World so it fell on bingo night. In any case, Orma did not last another ten minutes. Pleading a headache, she stood up, handing over to Hugh a box of whole-wheat pita and tahini she had brought along for refreshments. He was instructed to take them to the rectory. After resisting Mrs. Montague's request to bless her ("I already blessed you this morning") he set out with the cardboard box. Virgilio followed with the institutional coffeepot.

Most SRO hotels in the city had a sign in their lobbies discouraging visitors after ten P.M. The rectory, two doors down from the church, could have outdone them, had it chosen to put up its own notice: NO VISITORS, PERIOD. Cy Bellows, the pastor, did deserve a refuge from the ceaseless problems of the community. But whether he had the right to make Hugh's visitors feel unwelcome was another matter. After several skirmishes over this rule, Hugh tried to avoid the issue by sneaking in his guests. Virgilio was particularly adept at finding his way up to the third floor without being caught.

"Go on up while I put this stuff away," Hugh whispered at the door to the kitchen. Virgilio handed over the pot and gingerly, as the pine floors creaked, made his way to the back stairs.

"You through already?" Cy stuck his head out the door of the den as Hugh walked past.

"Mrs. Montague."

"Oh."

"There's some sandwiches in the fridge. I just put them there."

"Not Orma Link's, I hope."

Hugh shrugged. Cy grunted. Five years younger than Hugh, Cy nevertheless hadn't the slightest difficulty acting as if he were his father. Being bald helped in this regard, as did a minimal education. Cy was completely unself-conscious about saying "between you and I" and watched reruns of "Laugh-in" to pilfer jokes for his sermons.

"Well, uh . . . ." Cy began. Hugh braced himself. Had Virgilio been spotted? "I was wondering, Hugh, this friend of yours, Allen Bechstein. He's not a parishioner, is he? Why don't you see if you can get him to join up here? We could use people like him."

"Cy, he's a devout Jew."

"I see. Well, I suppose you want to turn in."

"Night."

Virgilio had once observed that Hugh's room was three inches smaller, lengthwise, than a cell at Riker's Island. There were bars over Hugh's window, which afforded a view of an airshaft, and a sink in one corner. The bathroom was down the hall. If Virgilio wanted to use it, Hugh would check to make sure the path was clear. A fellow Capuchin or two had, it was sad to say, informed on him in the past.

"Here," Hugh said after quietly shutting the door behind him.

Virgilio was stretched out on the vibrating bed that Hugh had inherited from the previous tenant, who had since left the Church to work for PaineWebber. Sitting up, Virgilio took the turkey leg Hugh had smuggled past Cy.

"Thanks, man." Cramming his mouth as full as possible, Virgilio rolled his eyes with a pleasure that was both real and mock.

Hugh knew that if it weren't for Virgilio, he would have given up long ago on the priesthood. It had all turned out so different from what he had imagined it would be. And also, when he had made the decision, he knew now that, in some respects, it hadn't been a very mature one. The thought of giving his mother the shock of her life was simply too delicious to pass up. Shortly after his divorce, Hugh had discovered in therapy that he had a huge store of resentment against Lettice. Their so-called close relationship was profoundly neurotic, like that between a memsahib and an Oxford-educated Indian of the Raj. The equality Lettice rejoiced in between them was a total sham. For behind it all was her power to disinherit him, to cast him aside just as easily as she had his father. Mr. Vanderbilt was an alcoholic—that was Lettice's excuse for her divorce. It was also Hugh's father's way of saying no to the Raj. Hugh himself came up with a slightly less destructive strategy. He called Lettice's bluff. She had told him that if he became a priest, she would guarantee that he would be penniless for the rest of his born days. She wasn't about to enrich the coffers of that bastion of Fascism. And he had to hand it to her, she had stuck by her word.

Lettice's threat was just the right spark to set off the fireworks for his declaration of independence. But all the powder's ingredients had been there for some time, lying inert. To begin with, Hugh had always been uneasy about how socially acceptable it was to be a Protestant, particularly a member of one of the more liberal congregations. There was something so much more earthy and appealing about the shoemakers and plumbers you were likely to sit next to in a Catholic church. Then there was his growing weariness at Union with all the intricacies of theology. He was good at it, having learned how to manipulate the right catchwords in a way that was fresh, even provocative. But it began to feel so sterile. If he hadn't taken a course with a priest from Madagascar, he might have given up altogether. Father Malubje confirmed his gut feeling that European theology had little relevance to what was happening in the world today. The voices that had to be heard all came from the Third World, and these voices were not abstract theories attempting to explain the mysteries of Atonement or the Incarnation. They were voices connected to living, suffering, exploited bodies. The Church, in other words, had to undergo a conversion herself. She had to repent and become what she was originally intended to be, the Church of the poor, the marginal.

The idea of repentance held its own attraction for Hugh at that time. Without Emily he found himself virtually addicted to lesbian pornography. And he spent a disturbing amount of time in vain attempts to make his fantasies come true. Decent women like Lisa and Nicky were out of the question. Lisa, in fact, had given him a good dressing down when she caught wind of what he was up to. He found himself haunting singles bars on First and Second avenues, sometimes with F.X., hoping to interest two girlfriends in trying something new. It had worked once or twice, but the women were either grossly overweight or so vulgar that he always promised himself, never again. In despair he had tried an escort service. The women he met through Champagne were definitely better looking and surprisingly intelligent. In fact, one of his favorites had an MBA and was going to law school at Fordham. The drawback here, aside from the predictable remorse, was the enormous expense. Lettice was beginning to ask questions, since he was borrowing more than ever before.

It was a vicious circle. Every time an experience disappointed him, he would say to himself, Fine, that's it, I'm through. But then he would think that maybe the next time would be better. If only the women wore rouge, all the heavy makeup of the fifties. His desire became more and more specific. They had to undress each other in a certain way, starting with their navy skirts and ending with the beige half heels. One of them had to be bossy, the other whiny, petulant, and both had to pretend he wasn't there. But no matter how carefully he rehearsed them, they would always screw up part of the script by maybe taking their shoes off too soon or, worst of all, giggling. Most of the escorts were dreadful actresses. He had to inject an exhausting amount of imagination into their performances to make them the least bit erotic.

All this was easy enough to discuss with his therapist. Between him and Dr. Waterman, they came up with plenty of reasons why he was fixated on two. Waterman thought that this was a reflection of Hugh's anima, which had somehow split in two and was trying to reunite. Hugh, in turn, had a notion that it was connected with seeing his father in a drunken rage once, forcing himself on Lettice. The sight of the hair on his father's back had severely upset the five-year-old Hugh and perhaps caused an aversion to anything masculine associated with sex. But all this theorizing did nothing to make him feel better about himself. He still felt the old shame he had brought with him to his marriage, the shame he had tried so hard to deny with overwork, or with sex with Emily.

What a relief it was, then, to make his first confession and, in fifteen minutes, with no elaborate explanations, emerge feeling forgiven, at peace with himself. Quite simply, it worked. It was what he had been looking for. Suffused with new hope, he thought there would be nothing better than to be able to do this for other people suffering from guilt. It was a real healing process—and cheap enough for anyone to afford.

So Hugh had plenty of good and bad reasons to find himself sneaking turkey legs past Cy Bellows. What he found difficult to reconcile himself to was that he had replaced a bad situation with regard to his mother, his divorce, his lack of purpose, with a worse. Surely, from the minute he had set foot in the seminary in Garrison, New York, he should have known that the Church was going to be every bit as trying a mother as his own. But he forged ahead, bristling at the pig-headed scholasticism, certain narrow-minded professors, knowing that if he dropped out it would give Lettice a field day. Transferring to a seminary in Mexico City helped a great deal. But then he was back in New York, face to face with the Mrs. Montagues of the world, who seemed to take up most of his time. He was a father, yes, but at forty-two he was treated like a child by his father provincial, Cy himself, and a fair number of parishioners. It would be intolerable were it not for Virgilio.

Hugh was not sure why he liked the man so much. There was nothing remarkable about his appearance, much less his intellect. Every third Sunday he was the lector at mass, reading in a dull monotone with only a slight accent. A naturally surly expression on his face had made Hugh steer clear of him for about a year. But then one afternoon Hugh and he wound up being the only volunteers to paint the Third World meeting room, and Hugh, to his surprise, found himself opening up to him as if it were the most natural thing in the world. He talked for hours about Cy, his teachers in the seminary, Emily, Lettice, his father. It wasn't long before Virgilio knew everything about him, even his obsession with lesbians. And never once did Hugh doubt that Virgilio, unlike Fay, could be trusted.

"So you saw Emily?" Virgilio asked as he adjusted the Magic Fingers on the headboard. He was lying down again, having made short work of the turkey.

Hugh was at his desk, proofreading the galleys of an article he had sold to a Jungian review published in Buenos Aires. It was actually an expanded version of a footnote from his dissertation.

In it he examined the forgeries that Thomas Aquinas had accepted as authentic, particularly the Pseudo-Isidorian Decretals. Blatant lies were an integral part of church history, not just an occasional exception, as some scholars would have it. Indeed, Hugh argued, the entire fortress of patriarchy is defended by infallible lies, a rewriting of history. To carry this out, the female must be silenced. For the female instinctively knows that the truth is not Platonic, as Augustine argued. No, the truth is sexual, passionate, messy. It is the very opposite of infallible; it is vulnerable.

"Hugh?"

"Huh?"

"I asked if you saw Emily tonight. Get your head out of those papers, man," he added as he lit up a cigarette.

Shoving his chair back, Hugh faced his friend, though his mind was still on the article. He had been reprimanded by his father provincial for an earlier article in *Tikkun*. Hugh wondered if this latest one, which was much more critical of the Church, would land him in real hot water. If he himself might be silenced. He wondered what he'd do then.

"Em? Yeah."

"Well?"

"It was great. We had a great time."

Virgilio seemed to savor each inhalation, as if he were smoking pot. "So you tell her about the father calling?"

"Mr. Brix? No, why should I upset her?"

"You seemed pretty upset."

"I was. But it doesn't have anything to do with her."

Virgilio tapped the ashes into a saucer on the floor. "What's eating you?"

"What?"

"That article, right? You're wondering if this one will finally do the trick."

"What are you talking about?"

"Get you kicked out. That's what you want, isn't it?"

"No, I just want to tell the truth, that's all. I'm too old to lie anymore."

"And you, you know the truth?" Virgilio made a smoke ring, which they both watched dissolve. "You, boy, you don't know nothing."

268

No one, not even Emily, could have said this to Hugh and not made him flare up—no one, that is, but Virgilio. Perhaps this had something to do with the fact that Virgilio had served time, twenty years ago, for armed robbery. Hugh had been more impressed by this than if Virgilio had told him he was on the board of the Rockefeller Foundation.

"By the way, you're coming to dinner Saturday, right?"

"You sure Lolita won't mind?"

"Mind? She kill me if you don't."

Lolita was Virgilio's common-law wife. She had a temper and would often leave Virgilio for months at a time. Hugh felt more comfortable visiting when she wasn't around. They lived on 128th Street, in a five-room apartment right over the hardware store Virgilio managed. When Lolita was there, not a doily was out of place. And she treated Hugh with such reverence that Virgilio often could not help laughing aloud, which, of course, would set her off. When she cursed, she would always get out her bottle of holy water and shake it over Virgilio and the furniture to rid the house of demons.

"Why do you say I know nothing?"

"Because it's true." Virgilio scratched a foot. He had kicked off his shoes. "You know nothing of women. Nothing of men. But don't worry. Most priests, they just like you. You fits right in."

"Fit."

"You preach about love, but you're angry all the time. Real mad. That's like most priests I know. They don't know the first thing about love. Haven't the slightest clue."

Hugh tried to sound sarcastic, but he was hurt. "So tell me, tell me the first thing."

"The first thing? Stop trying to be right all the time. Relax, take it easy."

"I can relax."

"I've never seen you relax. Your mind is always going. Something is always wrong. If it's not Father Bellows, it's Mr. Brix or Mrs. Montague or George Bush. You could've gone on that cruise with me last summer. Then you could've relaxed."

"To Norway? Lolita was supposed to go."

"Yeah, and when we fought, her place was empty. You

wouldn't had to pay a cent. We would've had a blast together, man, a real blast. We could've talked. And the food—it was out of sight."

"Cy needed me here."

"I don't believe that. You were just making him the heavy, like always."

"So what you're saying is, I shouldn't publish this article?" Hugh held up the galleys and gave them an irritable shake.

"Shouldn't? What's that mean? You either do or you don't. If you do, though, why not be happy, accept it? You've done something good. This writing, it takes a lot of work. If I did it, I'd be so proud I'd bust."

"Shhh."

Hugh had heard footsteps in the hall, and it sounded as if someone had paused outside the door. In a moment the footsteps went on.

"This is nice, huh?" Virgilio said, waving his cigarette at the door. "They think you are gay."

"Yeah, just great." Hugh deeply resented his brothers for having such small minds. They were all so terrified of friendship that any sort of intimacy was suspect.

"You hate them for that?"

"No, Virgilio, I feel sorry for them. That they don't have someone . . . like you."

"You blush, like a schoolgirl." He eyed him steadily. "Are you a virgin?"

"What?"

"With men. No experience, huh? You know, when I was a kid, we used to think all Wasps were gay. There's something about Wasp men, they're all so uptight you can't help wondering why."

"I asked my shrink once if she thought I was."

Virgilio barked with laughter. "God, if that isn't just like you sons of bitches. You got to ask if you are."

"Well, for your information, she told me I wasn't."

"Oh, I am so happy to hear this, sir. I feel safe now."

Hugh smiled, but Virgilio's mockery made him uneasy. "Look, what are you getting at? You think I'm in the closet or something?"

"Most Wasps aren't man enough to be gay."

"What? New York is overflowing with—"

"I'm not talking about that. I'm talking about your so-called straight guys. They're just terrified of being thought the least bit gay. You, for instance. It really grates on you that Father Bellows has you pegged."

"He doesn't. He's *wrong*. Hell, Virgilio, you know I've never done anything, never wanted to, even."

"Fine. So what's the problem? Why are you so angry?"

"Because it's not true. Cy is wrong, dead wrong. He doesn't have me pegged."

"Of course, my man. That's just the point. No one has anyone pegged. No human being can be classified with words, stupid words. It's impossible. That's something you little white boys will never understand."

"Oh, and you Latin lovers, you don't know the first thing about macho, huh? A guy looks crooked at you, and he's dead. He insulted your manly honor."

Virgilio, who had been sitting up by then, putting his shoes back on, reached out and grabbed Hugh's hand. "Good, now you're learning." He gave it a vigorous shake. "I'm as full of shit as anyone. That's your first lesson, my boy." On his way to the door Virgilio added, just in time, "And your second is this: Just let me walk out of here plain and simple. Don't go check the way first, understand?"

twenty-three

On hearing the news Emily's first impulse was to break the lease. She would pack up everything and move back to Louisiana to take care of her father. But Hugh thought she should give herself some leeway. Why not let him sublet her place for a while? That way, if she got tired of Louisiana, she would always be able to afford to come back to the city.

"But it doesn't matter if I get tired of it. I'm doing this for my father."

"Yes, I know. But what if he doesn't hold out long—I mean, it's possible. Then you're stuck."

"Oh, Hugh, Martha said it will be a while, a year at least. I won't want to come back after all that time."

Emily was surprised at how, if not joyful, at least relieved she was to be able to make this decision. It was as if a spell had been broken. Martha, in the unlikely role of Prince Charming, had awakened her, quite literally, at three in the morning with a phone call that had left Emily's heart pounding dully. In tears, Martha confessed that she was breaking a promise to Dolly, but she couldn't hold it in any longer. Their father had cancer; it had metastasized. There was no hope. Dolly herself had sworn not to tell anyone, but she had finally broken down and called Martha.

Then and there Emily made up her mind that she was going to devote herself entirely to her father. His last days would be made as comfortable as possible. She would read aloud to him, Ovid, Seneca, Virgil. She would help Dolly clean and cook. She would bake the New York *Post* chicken for her father—surely he would like it—and she would look up new ways to fix beets.

"You're going to live at home?" Hugh asked.

"Of course. I'll find some sort of work in town to make a few bucks. Why do you look at me like that?"

Emily was stretched out beside Hugh on the vibrating bed. He had smuggled her into the rectory after they had gone out for a couple of drinks at an Irish pub that catered to a grim, often homeless, clientele.

"Hugh?"

"I don't know. Somehow it doesn't seem right, going back to your parents'."

"But they need me. Mom can't do it all alone, not with her bad back. And Martha's got her own kids to deal with, three of them. Sandy's in Germany now, he can't help out. That leaves me." Emily gazed up at a water stain on the ceiling, beside the naked bulb. "Dad's going to make a fuss, I know. He's not going to want me to help. But I suppose he'll have to get used to the idea. I've made up my mind."

Stroking her hair, Hugh said, "What about your friends?"

"Allen? Well . . . I don't know, there was always something funny about our relationship. I love him dearly, but . . . He'll survive without me." She turned on her side to see him. "In a way, I'm glad. We were heading somewhere, Allen and me, our relationship, and I'm not sure how great it was. Hugh?"

"Huh?"

"I'm pretty screwed up, you know."

"What?"

"It suddenly occurred to me, after talking to Martha—I'm tired, I'm miserable. I've got to get out of this place."

Hugh reached up and switched off the ceiling bulb. The dim light from the lamp on the desk was enough, so much more merciful. "You're joking, Em. I've always thought of you as very centered."

"Centered, I hate that word. I hate people who use it."

"Thanks."

"Don't use it with me, please. And besides, how can you possibly imagine I'm centered? Does a centered woman give up her own flesh and blood, pretend she doesn't exist?"

"You did what was best for the child, what you thought was best," he said after a few moments, avoiding her eyes.

"The child? Her name is Priscilla. She's thirteen years old, a freshman at Sacred Heart, has a four point grade average, and she's never set eyes on me, not once. How's that for centered?"

"It took a lot of courage and integrity to keep your end of the bargain. No one thinks it's been easy for you."

"Don't you see, that's just it? It has been easy, too easy. I haven't suffered all that much, really. I've blocked her out as if she never existed. For years I've gone around like a total amnesiac. At first I had to force myself to forget, then it started coming naturally. Allen, my dear friend, hasn't a clue—and yet he thinks I've told him everything about me."

Hugh had shifted away slightly, though his arm still rested beneath her head. "What good would it have done for Priscilla to know? It would only have mixed her up, made her miserable. Besides, it's what Clara wanted, and you've been loyal to her. She couldn't have raised Priscilla otherwise."

"I don't know, it all sounds fine, logical. But it feels wrong. I've always felt wrong. And I've numbed myself all these years so I wouldn't feel it."

"So what do you want to do? Make a scene now with Clara? Tell her you want your baby back like in some stupid made-for-TV movie—based on *real* life?"

Hugh's sarcasm brought tears to her eyes. "I just want to feel the pain, that's all. Finally. And . . ."

"And?"

"And I think I'd like to tell Dad about her. After all, he is her grandfather."

"But—"

"Oh, shut up, Father—and hold me, hold me tight."

Hugh did as he was told, ignoring the approaching footsteps out in the hall.

*   *   *

The principality of Monaco and Central Park are roughly the same size, or so Clara had heard someone say. Emily doubted this information, but nodded agreeably as they walked past Cleopatra's Needle. She really didn't have time to see Clara. There were still so many details to clear up before she left—change-of-address notices for her credit cards and the post office, presents for her friends at work, one for Allen. Hugh would have to be warned about the super when he moved in, how to avoid him, since the landlord would fight any subletting in her building. The list seemed endless. But Clara had refused to take no for an answer. She had insisted that she and Emily get together for lunch before Emily left.

They had met at a restaurant on Madison in the 90s and found themselves squeezed between women on either side, with barely six inches between the tables. Perhaps this, and the fact that a neighbor's Agnes B shopping bag crowded Emily's feet, would have been tolerable if a bowl of soup didn't cost ten dollars and the coffee was not lukewarm. Clara, too, thought the prices were a sin, and wondered aloud about the friend who had recommended the place to her. It proved impossible to carry on a real conversation. Neither Clara nor Emily could altogether block out the competing talk, which was raised to a level of great excitement when an emaciated young gentleman with a rubicund nose joined the table to their left. Clara smiled stiffly at Emily, who did her best not to look annoyed at this waste of time. Once outside, Clara announced that she felt she should walk off the calories. And since it was so surprisingly warm for November, she asked Emily to accompany her at least partway through the Park. A walk would do Emily good, too. Not that she needed it, Clara hastily added.

By the time they got to the Great Lawn, Emily had taken off her cardigan jacket and Clara her peacoat. "You know, all the years I've lived here," Clara said, "I've never felt I belonged. I still feel like I'm just visiting."

Emily picked up a football that had skidded across the walk. She tossed it back to a shirtless young man—or attempted to. It wobbled only a yard or so and landed far in front of him. "Sorry," she called out automatically. He did not even give her a look.

"Is Hugh really moving into your apartment?"

"Looks like it."

"Are they allowed to do that, priests?"

Emily shrugged. They had climbed to an outcropping of rock just beneath Belvedere Castle. Clara had sat down, even though the granite seemed moist, while Emily gazed below at a straggling line of expert and inexpert folk dancers.

"Hugh needs some time to himself. He's got permission from his father provincial, for six weeks."

"And then?"

"I think he wants to go to Mexico. He's going to beg to be reassigned."

Clara looked vaguely disappointed. "Oh."

"You weren't thinking that he and I might . . ."

"Well, why not?"

"Are you crazy?" Though Emily smiled, there was anger in her voice. She was trying to forget how good it had been with Hugh, the night she had spent in the rectory. Though they had not made love, as she had hoped, she had not been disappointed as she lay beside him, talking over all the old hurts and wounds. Her amazement had overwhelmed any puny resentment she might have had when he told her, in great detail, about his fixation on lesbians. All those years she had lived with him, and not once had she had the slightest clue about what made him tick in bed. He had always been afraid to tell her, and probably rightfully so. She wouldn't have understood then. Yes, she probably would have been horrified, especially if she knew he had actually acted out his fantasies. Now it just seemed sad to her—and strange. "You still like the idea of two women?" she had asked, thinking confusedly that somehow his ordination had cured him. "Of course, I get turned on all the time." "Well, no wonder you married me in the first place." "What are you talking about?" "Don't you see?" she had said with a little laugh, "I'm two women." "You're nuts." "I know."

Clara had reached up and taken Emily's hand. "You and Hugh do love each other. And priests leave the Church all the time to get married."

"Don't be silly. The only reason Hugh and I can communicate now—"

"Communicate?"

"All right, love each other—in a strange way, I suppose—it's because we're not married." It was odd how constricted, narrow, her married life had felt. From her new vantage point she could see that this past was not at all as she had imagined it to be. The old familiar landmarks—Hugh's reserve, her constant anxiety—seemed to shrink as the horizon receded, becoming more vast. How sad that this tenderness she felt should be possible only as the distance increased.

Emily finally settled down onto a patch of frilly lichen while Clara went on and on about how wonderful marriage was, how it was the only way to really love a man. Once she had gotten this out of her system, Emily brought up something that had been troubling her. "Could you do me a favor, Clara?"

"What's that?"

"Would you let me tell my father about Priscilla?"

A breeze stirred Clara's tawny hair. Her face remained blank.

"I know I promised I would never tell a soul, but . . ."

"Why do you want to go and do that?"

"I don't know. I just feel I should."

"It's going to hurt him terribly."

Emily studied her friend's face, which was not as hard and defensive as she had thought it would be. "He likes you, though. A lot. And he should know, because whether I deny it or not, it's his future."

"Priscilla has nothing to do with him."

"He's her grandfather, her only grandfather."

"Not her only, girl. Don't forget, the guy you slept with, he has a father, too. Why don't we go all the way and fly him in to meet Priscilla. Then I can tell her, 'Now you know your daddy's daddy, and the daddy who had a one-night stand with your mommie. Now we're all one big happy family. You know the truth, aren't you happy, Priscilla? Now you got two daddies, two grand-daddies, two mommies—' "

"Stop it."

Clara had tears in her eyes. "I'm sorry."

"I didn't say anything about flying Dad here. He doesn't have to meet her. I just want him to know who I am."

"But you're not Priscilla."

Emily didn't need to be told this. She firmly believed that no parent owned a child. That was why, her therapist had told her years ago, so many children were in such conflict. Their parents assumed they owned the children, that they were part of their possessions. A child was not an extension of the parent. She was a gift, a trust, the parents always in one sense foster.

"You're not Priscilla," Clara insisted.

"I'm not saying that I am."

"No, but the next thing I know, you're going to want to meet her yourself, start taking her out to lunch. Aunt Emily."

"You forget, I'm leaving."

"For good?"

"I don't know. Probably."

When Clara spoke next, after a thoughtful pause, her voice was not so high, so strained. "So you're really not going back to Hugh?"

"No."

"Well, in that case, I suppose it wouldn't hurt . . ." She stirred the water in a small pool in the rocks. "Maybe, I mean if you're really leaving, Priscilla's at home now. You could come meet her if you like. I've mentioned your name before. She knows you're a friend."

"Clara, I can't bear the thought that I'm forcing you. You've got to do what you think is right. That's all that matters."

"Oh, Em, sometimes I think we've really screwed things up good. Nothing I do with her seems right. Every choice is wrong, the truth, lies, it doesn't matter, it's all going to hurt."

"Well, if it's all going to hurt no matter what, why don't we just try the truth?" Seeing the panic in her friend's face, Emily quickly amended, "I don't mean the whole truth, nothing but . . . Just let me look at her maybe, have a cup of tea."

There had been other people on the rocks, other conversations partly overheard, but easy to ignore. The closest was unseen, hidden by the angle of the granite outcropping. They were both Indians, two men from Calcutta. One of them had seen his only son die of cholera. The other had murdered his wife in a fit of drunken rage. They lived together now in a basement apartment off Central Park West, the stouter being the super in a brownstone, the leaner doing odd jobs as he had for years, bussing tables, washing dishes, picking up litter at the zoo, handing out flyers for discount clothes on lower Fifth Avenue and at some bars where women danced nude. The leaner held the stouter's hand as they talked, both gazing idly at the two women, who seemed, as they merged into the golden shade of a grove beyond the Great Lawn, farther west, to become indistinguishable, like one.